THE CURRENT

by

Jackson Peoples-Rosenblatt

ISBN: 0615819001
ISBN 13: 9780615819006
Library of Congress Control Number: 2014911404
ESC Press, San Diego, CA

For my mother- and father-in-law,

Shifra and Edward Cline, in loving memory

PART ONE: DEPARTURE

1973-74

There is a tide in the affairs of men

William Shakespeare—*Julius Caesar*

LAUNCH

Cooper's friends mostly got Volkswagens and BMW's for graduation, but his grandfather, grandmother, and two aunts had died at Auschwitz. A German car was unthinkable. He wouldn't have asked for one and knew he wouldn't have gotten it if he had. His oldest brother had received a Buick convertible. Nothing anti-Semitic about that as far as Cooper knew. Having other agendas, the twins didn't want cars at all. One of their uncles had escaped the Nazis and gone to Sweden, which made a Saab an appropriate choice for Cooper though perhaps not as sensible as a Volvo. His Saab was silver. It had a matte black hood, which was said to absorb the glare of oncoming headlights. It had mag wheels, fog lights, and a tachometer—all the boy racer accoutrements. Cooper had no aspirations with regard to the Monte Carlo Rallye, but it was nice to know that if he changed his mind he'd be prepared. Cooper had never been a Boy Scout, his parents considering him temperamentally unsuited to it. They had undoubtedly been correct in this estimation, but he shared that organization's reverence for advance preparation. Marco Rossini, the most popular boy in Cooper's graduating class, had been given an Alfa Romeo by his grandparents, and the Saab was far from being as glamorous as that. But Cooper considered it a much more serious car, a man's car as opposed to a gigolo's car. No one had ever accused the Vikings of being lightweights and lived to tell about it. Though the girls at school lined up for rides in the bright red Alfa, Cooper wasn't impressed either by Marco or his adoring fans. The first time the Alfa refused to start, or Marco was too ham fisted to put the top up with sufficient dexterity in a sudden rain shower to avoid being soaked to his alabaster skin, the mystique would burst like a popped balloon at a four-year-old's birthday party. Cooper had witnessed enough such debacles to know how this worked and took comfort in the certainty of his rival's impending discomfiture. Victory was sweetest when brought about by your adversary's incompetence. This entailed no effort on your part, while he was thereby reduced to the position of never having been a worthy competitor in the first place. Not only were you free of having to engage him, you didn't have to acknowledge him at all. He was insignificant and you remained unchallenged. It was hard for Cooper to imagine a better outcome than that.

Over the summer Cooper drove the Saab just enough to make it eligible for a free one thousand mile checkup at the dealer before his departure for college. While his friends cruised suburban boulevards and made midnight runs to the Jersey Shore, he worked double shifts at his parents' store and lived like a monk. He didn't really need the money. His Bar Mitzvah funds still sat happily accruing interest in the accounts his mother administered, the balances now enhanced by graduation checks. He was thrifty enough by nature to appreciate this more than the things he might have acquired, which by now would be worn out or cast off anyway. What he worked all that overtime for was something he thought of as insurance. It was a major component of his legendary imperviousness to that daunting phenomenon popularly known as Jewish guilt. He'd been waging guerilla warfare against it since toddlerhood and considered himself the only guy of his generation to be genuinely immune. This included his older brothers. His warfare against them had been the bitterest conflict of all—as the universe has ordained.

That morning he was up before dawn packing the Saab. Over the weekend he had measured the trunk space with a tape measure and laid out the cargo arrangement on graph paper. First to go in were his stereo components. In their original packaging they took up more space than he'd really have preferred, but this way their protection was guaranteed. After that were his record albums, crated alphabetically by performer's name. His clothes were next, carefully folded and organized in two large suitcases as if for his matriculation in a military school. His few books and mementos were in their own, smaller box, and that was enough to fill the trunk. This left the back seat, which in the Saab folded down handily, leaving space clear for a few bulky items of clothing and the two ice chests, one for drinks and the other filled with the perfectly uniform stacks of individually wrapped sandwiches which Nanny Freitag had made and stashed overnight in the freezer. They'd be fresh for days yet.

Satisfied with his work, he locked the car and went upstairs for breakfast.

———

At the last possible moment, Josh tossed his duffel on top of the things in the back seat, climbed in beside Cooper, slipped a cassette through the slot in the Saab's dash, and fastened his seat belt. Cooper didn't get the shaggy hair, granny glasses, sandals, and hippie beads thing. Not on guys, at least. And bell bottoms—weren't they for sailors? Still, it must be working. Girls of all ages and descriptions considered Josh irresistible. Cooper knew he was supposed to be jealous. As the engine whirred to life and Cooper adjusted the rear view mirror, the overture to *Little Mary Sunshine* boomed into the cabin.

They threaded their way through rain dampened early morning streets toward the onramps to the George Washington Bridge. Even this early in the day, traffic was heavy. Deplorable as ever, New Jerseyites returning home from night shifts in the city couldn't deal with the wet pavement. The challenge this posed gave a whole new meaning to the term "defensive driving." Halfway across the bridge, the overture ended and the forest rangers' chorus began. Josh sang along at half voice, a light, clear baritone that belied the impressive booming sound Cooper knew he was capable of producing onstage. The youngest of the Luxemberg boys, Cooper had a healthy respect for the obsessions of his family: Nanny Freitag, muttering like a sorceress over her recipes; Dad, ruminating over the business which kept a roof over their heads and food in their mouths; Mom, chain smoking and poring over the stock listings in the *Wall Street Journal*. And then his siblings: Ike, endlessly immersed in baseball stats; Jake, oblivious to all but his Zionism; and Josh, fanatically dedicated to musical theatre. The minute Cooper got to San Francisco he had to find a gym. God only knew what he'd look like after a layoff of nearly a week. Sitting on his butt in a car, for crying out loud. Could there be anything worse for muscle tone than that? Not to mention his hard won definition.

———

Josh was not happy. Not. One. Tiny. Bit. And he didn't care who knew it. This excursion had forced him to cut short his engagement with the stock company in Connecticut, his last—hopefully—and triumphant season with them. On his return from California he'd be off, newly minted diploma from Temple in hand, on his long awaited, meticulously plotted quest for Broadway glory. By next summer he'd be cast in a major role in a smash hit on the Great White Way and summer stock would be a thing of the past unless he felt like slumming. This prospect kept a smile on his face day in, day out. But this interruption was barely tolerable. Genghis Khan and Alexander the Great must not have had baby brothers. Or interfering mothers, though it was more pleasant contemplating a brother-free existence.

Cooper hardly needed a chaperone. Josh couldn't imagine anyone more capable of taking care of himself. Nobody who knew him could. Not with that chest and those shoulders. Dr. Frankenstein had assembled his monster out of fresh corpses. Cooper seemed intent on making a monster of his own body, slaving away endlessly in their basement gym. His ridiculous bulk was only the half of it. There was also that five o'clock shadow that generally showed up by lunchtime and that "take no prisoners" pugnacity. Worst of all was the way he wore his hair. That shiny flat top, like he'd just gotten back from bombing Hanoi. Of course, nobody was actually bombing Hanoi these days now that the war had been over for all of fifteen minutes. But Cooper's haircut was still inexcusable. Even when he let it grow out during the fall and winter it never reached as far as his shoulders. He was seventeen going on thirty, and the idea that he needed protection was absurd. Guidance, either. He was as stubborn as he was muscle bound and smart as a whip, at least with regard to practical matters. He'd have made an ideal artic explorer, melting ice for drinking water, staring down polar bears that got in his way, and communing with his sled dogs. To them, his lack of social skills would hardly matter. This needless errand was all because of Mom, who had somehow lost her bearings two years ago when Jake dropped out of Princeton to run off and join a kibbutz. Then last year, instead of starting medical school like he was expected to, Ike had taken a research job with Dow so he could marry his fiancée Cherie Landau. Cherie's first name was supposed to be pronounced with a heavy accent on the second syllable, but Mom persisted in screwing this up, pronouncing it like the wine when she didn't go completely off the rails and pronounce it like the fruit. Now in Boston helping take care of her first grandchild, Mom seemed positively querulous at the idea of her baby Cooper flying solo, which meant Josh was stuck with the job of escort/chaperone and in no position to argue the point. After all, he was going to have to ask Mom and Dad for rent and grocery money for the few months it might possibly take before his brilliant career was fully launched. The idea of moving back into his old room under the family roof on Riverside Drive was unacceptably bourgeois when what was obviously required of an aspiring Broadway sensation was *la vie bohemienne*. The one saving grace: Cooper, for all his natural boisterousness, had learned over the years when to keep his mouth shut, and, inexplicably, appreciated the Broadway and Off-Broadway classics, no matter how obscure or merely corny, almost as much as Josh did. Thus he made an ideal traveling companion if the journey absolutely must be taken. They wouldn't spend the next four days arguing the relative merits of Procol Harum and the Who, Cooper's favorites, versus the Moody Blues, who Josh pretended to love for the sake of argument though he could barely tolerate. Nanny Freitag had gone crazy over Paul McCartney when Ike brought home *Sergeant Pepper*, and that spoiled the Beatles for the whole household.

———

That summer Shoshonnah had finally, irrevocably, become a full fledged insomniac. It wasn't at all like her friends described it. Tossing and turning, frantic for sleep, tortured by the anxieties of the day—not her. Thoughts racing out of control didn't keep her awake. It was, rather, wakefulness that fueled her racing thoughts. Normal adults were said to need seven to nine hours of sleep a night. She might have reached adulthood in junior high but no one had ever mistaken her for normal, so it stood to reason, she supposed, that six hours was too much. She felt calm and clear headed on five, positively exhilarated on four and a half.

This had been her pattern ever since high school, but it wasn't until that summer that she stopped thinking of it as some sort of low grade disorder and embraced it with open arms. She stopped even pretending to retire before midnight. She stayed up far into the wee hours, talking on the telephone with her best friend, Rosie Stern Wallach, who was similarly, though not as contentedly, afflicted, watching whatever was on television—for the most part with the sound turned off—and pondering how she might manage her family more effectively.

She had finally reached the understanding that a life as rich and full as hers couldn't be shoehorned into a sixteen hour day. More waking hours were required for the proper appreciation, the savoring so to speak, of everything she was or possessed or reigned over. Cramming it all into a shorter duration only made her existence seem hectic and chaotic. An extra three hours or so of consciousness out of each twenty-four gave her life the expansiveness it deserved. Not to mention the solitude that as a wife, mother, and busy businesswoman she'd always missed.

She found pretty quickly, however, that solitude was overrated. It would have been nice, for instance, if Willi had joined her night owls' club at least once or twice a week, but he'd always slept like a log. Even if he tried to stay up with her he ended up snoring in his recliner. Even Rosie could only be depended upon until one a.m., just when Shoshonnah was getting her second wind most nights. Watching television with the sound turned off wasn't quite as entertaining as it might have been if there had been someone on the couch next to her to share the joy of creating alternate dialogue. But then God with His infinite sense of humor and/or irony intervened by making her a grandmother. She rushed to Boston as soon as Cherie's mother, Ella, was safely on her way back to Chicago. Genikayte, it turned out, was no more devoted to nocturnal sleep than her grandmother, and the love affair began.

Genikayte. Not Jenny Kate. Or even Jennifer Katharine, which Shoshonnah could have comprehended even though it seemed ridiculously goyish. No. Genikayte, even though the Landaus were as good a Jewish family as you could ever hope your son might marry into, though perhaps a little heavily weighted toward the Reform side of the equation. No Conservative Jew would have given her daughter a name like that. Shoshonnah held her tongue about the child's name, expressing her disapproval—or was it merely skepticism?—by persisting in her mispronunciation of Cherie in as many ways as she could think of depending on how the mood struck her. Which she knew she really had to stop doing. Even if she hadn't had the inclination to play nice, she had promised Willi.

Tomorrow. She would start pronouncing her daughter-in-law's name correctly tomorrow. Or the day after. Too soon and nobody would notice. She hadn't, she knew, been sufficiently obnoxious about it yet for her point to be fully made. So it would have to wait that much longer.

But also tomorrow or the day after because her current schedule left her a little confused about exactly when today ended and tomorrow began. Was it midnight Eastern, which really seemed too early, or midnight on the west coast, when the whole continent could be included in the new day that made the shift definitive? As Shoshonnah sat gazing at the baby gazing up at her, the first glimmers of the rain-gloomy morning obtruded on her reverie, asserting unequivocally that tomorrow had become today and reminding her of Cooper's scheduled departure. No worries about delay. Cooper was never late as long as he himself had determined the itinerary. Otherwise, all bets were off.

"Oh, baby girl," she murmured as the sleepless infant grinned, "have I got tricks to teach you. Your mother won't teach you these things, even if she can, because no mother would dare. But a grandmother can. A grandmother must."

Cherie and Ike first met at a love-in, of all places. It hardly sounded decent, but Josh had been there too and assured Shoshonnah that it was perfectly innocent. Cherie was devoted to all the latest fads. Since arriving, Shoshonnah had watched her do macramé, helped in the kitchen when she made those inedible granola cookies, and listened patiently to long orations on the virtues of macrobiotic diets. She even let Cherie, an avid amateur astrologer, do a reading for her. She drew the line at Tarot. It was too creepy. All of it seemed like gibberish to her, but she supposed it was what she got. In their day, she and Rosie had been bobby soxers, shrieking their guts out over the young Frank Sinatra. Their antics had driven their mothers to distraction. So it was fitting, Shoshonnah thought, that the one thing she and her daughter-in-law saw eye to eye on was that mysterious force known as karma. But she sure wished she could go to sleep and let the 'Seventies pass her by. There was something so fuzzy headed about what Willi referred to as the *zeitgeist*. She wasn't sure it was even a Yiddish word.

Once again she had her family buffaloed. It had been risky, she knew, playing the anxious little mother. Josh was the acknowledged thespian of the family, not her. And the casting was decidedly against type. She hadn't taken leave of her senses as she knew they all suspected. She wasn't suddenly menopausal. She hadn't lost her genius for calculation. She knew better than anyone how little assistance Cooper needed or indeed would accept from his elder brother. Cooper, the one of her sons as intrepid as his mother. She was certain Cooper had figured her gambit out. Otherwise, why the lack of resistence to her scheme on his part? Looking into Cooper's eyes had always been just like looking into a mirror. God help them both.

But Josh hadn't been himself, really, since Jake left them and went off to Israel. Twins don't find independent existence easy. She hoped by sending Josh on this errand he might discover some kind of brotherly connection to replace the one he obviously missed so badly. But she had needed an excuse to send him. Hence her act. Like everything else in life, of course, this was, at best, a crap shoot.

"Just wait, baby girl," she crooned. "Just wait until you're old enough I can teach you to shoot craps."

———

Rivka flushed, held the toilet seat at seventy degrees for a moment before dropping it with a crash that made her jump even though she was expecting it, and flushed again. Turned the water on and off, gargled like her life depended on it, faked a coughing spell violent enough to alarm an emergency room physician, flushed a third time, and rattled the door knob. In other words, she did everything she could think of to alert Sammie that his mother was about to emerge from the bathroom so as to encourage him to make sure he was decent.

It wasn't that she cared. What mother of three grown boys could muster the energy to bother? But with Maggie moving in soon there was lots of house training left to do. The girl might end up being her daughter-in-law someday, and Rivka hated the thought of being considered a failure as a mother merely because Sammie didn't approve of wearing a stitch of clothing in bed. Even though the bed in this case was the living room sofa. That fate was probably inescapable. Mother versus daughter-in-law was, she knew from bitter experience, one of the deadliest forms of combat on the planet. All these years later, she still had the scars. That Edith Fugelsang. She should rot in hell. Preferably one of those Christian ones, which somehow seemed so much worse than the Jewish variety.

Maggie was not officially moving in of course. But when your son and his girl-friend ended up at the same university and your son's apartment was just two blocks from his girlfriend's, it could only mean one thing. Some form of cohabitation was inevitable. Resistance was worse than futile, it was absurd. And your maternal skills, heretofore on display only sporadically, were subject to twenty-four hour a day scrutiny more or less. In Rivka's day, girls were assumed to be virgins on their wedding nights whether they actually were or not. And unmarried couples living together? Well, bohemians in Greenwich Village, perhaps. Everything was different nowadays. It made her feel old.

Maggie and Sammie's first date had been in eighth grade. Rivka couldn't imag-ine what a nice girl from a good family could possibly see in Sammie, who, it was already obvious, was his dead father resurrected. Handsome and charming, in other words, but, well, psychopathic wasn't too strong a word. Six years later they described themselves as going steady, and Rivka couldn't see any options for the two of them except marriage or murder. When Maggie graduated from high school and came north for college leaving Sammie back home in Encino, Rivka thought, "God bless her, she's made her escape". But then Sammie buckled down at community college and got himself accepted to the university as a transfer student two years later. Suddenly there was nothing standing between the two young fools and their fate.

Except maybe Sammie's cousin, Cooper. God only knew what had gotten Cooper interested in attending the same university as Sammie and Maggie. Nobody Rivka knew on the east coast had even heard of the place. She hadn't known quite how she was going to afford putting Sammie through two more years to finish his degree. His older brothers had nearly bankrupted her, and they'd both gotten scholarships. But with Nanny Freitag offering to pay the rent on an apartment for the two boys, that anxiety had largely evaporated. Rivka couldn't imagine those two sharing an apartment without killing each other, but they were legally adults, or close enough in Cooper's case, and it wasn't her problem. All she knew was, even with Sammie's pedigree she wouldn't lay odds against Cooper, who, she had been convinced since her first sight of him in his bassinet, had the heart of an assassin.

———

All his life people had treated Sammie like he was an idiot. It started with his two older brothers, Ben and Ethan, telling him that he was adopted when his resemblance to their late father was unmistakable. He played along to make fools of them. Then Mom and his grandparents cooked up that story about how Dad had died in an auto accident, as if nobody they knew would breathe a word to the contrary. Later, after they moved to California, it was the one about how the reason they never went back to New York to visit was they couldn't afford it. Sammie always knew better but didn't argue. Arguing with people gave them power. He retained what little he had by pretending to believe what he was told, and over time, by some magic analogous to the compounding of interest, his power increased enormously.

His teachers tried to convince him that knowledge is power, but by the time he was in second grade Sammie had figured out that ignorance could be power too. There was great strategic advantage to be gained from having your intelligence underestimated. It carried with it the potential element of surprise—*bam, I'm not as stupid as you think, sucker.* This, of course, had to be used judiciously or it wasn't surprising any more. There were practical advantages as well. If you seemed too stupid or inept to accomplish a given task, someone was likely to do it for you. Particularly if you had a mom like Rivka or a girlfriend like Maggie, who were as alike as twins, though this was one more thing everyone believed Sammie didn't understand about his existence. A young man would never choose such a thing on purpose, would he?

The most recent lie his family had told him was the one about Cousin Cooper. Or rather, about Nanny Freitag paying the rent on their apartment near the campus as her graduation gift to Cooper. Sammie was sure Cooper had already had his graduation present from Nanny Freitag, and what he was being told was just another of the transparent excuses his mother's family always came up with for their charity. Sammie didn't give a shit about this, however. There was great strategic advantage to be gained by exploiting your status as poor relations. Regardless of what his mother claimed, there wasn't anything humiliating about it.

———

Rivka had declared it girls' day out, which meant going shopping for the menfolk. If Tash or Rivka saw the irony in this, they gave no indication of it. It was far from lost on Maggie, however. She fumed as she steered the shopping cart along in their wake. It was enough to drive a girl to all out feminism.

"It's a shame to spend all this money on things for the apartment," Rivka said, tossing a bale of washcloths into the cart. "I should have brought all my old stuff from home. Boys spoil everything they touch. Scratch that, they spoil everything they look at. They don't have to touch it, just be in the same room with it and poof—it's garbage. All you can do is bury it in the yard or burn it. You can't even donate it to charity. It's that bad. I should have had daughters. I swear to God, I should have. I'd have been a fabulous mother if I'd had girls like you two."

"Then why are we doing this, Mrs. Fugelsang?" Tash asked.

"Grab six of those bath towels, Natasha dear. I know we got bath towels at the last place, but you can never have enough. Those two will probably shower three or four times a day, God knows. That many showers, and they'll still manage to be filthy. I'll never understand it."

Tash pulled a stack of bath towels off the display and laid them in the cart.

"We're doing this," Rivka said, glancing at her watch, "because Shoshonnah sent me a check. 'Get everything the boys will need for the apartment.' Those were her instructions. And the next time I speak to her, she'll want a full accounting. Down to the last penny, and every cent spent—to her specifications. That's

Shoshonnah. The more money some people have, the more they expect you to be careful with it."

"Couldn't you take all this new stuff home with you?" Tash suggested. "Maggie and I will be down in L.A. next weekend. We could bring all your old stuff back up with us. The boys will never know the difference. God knows they won't die if they have to go a few extra days before they change their sheets."

"Or a few extra months," Maggie grunted.

"If it were anybody but Shoshonnah's precious little Cooper," Rivka said, "I'd do exactly that. But she'll check what I tell her against what he'll tell her, and if it doesn't match up there will be hell to pay."

This, Maggie knew, was typical Rivka. Turning someone's generosity to her into an affliction. She had always felt close to Rivka. She thought of herself as the daughter Rivka never had. But the last two years had changed the nature of their relationship. Before Maggie came to San Francisco to school, she honestly thought of the two of them as kindred spirits. Her first visit home, for Thanksgiving week-end freshman year, had given her quite a shock. It was as if she'd never known Rivka at all, or as if some stranger had taken up residence in that familiar body.

The woman she'd known before, her boyfriend's mom, was funny, charming, a little kooky, and extremely cool. They had attended consciousness raising seminars together, staring at the reflections of their private parts in hand mirrors. They had burned their bras together—boy, Maggie's mom had a few choice words to say about that. They had even smoked their first joint together. That was still a secret, of course. They had been liberated women, no doubt about it.

The woman she was following up and down the aisles of this "housewares supermarket" was the consummate passive aggressive and potentially a very difficult mother-in-law. Maggie supposed that two years as a psych major had given her a completely new perspective on the woman. It was certainly true that she had developed a tendency to go around analyzing everyone she knew. She had always hated people who did that, and here she was turning into one. It must be an occupational hazard of her major. Maybe she should talk to her advisor about it. Then again, maybe she didn't want to know. It wasn't like she had any intention of going and changing her major to Art History.

But that wasn't what bothered her the most. She had always been told that men marry women like their mothers. If that was true, it meant she was either never going to marry Sammie, which might be a relief, actually, the way he'd been acting lately, or it was already too late and she had turned into Rivka without knowing it.

———

When Tash first heard that Sammie's cousin was planning to move to California to attend college, she thought *at last*. She believed devoutly in the duty of best friends to marry brothers, but Sammie's brothers weren't available. Worse than that, they were boring. Availability could vary over time, but boring was forever. She had read *The Joy of Sex* repeatedly, and if that book had one message, this was it. A girl had to avoid boring men. Because a man who was boring in conversation would almost certainly be boring in bed. That might have been good enough for her mother and grandmothers. But modern women deserved sexual satisfaction from their husbands, not just financial security. And since after this long a breakup between Maggie and Sammie didn't appear possible much less likely, Tash had been forced to reconsider her marital aspirations. The advent of an eligible cousin jump started her original intention, and she anticipated Cooper's visit over spring break with considerable excitement. She bleached her hair—again—lost five pounds and gained three of it back, and bought new underwear she imagined was sexy. Of course, truly liberated women weren't buying sexy underwear these days, so she didn't breathe a word about it to anyone. Maggie's sermons on the topic were like the feminist version of hellfire and damnation.

Maggie hadn't offered to show her a photo of Cooper, and Tash was too embarrassed to ask. Perhaps Maggie didn't have one. When Tash imagined Cooper, she thought of a sexy teddy bear with eyes the color of iced tea and perhaps a cute jewfro, though that was negotiable. Jewfros didn't suit everyone. She didn't speak of her interest, fearing ridicule from Sammie, who arrived from Los Angeles a day ahead of Cooper, and pity from Maggie. Instead she feigned complete indifference. She was certain that any overt expression of curiosity about Cooper would jinx everything.

Cooper's visit was a crushing disappointment. He had the haircut of a fascist. Really, it was a style only her father could love. And though he had the face of a European fashion model, from the neck down he bore a discouraging resemblance to the guys in the muscle magazines her brother Joe had kept hidden in his closet until Dad found them, jumped to an unflattering but ultimately accurate conclusion, burned the magazines in the back yard and threw Joe out of the house. There was no escaping it. Cooper was a freak. He was charming in his way. And if he could ever be convinced to wear his hair in a style that didn't label him as a psychopath from a previous generation, he might actually turn out to be handsome. But having met him Tash could only conclude that he was too much work. And poof! There went her marriage plans again.

—

"Of course you and Ike should go out to dinner on Saturday night," Shoshonnah said. "Don't worry about baby Genikayte and me. We'll be fine. I'll feed her a bottle and heat up some leftovers for myself. You deserve a night out."

Treat your daughter-in-law as you wish your mother-in-law had treated you. That was the advice Shoshonnah had read in a women's magazine on the plane from New York. Not having had a mother-in-law herself, she lacked experience of what the author referred to as the "relationship dynamic" involved. She thought she understood the concept, however, which seemed like good old common sense. Did it require a Ph.D. these days to possess that? She'd done her best to follow the author's advice during her visit. But the smell of patchouli in the apartment sometimes made her gag. And she wasn't sure that burning all that incense was good for the baby.

"Oh, Mama Luxemberg," Cherie cooed, "you're so good to us. It's so great having you here. My mom nearly drove me crazy. I thought she and Ike were going to kill each other. I love her, you know? But sometimes I can't stand her."

"That's the way it is with mothers and daughers sometimes," Shoshonnah said. "My sister and my mother were at it like cats and dogs until the day Rivka got married and left home. Then they only fought like that half the time."

"I'm going to call Ike at work and tell him," Cherie said, picking up the phone.

"Yes, do," Shoshonnah said. "I'm going out into the back yard for a moment."

She picked up the bag with her cigarettes and lighter. Before leaving New York she had promised Willi she wouldn't smoke in the house with the baby. Ella Landau smoked in the house when she was here. Shoshonnah smelled it the minute she arrived. But that wasn't her business. Willi was right. She should quit anyway. God knows what damage she had done to the boys, sitting at the table chain smoking while they had their breakfast all those years. Oh, well. You tried your best to be a good mother and next thing you knew they went and changed the rules on you.

According to the itinerary Cooper had taped to the refrigerator back home, Josh and he should be arriving in San Francisco tomorrow afternoon. She'd put money on their being within an hour of Cooper's estimated time of arrival. That boy with his plans and timetables. And people considered her obsessive. What a joke. How had she let them all gang up on her? What was he going to get up to out there three thousand miles away? With nobody but that idiot Sammie to keep a lookout. Cooper's three brothers she had never needed to worry about. They were good boys. They never got into trouble, but somehow she sensed it was only through lack of imagination. Cooper didn't get into trouble, either. But it wasn't lack of imagination, much less good intentions, in his case. He's just like me, she thought. He knows how to get away with things.

———

For a brief moment as the Bay Bridge came into view with the city skyline sparkling beyond it in the brilliant afternoon, Josh experienced an almost overwhelming wave of envy. It should be him, he thought, and not Cooper coming here to live. How could Cooper possibly understand a place like this? As far as Josh was concerned his brother was the quintessential philistine. Not because he had no appreciation for the finer things. He'd been taught good taste just as surely as the older Luxemberg boys. It apparently was because he believed there was nothing that couldn't be bought. There were no eternal values. There was only commerce. Josh had no evidence to base this judgment on. It was purely intuitive, but he knew he was right. And it dismayed him. Cooper inhabiting a place like this. What a deplorable waste.

Josh, on the other hand, would know exactly how to pursue the science of life in this exquisite setting. He could have appreciated it as it deserved to be appreciated, savoring the architecture, the natural beauty, the cuisine, the chaotic mixture of peoples and cultures, and the climate. He had the background, the education, the sensitivity for it. With his style and panache he'd take the city by storm. There was just one problem. Broadway was three thousand miles away.

But Cooper wouldn't do. He had no style, no panache, no *savoire faire*, just that bizarre persona. It wasn't quite swagger. It wasn't quite bravado. It was just a kind of steely truculence with occasional flashes of something that seemed like charm, or at least might pass for it in bad lighting. God help him.

———

Cooper had made his choice all the way back in fourth grade. The summer before, after their annual visit with Nannie and Grampa Freitag and Rivka and the cousins in Los Angeles, Willi and Shoshonnah had rented a car and driven the boys up the coast to San Francisco. It was, Cooper decided, Disneyland for grownups. Foresaking the charms of Fisherman's Wharf, they stayed in a tiny, European style hotel off Union Square. They spent days seeing the sights. They picniced on the grass at the Palace of Fine Art. They walked to the center of the Golden Gate Bridge. They went to the top of the Coit Tower. They ate Chinese food in Chinatown. It was the only place his parents had ever taken them that was as vivid as New York.

Back home, summer vacation over and bored to distraction with school, Cooper passed the time doodling scenes he remembered instead of solving arithmetic problems or working on his history report. The City by the Bay had gotten under his skin. New York was the center of the universe, of course. The visit to San Francisco hadn't shaken his faith in that eternal truth. But New York could only be inhabited. It couldn't be possessed. San Francisco appeared different in that crucial respect, and in Cooper's reckoning this meant everything.

He began his quest. He saw himself as he aspired someday to be, a handsome prince in a shining car driving the streets of that city, welcomed at every landmark, deferred to by every doorman and *maitre d'*, adored on every block. He dreamed of it the way other boys dream of glory on the football field or wartime valor. He was his parents' son and knew that only he could make his vision a reality, so he quickly taught himself the difference between dreams and plans. He pored over books and magazines in the public library. Long before any of his classmates, he found the college catalogues filed in the counseling office. He drew maps, constructed charts, studied rental ads in the classified sections of newspapers he bought with his earnings from the store, prepared budget proposals. He forced himself to study and keep his grades up. He wasn't a natural scholar like his brothers were with their straight A's, but he did nearly as well simply through perseverance and application. He left nothing to chance.

Then fortune intervened. Berkeley, his first choice of school, had become so notorious by the time he was ready to apply that he despaired of convincing his parents to let him study there. It was all drug dealers, hippies, and communists as far as they were concerned, and negotiations deadlocked as soon as they began. But then Cousin Sammie, stupid, corrupt Sammie, who had the personality of a thug tempered by the initiative of a tree sloth, elected to attend a university Cooper's parents had never heard of and were thus unequipped to object to. Bingo! If it was a safe enough, reliably American enough, school for Rivka to send Sammie there, how could Shoshonnah and Willi turn thumbs down?

JAKE

"Jesus Christ!" Maggie yelped. "What the hell are you doing?"

"What does it look like I'm doing?" Sammie grinned. "I'm eating a peanut butter and jelly sandwich. Which I had to make for myself, since it looks like nobody's planning to fix breakfast around here."

"It's Yom Kippur, you dolt."

"So?"

"So we agreed that we were going to fast this year," Maggie said.

"*We* didn't agree," Sammie said. "I seem to remember you and Tash and Cooper sitting around yammering about how nice it would be to attend services and then go out afterward for Chinese like our forefathers did in the desert, or some bullshit like that. I was trying not to pay attention because I was afraid if I listened too closely it would make me vomit. But *we* didn't agree to anything."

"God dammit, Sammie."

"What?"

"What am I going to do with you?"

"Listen, girl, I never said I was a good Jew. Nobody ever heard me say that. I would burn in hell for sure if I ever said such a thing. What I have said, lots and lots of times, is that I'm a bad Jew. You've heard me. A very bad Jew. Nobody better act surprised."

"Will you at least hurry up and go shower and dress so we won't be late for services?"

"Since you asked so nicely, I might. Just as soon as pretty boy gets out of the bathroom. But I might have to make another peanut butter and jelly sandwich first. Unless you want to make one for me."

———

"God," Maggie said, as Cooper emerged from his bedroom, "what a beautiful suit. You look like a model."

"He looks like a guy playing a gigolo on a soap opera," Sammie sneered.

"Thanks," Cooper smiled. It took a lot to propel Sammie on such a flight of eloquence. Usually he was, or pretended to be, indifferent to the appearance of anyone male. He went around looking like an unmade bed. Dressing up just made him look worse. It emphasized the deficiencies of his hygiene and grooming. But before Cooper could let loose with a caustic reply, Tash burst into the apartment.

"Oh, God, oh, God, it's terrible," she moaned.

"Morning Tash," Sammie said. "Come right in. Don't bother to knock. The coast is clear. Maggie has finished giving Cooper his daily blow job and now we're getting ready to play strip Scrabble."

"Asshole," Maggie spat.

"What's terrible?" Cooper asked.

"I can't believe you're not watching the news," Tash panted.

"It's Yom fucking Kippur," Sammie told her, "and Golda Meir here won't let me turn the television on."

"What's terrible?" Cooper asked

"They've attacked Israel," Tash said.

"My God," Maggie cried.

"Who attacked Israel?" Cooper asked, stepping toward the set.

"All of them. The Egyptians. The Syrians. The whoever."

"Fucking Arabs," Sammie yelled, showing the most enthusiasm anyone could remember in a long time.

———

There were a few Palestinan protesters standing in front of the Hillel holding picket signs. They stood silent, expressionless, avoiding eye contact. People were mostly pretending to ignore them. Cooper wondered how long that would last. It would be just like Sammie to take a swing at one of them. God only knew what would happen then. Other than Sammie getting himself beaten up. Cooper wasn't going to lift a hand to help him if he started something. Campus security had called in the SFPD for backup. Cooper thought the officers seemed tense.

He slapped his yarmulke onto his head, offered Tash his arm, and led their group through the entrance.

Inside, the place was packed. They bargained their way into four seats together. Even in a roomful of Jews no one could out-negotiate Cooper. Though they were half an hour late because of Sammie insisting on stopping for a burger, the service hadn't yet started. No one seemed certain when it would. No one even seemed to be in charge. Conversations buzzed all around, every one of them about the war.

"It isn't enough that the Germans killed six million of us," a young woman behind Cooper said, "now the Arabs want to finish the job."

It was his family she was talking about even though she didn't know it. His grandfather and grandmother, his father's baby sisters. It still hurt his father terribly to hear it spoken of, but to Cooper and his brothers it had always seemed as remote as Moses crossing the Red Sea. This was different. This was now. This was his brother Jake in danger. There were his aunt and uncle in Tel Aviv as well, and the cousins he barely knew. They might be strangers for all practical purposes, but they were his flesh and blood so they counted. He had no idea where Jake's kibbutz was located. His knowledge of Israel's geography was approximate at best. But it hardly seemed to matter. The country was tiny. Nowhere was safe.

Cooper had never given much thought to being Jewish. It was something you were, not something you chose. It was like being blue eyed, and he certainly didn't spend much time pondering that. It always seemed to him that people made a bigger deal about it than necessary. That was embarrassing. But for once he felt he understood. As long as their enemies made a big deal of it, he supposed his people had to as well.

———

Israel would win, they all agreed over Chinese food later when services were over and the sun had set. Israel always won. In 1948, in 1956, and most spectacularly six years ago in 1967—the Six Day War. It would be just like those times. There was nothing to worry about, really. Israel was invincible. The Arabs were stupid and cowardly and the whole world knew it. Case closed.

But Cooper worried. The victory, when it came, would not be without a price, and the price might include the life of his brother. The victory in 1967 had cost the life of his Aunt Yael, Uncle Marcus' first wife, who had been one of Israel's few civilian casualties. She had died in a rocket attack. Cooper had never been close to Jake. The twins had always been completely wrapped up in each other. There hadn't been room for anyone else, especially a snotty younger brother. They'd tormented him "to toughen him up", but he always gave back as good as he got if not more. Typical brother stuff, if the stories his friends at school told were to be believed. But this wasn't fun and games. This was life and death. Somewhere, thousands of miles away, some Arab wanted to destroy Cooper's flesh and blood.

———

"Your poor mother must be frantic." Over long distance, Rivka's voice was even more nasal than Cooper remembered it. "I can't imagine what she's going through."

"I haven't been able to get a call through to New York or Boston."

"It's probably too late by now," Rivka said, "with the time change."

Cooper knew it wasn't. Two a.m. was just the shank of the evening as far as his mother was concerned. He knew the reason he couldn't get through was because she and Dad were on the phone to each other. He had tried to call Josh too, but got no answer.

"Listen," Cooper said, "I think Sammie wants to ask you something."

Sammie was wildly pantomiming *NO!!!!!*, but Cooper handed him the phone anyway. He had to get out of the apartment. He grabbed a sweatshirt and went for a walk.

———

In the morning the news was bad. Israel was getting pounded. If they were going to beat the Arabs, who apparently weren't as stupid and cowardly as supposed, it wouldn't be soon. The others decided not to go to classes so they could monitor the news broadcasts, but Cooper didn't see how flunking out of school would help make the world safe for the Jewish people. He wore his Star of David necklace outside his sweatshirt, something he had never done before. He thought he noticed people on the street staring at it. On his way to campus he took a detour past the Hillel. There were more Palestinians holding picket signs out front and more campus police watching them than the day before. A couple of girls sat behind a banquet table just inside the entry. They were handing out flyers. Cooper signed their petitions and dropped twenty dollars in their collection box before heading for his algebra class.

———

A bunch of Jesus freaks was staging some kind of event in front of the student union when Cooper went to lunch. You could hardly call it a demonstration. It seemed more like a flashback to the Summer of Love. A band was playing "Jesus Rock", and "groovy" looking girls were handing out flyers. The war was great news, a six foot tall Barbie doll with a southern accent assured him, for everybody who had accepted Jesus as personal savior. It was surely a sign of the End Times. The last great earthly conflict that would usher in the Rapture would start with war in the Holy Land. It said so in the book of *Revelations*. This could be it. In fact, it almost certainly was. Would he like to give his heart to Jesus Christ this afternoon, while there was still time? She'd be glad to pray with him.

He wouldn't, thanks. He walked away disgusted. How could anybody fall for that bullshit? It wasn't a religion. It was a cult. Sammie's oldest brother Benny had joined Jews for Jesus his freshman year at UCLA. Rivka was frantic. She tried to borrow money from Nanny Freitag to pay a deprogrammer to kidnap him. Mom and Dad put a stop to that. Not that they didn't think Benny was crazy; they just didn't like the sound of the deprogrammer's methods. Mom was of the opinion that there was nothing a Conservative rabbi and a strict Freudian psychotherapist working in collaboration couldn't clear up. The grownups were still fighting about it when Benny met a nice Jewish girl, a rabbinical student's little sister who immediately brought him back into the fold. He had actually turned into kind of a super Jew. But even now Rivka foamed at the mouth when it was mentioned. For once, Cooper was on her side. And these lunatics today. They were as bad as the Nazis, making his people disposable for the sake of some crazy idea about history.

———

When he got to the apartment late that afternoon, Maggie and Tash were up to their elbows in granola cookie dough and kvetching like mad about the latest news bulletins.

"Where's Sammie?"

"He's gone to the Israeli consultate," Maggie said.

"There's an Israeli consulate?" Cooper was astonished. "He'll get lost trying to find it. We'll never see him again."

"To enlist," Tash said.

"You're kidding."

"It's bad, Cooper." Maggie brandished a spatula at him as if preparing to fend off an invader. "The Israelis are losing."

"But Sammie in the army? Who the hell thinks that's a good idea?"

"I think he's very brave," Tash said, looking at Cooper meaningfully.

———

"When do you ship out?" Cooper asked when Sammie came in later.

"Bastards wouldn't take me."

"Of course they wouldn't take you," Maggie said. "Look at you. Pudgy as Elmer Fudd. And you don't know your left from your right. They want to win this war, not lose it."

"They'd take Cooper in a second, I bet," Tash said.

"They wouldn't look twice at Cooper," Sammie snarled. "They know a candy ass when they see one."

It would have been so easy to take a swing and put Sammie out on the floor. So very easy. But it wouldn't solve anything.

"I'm going to the gym," Cooper said.

"Don't go," Tash pleaded. "He didn't mean it."

"Sorry, did he say something? I must have missed it."

"Cooper."

"Tash, I'm going to the gym. That's all."

———

When he got back to the apartment several hours later, the door to Sammie's room was closed and Tash was camped out on the living room sofa, snoring. There was a note for him on the kitchen counter. He was to call his mom. In New York.

She answered on the first ring.

"I thought you were in Boston."

"I came back as soon as this started," she said. "I couldn't leave your father and grandmother here alone."

"Of course not."

"Your father is beside himself."

"You don't sound so great either."

"There were three screaming babies on the flight from Boston. I thought I was going to have to kill someone."

"Seriously, Mom, is there anything you need me to do?"

"Stay put. Don't do anything crazy. I can just about get through this if I only have your brother to worry about."

"You know me better than that."

"Do I?"

"Of course you do," Cooper said.

"Well, I thought I knew your brother, didn't I? Ike was always the one with the weird ideas. And now look."

"Ma, I'm sure Jake is fine. The kibbutz is probably nowhere near the fighting."

"He's not fine. He's been wounded. He's in the hospital. Anat called from Tel Aviv to tell me. She didn't know any details."

"What happened? Was the kibbutz attacked?"

"There is no kibbutz. There never was a kibbutz. It was just a story Jake made up. The minute he got over there, your Uncle Marcus helped him enlist. That was his plan from the start. He's a sergeant already."

"What?"

"Great, now you're going deaf?"

"No, Ma. Sorry. How bad is it? Is he going to be O.K?"

"I don't know, Cooper. Anat didn't have any details."

"How are they?"

"Your uncle is fine. Anat has spoken to him several times. Your cousins are all right the last she heard. Rafi's flying missions, she assumes, and Gil was mobilized but she didn't know where. She and the babies were clearing out to a shelter, so I can't reach her. I just have to wait until she calls. With the time difference that could be any minute. Or not."

"Ma, listen. It's going to be fine."

"Is it? You know that for a fact?"

"Ma, we have to believe it."

"You're right, sweetie. Sorry I snapped at you."

———

Cooper tried, but failed, to imagine Jake in uniform. Jake carrying a rifle. Jake riding on a tank. Jake tossing a grenade was the hardest. He had always thrown like a girl. Cooper tried to imagine Jake with his mop of golden curls brutally cropped, his green eyes squinting against the desert glare. Perhaps he had grown a mustache. That would certainly help toughen up his appearance. It was the same face as Josh—way too pretty for a warrior. But really, the whole thing was absurd. Neither of the twins had ever shown any interest in playing soldier, and now this?

———

"Why don't you want to enlist?" Tash asked the next morning, watching Cooper mix his protein shake.

"Why do you think, Tash? Didn't Sammie explain it to you? I'm a candy ass who isn't man enough to do really courageous things like get drunk and make a nuisance of himself at the Israeli consulate."

"That's not fair. Sammie didn't mean what he said. He was just frustrated."

"That's how he gets away with everything around here. You and Maggie constantly make excuses for him."

"You're really good at it, you know."

"Good at what?" Cooper asked.

"Good at deflecting things," Tash said. "I asked a question about you, and all of a sudden we're talking about Sammie."

"Deflecting. That's a good word Tash. A college word, some might say."

"Why does everybody think I'm stupid? I'm not stupid, really."

"I don't think you're stupid," Cooper said. "I think you pretend to be stupid. I have no idea why."

"God, just what we need. Another would-be shrink around here. And you're doing it again."

"What?"

"Evading the question," Tash said. "What about enlisting?"

"Tash, the Israeli army doesn't need us. We're American teenagers."

"Sammie's twenty."

"With no military training. No skills. No experience, except at being American teenagers. We'd just get in their way."

"So don't enlist," Tash said. "But there must be something you could do over there."

"How am I going to get there? Swim? There are no flights. By the time there are, it'll be over."

"You're always so practical."

"I guess that's a step up from being a candy ass," Cooper said.

———

On day four, Mom called just as Cooper was about to leave for school. There was still no word about Jake. Uncle Marcus' troops had suffered heavy casualties, but he was safe. Gil was safe, too. Rafi had shot down at least one MiG. Rafi's wife Rebekkah's hospital was overrun with wounded. Gil's fiancée, a research scientist, had been attending a conference in Switzerland when the fighting broke out and now couldn't get back to Tel Aviv. Anat and the babies, four year old Avi and two year old Zev, were staying with her mother and were safe for now. Anat's new baby was due any minute. And Mom's best friend Rosie and her new husband Lou were caught in Haifa. Their honeymoon had taken an unexpected turn. The State Department was working on organizing evacuation flights for U.S. citizens stuck in the country, but it might be days yet.

So it wasn't just Jake they all had to worry about, to pray for.

On campus, there were tense confrontations between Palestinian students and supporters of Israel. The university administration issued a statement calling for calm. Cooper was anything but calm. Calm was for someone else, a luxury he couldn't afford just then.

II

Cooper imagined his mother sitting up alone, chain smoking and worrying, and he called. He knew that what worried her most was that she couldn't do anything. Her natural inclination would have been to go immediately to take care of Jake, but travel to that part of the world was impossible. Trouble had never been her nemesis. Inactivity in the face of trouble was. She frequently took up her six-shooters and got on her white horse and galloped off to someone or something's rescue. She was fearless at times like those. It was on the rare occasions when she could do nothing that she found it hard to cope. And without her beloved Rosie to talk to by the hour, she must be going out of her mind. Cooper knew all this, so he called every night. He didn't have much to say. He knew nothing he could say would make her feel better. He just listened.

—

The catastrophic reverses of the first few days of war eventually started to correct themselves. Good news about the military situation began to come in dribs and drabs. Before long it was apparent that Israel had rallied and once again would successfully defend itself against any and all invaders. The God-ordained order of things was preserved but at a cost far higher than Tash and company had anticipated. In the days immediately after the eventual outcome became obvious, the Palestinian demonstrators disappeared from campus as if they'd never been there. The Hillel returned to its previous sleepy obscurity. The news reports were now full of rumors and speculations centering on the U.S. and Soviet Union each attempting to turn the situation to advantage. This was nothing new, of course. It was just another chapter in the long history of Cold War maneuvering. But Cooper thought it was nauseating to have his people used as pawns in this way. Geopolitics was apparently the devil's work. There had been concern in the early going, with the Arabs advancing on all sides, that the Israelis might use the nuclear weapons they had never admitted to having but which everyone else seemed to assume they did. The Jesus freaks on campus were particularly fervent on this point. You could almost see the mushroom clouds blossoming in their eyes as they spoke of it. As the Israelis finally began to push the Arab forces back and that threat receded, their disappointment was palpable. Armageddon, long and fervently anticipated, was slipping from their grasp. It began to look as if they might have to continue inhabiting planet Earth alongside everyone else indefinitely. Served them right, Cooper thought, for their insanity.

—

The people Cooper shared the apartment with were nearly as silly as those Jesus freaks. Their triviality was matched only by their petulance. They squabbled constantly, and not even the most routine of domestic tasks got done unless he took charge of it. It felt like he'd been drafted as substitute teacher in a day care center. He spent as much time as he could in the library or at the gym in order to minimize his exposure. Inactivity was as poisonous for him as for his mother. But after several sleepless nights, he'd come to certain conclusions. He hadn't been crazy enough to convince himself that anything he could do would affect the outcome of the war, but he'd formulated a plan he considered appropriate for a young male American Jew.

Defeat for Israel wouldn't be the end for his people unless American Jews gave up the fight. Because even if there were no Israel there would still be the Jews of America. And as long as American Jews stayed strong, their people had a future. But strength, as Cooper understood it, wasn't a group project. It required solidarity, of course, but it depended on more than that. It was something individuals achieved, each on his own, each in his own way. It took many forms. Political, obviously, though Cooper suspected that was of limited usefulness. Intelligence, tenacity, initiative. These were strengths a young American Jew could aspire to and offer to the life of the community. They were things he could work toward every day.

Cooper wouldn't understand until much later that the only thing he'd gotten wrong in his calculus was a kind of reversal of causes and effects. He believed in his plan because he believed that the strengths he had identified reflected the ongoing needs of his people. But what he had actually done was assume the existence of a set of needs that reflected the strengths he most wanted to believe he possessed, or at least was capable of developing.

———

Finally the war ended. Unlike in 1967 there was no euphoria, no sense that anything had been resolved, that a bright new day was dawning for the State of Israel. But still Cooper felt a kind of quiet joy that the killing was over, for the present at least. And that the people he loved were, if not truly safe, at least out of immediate danger. That night when he called home ready to share his jubilation with her, his mother was almost too busy to talk. She was packing and simultaneously preparing her household for her absence. She had a flight to Israel the next morning. Jake needed her whether he knew it or not. There was nothing to do but go to him as quickly as she could get there.

III

Sammie didn't understand or appreciate Cooper's insistence that they drive both cars to Los Angeles for Thanksgiving weekend. It seemed like a waste. They really all should go in his Oldsmobile. It would save on gas, which had gotten disastrously more expensive since the war back in October. Fucking Arabs again. There was plenty of room in the Oldsmobile. His stereo system was inarguably superior. But every reason he cited drew Cooper's objections. That damned showoff Cooper, engaging him in another pissing contest. He always had to disagree. If Sammie said the sky was blue, Cooper found a way to argue the point. It was so old, so very boring. Then on the Monday before they were to leave, he and Maggie had the mother of all fights and she refused to ride with him, among other things, and what had seemed to him a ridiculous proposition became, at least to the others, an absolute necessity. Nobody wanted to spend hours in the car with Maggie and Sammie silently feuding. Which made him like Cooper's plan even less. Then, Wednesday night, fifty miles short of their destination, a radiator hose gave way, leaving all his coolant in a pool on the freeway, and Sammie at Cooper's mercy. It was like something out of the book of *Job*.

———

After driving Sammie to a phone so he could call AAA and then driving him back to the Oldsmobile to wait for the tow truck, Cooper insisted on taking Maggie and Tash to their homes. It was nearly midnight, and he said he didn't see why they should all wait on the side of the road along with Sammie, who never lost an opportunity to explain to anyone who would listen that he was a big boy and could take care of himself. Maggie had the good manners not to mention that if Cooper hadn't driven the Saab they'd all have been stranded and freezing, but everybody knew that's what she was thinking. Before they left him, Tash made sure Sammie had a Fresca and a supply of granola cookies, both of which he hated. Sammie knew Tash knew he hated them. Could you get a divorce from your girlfriend's best friend?

It was just like Cooper to get in the middle of one of Maggie and Sammie's fights without seeming to try. Always the good guy. Always the bigger man. It made

Sammie want to puke. And when Cooper returned from dropping off the girls to wait for the tow truck with him that just made Sammie madder. What a schmuck.

———

When they finally got to Rivka's house in Encino, Sammie's brother Ethan was sitting staring at the television screen where some car dealer was promising to stand on his head to beat any competitor's prices. Cooper hadn't seen Ethan since way back in grade school. The man on the couch had the eyes of a drunk, the skin of an infant, and the hair and beard of an Old Testament prophet. He greeted Cooper like he had just offered to buy a round of drinks for the house.

———

"Have you spoken to your mother?" Rivka asked, bustling around the kitchen the next morning.

"Not since she left for Tel Aviv," Cooper said, draining the last of his protein shake. "Dad speaks to her every couple of days."

"Yeah?"

"He says it's a good thing they own AT&T stock."

"I'll bet. So how's Jake?"

"Mom says he's fine. It was just a flesh wound. Once they stopped his bleeding and transfused him, it was pretty much done. He's back on normal activities."

"Why, that's wonderful," Rivka said.

"It would be, but you know Dad. He thinks she's lying about it. He's sure it's much worse than she says."

"What do you think?"

It was entirely possible that Mom was lying to Dad. Cooper knew she was capable of it. As far as he was concerned, he was the only member of the family she couldn't lie to. He'd never have said it aloud. Either he'd be proven wrong or he'd lose the advantage of holding onto the secret.

"I think he worries too much," Cooper said.

"Of course he worries. How can he help it? Losing his family the way he did."

"Well anyway, he's not going to believe her as long as she stays over there. The proof he needs is being able to look her in the eye. Preferably in his own kitchen."

"You know, dear, I'm choosing to believe that everything's fine," Rivka said. "I need something extra special to be thankful for today."

———

Cooper and Sammie went to the supermarket to pick up the Thanksgiving dinner Rivka had ordered from the deli department. Nanny Freitag prided herself on being a wonderful cook, a literal wizard in the kitchen, but she hadn't passed her love for the skill on to her daughters. Sammie professed deep respect for Maggie's mother's cooking, but Cooper had eaten it when she visited them for parents' weekend and didn't share Sammie's enthusiasm. He was gratified to see each container emerge from behind the counter and nestle safely in the grocery cart. Leave it to professionals, was his motto. He'd fill up at Rivka's, and then when he and Sammie went to the Maurers' later he'd just nibble.

———

It was surreal belching turkey and stuffing and standing on the beach watching the surfers. Thanksgiving in New York was never like this. Maggie and Sammie strolled along the edge of the water hand in hand like lovers in a television commercial. Beside Cooper, Tash shivered despite the balmy temperature.

"They're so lucky," she sighed, staring at Maggie and Sammie.

"Oh?" Lucky wasn't really the word that came to mind when Cooper thought about those two. Masochistic, more like.

"They've got each other," Tash explained. "Don't you wish you had somebody special in your life?"

"I do have somebody special in my life. Me."

"You big dummy. You're never serious about anything, are you?"

"You have no idea," Cooper said. He just wasn't serious about the same things as the people around him. That was all.

"You never joke around, but somehow you always seem like you're laughing at everything."

"I have no idea what you're talking about."

"Right," Tash shook her head. "I just get so lonely."

Cooper had no response to that one. He knew she was lonely. It was mostly self-inflicted, but how did you explain that to her?

"I've been thinking a lot about Ethan," Tash said.

"Ethan? Our Ethan? Ethan Fugelsang?"

"What other Ethan would I be talking about?"

"Tash, Tash, Tash, Ethan is a psychopath. He hasn't had a job since he got out of college. His last girlfriend finally got tired of his mooching off her and threw him out. Now he lives with his mom. He hardly ever moves off her family room sofa. You know all this."

"It's so easy for you to be critical, Cooper."

"Huh?"

"After all, nobody ever meets your standards."

"Tash, this has nothing to do with me."

"That's right. Nothing ever does."

"You could do a lot better than Cousin Ethan. That's all I'm trying to say."

She stomped off. Cooper stared at the surfers. Here he was in beautiful Southern California, the scene spoiled only by idiots, and eight thousand miles away Jake was probably in bed asleep. Unless his wound kept him awake. Either that or nightmares of what he'd seen in combat. There were beaches in Tel Aviv, too. Cooper wondered if guys went surfing there. Perhaps he should try to ship Jake a board. But if Dad was right, and Mom was lying to them all and Jake was a paraplegic or something it wouldn't be a very thoughtful gesture.

———

All Cooper could remember about the movie was the first ten minutes. He had fallen asleep after that. It had to be a pretty good movie to keep Cooper awake, and the ones Maggie and Tash chose were never up to the task. Still, the one time you could depend on Maggie and Sammie not to fight—when they were in the same room, at least—was at the movies.

Cooper would rather have spent the time at the gym. But he had no idea where you would find a gym anywhere near Sherman Oaks that was open on Thanksgiving night. This seemed ridiculously counterintuitive. When would people ever need a gym worse than after stuffing themselves to the gills with all that food? He felt like a beached whale himself, and he had been reasonably careful about his intake. He hadn't touched the tub of popcorn Tash wheedled him into buying at the concession counter. Still, when he woke up during the final credits, the damned thing was empty.

The theater parking lot was nearly deserted by the time they got out. Sammie wanted to go cruise Mulholland Drive, but Maggie vetoed the idea. Sammie sulked all the way to Maggie's house. Cooper knew what Sammie was planning once the girls had been dropped off, so he got out there, too. Let Sammie head off on whatever dunderheaded escapade beckoned him. Cooper wanted no part of it. Maggie invited him inside and Tash seemed particularly frantic about it, but he just wanted to be rid of them all. Maggie offered to drive him to Rivka's in her father's Buick, but ten blocks of quiet surburban streets held no terrors. He insisted on walking.

———

Ethan was watching that same used car commercial when Cooper walked in, and Rivka was emptying the dishwasher.

"Where's Sammie?"

"He said he was going to meet up with some friends," Cooper said.

"After midnight? On Thanksgiving?"

"That's what he said."

"What kind of friends would they be that he would meet them at this time of night?" Rivka asked. "I wonder."

"Just friends, I guess."

"You need to call your mother in the morning."

"She's back from Israel?"

"She got in this afternoon," Rivka said.

"What did she say?"

"Everything's fine."

"But what?"

"But nothing," Rivka said. "We didn't talk but for two minutes. She's very tired, that's all. You'll speak to her in the morning."

But Cooper knew. He could feel it. She was waiting up to hear from him. As soon as Rivka went to her room, he picked up the phone and dialed. Mom answered on the second ring.

"Mom."

"Cooper, honey."

"Mom, how are you?"

"Fine. Now that I'm home and it turns out your father and grandmother didn't burn down the building or poison each other."

"Great. And what about Jake?"

"There's no more Jake, Cooper."

"What do you mean? What happened? I thought he was recovering."

"Physically he's fine. He's already back with his unit."

"I don't understand."

"He's not our Jake anymore, is all," she said. "He's somebody else now. He's changed his name. He's calling himself Yakov."

SCHOOLBOYS

The guy was waiting for him just outside the entrance to the gym. Cooper had noticed him inside earlier, halfheartedly messing around with the weight machines. He didn't know a barbell from a hole in the ground and his eyes were as shifty as a shoplifter's. He obviously wasn't there to work out. He fell into step beside Cooper like they were pals. The California rainy season was going into extra innings—April, and it showed no signs of letting up. Cooper found it amusing the way the natives fled in terror from a light sprinkle like the one this afternoon.

"Hey," the guy said. Wooly hair, glasses, and a stereotypical nose. He looked like someone Cooper might have gone to high school with.

"Hey."

"Crappy weather."

Is that the best you can do? Cooper thought.

"Hardly notice it myself," he said, just to be argumentative.

"You, uh, ever had your dick sucked?"

Given the guy's body language inside the gym, Cooper wasn't surprised at the question.

"Who hasn't?"

"By a guy?"

"You offering?" Cooper asked.

"My place is just five minutes from here," the guy said, "unless you know of somewhere closer."

—

It was the thickest, shiniest, most perfectly coifed head of blond hair Cooper had ever seen on a man. Seriously, it must take this guy an hour to get ready to leave the house in the morning. With a different haircut, he might actually be cute. Cooper didn't often allow himself such musings. What guys looked like wasn't the point. At least within reason. He had to be able to function.

"You have to promise not to come in my mouth," the guy said, staring as Cooper pulled his sweatshirt over his head.

There it was—that accent. Something European.

"What's the problem?" Cooper asked, pulling down his jeans. "Afraid it might poison you?"

"Please," the guy said, "what I really want you to do is mess up my hair. Please."

—

"Is this the best pizza you ever ate?" Rick enthused.

Cooper had had better, actually. People on the west coast just didn't get pizza. But he didn't want to be a wet blanket. Besides, he apparently wasn't paying. Free pizza had to be a lot worse than this to elicit his disapproval.

"Great," he said, reaching for another slice.

"I don't see why we couldn't have tried that kind with Canadian bacon and pineapple," Cindee sulked.

"You just won't let that go, will you?" Rick grunted.

"For a change," Cindee said, "just once in a while, you know, I'd like it if we could do things my way."

"Women," Rick laughed.

Cooper shrugged.

"It's too bad you don't have a girlfriend," Cindee said. "It would be fun to go on double dates."

"Give a guy a break," Rick said. "There's nothing wrong with playing the field."

"I've got a couple of friends you might like," Cindee smiled.

She was prettier, Cooper thought, when you couldn't see her teeth.

"Can it, chick," Rick said. "Does Cooper look like the kind of guy who needs help in that department?"

"Maybe he's shy," Cindee suggested. "Lots of cute guys are shy."

"He's not cute," Rick said. "Don't call him that. How many times do I have to tell you? Guys are never cute. If you have to call him anything, you should say he's handsome."

"That sounds so old fashioned," Cindee complained.

"Then say he's hot," Rick said. "Say he's a fox. Anything but cute. Right, Cooper?"

"Call me anything you want," Cooper said, wondering how it was he always ended up hanging out with couples and if every couple in the world constantly bickered, "just don't call me late for dinner."

"Cute and funny," Cindee giggled. "Suzette would love you."

"Chick, stop," Rick said. "You're really starting to piss me off."

———

Back at Rick and Cindee's apartment, Rick got out his stuff and starting rolling a joint.

"Ought to be heading home, I guess," Cooper said.

"Don't be stupid, guy," Rick said. "You haven't had dessert yet."

"Uh, I don't really smoke the stuff. I'm in training."

"Not talkin' about that. Cindee's pussy. It's the sweetest thing in the Bay Area. Just wait till you slide it in there. Man, she'll drive you crazy."

So it was like that. He thought he'd had them figured out over pizza, but he wasn't sure. As for being driven crazy, Cooper was skeptical. Girls were all right, but they didn't drive him crazy. The best he could say about girls was that they would do in a pinch. He tried to avoid them, though. They always wanted you to call them afterward. Guys generally knew how the game went and didn't make demands. But girls seemed incapable of no strings attached sex. That was how he always explained his aversion to girls. It was like he had an allergy to emotional entanglements. He hadn't met a guy yet who didn't agree, or at least accept his position at face value. It was the perfect explanation for not having a girlfriend of his own.

"So?"

"She really thinks you're hot, Cooper. Didn't you see how squirmy she was at the pizza joint? She's gonna love having you fuck that sweet pussy of hers."

"Man, I don't know." Cooper had learned that in such situations acting a little reluctant generally made the boyfriends that much more insistent.

"It's cool, guy. I love watching some real hot stud giving it to her like nobody's business. It is just so fucking hot. And when you finish doing that, I'm going to suck your cock so hard it's going to blow your fucking mind. I love the taste of her pussy juice on a hot guy's tool. I bet you're packing at least eight inches."

———

"I miss her so bad," Julian said, slumped on the sofa. "I never should have let her join the Peace Corps."

Julian was in Cooper's chemistry class and had suggested they get together to study for their upcoming midterm.

"That's rough," Cooper agreed. He had lost count of the guys he'd met this year whose girls had deserted/cheated on/dumped them. The women's libbers had a lot to answer for. Or at least they would have if Cooper believed half of these guys' stories. Trouble was, he didn't. The absent girlfriend, he had quickly figured out, was one of the handiest excuses in the book. He always knew he was home free when they started whining about how bad they missed the absent girlfriend. He gave it twenty minutes, max, before Julian made his move.

———

"Those two over there," Rory muttered into Cooper's ear. "They musta been cheer-leaders back in high school, you think?"

"Possibly."

"Hot and spicy," Rory laughed. "Let's go over."

"O.K."

The last time Rory and he took two girls back to Rory's apartment, Rory insisted on getting out his thirty-five millimeter Leica and taking pictures while the girls worked Cooper over. He wondered what ever happened to all those photos.

"Know what?" Rory muttered into Cooper's ear.

"What?"

"I can't wait to lick your come out of those hot snatches. Sure hope you've got two loads worth saved up."

———

"Haven't seen you lately," the guy said, falling into step with Cooper.

"I'm here every day."

"Yeah," the guy said, "leaving with some blond surfer dude."

"I thought you said you hadn't seen me."

"You know what I mean."

"Do I?" Cooper asked.

"Don't play dumb. Who is he anyway, your boyfriend?"

"I don't have a boyfriend."

"Sure, Mary."

"Oh, now, don't get all like that."

"Like what?"

"That queer stuff," Cooper said.

"Oh, please, like you're not queer yourself."

"I never said I wasn't. Just don't call me Mary. Ever."

"Oh. Think you're too good for the rest of us nellie queens, do you?"

"Listen," Cooper said, "do you want to suck my cock or do you just want to argue?"

"My place is right. . ."

"I know where your place is."

———

Kyle from Cooper's philosophy class had an idea about how they could make some money. Cooper was living well within his budget, but he believed in free enterprise. More money was always a good thing. Kyle was so serious about the plan he made all the arrangements and even fronted the money for their costume rental and new, sexy underwear.

At the appointed time, uniforms immaculate and their hair greased back, they lurked outside the appointed apartment. At the arranged signal—Kyle's flatmate Estelle, sister of the bride, was inside—Kyle pounded on the door, which opened almost immediately.

"Sorry, ladies," Kyle growled, "I'm afraid there's been a complaint about your little get together here."

"What complaint, officer?"

"Let me see," Kyle said, checking his notepad. "Ah, here it is. The problem is . . . my buddy and I weren't invited."

A chorus of whoops greeted them as they entered the apartment. Kyle already had his shirt unbuttoned.

———

Several hours later, Kyle tumbled into the back seat of the taxi beside Cooper as Estelle pounded on the trunk lid with her fist.

"That was so fucking crazy," Kyle panted.

"A hundred apiece you said?"

"Plus whatever we took in tips," Kyle said.

"Not bad," Cooper said.

The next thing he knew, Kyle's tongue was halfway down his throat.

———

Cooper knocked on the office door.

"Come in."

His English T.A., Gregory Yates, got up from his desk and took off his glasses. Cooper had always suspected they were a prop.

"Ah, Mr. Luxemberg, right on time."

"That's me, prof."

"Take a seat."

"What's up?" Cooper asked.

"I just wanted to go over this essay with you."

"Something wrong with it?"

There'd better not be. Cooper had paid good money to the tutor, in addition to consenting to receive a perfectly adequate blow job, which he figured counted as his tip.

"Nothing serious," Gregory Yates said, "but I thought you might benefit from a few pointers. For the next essay."

"Sure," Cooper said, seeing how the land lay.

"Now, here at the end of the first paragraph," Gregory Yates said, "where your thesis statement should appear. . ."

"Listen," Cooper said, "do we really have to go through all this?"

"What do you mean?"

"This whatever we're playing here? Evening of Kabuki, is it?"

"I don't understand."

"Because if you want to have sex with me, all you have to do is say so."

———

"Cooper. Shit, man, I haven't seen you in, God, when was it?"

"Hey, Rick."

"Listen, I can't wait for you to meet my new girlfriend. Name's Suzette. God, she knows how to do things that will just—I mean, wow, guy. You'll never want to put your cock anywhere else."

"Really."

"Except in my mouth," Rick said. "So like, you know?"

"Whenever."

"Soon, O.K?"

"Sure," Cooper said.

———

"Hey, Coop."

"Hey, Kyle."

"This is Wayne."

"Hey, Wayne."

Wayne was a tall, broad shouldered, foxy brunette who looked, Cooper thought, like a really good time.

"Wayne is going to come along next time we do one of our jobs," Kyle said. "We can use a third man."

Which, Cooper thought, was as good an excuse as any to make a new friend.

"Cool."

"We're on our way to my place," Kyle said. "Do some brainstorming about, you know, our routines and stuff. You should come along."

"Really," Wayne nodded.

———

"Come on, now," Cooper said, "don't cry."

This just made Judy from his psych class cry harder. He should have known better. She had said she needed a favor. Would he come by her place and have a look at her research paper? He never saw it coming. Usually he read girls better.

"Tell me what's wrong," he said. "Did I hurt you?"

"No," she sobbed. "I'm just stupid, that's all."

"You're not stupid."

"Yes, I am. The other girls all manage to lose their virginity and it's no big deal. Me? I get all emotional."

———

"Better not say anything to Wayne about this," Kyle said, wiping himself off with a wet washcloth. "He kind of thinks we're boyfriends now."

"Right," Cooper chuckled.

———

"You want to do what?" Cooper asked.

"I want to shave off all your pubic hair," Rory said.

"You're joking, right?"

"It'll make everything look bigger. For the photos I'm going to take."

"Photos?"

"I don't see what the big deal is," Rory said. "You already shave everywhere else."

"Not my eyebrows."

"I won't get anywhere near your eyebrows, I promise. And I'll make it worth your while. Don't worry."

———

"I don't do couples."

What Cooper meant was he didn't do couples until he had some idea of the ground rules. There had been a couple of awkward scenes. It turned out some guys with girlfriends didn't like to suck cock.

"That's O.K.," Renee giggled. "We're not a couple."

"Just roommates," Jordan confirmed. "She likes guys, and so do I. Surprise, surprise."

"I guess it's nice for you to have something like that in common," Cooper laughed.

"We've got this bet going," Renee explained. "Which one of us bags you first."

"So?" Jordan raised his eyebrows.

"Now how am I supposed to make a choice like that?" Cooper asked.

"I don't know," Renee said, batting her eyelashes.

"How about eenie, meenie?" Jordan suggested.

"We could all three. . ."

"Maybe another time," Renee said. "It's just this bet. We have to settle it before spring break."

"Come on, big guy."

"I hate to do this," Cooper said, "but I'm afraid you lose, Renee."

———

"Well, the thing is," Gregory Yates said, sliding off his glasses, "I think I've fallen in love with you, Cooper."

Just in time for midterms, Cooper thought.

———

"Better not tell Kyle about this," Wayne said, pulling up his undershorts. "We're kind of dating."

"My lips are sealed," Cooper said.

———

The guy was waiting for him when he came out of the gym.

"Hey," he said, falling into step.

"Hey yourself," Cooper said.

"Haven't seen you in a while."

"I'm here every day."

"You know what I mean," the guy said.

"So, I'm, like, supposed to just knock on your door? Is that it?"

"You could do that."

"I suppose," Cooper shrugged.

"You don't have to be on the rampage all the time."

"Rampage?"

"Really," the guy said. "You should think about settling down."

"Rampage."

"You're almost through with freshman year, you know."

"Who says I'm a freshman?"

"Everybody knows about you. Seriously. You're practically notorious. What you need is a boyfriend."

"Are you offering?" Cooper asked.

"Yes, Cooper, I am."

"Huh?"

"That's right. I know your name."

"And you are?"

"Zeb."

"I'd say pleased to meet you, but under the circumstances. . ."

"You're not pleased?" Zeb asked.

"I think we already met."

"Right."

"You know, Zeb, I'm really flattered, but I'm not looking for a boyfriend."

"Why not? Are you afraid people will figure out you're gay? Because I've got news for you. It's way too late for that."

"I don't give a shit what anybody thinks," Cooper said.

"Then you must be afraid of commitment."

"I'm not afraid of anything."

"No? Well there must be some reason you don't want to settle down. Let's see, could it be. . .?"

"Oh, goodie, multiple choice," Cooper said. "The answer is 'E, none of the above'."

"What's the problem?"

"The word 'boyfriend' has the word 'boy' in it," Cooper said.

"Oh, please. You really are a closet case."

"Not so, oh wise one," Cooper laughed. "Think a little harder. The opposite of 'boy' isn't always 'girl'."

MAGGIE

I

"Thank God you're back," Tash said, unlocking the door of her sunflower yellow Renault. "I think Maggie and Sammie are really going to kill each other this time."

She had lost weight over the summer and done something strange to her hair. Cooper almost didn't recognize her.

"I mean seriously," she said, as he stowed his bags and slammed the hatch, "it's never been this bad. Never."

"Hi, Cooper, it's great to see you. How was your summer vacation?""Fine, thanks, Tash." "And the flight?""Flight was fine, Tash. Two stewardesses slipped me their phone numbers." "Really? Were they pretty?""All stewardesses are pretty. Say, you're looking very nice yourself this afternoon—that a new dress?"

"God, Cooper," Tash said, stalling the engine, "you are such an asshole, you know that? And at a time like this."

"Thanks for picking me up," Cooper said. "I know how you hate coming to the airport."

———

"Oh, it's you," Sammie grunted.

"Hey, cous, nice beard," Cooper said.

"Sarcastic bastard. Where's Tash?"

"Said she had some errands to run."

"She's always running errands," Sammie said. "Ask me, it's why she never gets anything done."

"Maggie around?"

"Gone to the doctor. Some stomach thing she can't seem to shake. Hell of a time for her to turn into a hypochondriac."

———

"Pass the fried rice, please."

"Trade you for the barbecue pork ribs."

"Is there any more of the lemon chicken?"

Chinese takeout—how Jews celebrate everything, Cooper thought.

"Isn't this nice?" Rivka crowed. "Everybody back together. It makes me feel young again. How was your flight, Cooper?"

"Great," Cooper said.

"Not too much turbulence?" she asked. "I hate turbulence. It sets me on edge so bad. All that bouncing, I can't think of anything but a wing falling off."

"No wings fell off," Cooper said, "that I noticed."

"Shoshonnah and Willi? They're O.K?"

"They're fine. We shared a taxi to Kennedy this morning. They're off to Israel."

"She worries about Jake terribly," Rivka said. "It's heartbreaking how she suffers."

"Why? Did she say something to you about Yakov?"

"No, dear. I'm a mother. I just know. Tell me, you don't really go along with that 'Yakov' silliness, do you?"

"It's his name now," Cooper said. "He changed it legally. He wrote to Josh about it. Josh showed me the letter."

"Well, he'll always be Jake to me," Rivka asserted. "Sweet little Jake. Always such a serious boy. An old soul. That's what they call someone like that. Josh was always the outgoing one. How is Josh? Anything new with his career? Any parts?"

"Just chorus work for now. He's auditioning all the time. He's got his little place down in the Village. Mom says it's a roach factory, but he likes it."

"That's nice," Rivka said. "And you, Maggie, look at you. You've hardly eaten a thing. You'd better get down to business before the boys gobble everything up."

There was no danger of that. When Rivka ordered takeout it was like she was feeding an army. There would be leftovers in the fridge until Cooper threw them out.

"Leave her alone, Ma," Sammie said.

"I just said. . ."

"She doesn't feel good. I told you she went to the doctor today."

"That's right, Sammie, you did. What did the doctor say, dear?"

"He did some tests," Maggie said, looking like she wanted to disappear. "Routine stuff. He wanted to rule some things out. It's probably just a virus. Or maybe stress."

———

"She's pregnant, isn't she?" Cooper asked.

"Of course she's not pregnant," Tash snorted. "Don't be ridiculous."

"Don't lie to me Tash. That stuff might work with lightweights like Rivka and Sammie, but I'm the human polygraph."

Sammie had taken Rivka back to her hotel and Maggie had gone with him for the ride. Cooper hoped they would finish fighting before they got back. He was still on Eastern Daylight Time and didn't want to be up for hours yet helping Tash referee.

"She's not pregnant until Dr. Wasserman says she's pregnant."

"A technicality, Tash. You know I have no patience with technicalities."

"It could be a false alarm."

"Could be," Cooper nodded, "but isn't."

"No, Cooper. It could be. It really could. She's had them before, you know. Anyway, you can't say anything."

"Mum's the word. Or is it Mom?"

"I mean it. Especially not to Sammie."

"Sammie doesn't know?" Cooper asked.

"You heard him at dinner. He thinks she's having stomach trouble. They went to Acapulco last month. He thinks she drank the water."

"He has to suspect something."

"Sammie suspect something? You're joking, right?"

"Guys aren't as dumb as girls think."

"Sammie is," Tash insisted, "and then some."

"Maybe. But he'd have to be an inanimate object not to suspect something the way you and Maggie go around being all dramatic. I swear, the two of you are like outtakes from Chekhov. All I'm saying is she can't expect to keep it under her hat much longer. It'd be better if she goes ahead and tells him."

"She won't."

"Why?" Cooper asked.

"That's her business."

"Why isn't it his business, too? I mean, it's his baby as much as hers."

"That's right," Tash said, "side with him."

"It's his baby, right? So he has a right to know it exists."

"Sure," Tash said, looking about ready to crawl out of her skin.

"Tash? It is his baby, right?"

"Who else's would it be?"

"What an interesting question," Cooper said. "Some other guy's maybe."

"No," Tash stammered. "No. Are you crazy? Of course the baby is Sammie's."

"I thought it was just a false alarm."

"God dammit, Cooper. Sometimes I really hate you."

"Not so," Cooper said. "You always hate me. But that's beside the point. Is the baby Sammie's or not?"

"Maggie's really not sure. But you absolutely, positively can't say anything to anyone. Promise?"

———

It wasn't the first pregnancy scare they had been through. Tash was right about that. But those other times, Maggie had told Sammie nearly as soon as she told Tash and Cooper. That's what worried Cooper. He didn't doubt that Sammie was a real bust in the sack. For all his he-man talk, Sammie seemed to have the libido of a hundred year old sea turtle. A girl like Maggie, pretty and with that line of salty talk, attracted all kinds of attention. In Cooper's book she could hardly be blamed for indulging in a little something on the side. But why, oh why wasn't she on the pill? Any girl with a boyfriend like Sammie was a fool if she wasn't on the pill.

———

"Oh, Missa Coopa, how you been?"

"Hello, Mr. Chang. Fine, thanks. And you?"

"Pre'y good, pre'y good. Not see you long time."

"I was in New York for the summer."

"They not have barber in New York?"

"Nobody there understands my hair like you do, Mr. Chang."

"That right? Well, have sit. You next."

Cooper grabbed a copy of *Rolling Stone,* which seemed out of place in a barbershop where the clientele consisted almost exclusively of Chinese immigrants. But he'd met Mr. Chang's grandsons. They were as American as he was. The son and grandson of immigrants himself, Cooper knew how that worked. Outside the shop, Chinatown paraded past. After this, he would go have lunch in North Beach. Let the craziness back at the apartment go through a few more rounds. Tash could play nursery school teacher twenty-four hours a day if she wanted, but Cooper wasn't planning to hang around any more than necessary.

———

That afternoon the campus was sleepy under the perennial fog. Registration didn't start until next week. Cooper found a parking space without having to look and headed for the gym. Inside was even quieter than outside, and he settled in for a nice, hard workout.

———

"Coop," Kyle yelped, finding him in the shower. "When did you get into town?"

"Late yesterday."

"Lookin' good, man. But seems like you didn't get much sun over the summer."

"Double shifts at my dad's store. Barely had time to wipe my butt."

"I bet you still managed to squeeze in plenty of action."

Actually he hadn't. He hadn't so much as tried. It promised to be as easy in New York as all last year on campus but seemed pointless somehow. Staring at himself in the mirror after workouts, he had seen the result of concentrating completely on his exercise program and was satisfied with the tradeoff. Celibacy didn't have to be forever, and if it got you results like those, so be it.

"Seen Wayne?" he asked.

"Bastard got himself engaged over the summer."

"Uh oh."

"It was going so well, Coop. I never figured him for the type to go and do something like that."

"Engagements are made to be broken," Cooper suggested. "For that matter, I did lots of guys last year who had girlfriends."

"You did, maybe," Kyle frowned. "I don't know if I'm up to it. Guys like that are too much work."

———

"What a handsome haircut," Rivka said, fastening her seat belt. "Wherever do you go for that, honey?"

"A little place I know," Cooper said.

"Well, I wish you'd take Sammie there already."

When pigs fly, he thought, wrestling with the gearshift, which, since the Saab had been sitting in the garage all summer all of a sudden didn't want to operate properly. He had his suspicions about what had caused it.

"On second thought, maybe that's not such a good idea," Rivka said, adjusting her sunglasses against the nonexistent glare. They were exactly the style Sopia Loren had worn in that movie Rivka always said was her favorite. "Can you imagine the poor barber? And you, Cooper, having to hold a gun to Sammie's head to make him sit still for it."

"Sammie's not so bad."

"No? Well he certainly looks bad."

"It's the fashion."

"Fashion, shmashion. He has no self respect, is what it is. The curse of the Fugelsangs."

"I sort of got the idea they had too much self respect," Cooper ventured.

"It skips generations apparently," Rivka said. "Now dear, I know you and I don't often see eye to eye. . ."

It was his mother she was actually speaking to, Cooper knew. But he didn't bother pointing it out. Whatever tangent she was off on, he preferred not to redirect her. Some of his best intelligence came from letting her free associate.

"But I'm awfully glad you're living under the same roof with those two."

"Huh?"

"You're a good influence, whether you know it or not," Rivka said.

Cooper profoundly doubted this. He didn't even think she meant it. She was up to something.

"Natasha is a nice girl, and all. But she fills Maggie's head full of—well, I shouldn't say nonsense, I suppose, because you young people certainly have your own way of looking at things, and I wouldn't dream of standing in the way of progress, but really, some of that girl's ideas. Does her mother know she says things like this? I ask myself, you know. But you're back now, so that's all right. Maggie will settle right down. I mean I know my Sammie is a handful. If Maggie had any sense at all, she'd probably give him the heave-ho. But since she chooses to stay with him, is it too much to ask that they should get along? Even a little bit?"

"All couples have their ups and downs," Cooper said.

"You know that?" Rivka's eyes riveted his in the rear view mirror. The effect was not comfortable. "You know about relationships? You fascinate me."

"It just stands to reason."

"Yes, you're right, I suppose. But listen, I need to speak to you about something important. How is your grandmother doing? Really?"

"Nanny's fine," Cooper said, dreading where this might go.

"Fine?" Rivka asked. "Fine enough Shoshonnah and Willi should go off for three weeks to Israel and leave her alone like that?"

"She's not that forgetful, really," Cooper said. "She spends all day at the Jewish Community Center playing mahjong with her friends and having lunch. Aunt Rosie will check in on her in the evenings and help her get settled for the night. And if anything serious comes up, Josh is just down in the Village."

"Fine," Rikva said. "Huh."

—

"Thank God that woman is finally gone," Sammie said as Cooper came in the door. "Maybe we'll have some peace around here now."

"I don't know what you're talking about," Maggie said. "I was very nice to your mother. I'm always nice to your mother."

"That's your problem. She runs all over you and you don't say a thing about it. You need to put her in her place," Sammie grumbled, "like I do. She is gone, isn't she? You did see her get on the plane?"

"Yes," Cooper said, "the coast is clear."

"Not a moment too soon," Sammie yawned. "Now maybe this one will finally be able to keep some food down."

"I told you, you idiot," Maggie sighed, "it's a virus. It has nothing to do with your mother being here."

"Well, don't tell her that," Sammie said, "whatever you do. She doesn't need encouragement."

II

"You're going to the doctor again?" Sammie asked a few mornings later.

Cooper went on measuring out protein powder for his morning shake. He wondered how long Maggie was going to keep her charade going. He wondered how long he was going to be able to hold his tongue. Sammie was a goon, sure. But didn't he have a right to know about it if he was going to be a father? And even if he wasn't, shouldn't Maggie let him know what was going on? If there was some other guy in the picture, Sammie really shouldn't be the last to know about it.

"I told you," Maggie said. "The pills he gave me for my stomach aren't working. He said I should come back if I didn't feel better."

"If I didn't know better, I'd think you were having an affair with that Wasserman character."

"What does that mean? *If you didn't know better*. Is it too much to think that a handsome young Jewish doctor might find me attractive? Really?"

"You're not having an affair with Wasserman," Sammie said, "because the good doctor is a big old homo."

"He is not."

"Is so," Sammie insisted, "and don't ask me how I know, because I just might tell you."

———

"Cooper, great to see you, man."

"Hey, Wayne."

The line—the third one Cooper had been in in the last two hours—inched toward the banquet tables where he hoped he'd finally write his check and be done.

"Didn't expect to see you here. Heard you were still off mountain climbing in Tierra del Fuego."

"You're so full of shit," Cooper laughed.

"You wouldn't believe how many people I've run into today that fell for it. *'Who told you that?'"*

"Telling people fake rumors about themselves? That your idea of a good time?"

"As good as you can have standing in these lines," Wayne said. "Say, when we get through here, you want to come by my place?"

"Huh?"

"Been thinking about that monster of yours all summer," Waybe said. "Most guys with equipment that big have no idea what to do with it."

"I heard you'd gone straight."

"You must have talked to Kyle."

"That's right."

"I had to tell him something, Coop. He was getting all clingy. Like we were boyfriends or something. I couldn't deal with it. I'm not even sure I'm gay."

"Right."

"No, Coop, I mean it."

"Then let me clear it up for you," Cooper said. "If you spent all summer thinking about my cock, you're definitely gay."

"Ssh. Not so loud," Wayne said. "Listen, it's not that simple."

"So your fiancée—real or fake?"

"What do you think?"

"Doesn't matter what I think. Except I have to tell you, either way, it's a really bad idea."

"How so?"

"You'll never get away with it."

"Worth a try," Wayne said. "So how about it? My place?"

"I made a resolution. Sort of happy new school year thing. Want to hear it?"

"I don't know. Do I?"

"Don't fuck where you eat," Cooper said.

"What does that mean?"

———

Predictable as Big Ben, Zeb was waiting at the exit to the gym.

"Hey, Cooper. Heard you were back."

"Huh?"

"Sightings have been reported."

"Good to see you too, Zeb."

"Oh, wow."

"What?"

"I had a bet going with myself," Zeb said.

"Oh?"

"I didn't figure you'd remember my name."

"So I guess you lose," Cooper said.

"Or maybe I win. Coming over?"

"Your sources didn't tell you my news?"

"No."

"I'm turning celibate," Cooper said.

"And I'm Lucy Arnaz."

"Seriously," Cooper said. "No sex with anyone I meet inside a two mile radius of this spot."

"I'll believe that when I see it."

———

Cooper wasn't joking. Last year he'd managed to sleep with a large proportion of the gay, bisexual, and merely confused population of the university. No question about it, the sex had been great. But the guys themselves left a lot to be desired. Not in the looks department necessarily, but in just about every other respect. It had been good enough action for a college freshman, but he couldn't imagine spending the rest of his life that way. There had to be a better way of keeping himself satisfied.

He'd known for a long time that he was gay. It wasn't a big deal. Your dick liked what it liked. End of story. The only surprise involved was how much agonizing other guys went through over it. It seemed like such a waste. What they should be doing was what he had done. Figure it out the same way he figured out everything else about his life. And as for what their parents, rabbis, priests, and friends all said on the subject, well, it was nobody's damn business. But the guys he encountered on campus didn't see it that way. Either they claimed not to be gay at all, which was ridiculous considering how desperate they were to have his cock in their mouths and asses, or they seemed to believe that coming out had to be traumatic. That it inevitably entailed tears and dramatic scenes and ample helpings of loneliness, misery and despair. Everybody he discussed it with seemed convinced that when he claimed he hadn't experienced anything like that he was lying about it.

He simply didn't have the patience for them and their game playing and hand wringing. San Francisco was supposed to be full of gay men. Surely there must be some of them whose outlook matched his own.

———

As always when he was embarking on a new endeavor, Cooper did extensive research. He hated surprises and he believed that the knowledge he carried with him into new situations gave him power. The resulting confidence proved invaluable time after time. Armed with it, he had mastered countless eventualities stretching all the way back beyond his first day of kindergarten. He could no more have imagined being without it than leaving the apartment without any pants.

He had been dreading the quick stop at home to change clothes, where God only knew what questions he'd have to field, what disputes he'd be called on to arbitrate, what delays he'd have to evade. But when he arrived at the apartment it was unexpectedly deserted. He wasted no time pondering the significance of this. He simply went about his business quickly and efficiently as a neurosurgeon or the pilot of a transatlantic jetliner. He had already planned his wardrobe. Faded Levis a size too small and worn without underwear. An equally snug athletic shirt white enough to screen vacation slides on, and a buffalo plaid flannel shirt over that because less than a week after Labor Day the nights were nevertheless chilly. Crew socks as white as the a-shirt and a pair of black penny loafers with genuine New York subway tokens instead of the titular coins in the slots finished him off. This ensemble was not especially fashionable, nor did he consider it at all flattering.

What it was, his homework had established, was a kind of uniform. More than anything he was determined to look like he belonged there.

Unwilling to subject the Saab to whatever conditions prevailed in that unfamiliar neighborhood and to trust to the vagaries of San Francisco parking, he walked several blocks to a bus stop—not the closest, but the one where he was least likely to encounter anyone he knew. This was no more than a slight possibility at this time of evening but not something he wanted to risk. There would be questions, there would almost certainly be an offer of company no matter how he described his outing, there would be delay. There would, worst of all, be the slightest loss of control over the situation.

———

Considering the minimal distance involved, the trip took a long time. It would have gone faster in Manhattan. But he had expected this, so it was fine. He had to change buses twice. And, as was typical in the city, each bus route attracted its own distinct clientele. On the last leg, he was gratified to notice several young men dressed just like he was, and even more so, that he was sufficiently noteworthy to have become the topic of their conversation.

———

When he stepped off the bus, there was nothing about that stretch of the street to hint at anything out of the ordinary. With its hardware stores, pharmacies, picture framers, and corner groceries, it could have been any middle class neighborhood in the city. That was the point, he supposed. Just like his clothing, suggestive as it was of working class origins and pursuits, this drab ordinariness was a form of camouflage. He was under threat here just as surely as his brother Yakov would have been walking the streets of Jerusalem on patrol. Hopefully, Cooper was as well armed.

———

It was a simple greasy spoon with no pretentions of any kind. The clientele was almost exclusively male, which might have raised eyebrows except that there was nothing stereotypical about these habituees. They were as camouflaged as Cooper was. It might well have been a gathering of plumbers or bricklayers. He scanned the menu quickly, then ordered the day's special off the chalkboard behind the counter. The waiter was a sad faced young man. The first hint so far of the true nature of the establishment was the avid look in his eyes and the barely discernable innuendo in his quiet patter.

————

There was nothing special about the bar, either, except that it existed. Stepping inside, Cooper was assaulted by the thick pall of cigarette smoke, which he found both barely tolerable and strangely comforting. It was just another bar with bad air quality. It was stifling, as well. He quickly realized why they kept it so warm, and followed the example of a large proportion of men present by immediately shedding his flannel shirt. There was a jukebox, there was a pool table, there was truly atrocious carpeting on the floor. God only knew what sort of filth he'd be tracking home when he left. At a table in a corner sat the first drag queens Cooper had ever seen in real life. He was far too well prepared for this spectacle to stare.

He spent the evening sipping drinks purchased for him by a succession of men old enough to be his father. They were genial and they didn't exert enough pressure on him for it to become unpleasant. The only men his own age who spoke to him were the guys at the pool table and the guys playing darts. They exerted considerably more pressure than the older men had, and he didn't consider that unpleasant at all. There were several guys he wouldn't have turned down under normal circumstances and an even larger number of reasonable possibilities. If this had been a hunting trip rather than a reconnaisance expedition, he wouldn't have gotten home before morning.

————

The bus ride home would have been an anticlimax for anyone else. For Cooper, it was an opportunity to analyze and catalogue his impressions of the evening prior to surrendering his consciousness of them to the racket and disorganization of his habitat. The whole thing had been a notable success. It lived up to his expectations in every possible way. There was nothing to prevent him from returning. On the occasion of his next visit, he resolved to go as a native rather than a tourist.

———

When he got home, Sammie was snoring on the couch, and the door to his bedroom was closed. Cooper hung his clothes out the window to rid them of the smell of cigarette smoke and took a long shower before going to bed.

———

"Where the hell have you been?" Tash fumed, striding up to the table where he was eating lunch.

"Minding my own business," Cooper said. "You?"

"Dammit, Cooper. Things are falling apart, and you do one of your disappearing acts."

"Classes start Monday," Cooper said. "Today is Friday. Any of you registered yet? Any of you have any plans at all beyond staging your private soap opera?"

"As a matter of fact, we're here for late registration," Tash said. "Maggie's meeting with her advisor right this minute."

"What about Sammie?"

"Who knows? Still in bed, probably."

"On the sofa, last I saw. Where did you sleep last night, Tash? In your car? I know you didn't go home. I saw the Yellow Peril parked out front when I got in."

"Maggie didn't want to be alone."

"You two better watch out. Sammie is the jealous type."

"Right."

"So is she or isn't she?" Cooper asked.

"She is."

"Is that what the big fight was about?"

"What big fight?" Tash asked. "Was there a fight?"

"Has to be a big fight for Sammie to sleep on the sofa."

"She hasn't told him yet."

"God dammit. What is she waiting for?"

"She's afraid, Cooper."

"Of what? That he won't want to marry her? Or that he will?"

———

Zeb was waiting for him outside the gym, flanked by Kyle and Wayne.

"We're calling your bluff," Kyle said.

"That right?"

"Rory's at my place, setting up lights and cameras. A couple of my friends are already there," Zeb said.

"It's a 'welcome back to school' orgy," Wayne leered.

"And we're not taking no for an answer," Kyle said.

"Huh."

"So let's go," Wayne said.

"Be sure to let me know how it turns out," Cooper said.

"What?"

"You can't call my bluff," he said, "if I'm not bluffing."

—

There were lights on at Maggie and Tash's apartment but there wasn't a sound from inside. Usually, if they were there at all the television was on full blast. Cooper had often thought it must be so they wouldn't have to talk to each other. He knew they were home because both of their cars were out front. He knocked. Ordinarily he'd have gone right in after that non-verbal announcement, but ordinarily they would have been expecting him.

Tash opened the door.

"I'm not here to argue," he said.

"Good. Maggie just got to sleep. She's exhausted."

"Let's go for a walk."

"Why?"

"So you can explain to me what's going on," Cooper said.

"Really?"

"Yes, really. You might want a jacket. It's pretty chilly."

"Hang on."

He watched her peek in on Maggie. Then she grabbed a sweatshirt and pulled it on.

"You're really not going to argue?"

"I'm really going to try not to argue."

"Cooper."

"Sorry. That's all I can promise."

"Oh, all right."

They went down the stairs and out onto the street. The block was extremely quiet for a Friday evening. Cooper thought it was like one of those zombie movies before the nice kids got attacked.

"There's something about all this you're not telling me," he announced. "If Maggie made you promise not to, I understand. But the whole thing doesn't make sense without that piece of information. And what it does is—I don't have any idea how to help. Not trying to start a fight, Tash. Just where I'm coming from, right?"

"I guess."

"So the baby—it's Sammie's?"

"She's honestly not sure," Tash said. "That's one reason she hasn't told Sammie yet."

"What about the other guy? He know about this?"

"No."

"Why not?" Cooper asked.

"He's not somebody she actually knows. She just gets—well, you try being Sammie's girlfriend."

"No thanks," Cooper said.

"Anyway, every now and then she's had enough, and things just happen."

"I see. So this guy is just a guy."

"Right," Tash said.

"O.K. Then the only other reason she might not want to tell Sammie about the baby is she's considering not keeping it."

"I don't want to get into a whole thing about that."

"Not trying to start something," Cooper assured her. "Just telling you how I read things."

"O.K. Yes, she's thinking about not keeping the baby."

"I get that," Cooper said, "and at the same time I don't get it. I can see that she might think Sammie's not ready to be a dad."

"Obviously, he isn't."

"On the other hand," Cooper said, "and I'm playing devil's advocate here: is he going to be any more ready in the near future? Say the next year or so? So unless she's really committed to not being with him long term, she might as well go ahead and bite the bullet."

"See, Cooper, your problem is you make too much sense. You work things out logically, but that's not how people are."

"I know, Tash. But what's wrong with trying to inject a little reason into the situation? I mean, really?"

"Nothing at all," Tash said, "as long as you understand nobody's going to pay any attention to it."

"Fair enough, I guess," Cooper said, "but if she's going to have Sammie's kids eventually, I don't see the advantage in waiting. By the time the kid gets here, she'll practically be graduated. She can start her career and Sammie can be a stay at home dad. Since he'll probably be staying at home anyway."

"Just stop."

"What?"

"I told you you make too much sense," Tash said, "and you don't stop. You just keep on going. That's your other problem. You're stubborn."

"So what is it? What am I missing?"

"You think this is just about Maggie and Sammie," Tash said.

"Didn't you just say the other guy was just a guy?"

"*That* other guy, yes."

"Uh oh. There's another other guy? That's why she doesn't want to keep the baby? Because there really is somebody else?"

"There is and there isn't," Tash said.

"Huh?"

"There's this guy she likes," Tash said. "Actually, there's this guy she thinks she's in love with."

"And she figures that with a kid in tow she has no chance with him, right?"

"That's about the size of it," Tash said.

"And without a kid, she thinks she does?"

"I've tried to talk her out of it. He's not right for her."

"It's certainly no reason to have an abortion. Just on the off chance some guy might take a shine to her."

"Exactly," Tash said.

"So this guy? If I knew him, would I agree with you that he's wrong for her?"

"Oh, yes, Cooper, you of all people would agree."

"Huh? I of all people? What's that supposed to mean?"

"It's just a figure of speech."

"Tash?"

"What?"

"Oh, no, Tash, she can't be."

"I've told her and told her," Tash said. "Maybe you want to try yourself."

"How could I even bring it up?"

"Easy. Tell her you've noticed how she is around you. Tell her I told you. I don't see how that could hurt at this point."

"Oh, Tash. She doesn't know me at all."

"Tell me about it."

———

"Before you walk away," Kyle said, "would you at least listen? It's strictly business, I swear."

"Who's your friend?" Cooper asked.

"Hey," the friend said, "I'm Stone."

Stone was—well, after studying him for a moment, Cooper saw that Stone was, more or less, a blond, Scandinavian version of himself. Really, if he got a tan—if he *could* get a tan that deep—and bleached his hair, Stone was roughly what he'd look like. Cooper couldn't help being intrigued. It was enough to make him question his resolution.

"Stone and I are teaming up," Kyle said.

"Interesting thing to call it," Cooper laughed.

"It's business, Coop," Kyle said. "I told you."

"O.K., talk."

"Remember how much cash we made last year? Tax free American dollars?"

"Yeah."

"So?"

"Is Wayne in on this?" Cooper asked.

"Thing is," Kyle said, "we're changing our approach."

"Different costumes?" Cooper suggested. "Beethoven and Chopin exclusively for our dance music? I don't recommend it."

"Different audience," Kyle said. "We'll still do women's parties, of course."

"Uh-oh."

"Gays have lots of money," Kyle pointed out. "They like to watch hot guys take off their clothes at least as much as chicks do."

"I didn't mean uh-oh for me," Cooper said. "I'll drop trou for anybody who's waving cash at me. I meant, uh-oh, Wayne won't like that."

"So you're in?"

"I'm prepared to be talked into it," Cooper said, getting meaningful eye contact from Stone.

"Fair enough," Kyle grinned.

———

"Chinese takeout?" Maggie asked. "Why Chinese takeout?"

"Why not?" Sammie asked. "Gotta eat something, and nobody cooks around here these days. Somebody pass me the barbecue pork ribs."

"Cooper's paying," Tash said, a Mona Lisa smile on her face.

"And you'd better eat something, girl," Sammie said. "Tired of you complaining about your stomach, you hear?"

"Some rice, at least, Maggie," Tash suggested. "Surely you could eat a little rice."

"The reason I called this family meeting," Cooper said, figuring there was no time like the present, "is I have an announcement to make."

"What?" Sammie asked through a mouthful of barbecue. "Got some chick pregnant and now you have to marry her?"

"I'm gay," Cooper said.

"You're what?" Maggie cried, eyes huge.

"I knew it," Sammie snorted, a look of profound satisfaction on his face. "I knew it all along."

"Thank God," Tash giggled. "Pass me the Orange Peel Beef."

PART TWO: FULL SAIL

1974-1977

GYM RATS

I

"Spot you?"

The guy was several years older than Cooper. His blond hair was unfashionably short and oiled into place as if he'd missed out on the last eight years or so of American history. His blue eyes twinkled. He was built like Cooper planned to be in a couple more years. Meeting guys like this was exactly what Cooper had been hoping for when he came to San Francisco.

"Sure," Cooper said, getting into position on the weight bench. "Thanks."

———

"Haven't seen you in here before," the blond said.

"Just joined a couple of days ago."

"And immediately became a subject of gossip."

"Huh? How'd I do that?"

"Well," the blond said, "gossip's probably not the right word. Let's say speculation."

"Do we have to?" Cooper asked. "Can't we just ignore everybody else and focus on working out?"

"We could. But we won't."

"Why not?"

"It's O.K. that you don't understand how it works. You're not from around here."

"It shows?" Cooper asked.

"That accent."

"I could say the same thing about you."

"My husband and I constantly argue the point. Which one of us has the accent? Our friend Nick says we both do."

"Where's your husband from?" Cooper asked, secretly thrilling to the thought of a bodybuilder as hot as this guy casually saying "my husband". This is what King Arthur would have felt like sighting the grail.

"Right around the corner from your house would be my guess."

"New York?"

"Brooklyn to be exact."

"Manhattan," Cooper said, poking himself in the chest with his index finger.

"Italian?"

"Jewish."

"Ah. Stefano is Italian."

"And you are?"

"Scots-Irish, on my father's side."

"No, man, your name. Me Cooper, you. . ."

"Tristan."

"Pleased to meet you."

———

Cooper couldn't believe he hadn't thought of it sooner. Ordinarily he was smarter than that. There, just a few miles from the apartment, the campus, all that annoying fauna, was Nirvana. A real, honest to God, hard core gym, where real, honest to God, hard core bodybuilders worked out. At least a handful of them gay. No more hopeless college boys cluttering up the place and getting in the way of the handful of serious lifters. No more easy temptation and rampant distraction. No more juvenile game playing. This gym wasn't convenient, but so much the better. It would require planning and a greater degree of commitment, two things Cooper excelled at. He was always looking for excuses to get away from campus. This was the ultimate one.

———

"You see, what did I tell you?"

It was two days later, and that was unmistakably Tristan's voice. Cooper only kept from looking in that direction by a supreme effort of will, maintaining his concentration on his set.

"You're right. It's a very strong resemblance."

The answering voice spoke the flattened, almost dimensionless vowels of the upper Midwest. That left the husband out. It must be the friend. Cooper couldn't remember his name. He continued lifting. If they were going to watch, to talk about him, he was determined to present them with exactly the right things to remark on. And to pretend he didn't hear them.

"He really could be Big Steve's baby brother," Tristan said.

"Or love child. Big Steve could have a son that age."

This finally was too much for Cooper. He finished his set. He replaced the bar in the rack carefully, determined not to let them see him rush. Readying his most dazzling smile, he turned. And was, uncharacteristically for him, stupefied by what he saw.

The man next to Tristan, wearing gym shorts and a deeply scooped tank top, was everything that had impressed Cooper so much about Tristan the day before, yet more so. Taller, broader in the shoulder, denser and more massive overall. His hair was blonder, fashionably blow dried instead of greased down. His blue eyes were deeper blue. He was the king of the Vikings.

"Hey, Tristan," Cooper managed to stammer. "I wondered if I'd run into you again."

"Cooper," Tristan smiled. "That set looked pretty fierce."

Cooper managed to recover himself enough to at least attempt a blasé expression, though he knew he'd been putting on an act for them.

"This must be the friend you were talking about," he said, anxious not to seem too curious.

"Hi," the man said, "I'm Nick."

———

If that wasn't husband material there was no such thing. That's all there was to it. That was Cooper's last thought that night and pretty much his first thought the next morning. All those guys on campus with their incessant whining about boyfriends were barking up the wrong tree. What a ridiculous waste of time his freshman year had turned out to be. Why hang out with beagles when what you wanted to join was a wolf pack?

———

"You been sick?" Chet asked, pulling up a chair across from him in the student union.

"Why?" Cooper asked. "Do I look sick?"

"Haven't seen you at the gym in over a week," Chet said. "Nobody has. And boy have you been missed. People are talking."

"Really. What are they saying?"

"You don't want to know."

"You know, you're right," Cooper laughed, "I don't. But here's what you can tell them. I'm giving it all up. I'm going to turn into a pencil neck geek. I'm going to go shopping for some really thick glasses. This afternoon. From now on if they want me they'll have to look for me in the library."

"Like anybody will believe that," Chet said, rolling his eyes. "So tell."

"Sorry," Cooper said.

"But your friends want to know what's up with you."

"Guess you'll all have to chip in for a private investigator."

———

Tristan's husband was the biggest bodybuilder Cooper had ever seen. In his experience, guys much over six feet tall never seemed to pack on enough bulk to be really impressive. But Stefano was a giant, six and a half feet tall and massive in every direction. He dwarfed Nick, who was a big guy by any reasonable standard, and he made Tristan look positively petite. In their company, Cooper felt like a puppy. He tried not to act like one by following them around making a nuisance of himself. But it wasn't much of a problem. Their company was elusive. He found himself spending more and more time at the gym just to get a glimpse of one or the other of them. Some days all he got was a flash of Tristan's glistening hair or Nick's spooky eyes, which alternately smoldered or froze. Sometimes the only hint of their presence was the distant rumble of Stefano's basso profundo. Some days one of them, some days two, occasionally but rarely all three at once graced the precincts of the establishment like princes on a royal progress through the remoter hinterlands of some fantastic empire.

They absolutely ruled the gym. Hank, the owner, didn't so much as change a light bulb without their permission. The regulars greeted Stefano's pronouncements with a degree of reverence typically reserved for texts carved onto stone tablets and schlepped down desolate mountainsides. A goodly portion of gay San Francisco seemed to drop by on a regular basis just in case one or the other of them happened to be there, hopefully with his shirt off. When one of them showered, the resulting crowd scene was both deplorable and comic. Individually and collectively they were the subject of endless talk, the bulk of it all too obviously uninformed. Cooper watched more than one hunk-in-waiting appear foolish by attempting to shoehorn himself into greater intimacy with them than they were prepared to grant. They never went out of their way to make such individuals unwelcome but neither did they encourage the overtures. Invitations were not issued. Offers of various kinds were not taken up on. Proposed favors were quietly but firmly deflected. Desperation was not acknowledged, much less rewarded. The implicit lesson of this wasn't lost on Cooper, who, though cordial when one or the other of them spoke to him, always kept his distance. If he was going to be one of their crew, it would be because they chose him, not vice versa. Obviously.

The three men represented a species Cooper hadn't previously suspected the existence of. They were men who loved men yet were resolutely men themselves. He had resigned himself to being the sole exemplar and exponent of this type— almost its originator, since until meeting them he'd had no indication anyone in the universe shared his vision. But here they were, fully actualized, realer than real, more authentic, indeed, than anything he had been able to imagine. They had already gone where he was still planning to venture, and he wanted to know everything about them.

———

"Didn't I tell you gay men were better tippers than straight chicks?" Kyle laughed, counting out bills.

"You were right, oh wise one," Stone laughed.

"We'll never doubt you again," Cooper said, "until next time."

"We should go get pizza," Kyle suggested.

"Gotta see a man about a horse," Stone said, looking cryptic. "Take a rain check, though."

"Cooper?"

"Early study group," Cooper said, on a hunch.

"Some strippers you guys are," Kyle complained. "Real sexual outlaws."

"What's that got to do with pizza?" Cooper asked.

"I just thought. . ."

"Sorry, man," Stone said.

"Next time," Kyle said.

"Sure," Cooper nodded.

———

"Quick on the uptake," Stone grinned. "I like that in a pal."

Cooper slid into the booth across from him. He had followed Stone at the distance of half a block for exactly twelve minutes, hoping that when he got wherever they were headed it wouldn't seem too creepy of him.

"More a case of Kyle being slow on the uptake," Cooper said.

"Sometimes I like that even better."

"Nice place."

"No, it isn't," Stone said. "Not even close. But nobody I know comes here."

"I like that in a diner."

"What are you having?" Stone asked. "I'm paying. I just came into some money."

"What's good here?"

"Nothing on the menu, that's for damned sure."

"Is your solitude really that important to you?" Cooper asked, scanning the document. "You'll eat crappy food just to be left alone?"

"The night chef does this special for me. He pulls the skin off a couple of chicken breasts and grills them. Serves it sliced on a bed of raw spinach. I squeeze lemon juice on it. It's not bad."

"Sounds really healthy," Cooper said.

"That's me."

The waitress arrived, popping her bubble gum.

"Hey, Stone, who's your friend?"

"I'm Cooper."

"I'm Stella."

"Nice to meet you."

"No, it's not," she giggled.

"Tell Tiny hi for me," Stone said, "and tell him to put two specials on."

"Anything to drink?"

"Just water," Stone said.

"And you?"

"Water," Cooper said. "Slice of lemon in it."

"Coming right up, boys."

"You're friends with Stefano and T.," Stone said. "I see you with them at the gym."

"I don't know that we're friends," Cooper said.

"I hear how they talk about you when you're not there," Stone said. "They're getting ready to adopt you."

"Really."

"Unless you don't want to be adopted."

"You've got the right look," Cooper said. "Maybe they'll adopt you, too."

"Stefano doesn't approve of me," Stone said. "I'm too commercially oriented."

"Sounds like him, all right. For a libertine, he's a real prude."

"Hell, I don't blame him," Stone said. "I don't approve of me, either. But a boy's got to get by."

"Right."

"Too bad you took yourself out of circulation."

"I'm not out of circulation," Cooper said.

"What I heard."

"I just got bored with college guys. They're too stupid to live."

"So true. It's all hearts and flowers with them. 'Let's be boyfriends, Stone'. Enough to make you barf."

"Exactly," Cooper nodded.

"Either that or 'god, I was so drunk last night, I can't remember a thing'."

"Or 'you should come over. My girlfriend's out of town for the weekend'."

"My personal favorite," Stone said, "is 'my girlfriend's in the Peace Corps'."

"I know that guy," Cooper laughed.

"Everybody knows that guy."

"Right."

"Anyway, I'm glad you showed up," Stone said.

"That's good," Cooper said, "I guess."

"Got a little proposition for you."

"I'm really not commercially oriented."

"Not business," Stone said, "personal."

"Oh?"

"There's this thing I never do with my gentlemen," Stone said. "Once you do, your business is never the same. Not the way I really want things to go. Got to take a long term approach."

"I see."

"But see, I really like doing, um, that certain thing. Just not professionally."

"Wait," Cooper said, "you want me. . ."

"Everybody says you're really good at it," Stone said.

"Oh."

"Like, really, really good."

"How do you know I won't fuck you and then run off and tell all my friends about it?" Cooper asked.

"Hey, if you're such a boy scout that Stefano and T. are ready to declare you their love child, I can trust you."

———

Cooper found that the mysteries of the secret kingdom revealed themselves to him with a speed and ease of effort he wouldn't have considered possible if he had been anyone else. Almost before he knew it, all the arcana of the habitat was neatly categorized and prioritized and filed away in his memory, much like the specialized knowledge of an ornithologist, lapidary, or amateur astronomer. He learned which bar was appropriate for a quick drop in visit early on a Tuesday evening before an important midterm, which one was most promising if he were in the mood to shoot pool or play darts without having to fend off admirers, inside which one resided the jukebox offering the least objectionable repertoire, and which one was most likely to be festive—or merely frenetic—with drag queens on the night of a full moon. He knew which bartenders could be relied on to serve him club soda when a prospective suitor tried to get him drunk, which restroom windows were good for a quick escape when unpleasantness, or merely boredom, loomed, which handsome former athlete determined to catch his eye was most likely to be a plainclothes cop or a psychopath.

He knew the styles of the neighborhood as well as he knew the schedules and rhythms and species of the other fauna. He knew to a millimeter how long he should have Mr. Chang trim his hair. He knew exactly how much cologne he could safely wear in daylight or after dark, and which brand. The faded blue of his jeans, their tightness, and their length he could unconsciously calibrate as precisely as a gunnery sergeant could direct mortar fire against an enemy fortification. He knew the styles so well that he knew exactly to what extent they could be violated to exquisite, rather than disastrous, effect. This, he understood, was perhaps even more important than his looks and physique.

He learned all of this the way fish learn about water.

The men he went with were pretty much the same physical type as the ones he now avoided back on campus. A few years older, they had careers and apartments. They had settled routines. They had cats, or even, depending on their landlords, dogs. They had conversation more comprehensive than any undergraduate he had yet encountered. They had fewer opinions, though still enough that he sometimes found it obstructive. More importantly they had experience, both in and out of bed. Best of all, they seemed to have lower expectations, not sexually, but in every other respect. They didn't make a case out of everything, just half of it. They knew the rules. They did not expect to invent new ones but merely to follow established practice. Though there were occasional unpleasant surprises, for the most part they were amazingly accommodating. If they found some activity he advocated not to their taste, they quickly, and unprompted, came up with acceptable and sometimes gratifyingly inventive alternatives. His schoolmates obsessed over penis size and who did what to whom, while Cooper found the condition of the sheets on the bed he'd be sharing and the cleanliness of the shower he'd be stepping into afterward far more crucial questions. Sex was just sex, but hygiene was elemental.

———

"Cooper. Over here."

It was like he could feel Stefano's growl through the soles of his feet. Stefano and a guy Cooper didn't recognize stood on the other side of the gym.

He had noticed them when he came in, having what looked like a serious conversation.

"What's up?"

"Giving Denny some pointers," Stefano said. "Got a few minutes?"

"Sure."

"Take off that shirt."

Cooper pulled the t-shirt over his head. Stefano reached over and smoothed his hair down like he was a four year old. Cooper had seen him do the same thing to Tristan. He tried not to bask too obviously.

"What you got on under those sweats?"

"Jockstrap," Cooper said.

"Drop them," Stefano said. "You mind?"

Cooper undid the drawstring, slipped the garment over his quads, and let it fall.

"Thing is," Stefano said to Denny, a guy about Cooper's height with brown hair and a mustache that was trimmed to Folsom Street specifications, "Cooper's got great size, as you see, but also he's really cut. Most guys, it's one or the other. They're defined but undersized, or they have the mass but not the cuts. You can see that Cooper has been really careful not to get too big too fast and lose all the refinement and detail."

"Right," Denny said.

A little too avidly, Cooper thought.

"And he's what, twenty-one?" Stefano observed.

"Turning nineteen in a few more weeks," Cooper said.

"All right then," Stefano said, "let's go over it in detail."

Denny nodded.

"Just relax, Coop," Stefano muttered, beefy hands taking him by the shoulders. "Going to put you into a few poses, right?"

Cooper relaxed into it, glad that he had shaved all over the night before. A shove here and a nudge there, murmuring to him from time to time, all the while keeping up the patter, Stefano put him through the regulation poses of a competition routine. Cooper knew them by heart from reading the bodybuilding magazines, but except in his imagination had never actually executed them. He hoped he didn't look as awkward as he felt. Stefano's hands roamed all over him, tracing a line here, emphasizing a contour there, demonstrating the tightness of the skin over his abs and pointing out the separations between his serratus muscles. Stefano suggested strategies for improving certain areas, proposed further development in others, discussed overall potential. Observing him working with Tristan and Nick, Cooper had formed an impression of Stefano as the consummate expert and authority. Now he knew first hand. Stefano was Phidias; he was Michelangelo; he was Rodin. Eventually, hypnotized by the deep voice and overpowered by the proximity, Cooper lost track of what Stefano was saying; moved to the imperatives of those virtuosic hands.

Recalling it afterward, it seemed to him it was the sexiest thing he'd ever experienced, though there had been nothing explicitly sexual about it.

———

"Gotta hand it to you, cous," Sammie smirked.

"Huh?"

"Brilliant move, that line of yours about being gay."

"It wasn't a line."

"Right," Sammie nodded. "Your secret is safe with me. Sure got the girls' attention, though. Seems like all they and their little friends talk about these days is which one of them is gonna convert you back. Wish I'd thought of it myself. It's sure as hell like having a license to steal."

"That's not why I told you guys."

"It is what it is," Sammie shrugged. "Never gave you credit for being that smart, is all."

———

"You should let me train you."

Determined not to betray his surprise, Cooper didn't move a muscle for a count of two. Then he turned, flashing that "aw shucks" grin he'd been practicing in the bathroom mirror.

"Hey, Big Steve. Didn't know you were in the gym this afternoon."

Last week, Cooper had graduated from calling the man Stefano to calling him Big Steve like Nick and Tristan did. It still felt a little strange.

"Think about it," Big Steve said. "You've got serious potential."

Since joining the gym, Cooper had heard well over a dozen guys begging, pleading, cajoling, offering money, and promising favors—to no avail. Word was, you didn't approach Big Steve. He came to you. Except he almost never did. You could count his protégés on the fingers of one hand with your thumb left over. Tristan and Nick, of course, and a silver haired, baby faced monster with an intermittent stutter everybody referred to as J. B. There was also some airline pilot that everybody talked about but no one ever actually saw. Cooper wasn't sure he'd ever heard that man's name.

"I don't have to think about it," Cooper said, extending his hand, "just say thanks and when do we start?"

"We'll set up a schedule," Big Steve said, "but it would help if I knew what your goal is."

"Get big. Achieve my full potential."

"Everybody says that," Big Steve said, "but who knows what it means? It's an abstraction as much as a cliché. A man needs something more concrete than that to focus on. A specific image, you know. What he sees himself looking like someday."

"Tristan and I," Cooper said, determined not to sound like he'd rehearsed this speech though he had, "have the same body type. I could look like that, given time and hard work."

"Good call," Big Steve nodded. "Your hips are a little narrower and your shoulders are a little wider. Talking bone structure, you understand, not actual size at this point. He's probably got twenty-five pounds of lean muscle mass on you right now."

"Sure."

"Looks to me, too, like you might just put on more fullness in the pecs than he's been able to, but we'll have to see."

"I'll tell him you said all that," Cooper chuckled.

"He knows," Big Steve said. "We talked about it. Hell, it's not personal."

"No." Cooper said, wondering what it was, if not that.

"What we don't know," Big Steve said, "is how much lean muscle mass your metabolism will support. What kind of diet will work best for you. How much recovery time you'll need between workouts to promote optimum growth. And then there's the whole psychological component that's involved. That's probably more important than anything. Everybody's different, but having an advanced bodybuilder similar to you to measure your progress against is a big advantage."

II

It didn't look much like Valhalla. It had been silly of Cooper to expect something as grandiose as its inhabitants. In real life, Stefano and Tristan were just a couple of police officers. They lived in this modest Tudor cottage, two storied, half timbered, slate roofed. Nick and J.B.'s motorcycles parked in the driveway were the only indication that Miss Marple wasn't the resident.

———

Tristan was adamant when he issued the invitation. Sure, it was Big Steve's birthday, but no cards, no gifts, no bottle of wine—just show up. Still, Cooper felt awkward arriving empty handed. It was a surprisingly small gathering to celebrate such a luminary. There easily could have been dozens or even hundreds present. Realizing the intimacy of the event, he was flattered that he'd been included.

Nick was there of course, grinning that grin that was an offensive weapon and looking like the captain of a band of Swedish speaking pirates. Hulking, monosyllabic J.B. was there, devouring Cooper with those famished eyes of his. And in the kitchen, a woman nearly as tiny as Nanny Freitag was transferring meatballs from a baking sheet to a pot of fragrant Bolognese sauce.

"Auntie Violetta," Tristan said, "I want you to meet our buddy, Cooper."

"Oh, Cooper," she said, wiping her gem encrusted hands on a dish towel and turning to greet him. She reached up, grabbed his face with both hands, and pulled him down for a kiss. "My Stefano has written to me about you, his new young friend. How happy it makes me to finally meet you."

"Nice to meet you, too," Cooper said. He hadn't thought of Big Steve as actually having family. Except perhaps some residing on Mount Olympus.

"I hear you're a nice New York boy."

"Manhattan," Cooper nodded.

"Where in Manhattan?"

"Riverside Drive."

"Oh. So nice. And your papa? What does he do?"

"My parents own a jewelry store."

"*Vero*? Which one, please?"

"Luxemberg's."

"No," her jaw dropped. "My favorite. I shop other places, but I never buy anything anywhere else."

"Cool."

"But wait," she said breathlessly. "That must mean that you are Shoshonnah's boy, no?"

"No," Cooper stammered, "I mean yes."

"Oh, dear, dear Shoshonnah. She helps me personally, you know, whenever I am in the shop. Such a sweet, lovely woman. Oh, Cooper, *caro*, this meeting fills me with such joy. Truly. Come, let me kiss you again and say *benvenuto*. Welcome to the *famiglia*."

———

"Is she really Big Steve's auntie?" Cooper asked, once she had shoo'ed them out of the kitchen.

"Just about his only family," Tristan confirmed. "She raised him pretty much single handed. He was apparently a real handful."

"Amazing. Does she realize she's in a house full of homosexuals?"

"She played matchmaker for Big Steve and me."

"You're joking."

"We wouldn't be together today except for her."

———

Just before dinner was served, the last of the guests arrived. The airline pilot Cooper had been hearing about at the gym was named Matt. He had Tristan's haircut, Nick's mustache, and J.B.'s physique. Cooper recognized him on sight. He'd placed third in the Mr. America contest a couple of times, and Cooper remembered seeing him on the covers of half a dozen bodybuilding magazines over the years. His boyfriend was noticeably younger, probably no more than a few years older than Cooper himself. His name was Ashby, and he was introduced as a medical student. With smooth black hair and eyes the color of honey, he was handsome in the fashion of one of those 1930's matinee idols. He didn't look like he'd ever spent a minute in a gym. Cooper thought that was fascinating.

———

Nick and Tristan consumed their meatballs without sauce or pasta. Their big contest was just two weeks off. Cooper admired their will power. The meatballs were about on a level with manna from heaven, but then, the more he observed her, the more Auntie Violetta seemed to take on the aura of a supernatural creature. No surprise, really, if she had truly raised Big Steve on her own.

"Will you be attending the contest?" Ashby asked him.

"Sure," Cooper said.

"He'll be in the pump room with us," Big Steve said. "We'll need his help prepping our two competitors."

This was the first Cooper had heard of it. His cup was certainly running over.

———

"And for dessert," Auntie Violetta announced, bearing a platter in from the kitchen, "Stefano's favorite. Auntie Violetta's special cannoli. Tristan, darling, you and Nick will share one. I command it. Your abdominals will recover in time, I promise."

III

"Thanks for taking Auntie Violetta out to lunch last week," Big Steve said, loading gym bags into the back of the Land Rover. "She had a great time. She said to tell you you're a true prince. *Un' principe assoluto*."

"That's sweet," Cooper said. "She reminds me of my Nanny Freitag. Eighty-nine pounds dripping wet, hot as a pistol, and tough as a crocodile. Violetta's much younger, of course."

"I pity any guy who doesn't have a woman like that in his life," Big Steve laughed.

"She get back to Brooklyn all right?"

"Yeah. She'll be out here next month for Tristan's birthday. She'll stay through New Year's. And you'd better make time for her in your calendar. She'll insist on seeing you."

"Can't wait."

"You been to one of these things before?"

"Never," Cooper said. "Read about them in the mags is all."

"You're in for a treat."

"You ever compete yourself?"

"Not for a while," Big Steve shook his head.

"You're the biggest guy I've ever seen," Cooper said. "No joke. And you're in at least as good a condition as Nick and Tristan are. I'd be surprised if anybody out there could beat you."

"There's a certain body of opinion," Big Steve said, "to the effect that I don't complete because I'm afraid of losing. The real reason is I've got nothing to prove. When Nick competes, he's sending a message to the whole world. And Tristan thinks he has something to prove to me. He's wrong about that, but you'll never convince him of it."

"What are their chances tonight?" Cooper asked.

"What do you think?"

"It's hard to imagine anyone beating either of them."

"Time will tell."

"What about J.B.? He ever been in a contest?"

"It's a confidence thing with J.B.," Big Steve said. "His upper body is certainly at the same level as Nick's. No question about it. But there's a reason you've never seen his legs."

"Not up to it?"

"They're fine. Thing is, his left calf is scarred up. He was wounded in 'Nam. The doctors wanted to amputate just below the knee. He fought like hell and he kept the whole leg. It doesn't look as bad as he thinks. He'd be competitive even with those scars. But, well, having Nick and Tristan for your best friends doesn't make it easy. It's hard for him to be objective about his body."

———

The venue for the event was a high school way down the peninsula. The pump room wasn't a room at all, just backstage space in the auditorium where benches and weights had been arranged so the competitors could warm up. The competitors were divided into three classes: teen—for competitors under twenty years old, junior—for less experienced competitors who had been in six or fewer contests, and the open class, so called because there were no restrictions on the entrants except for amateur status. It was the largest class, with over forty competitors, but realistically only half a dozen men had any chance at all of winning it. The overall winner of the competition would be selected from the open class.

"Here," Big Steve said, handing Cooper a bottle. "Oil Tristan up. Just watch J.B. working on Nick and do what he does. You'll be fine."

Cooper hadn't anticipated this. But Tristan didn't seem the least bit concerned, so Cooper got to work. The feel of Tristan's body in his hands was nothing less than revelatory. The opulence of the contours, the firmness of the flesh, the satiny smoothness of the freshly shaven surfaces. If Big Steve had the least inkling what he was thinking or feeling, Cooper was sure he'd have his neck broken. Looking over at J.B. and Nick didn't help. It wasn't the distraction he hoped it would be. It just made what he was feeling more intense.

———

From his vantage point in the audience, it looked to Cooper like Nick was unbeatable. It was harder to be sure about Tristan's placing. There was a black guy from Oakland who might beat him for second. Sitting between J.B. and Big Steve, Cooper felt like a whippet in a kennel full of greyhounds.

———

The men on stage were astonishing. Cooper had seen them up close in the pump room, and the best of them had been impressive enough. But from the audience, under the lights like that, they so totally eclipsed average men that they could almost have been members of a different species. Cooper wasn't sure if he'd ever want to compete, but he certainly wanted to look like them. He was going to have to really get his ass in gear in the gym.

———

"Pizza," Tristan moaned in a bad imitation of a zombie. "Must have pizza now."

"Congratulations," Cooper said, slapping him on the back. Tristan had come in third, behind Nick, the winner, and the black guy from Oakland. Back in sweats he didn't look like a god at all, just a goofball gym rat.

"Seriously," Tristan said, breaking character, "if I don't ingest some carbs soon I may pass out."

"Here," Big Steve said, handing him a bar of dark chocolate. "This will keep you conscious until we get to Angelotti's."

———

Sitting between Tristan and J.B. in the back seat of the Land Rover, Cooper finally got why all those jocks back in high school had been so crazy to make the squad. Though he had always been a lone wolf, the feeling of belonging was intoxicating.

"Next stop North Beach," Big Steve said, shifting gears.

"Pizza," Tristan muttered. "Need pizza."

———

"Congratulations again," Cooper said. "You looked great."

They were back at Big Steve and Tristan's house, and the party was breaking up.

"And you make a terrific team mascot," Nick said. "Next year, it's going to be you up there on the stage."

"Don't know about that."

"You've got all kinds of potential. And Big Steve says you're a really hard worker."

"I guess you guys kind of inspire me," Cooper said.

"We should go out," Nick said. "You free next Friday?"

IV

Cooper couldn't remember ever having been so horny. He'd hardly understood the meaning of the word until Nick asked him out. It seemed like Friday would never come.

———

"Nice place," Cooper said, looking around the restaurant.

"You don't have to be polite," Nick laughed. "The atmosphere sucks. But the food here is great. And they're sympathetic people."

"I know absolutely nothing about Eastern European food."

"I'll order for you," Nick said, "if that's O.K."

"Sure," Cooper said. "I'm completely at your mercy."

"I like the sound of that," Nick said.

He was just the most amazing man in the world, Cooper thought. This might be the night that changed his life.

———

"You were out with Nick Romanovsky Friday night," Stone said, falling into step beside Cooper. "I saw you."

"Yes," Cooper said. "We went out."

"How was it?"

"Weird."

"Weird how?"

"We went to dinner. We went dancing. We went for a long walk. We talked about all kinds of things. I thought we were connecting. Hell, I know we were connecting."

"Yeah?"

"We even made out a little," Cooper continued. "I was sure we were getting ready for the main event. Next thing I know, he's dropping me off at my car. He gives me a firm, manly handshake, flashes me a grin—you know that grin of his? Shit, everybody knows that grin of his."

"Right."

"And then all of a sudden he's off into the night on that BMW. And I'm standing there thinking, what gives?"

"My fault," Stone said.

"What?"

"My fault. I never should have let him fuck me."

"Explain, please."

"Nick doesn't take it up the ass," Stone said. "Ever."

"Uh huh."

"I mean, ever," Stone said. "So when we started dating, I thought, well, he's just so damned hot. And he's a really great top. I like being fucked by a really hot guy. You know that, Coop."

"Sure."

"But, see, after a while he started talking about us being exclusive, and I just couldn't do it. I like pitching, too. I like it a lot."

"And?"

"That's how the story ends, man. I couldn't turn myself into a bottom for life. Not even for Nick Romanovsky. He didn't have that problem with the next guy."

"Oh."

"No sir, the next guy he dated made me look downright reasonable. But for some reason that didn't work out, either. I'm guessing by the time he dropped you off Friday night, he'd figured you out."

THE WEDDING CAKE HOUSE

The first time Cooper saw the house was by moonlight. The ornately sculpted stucco of its façade seemed to glow. It appeared to produce its own light rather than simply reflecting the moon. It was an extraordinary effect, and it elicited an extraordinary reaction from Cooper. Long a fancier of architecture, he had nevertheless waited until that moment to think of a house as a poem. Though in this case "house" was hardly an appropriate term. "Temple", "mauseoleum", and "villa" all came to mind, but he quickly discarded these terms as too literal. Really, it was a kind of dream realized in concrete, wood, stucco. But a particular type of dream. Finally it came to him. It was a giant wedding cake.

"You live here?" he asked the black clad figure leading him past the side of the house. He asked silently, unwilling to betray his astonishment, but he asked nevertheless. His astonishment surprised him. He considered himself immune to the feeling. He tried his best not to have feelings of any kind, preferring instead to focus on his instincts and his reason. Feelings were trivial and astonishment seemed to him to denote weakness, in this case a failure of his imagination.

The black clad figure led him around to the rear of the house, which as far as Cooper could tell presented an aspect as elaborate and monumental as did the front. Indeed, it was only the building's orientation to the street that determined which elevation was front and which rear. The building's appearance, except for the stately entry plaza and steps leading to the portico, indicated no hierarchy between the two facades, since the rear had its own terrace and broad stairs leading down to the swimming pool, itself reminiscent of a reflecting pool set in the precincts of a temple.

"You live here?" Cooper asked again, once more inaudibly.

"Almost there," the black clad figure said. He spoke with what Cooper thought was almost but not quite an accent. Like someone who had come to America as a small child but whose speech was still subtly flavored by that other, all but forgotten, speech of his homeland. They approached another structure, equally as fanciful as the main building but somewhat smaller and equipped with a row of garage doors. They climbed a set of stairs built into its side. At the top, they walked along an arcade looking out across the pool toward the rear of the mansion.

"You live *here*?" Cooper asked a third time, as the black clad figure turned a key in a french door off the arcade. But what actually came out of him was, "wow, some place you've got here."

"My landlords are unusual guys."

———

It fit, Cooper thought later, standing naked and gazing out the french door at the mansion. However Christopher happened to acquire this apartment, he had placed himself in the perfect setting. Somehow, though Cooper couldn't have explained it, Christopher seemed to belong there. They had met that evening outside one of Cooper's favorite bars. He was on the point of entering when that smoky voice said in that almost but not quite accent "you don't really want to go in there. Let's go somewhere for coffee instead."

Cooper turned, looked, and was amazed. The man, two or three years older than him at most, was breathtaking. Other than Big Steve's crew and Cooper's pal Stone, nobody was breathtaking like that. It was reflex as much as anything when Cooper shrugged, grinned, let go of the door handle, and said "O.K."

———

Christopher's father was from Connecticut, his mother from Guadalajara. He had graduated from the University of Paris. He was a third year medical student. Cooper didn't learn any of this over coffee. They didn't talk about anything of consequence until after sex. The sex—hours of it—had been revelatory. Christopher was Cooper's perfect match, the magnetic south to his north, equal to him in expertise and intensity, his opposite in exactly the right technical aspects. Cooper's disappointment over Nick Romanovsky died silently and unmourned that night in Christopher's bed.

———

Who knew that the brain was an erogenous zone? Perhaps the biggest, most sensitive one of all? Thinking back, Cooper realized that Big Steve and Tristan had tried to tell him as much, but his first few times with Christopher demonstrated the reality of it in ways he couldn't ignore. He spent every waking hour in a fog of amazement that something he had considered himself such a master of—dozens of satisfied customers!—could have this unsuspected dimension.

———

Christopher was remarkable. But also, Cooper thought, a little mysterious. Not to mention far less available than Cooper would have liked. Accustomed to bowling over his conquests, he found that Christopher defied being shoved into that category. Nor could Cooper chalk him up and move on. Every time they were together he felt they left something undone, or perhaps it was that he had glimpsed something as yet undiscovered which necessitated further explorations. These, though satisfying, continued to be inconclusive, necessitating yet more. Christopher seemed to withhold as much as he gave, and comprehending this Cooper recognized for the first time his own withholding nature. He finally understood that as lavish as he was with his body, his generosity pretty much ended there. It was funny how easy it was to recognize the quality in someone else; ironic that he had to learn the lesson from someone whose tendencies in that regard exceeded even his own. It wasn't the kind of insight that prompted to him to change. It simply enlarged his understanding.

But it was a frustrating trait to deal with in his—whatever Christopher was. Cooper had had lots of sex but never really a boyfriend. That term, however it might be understood, seemed singularly unsuitable for the present case. Labeling it at all felt like too much trouble. What they were together, in bed at least, transcended the whole notion of labels. Why bother naming something when its real meaning was in the doing? Why bother to contemplate its significance while you were apart when a much better use could be made of your time preparing for your next encounter? Which, considering the rigors of Christopher's schedule might be the next night or never.

———

Sometimes, preparing for his next encounter with Christopher occurred simultaneously with something else, Cooper mused, feeling Stone's muscles clench around him, surveying the broad, smooth expanse of Stone's back with its extravagantly flaring latissimus muscles bulging inside the satiny skin, burying his fingers in the golden silkiness, the dense luxuriance of Stone's hair.

If Christopher was the magnetic south to Cooper's north, Stone was his photographic negative: deeply bronzed skin, tawny eyes, blond hair. Two distinct metaphors, but they both signified oppositeness. How could two opposites of the same thing be so completely different from each other? How could doing the same thing to both of them feel so completely different when he was doing it? Yet when Cooper attempted to describe the difference to himself, why should it be so impossible to find the words for the task?

———

They met in front of the Castro Theater, in front of City Lights Bookstore, in front of the opera house, in front of Grace Cathedral. Always in front of somewhere, never inside. On the way to Christopher's apartment, it was time for "how was your day?" or "I missed you the last three days" or once even, "I can't believe that it's been a whole week." In bed there was no talk. After sex someone always fell asleep or someone had to leave or both of them did. Sometimes, looking into Christopher's eyes, Cooper felt like he was looking into a mirror. Sometimes, looking into Christopher's eyes, he felt like he was looking into deep, turbulent waters. Sometimes, looking into Christopher's eyes, he felt like he was looking at smooth concrete.

———

One night, while Cooper and Stone were standing around in their second favorite bar trying to figure out if they were bored enough to go fuck, Christopher entered, looked around, saw them, sauntered up, and kissed Cooper full on the mouth. It was so obviously a grandstand play that Cooper almost turned and walked away. He sensed nothing authentic in the act, and that made it detestable.

"Let's go," Christopher said.

"Stone and I kind of had plans," Cooper said.

"Oh, Stone's coming, too."

"You two know each other?"

"Christopher knows everybody," Stone said.

"So does Stone," Christopher smiled. "I like a good threesome."

———

"You should have told me you were seeing him," Stone said the next time they met.

"Oh?"

"You should have," Stone nodded.

"Would it have mattered?" Cooper asked.

"Don't be stupid," Stone said.

"Then why mention it?"

"I could have given you some pointers."

"I need pointers?" Cooper asked.

"With that one," Stone said, "everyone needs pointers."

"Stone, who are you talking to?"

"Has he introduced you to his uncle?"

"What uncle?"

"The uncle whose boyfriend owns the big house," Stone said. "What? You thought he just found that apartment? Like in the classifieds?"

"I had no idea."

"And you think you know who you're dealing with," Stone laughed.

II

The first time Cooper visited the big house he felt like he was entering a movie set. He dressed up a little because though Christopher hadn't said he should he wanted to make a good impression. And when the seven foot tall butler greeted him at the door, he was glad he had. The man's glare couldn't have been more intimidating if he'd been a prime minister.

"The *messieurs* are expecting you," he said as Cooper stepped inside, making it sound like an accusation.

Everything about the entry hall of the house was imposing, from the slick marble floors to the suits of armor on pedestals at intervals around the perimeter of the cavernous space. Nothing about it said San Francisco. Very little about it even said twentieth century. The dim chandelier overhead could easily have been illuminated with real candles.

———

Christopher's Uncle Rene had the slicked back hair and pencil line mustache of a 'Twenties gigolo or a famous vampire of the silver screen. He was strikingly handsome in a pale, slightly anemic way that reeked of European decadence. His English was thickly accented, and when he spoke it sounded like he was reading from a script. His expression said that while he might be too impotent to rape you, he'd gladly pay someone else to tie you up and do it—a whole gang, preferably—while he watched. There was a strong family resemblance between Christopher and his uncle. It was a little spooky to think that Christopher might well look like that in twenty years or so. It was even spookier to contemplate the possibility of internal similarities between the two.

Jules, the actual owner of the house, looked like a gorilla dressed up for the senior prom. He didn't speak any English, and Cooper was relieved when Christopher told him not to bother addressing the man. It was almost impossible to believe that he was an internationally famous film director, the kind universities taught seminars about. If he was so great, shouldn't Cooper have heard of him?

"He learns everything he needs to know from watching you," Christopher explained. "He's the most totally visual man you'll ever meet. He's like a deaf man whose powers of visual observation have become heightened in compensation for his disability. Except he's not actually deaf—just too lazy to bother learning English. His French isn't that good either."

"I thought he was a Frenchman."

"He's a French citizen," Christopher nodded, "but Rene says it's not by birth. He was naturalized."

"Where's he from, then? What language does he speak?"

"Nobody knows for certain."

Cooper couldn't help being suspicious of the story. It seemed too much like the plot of a movie. And what else would an eccentric director do but replace his own biography with a script?

——

Dinner was served in a grand hall large enough to host a banquet. The dark wooden paneling was gothic in design, and once again there was a chandelier that provided surprisingly little illumination. The butler presided, but the actual serving was done by half a dozen uniformed young men all of whom looked like Rene's offspring. A similar cohort performed chamber music in the gallery overlooking the room. The meal consisted of a parade of courses, all of them exquisite, though none of the portions was large enough to provide more than a couple of mouthfuls. It was like prolonged foreplay, Cooper thought. The conversation at the table was desultory and mind numbingly trivial. Cooper was left with the strong impression that everyone was there to be seen and not heard.

——

"I can't ask you to stay the night," Christopher said, giving him a quick kiss at the front door.

"I've got an early exam anyway," Cooper lied, faking a yawn. The whole thing had been at least as anti-climactic as his date-that-apparently-wasn't with Nick Romanovsky six weeks earlier.

"Don't forget the party next weekend," Christopher said.

III

"Is that what you're wearing?" Cooper asked.

"You don't like my outfit?" Stone grinned, doing a surprisingly agile pirouette given his bulk.

His outfit consisted of gleaming motorcycle boots, black leather short shorts, and a matching body harness. He had greased his hair back into a glistening skullcap. It was undeniably a hot look, but Cooper wondered if it wasn't a little too blatant for the occasion. His own black leather jeans and white tank top seemed demure by comparison.

"Just thought it might be a little drafty."

"I've been to their parties before," Stone said. "They'll have the heat turned up. Don't worry."

———

Jules must have paid off the neighbors. Traffic was backed up for blocks. The house was blinding in the glare of spotlights. Searchlights slashed at the low hanging overcast like daggers. It was like a movie premiere. Jules knew all about those, so it wasn't surprising. But for a gay party? Cooper would have expected something more discreet.

At the front door, a team of beefy guys in dark suits scowled intimidatingly. Cooper reached into the pocket of his jeans for his invitation.

"Don't bother," Stone said. "They're not here to keep guys that look like us from getting in. Their job is to keep out fatties, drag queens, women, and anyone over the age of thirty who doesn't meet certain income guidelines."

———

In the entry hall, six nude bodybuilders stood in a circle facing outward, their shoulders just touching. Their skin glistened with oil. Arriving partygoers paused there to stroke, fondle, or merely admire.

———

A bodybuilder with straw colored hair reclined on the desk in Jules' study. In his hands was an enormous black dildo.

———

Two bodybuilders lay on an overstuffed sofa in the library, heavily involved with each other. They seemed oblivious to their onlookers.

———

Two nude bodybuilders lay on their backs on the dining table, their feet almost touching. They were surrounded by a spectacular array of *hors d'oeuvres* arranged on silver trays.

—

In one end of the room, two nude bodybuilders worked out. They alternated doing bench presses and military presses. There wasn't a barbell in sight. They lifted naked go-go boys.

—

In the other end of the room, two pairs of nude bodybuilders performed an elaborate adagio routine, the kind ordinarily featuring male and female pairs of acrobats.

—

A trio of naked bodybuilders had been collared and leashed. A fourth bodybuilder, naked except for a peaked, military style cap with Nazi badges on it led them on all fours as they made a meandering circuit of the house

—

Naked go-go boys wandered through the rooms bearing trays of desserts, glasses of champagne, finger sandwiches, *hors d'oeuvres*, joints.

—

The marble plinth in the center of the gallery off the first floor landing of the grand staircase usually held a medieval suit of armor silhouetted against the great Tiffany window. Tonight a bodybuilder posed there, his body completely covered in what looked like silver leaf. His nipples were adorned with huge golden sunbursts of filigree work and gemstones.

"Must be glued in place," Cooper muttered. "Spirit gum or something like that."

"If you look closely," Stone said, "you'll see that they're secured to his piercings."

Cooper noticed that the head of the man's penis was similarly decorated.

———

In the taverna, bodybuilders pranced back and forth on top of the bar, stroking their erections.

———

In one bathroom, a tattoo artist was hard at work. In a second bathroom, a gentleman was performing piercings. In a third, two men in leather body harnesses were using straight razors to shave the body of a young redheaded bodybuilder. In a fourth, the toilet seat had been secured with yellow police tape, and a bodybuilder lay in the bathtub, his bare skin glistening with urine.

———

A wrestling ring had been set up in the conservatory. Pairs of oiled bodybuilders grappled until someone was defeated. Then things got really interesting.

———

Steam rose off the water of the swimming pool, where naked bodybuilders cavorted with anyone who chose to join them.

———

In the basement, a number of vignettes were on display. A naked bodybuilder stood with his forearm up to the elbow in a place Cooper wouldn't have thought it could go. His partner looked like a go-go boy. Next to this pair, a man lay face down as a naked bodybuilder inserted links of heavy gauge chromium chain into his ass one by one and then slowly pulled them out again.

———

A bodybuilder was shackled with his face to the wall, and guests stood in line to flog him with a whip or spank him with paddles and belts.

———

Another bodybuilder had been strapped into a sling, helpless and apparently available to all comers.

———

In a corner of the room, a bodybuilder was shackled to a lab table. Electrodes had been attached to his nipples and shaven scrotum, and a sort of electrical collar was around the base of his penis. An operator administrated shocks, and the guests oohed and aahed at the man's spasms.

———

On a similar table in the opposite corner of the room, another bodybuilder was gradually being encased in wax that hardened as guests dripped it onto his skin from burning candles.

———

At a third table, a foxy latin lover type in a lab coat was sliding a long metal rod deep into and back out of the urethra of a bodybuilder who was chained in a spread eagle position and blindfolded. Every few moments the "scientist" discarded the rod he'd been using and took up another one of a heavier gauge.

———

In a small anteroom off the main space, another naked bodybuilder lay shackled to another lab table. Cooper recognized the young man in the white coat. He wasn't sure he wanted to watch as "treatments" were administered.

———

Back upstairs in the ballroom, the dance floor was packed. On the stage at the far end of the space, an elaborate tableau unfolded continuously. At center left, a drag queen wearing a sequined gown and a three foot tall headdress of ostrich feathers and rhinestones pantomimed an opera diva in full cry. She sang to a bloody dagger clutched in her left hand. At center right, a trio of bodybuilders moved through an unending series of poses in a stately slow motion rhythm. At extreme downstage left and right, two bodybuilders stood in profile, their backs to the proscenium arch. Shadowy figures knelt in front of each of them head to crotch. And on a spot-lit platform at center stage, two bodybuilders took turns slowly fucking each other.

———

"They must have emptied out every gym in the Bay Area," Cooper muttered. "Except ours."

He hadn't seen anyone he recognized from there.

"Actually," Stone said, "there's hardly any local talent here. Jules flies them in from all over. New York and Montreal mostly. Charters a jet."

"Really."

"That and a couple of busloads from L.A."

"All I know," Cooper said, "is I've got to get to work back at the gym. I look as scrawny as an eighth grader next to these guys."

"You do not," Stone laughed.

"All right, a tenth grader."

"Most of them have ten to fifteen years on you," Stone said, "and most of them are on the juice."

"Seeing these guys is about enough to make me start using."

———

"Oh, good," Christopher said, giving Cooper a quick kiss on the mouth. "You two made it."

"Hi."

"Having a good time?"

"Having an interesting time," Stone said.

"You always do, Stonie," Christopher grinned.

"Usually I'm the one who's interesting," Stone said.

"You guys should get naked," Christopher grinned. "Stone practically is already. The two of you would fit right in."

"No thanks," Cooper said.

"You sure about that?"

"Speaking of interesting," Stone said, "we caught your routine downstairs. That was some nifty work with the syringe. They must be crazy about that act over at the medical school."

"You have no idea," Christopher laughed. "You sure you two aren't bored just being spectators?"

"Bored? Cooper and I make our own fun."

"I'll bet. Well, don't forget to show Cooper the screening room. You know the way."

———

"What's on in the screening room?" Cooper asked.

"More of the same, just on film. Let's get out of here. I'm bored."

"What's on in the screening room that Christopher wants me to see and you don't want to show me?"

"You won't like it."

"Come on, Stonie."

"Don't call me that."

"Then take me to the screening room," Cooper said. "If you don't, I'll just ask some nice bodybuilder for directions. And no telling what else."

———

The film featured three bodybuilders. Two were blond. The third was raven haired. The smallest of them, one of the blonds, was still noticeably larger than Cooper. The second blond was substantially larger than the first, and the black haired man was a monster. The two larger men began the action by undressing their companion. He was extremely handsome in a boy-next-door kind of way. They sheared off his luxuriant hair with electric clippers. Then they shaved his body with straight razors. In a closeup, Cooper could clearly read the tattoo which ran along the length of his penis—STEFANO, in block capitals. Glancing at the line of irregularly shaped blotches in the showers at the gym, Cooper had taken it for a strangely located birthmark.

He sat through the rest of the video astonished.

———

"It was almost a year ago," Stone said in answer to Cooper's unspoken question. "They're not proud of it. Big Steve blames himself for not seeing through Jules' promise that he only wanted it for private use. Nick blames himself for falling for Christopher in the first place."

"You've seen it before," Cooper said.

"Jules shows it at all his parties."

"Let's get out of here."

———

As they trudged down the hill toward Cooper's car, the house loomed behind them like the temple of an ancient cult. The searchlights and spots had been turned off but the house still gleamed. The gods had sent moonlight.

"Just wait 'til the New Years Eve party," Stone said. "There won't be a body-builder in sight. Except for invited guests, of course. The theme will be gymnasts and swimmers. And it'll be so depraved it will make tonight's action look like Wednesday evening prayer meeting."

———

"I can't imagine what Big Steve's crew would have thought of all that," Cooper said, staring into his coffee cup.

"Big Steve doesn't disapprove of anything consenting adults do," Stone said, "so in itself nothing there tonight would have bothered him in the least. What he would have hated was that hardly any of those guys consider themselves gay. They never do any of those things in real life. They wouldn't dream of having sex with a man under normal circumstances. They only do it for the money. They show up, they do all that shit, and Jules pays them. Handsomely, needless to day. Then they're off home to their wives and girlfriends. They won't touch a man again until the next time Jules summons them. It's not the money thing that Big Steve would disapprove of. He doesn't expect people to give anything away. He just thinks if you're going to be paid it should be for doing something you'd do anyway, and doing it extremely well. Lack of authenticity is the only sin he recognizes."

"That covers a lot, when you think about it," Cooper said.

"Just about everything," Stone nodded.

"Makes sense I guess," Cooper said.

"Jules, on the other hand, thinks anything you can buy is worth having," Stone said. "He doesn't care if things are real or not."

"It all looked pretty real to me," Cooper said.

"It was just bodies, Coop."

"What does that mean?"

"Only what goes on in your brain is real."

———

It wasn't Christopher, Cooper thought, driving home from Stone's place. It was Jules and Rene who were behind the whole thing. Christopher was just a simple medical student who happened to have a kinky uncle.

———

It was basically harmless, in any case. Everyone there—like Stone said; they were all consenting adults.

IV

"Cooper," Big Steve barked, "take off that shirt."

Cooper pulled the garment over his head and tossed his hair back into place.

"Nice. Very nice," Big Steve said, then poked him in the sternum with a fore-finger that somehow seemed like the barrel of a gun. "What did I tell you about working those lower pecs? I was right, wasn't I?"

"You're always right, Big Steve," Cooper answered.

"Does our friend seem a little, um, nervous to you, Big Steve?" Tristan asked.

"I'm not nervous," Cooper said.

"He says he's not nervous, T."

"Maybe it's because he went to a certain party last weekend," Tristan suggested, "and viewed a certain masterpiece of the cinematic art."

"Do you think so?"

"We know he was there," Tristan said. "There were witnesses."

"What film?" Cooper asked, unable to look either of them in the eye.

"Pull down the sweatpants," Big Steve said. "Need to have a look at those legs."

"Seriously, Cooper," Tristan said, "if you saw the movie, you saw the movie. You'll get over it. We did."

"Eventually," Big Steve said.

"Sure," Cooper said, feeling anything but.

"Nice definition you're starting to have in those quads," Big Steve said.

"One thing," Cooper said.

"Yeah?" Tristan's right eyebrow tilted about a millimeter and a half upward.

"Christopher," Cooper said.

They both looked at him.

"Is he? I mean, did he? I mean—he and Nick?"

"Yes," Tristan said, "Christopher's the one. Christopher and Nick. Choose your preposition from this extensive list."

"And your verb from column B," Big Steve added.

"So how mad is he?"

"Nick?" Tristan asked. "At you?"

"He doesn't blame you," Big Steve said.

"He just hopes you'll get out before you get screwed."

"Unlike Niko himself," Big Steve said.

———

"You know," Stone said, "I love listening to you on the phone with loverboy just after you and I have fucked."

"Sorry," Cooper said. "I should have let it ring. It's just so hard for us to stay in touch. His schedule is really chaotic."

"That's what you get for dating a medical student," Stone laughed. "I just think it's funny how he always seems to call right when I'm thinking about getting up to leave. Five minutes later, I'd be out the door and I wouldn't know he exists. You could have two boyfriends who don't know about each other."

"As opposed to two fuckbuddies who do know about each other," Cooper grinned. "Who probably fuck each other when I'm not around."

"I do fuck him when you're not around," Stone laughed, "but out of loyalty to you, I don't allow myself to enjoy it. It's just another job. One that doesn't pay particularly well. But there are fringe benefits. He has the hungriest ass on the West Coast."

"Does he?"

"Don't tell me you haven't noticed."

"T. says Christopher is not to be trusted."

"You went to his party," Stone said, "and you had to have T. tell you that? Boy are you dense."

"Do you trust Christopher?" Cooper asked.

"I don't trust anybody."

"Except me."

"Do I trust you?" Stone asked, looking serious.

"Of course you do."

"And you trust Christopher," Stone said.

"I don't know. Do you think I should?"

"I think you should shut up and get back to work," Stone said. "I've got an empty asshole sitting here getting bored."

"I'm meeting him later," Cooper said. "Maybe."

———

Nick would have made the perfect boyfriend if it hadn't been for what he wanted to do in bed. Christopher would have made the perfect boyfriend, except, apparently, for what he wanted to do when he wasn't in bed. The same could be said for Stone. Cooper seemed incapable of getting Christopher's undivided attention with anything but his penis. That went a long way, but Cooper knew it wasn't what kept Big Steve and Tristan together. Or Matt and Ashby. There had to be something else. Something he hadn't discovered the nature of.

None of it mattered. He wasn't looking for a boyfriend. His interest was purely academic. He wanted to know how things worked.

———

Cooper walked into chaos. A babble of voices, the smell of frying potatoes, some-one singing about dreidels on the stereo. After having the apartment to himself for weeks, the circus was back in town. Stone had been snoozing when he left for the gym. Cooper hoped he had cleared out before this bunch arrived.

"Cooper, honey," Rivka shrieked, "there you are. It's time to light candles."

She had done something extremely questionable to her hair since Thanksgiving. Tash had done something similar to hers. Cooper wondered if either of them knew what a mirror was. Sammie, fatter than Cooper recalled, sprawled on the couch looking like a particularly hairy variety of fungus that had grown there. Only Maggie's sardonic grin was unchanged.

"The latkes smell great," Cooper said.

"Come on, everybody," Rivka said. "Let's light the menorah."

———

"Such a tragedy about Maggie's miscarriage," Rivka said. "Still, she seems better now, don't you think?"

"Yes," Cooper said. "Better."

Sammie had driven the girls back to their apartment. Rivka seemed to be expecting him back. She was making up a bed for herself on the couch. But maybe she just didn't want to sleep in Sammie's bed under any circumstances. Cooper wouldn't blame her. You could change the sheets, certainly, but that mattress.

"It's nice that we can have a chat," Rivka said, "just the two of us."

"Sure."

"So how are you, dear?"

"Great," Cooper said, regretting that one last latke. Nobody made latkes like Nanny Freitag. Hers never made him feel like this.

"Yes?"

"Sure," Cooper said. "Of course. Why not?"

"The girls told me," she said. "You know."

But he didn't know. He had no idea what she was getting at for a long, awk-ward moment.

"Sammie thinks I made it up," he finally laughed. "It's supposed to be a fiend-ishly clever gambit to attract women."

"He what?" Rivka pretended to be shocked, which meant she was already familiar with this theory. "Well, he would say something like that, wouldn't he?"

"Sammie," Cooper said, as if the name itself explained everything.

"So, uh, have you. . ?"

"What?"

"Have you spoken to Shoshonnah and Willi about this?"

"No," Cooper said. "Not yet."

"I see."

"Not sure how they'll react," he explained. "Anyway, there's really no hurry."

"I suppose not."

"You think I should tell them," Cooper said.

"It's not my business, dear."

Her unspoken "but" ricocheted off the walls. Her refusal to meet his eye emphasized it.

"You think I should tell them."

"In your own time, of course."

"Oh, I plan to," Cooper said, "when I'm ready."

"It's just," she shrugged.

That shrug. It came straight from the old country. Some ancestor of theirs had shrugged like that on the dusty main street of the *shtetl*.

"Why? What's wrong? Is it Nanny?"

"Nothing's wrong, dear. Your grandmother is as fit as a fiddle. A little out of tune, sure. It's just, if you're worried about how Mom and Dad will take it, you should relax, already. They've been through it all before."

"What?"

"With your brother, of course," she said. "Oh my God, they haven't told you."

"My brother? Josh? Joshua is gay?"

"Joshua? Who said anything about Joshua? No, darling, it's Jacob."

"Yakov?"

"Who's Yakov? Oh, that's right. I always forget," she said. "Jake. Jacob. Jacob is gay. Shoshonnah found out about it when she went to him in Israel last year after he was wounded in the war. In the hospital he and his doctor fell in love. Isn't that romantic? They're living together. They have this little apartment in Tel Aviv. At least they are when Jacob isn't on maneuvers or whatever it is they do when they're not fighting Arabs."

"Yakov?" Cooper said, shaking his head.

"But I'm warning you," Rivka said, "first thing Shoshonnah is going to ask you when you tell her is are you seeing someone? So be ready for that."

"Actually," Cooper said, "I am seeing someone."

"You are? Well, I hope he's nice."

"Me, too."

SONNY

"I'm going to miss you," Sonny Dallas said.

"Why?" Cooper asked. "Are you going somewhere?"

"No. But you are, aren't you?"

Sonny had had several affairs with college men. It was convenient that they were always going somewhere. Christmas. Spring Break. Summer vacation was especially useful. A twenty year old's attention span was simply too short to allow him to sustain an affair from May all the way to September. It was a law of nature, and Sonny relied on it just as ancient mariners relied on the unvarying position of the stars. By the time Sonny's beau could manage to return for the fall term, Sonny would be well embarked on a new adventure with a new playmate, as often female as male. All Sonny required in an inamorata/o was to be allowed always to maintain the upper hand.

"Am I?" Cooper asked.

"Well, aren't you? Don't you have final exams soon? Surely your parents will be expecting you back in New York."

"You know," Cooper began, then left off for a moment as he stretched himself luxuriously, like a panther rousing itself from that near-somnolent alertness all felines seemed to specialize in. "I was really thinking. . ."

Another pause as Cooper pulled back the sheets. Getting out of bed? Yes? No? Cooper didn't do anything quickly. And he appeared always to be posing. It was if he planned every move so as to show himself off. There wasn't anything overtly narcissistic about it, but it certainly seemed calculating. The word "thinking" on those full lips alarmed Sonny. He didn't like it when they thought. Actually, what made him uneasy was being reminded that they were even capable of thought.

"I might not go home this summer," Cooper finally said while running a hand through his hair.

"Not go home for the summer?" Sonny was horrified. But on the other hand, that pectoral development was truly extraordinary for a nineteen year old. Actually, it was extraordinary, period. "But what would you do here?"

The idea of a young man cluttering up the place for weeks on end—it was unthinkable. Even a young man as spectacular as Cooper Luxemberg. Sonny simply couldn't allow it.

"You could look for a job, I suppose."

"I was thinking," Cooper said, idly stroking his right pectoral and stifling a yawn, "of going to school."

"Summer school," Sonny said, feeling like a drowning man who has just noticed a life preserver drifting toward him on the current, "summer school. Now there's an idea."

"Not summer school," Cooper said. When he shook his head like that, the floppiness of his hair was exquisite. The shine was nearly blinding.

"I don't understand."

"I was thinking of getting my real estate license over the summer. Then maybe some nice broker will give me a job and I won't have to go back to the university in the fall."

———

Sonny wasn't used to having trouble saying no to anyone and he didn't see why the present situation should be any different, but somehow it was. His "friends", particularly the male ones, were ordinarily very compliant. Keep them fed, keep them mildly intoxicated, keep their cocks expertly, thoroughly sucked. What more should it require? It really wasn't any more complicated than that. And he even let Cooper fuck him, which wasn't his usual modus operandi. Some appreciation certainly seemed in order. Some quid pro quo.

Perhaps that was the problem. Perhaps allowing Cooper that particular liberty had sent a strategically unfortunate message. But really, contemplating that long, unusually, um, sturdy organ—not to mention what it was attached to—it had seemed to Sonny that there was only one place, really, that could appropriately accommodate it. He didn't regret the act or its subsequent repetitions at all.

But.

Yes, but. Now he was having the greatest difficulty saying no to anything Cooper suggested.

"I can't imagine your parents would be pleased if they knew you were thinking about dropping out of college."

He had to say this quite loud. The bar was crowded and extremely noisy.

"I don't see why," Cooper yelled back. "Neither of them went to college. They've done fine without degrees."

"Aren't you hot in that shirt?" Sonny asked. He was absolutely roasting in his cashmere sweater.

Obedient as a corporal facing a general, Cooper shed the garment. With considerable panache, it had to be acknowleged. It wasn't enough to be seen taking one's shirt off in a bar or even taking it off to reveal such a stupefying physique. The real test was the manner in which the garment was removed. Sonny knew this because he had watched spectacular men perform the act on four different continents. He considered himself a connoisseur.

"All the more reason," he suggested, "for them to want you to get your diploma."

"It will save them a boatload of money if I don't."

The blond Adonis across the room from them had caught Sonny's eye even before his shirt came off. He lacked only about five pounds of lean muscle mass to be Cooper's equal in the physique department, and he was as handsome as a Nordic god. Sonny wondered if his name might happen to be Sven or Olaf or Jorg and if he might turn out to be more compliant than Cooper had been lately. Sonny decided that he'd like to know all kinds of things about the young man. He just needed to hit on the right approach.

"You've been staring at that guy for the last ten minutes."

"What guy?" Sonny asked.

"The big blond over there."

"I have not."

"You have."

"Honestly, Cooper."

"It's almost like—I don't know—you were thinking about asking him home with us for a threeway."

"I wasn't," Sonny insisted, though this was exactly what he'd been thinking about. Threeways were not something he had proposed to Cooper so far. He preferred to feel more securely in control of his "friends" before making that kind of suggestion. Still, since the opportunity seemed to have presented itself. . .

"Wait here," Cooper said. "We'll be right back."

"Cooper, no," Sonny said, but not loud enough that Cooper could possibly hear.

———

"I suppose," Sonny said the next day at brunch as he savored the recollection of Cooper slamming his long, unusually, um, sturdy organ into the blond's muscular backside—muscular, extremely appreciative backside, as it turned out—It couldn't hurt for you to attend real estate school. But I don't think you should plan to leave college. I feel really strongly about that. You only need four more semesters to finish."

Sonny remembered real estate school all too well. It had been the most boring experience of his life. Excruciating. Like some arcane form of torture. Nothing seemed as likely to deflect Cooper from this insane scheme of his as four days of real estate school. Five days, max.

"So you'll. . .?" Cooper grinned.

"No promises, darling," Sonny said. "No promises."

———

"Did I already know Stone?" Cooper looked shocked. "What do you mean, did I already know Stone? Of course I already knew Stone. I never told you I didn't."

"I had a clear impression that night," Sonny said.

"A clear impression? What? That when I brought him to meet you in the bar he was a complete stranger?"

"Well, yes, actually."

"Did I say that?"

Sonny considered this. Cooper hadn't said anything of the sort. He had to admit it. Sonny had assumed it because he wanted it to be true. Now he sincerely wished it had been. But that wasn't Cooper's fault.

"Why does it matter?" Cooper asked.

"Well, the two of you are just such chums," Sonny said.

"What's that supposed to mean?" Cooper asked. "No, wait. I get it. You think that night at the bar was a setup. You think Stone and I arranged to meet there so I could bring him home with us."

"Well. . ."

"You do. You rich guys are all paranoid."

"I'm not rich," Sonny said, knowing how ridiculous he sounded.

"Right."

"Not really rich," he maintained, feeling stupider and stupider. "Not like the Rockefellers and the Kennedys."

"Richer than Stone, at least."

"I wouldn't know," Sonny said. "He's your friend. Where do you know him from, anyway?"

"The ultra-exclusive male brothel where we both work."

"Don't be facetious."

"The gym," Cooper said. "And we do occasionally work together."

"Aha!"

"As exotic dancers at bachelorette parties, birthdays, that sort of thing. I'll quit if you want me to. Been thinking about it already, as a matter of fact. Probably not the best part-time job for a guy interested in starting a professional career."

"That's all?" Sonny asked.

"What's all?"

"You and Stone?"

"What? You think I'm his boyfriend? Sonny, Sonny. Stone doesn't have boyfriends. Actually, that's not true. He does have boyfriends. Dozens of them. Some of them he hasn't even met yet."

"There's just something. . ."

"What are you talking about?"

"When the two of you are—um. . ."

"When I'm fucking him," Cooper said.

"Yes," Sonny nodded. "You seem so compatible."

"We've had lots of practice," Cooper grinned.

"That's my point," Sonny said, "exactly."

"You don't understand," Cooper said. "The guys Stone goes with—the way he looks, they expect him to just top the living daylights out of them. It's kind of his vocation. But sometimes he's in the mood to catch instead."

"And that's where you come in."

"He can't do it with just anybody," Cooper said. "It would be bad for business. He needs someone discreet."

"Isn't he worried that I might tell everyone I know?" Sonny asked.

"I asked him that," Cooper said.

"What did he say?"

"He thinks you enjoy watching us too much to want to mess up the arrangement."

"I'm going to have to think about that," Sonny said. "He might be right."

"You know," Cooper said, "if I didn't know better, I'd think you were jealous."

"Jealous?" Sonny laughed as if the suggestion were preposterous. The problem was he was jealous. And the only thing he hated worse than being jealous was the idea that anyone, Cooper included, could make him feel that way.

II

Sonny's wife and two younger daughters lived in a Mediterranean style villa in Hillsborough, but he spent most nights in the city. The oldest daughter was studying art history in Paris. Cooper had never asked her age, but was pretty certain she had a couple of years on him at least. Sonny had what he referred to as a *pied a terre* in a building on Nob Hill. Cooper, familiar with Manhattan apartments, thought of it as far too grand to deserve that description. The building seemed full of aging widows with tiny, yappy dogs. He quickly learned to tread carefully when he got on the elevator. And his New York upbringing came in handy when dealing with the doorman, a gentleman who gave a clear impression of having served in the military though Cooper wasn't sure exactly whose, and who obviously disapproved of Sonny on all imaginable grounds. Which should have come as no surprise. And, for that matter, indicated good judgement on his part.

The décor of Sonny's apartment wasn't to Cooper's taste, but he certainly admired the craftsmanship. The marble fireplace in the living room, an art nouveau masterpiece, was enough to sell the place more or less on its own. Sonny's furniture wasn't what Cooper would have expected of such a man of the world. It reminded him of Nanny Freitag's stuff—heavy and old fashioned, though of the highest quality. Only one room wasn't crammed to the rafters with tchotchkes, the second bedroom. It was almost totally bare. There was a bed in there, but it didn't seem likely that anyone had ever slept in it. It was apparently reserved for recreational purposes. The tipoff was the rubber matting on the floor, like in a gym. The night Cooper and Sonny met, Cooper almost ended up in there instead of the master bedroom. If that indeed had happened, Sonny would never have seen Cooper again. Cooper had nothing against tricking, but he did believe there was a difference between a trick and a date. A trick, by definition, couldn't be repeated, while a date might. And if Sonny had insisted on the "playroom", Cooper would have read the encounter differently. He had seen that momentary indecision in Sonny's eyes and took charge, propelling them into the master bedroom, with its Persian rug, damask curtains, Tiffany lamps and Louis Philippe furniture. It had been a close call.

———

Real estate school was heaven. Cooper's university classes seemed hopelessly soporific by comparison. Most people would have seen it differently. He understood that. Most people would have found it dry and boring, but that was because they had no connection to what lay behind it all. Most people would have gone crosseyed over the myriad tiny details. Most of his classmates had trouble staying awake. Every day, he heard someone in the room snoring. Nanny Freitag always said "there are no boring things, only boring people", and she had known what she was talking about. Cooper had never seen a more boring bunch. He shuddered to think what their lives were like.

Cooper loved real estate school because it wasn't about dead kings, esoteric trivia, and crazy theories that didn't stand up to critical appraisal. It was in the name itself. It was real.

———

"This is my friend, Stone," Cooper said. It had finally been long enough that he could approach Nick without feeling awkward, even with T. and Big Steve nowhere in sight.

"We've met," Nick said. "Hey, Stonie."

"You're not supposed to call me that," Stone said.

Cooper knew Stone well enough that he could tell the fake pout from the real one, so it was O.K.

"Stone needs some legal advice," Cooper said.

"You in trouble?" Nick grunted.

"Always," Stone said, "but not of the legal variety."

"Just a matter of time," Nick said.

"Ha, ha."

"Play nice, you two," Cooper said.

"You know I'm not supposed to moonlight," Nick said. "It's against the policies of the prosecutor's office."

"So don't charge him anything," Cooper said. "Then you'll be off the hook."

—

"Ladies and gentlemen," Fred Finkelstein, their instructor, said, "congratulations to you all. Everyone passed our first exam. Special congratulations to Mr. Luxemberg. Ninety-four percent. Head of the class."

—

"You know he's married," Tristan said.

"They hardly ever see each other," Cooper said. "They haven't had sex in years."

"You believe that?"

"Certainly not," Cooper said. "It's the kind of thing married guys always say, isn't it?"

"I wouldn't know,"

"Of course you do. Everyone knows that."

"Maybe I've heard something about it," Tristan admitted.

"I get it, you know," Cooper said. "Big Steve doesn't approve. I really didn't expect him to."

"Next you're going to say it's none of our business."

"I would never say that."

"But you might think it."

"Let's pretend I don't," Cooper said.

"All right."

"I know Big Steve has an opinion about it because Big Steve has an opinion about everything. So you might as well come out with it."

"Why can't you date someone closer to your own age?" Tristan asked. "That's what Big Steve would like to know."

"Just about anyone would be closer to my age," Cooper said.

"That's the point."

"I can't believe Big Steve thinks I would be better off with a forty-one year old than with Sonny. That's closer to my own age. Substantially."

"True."

"Then again, Christopher was very close to my age and Big Steve really hated that."

"Point taken," Tristan said.

"He must have something more specific in mind than what decade my prospective boyfriend was born during."

"That Stone seems nice."

"Stone is many things," Cooper said, "but nice isn't one of them."

"Nice enough."

"Perhaps you should talk to Niko about that."

"You're not allowed to call him Niko," Tristan said. "Only Big Steve is allowed to do that."

"And me."

"No, not 'and you'."

"We'll see about that," Cooper said. "But just ask what's his name to fill you in on my pal Stone."

"Why, what's he done?"

"Taken himself off the market, is what."

———

"That Nick is a genius," Stone said. "A fucking genius."

"Did you fuck him?"

"It didn't seem fair to expect him to work for free. Not to mention auld lang syne."

"That was very considerate of you."

"That's me all right," Stone grinned.

"What's he like?"

"Oh, that's right. You never did him, did you?"

"Somebody told me we're sexually incompatible," Cooper said.

"Being fucked by him is exactly like being fucked by you," Stone said. "If the two of you blindfolded me and took turns, I'd never be able to tell the difference."

"Really."

"Honest to God," Stone said, "but that's beside the point. You won't believe what all he got out of Esteban. A monthly allowance, an apartment, and a car. For starters."

"You're joking."

"The apartment is just a studio," Stone said, "but in a good location. And the car's not going to be mine, just 'for my exclusive use'. That's what it says in the contract."

"Contract? You've signed a contract?"

"Not yet. But Esteban has, and I don't see any reason not to. Nick drew it up, so it must be kosher."

"Well in that case," Cooper said, "congratulations. If it's what you want."

"Thanks."

"I guess there won't be any more of this."

"You guess wrong," Stone laughed. "I'm required to be available to have sex with him at least twice per week at mutually agreed upon times, but we're not exclusive. I'm allowed to sleep with other people. I'm guaranteed at least two nights off per week."

"You're right," Cooper laughed. "Nick's a genius."

"It's only fair, since Esteban will still be sleeping with his wife."

"Good point."

"I pay a fine if I give him any diseases. Or if it turns out I've been using drugs."

"But you don't use drugs," Cooper said.

"Esteban doesn't know that," Stone said. "It's what Nick calls a bargaining chip."

"Right. What other terms are there? I mean, this isn't a permanent arrangement is it?"

"Renewable annually," Stone said. "Automatically. Either of us wants out, that has to be negotiated."

"Wow," Cooper said. "So you're more or less set."

"All I have to do is sign and have my attorney return the contract to Esteban's attorney. Really, Cooper, you ought to get Nick to help you out with Sonny."

"I think I'd rather keep my options open," Cooper said. He could just imagine Sonny's reaction if he showed up with something like that in his hand. But that wasn't his most serious objection. It was fine for a guy like Stone, who despite appearances really did need to have his interests protected. Sugar daddies could be a rapacious, exploitive breed. But Cooper took too much pride in his ability to take care of himself. He'd never be able to look himself in the face otherwise.

———

"Whatever happened to that little friend of yours?" Sonny asked.

"Who?"

"What was his name? Storm?"

"Stone."

"Yes, Stone. It seems like he dropped right off the face of the earth."

"Stone's still around," Cooper said, wondering if Sonny was trying to set some kind of trap.

"Is he? You see him regularly?"

"At the gym," Cooper said.

"Well, that's regular, certainly," Sonny observed. "You seem to have gotten bigger just since we've been seeing each other."

Cooper wasn't sure whether this was a compliment or not.

"Do you think Stone might like to join us for dinner some evening?" Sonny asked.

"I'll ask him," Cooper said, careful not to sound too enthusiastic. "If you'd like me to."

"Yes," Sonny said, "I believe I would. See if he's available this Thursday. I'll book us a table at *L'Etoile*. Say eight o'clock."

———

They stopped in front of a storefront with blacked out windows. Sonny pulled into the parallel space with what Cooper considered shocking disregard for the Rolls-Royce's bumpers.

"Bring your gym bag," Sonny said.

On the door, block letters in silver leaf: Lance Garrison Photography. There was something familiar about the name, but Cooper couldn't place it.

"Lance is an old friend," Sonny said, in a tone that Cooper knew meant absolutely nothing.

———

Cooper recognized Lance on sight, but read the warning in his eyes as Sonny introduced them.

"Great to meet you, Lance."

"Likewise, Cooper."

Lance was only a few years older than Cooper. He was handsome in the manner of the men on the covers of the romance novels Maggie and Tash left lying around the apartment. From the neck down, he was built like Tristan Bentley. Cooper had met him at the first bodybuilding contest he attended with Big Steve and company. He was a sort of official photographer of the sport. He looked like he'd be a sure winner if he ever entered one of the contests himself.

"Oh, good," Lance said. "You've got your gym bag. Posing trunks in there, by any chance?"

"Sure."

"What color?"

"Navy."

"Perfect. They'll read as black in the black and white photos. And in the color shots they'll be fine."

"Don't forget to oil him up," Sonny said.

———

It was strangely like working on his posing with Big Steve. Lance's hands on him adjusting his posture, touching up his hair, positioning his head, were just as expert, just as sure and strong, just as impersonal. He extended Cooper's poses in exactly the way Big Steve would have, stretching him just that little bit further into attitudes that felt grotesque, but, he presumed, would be perfect on camera. Even Lance's voice was strangely like Big Steve's, though there wasn't a whiff of New York in his speech. It was something in the gruff tone, the deep pitch, the softness of his words. There wasn't a wasted syllable. There was no apparent emotion. Often he was barely audible. He exuded exactly the same confident masculinity Cooper so prized in Big Steve, totally unconscious and natural. The intimacy of the encounter was devastating, yet completely non-sexual. It was so enthralling that Cooper quickly forgot the presence of the camera, not to mention the presence of Sonny lurking silent in the shadows at the rear of the studio and thinking about God only knew what.

———

"You know what he wants next, don't you?" Lance murmured into Cooper's ear.

"Nudes, I expect."

"You O.K. with that?" Lance asked. "It's good money for me, but if you're not into it we'll call it a day right now. I tell him I'm out of film."

"I'm O.K. with it," Cooper said. "It's nothing he hasn't already seen."

"Got it."

———

"Excellent, excellent," Sonny called from back in the shadows. "Now could we have both of those sequences again? With his hair greased back this time?"

———

"Give my regards to Big Steve and Tristan," Lance muttered under his breath as Cooper and Sonny were leaving.

Cooper nodded.

"Thanks for bringing him by, Sonny. He's a natural. Great body, terrific look. I think you're going to be very pleased when you see the proofs."

"I'm sure I will."

———

"What was that Lance said to you?" Sonny asked as they got into the car. "Trying to make a date? You'll want to be careful with that one."

"I don't think he's even gay," Cooper said.

"Haven't you figured out yet that labels are meaningless?"

"What's that supposed to mean?"

"I saw how he was looking at you," Sonny said.

———

Cooper knew Sonny was a little dubious about Stone's wardrobe. You couldn't show up at *L'Etoile* wearing just anything. They wouldn't let you in. He arranged to meet Stone early enough that they could swing by Cooper's place if necessary and raid his closet. Since they were pretty much the same size, there wouldn't be a problem changing Stone into something more suitable as long as they had time for it. Sonny had no patience at all with tardiness. As it happened, there was no need for worry. Stone looked as sharp as Cooper did himself.

"Nice threads, bud," Cooper said.

"I just hope we don't run into anybody I know," Stone said. "Who's going to believe me talking dirty to them when they've seen me in this getup?"

The impact of their perfectly timed entrance at L'Etoile was blunted by the presence of a familiar face at the table with Sonny.

"What the hell's Christopher doing here?" Stone muttered as they followed the hostess toward the table.

———

Cooper had almost forgotten how attractive Christopher was. That face, that hair, that Olympic gymnast's body. At the restaurant, he flirted with the waiter in French, for God's sake. Sonny must have heard something about their history. Cooper was beginning to understand Sonny's perverse streak. Why else would Sonny have brought Christopher and him together?

But there was something Sonny couldn't have known about. Exquisite as Christopher was—and there was no denying that—what Cooper had found most compelling of all in the escapade was the sensation as he eased into Christopher's ass and the length of his cock slid along the length of Stone's, already in place there, hot and hard, twitching slightly. It was a connection he'd never experienced with anyone. Good old Stone. Maybe Sonny needed to be jealous of Stone after all. It almost made Cooper believe in mysticism.

———

"That was weird," Stone said the next day at the gym.

"I thought I'd seen the last of him," Cooper said. "At least I hoped I had."

"You didn't really think you could get clear of him that easily."

"I guess I did."

"You have to admit," Stone said, "it was kind of hot."

"No doubt."

"But every time I see him, I can't help thinking there's a really nasty picture of him stored in the attic."

———

"Ladies and gentlemen, once again Mr. Luxemberg is head of the class with a score of ninety-eight."

So much for the queen in the front row. Cooper had heard him in the hall, saying that a certain young man was nothing but a pretty face.

———

"Sonny would like you to meet us for dinner next Thursday," Cooper said, handing Stone his club soda.

"What next?"

———

"Gentlemen," Sonny said, "As you see, Veronique is prepared."

Veronique giggled. She lay on the bed, completely naked and glassy eyed. Cooper wondered what she had ingested in addition to the champagne Sonny ordered with dinner. He knew Sonny had a doctor friend who supplied him with various pharmaceuticals which Sonny himself never seemed to take. He offered some to Cooper once and seemed pleased when Cooper declined.

"First, I'd like the two of you to undress each other," Sonny continued. "Taking your time. Then you'll do whatever you can think of with Veronique for as long as you wish."

Stone looked into Cooper's eyes. Cooper could see he was about to start giggling, which would spoil Sonny's mood. The results were potentially disastrous. He grabbed the collar of Stone's shirt with both hands and yanked as hard as he could. As he hoped, the garment ripped. That was enough to focus Stone on their task.

———

"What the hell was that?" Stone asked when they ran into each other at the gym the next afternoon.

"Search me," Cooper said.

"Kinda hot, though," Stone said.

"Ever done anything like that before?" Cooper asked.

"Fucked a woman in the ass? Hell, yes. Used to be my specialty."

"No, man, I mean, with another guy next door."

"No," Stone said. "That was a new one. Sonny ever asked you to do that kind of thing before?"

"He's never brought a woman in with us," Cooper said. "It's just been the two of us except for those times with you. And that night with Christopher, of course."

———

Cooper was still wondering that on Sunday morning when he met Sonny at brunch to find a small package sitting at his place.

"What's this?"

"Unwrap it," Sonny said.

It was a bracelet of heavy gold links. From Tiffany.

"Sonny?"

"We're celebrating. I spoke with your teacher. He's an old friend of mine. He told me you're at the head of your class."

But Cooper couldn't help feeling that they were actually celebrating something else.

III

"These gentlemen are Derwent and Mick," Sonny said. "Mick is charge."

Cooper nodded, and Sonny settled himself to watch.

———

"You must be so proud," Mick said at brunch a few days later, "your boy was very good. Very, very good for a novice."

"Very good, you old goat," Derwent giggled. "He was spectacular. Didn't you think so, Sonny?"

"He was a very pleasant surprise," Sonny admitted. In his mind, he dubbed the episode "The Torturer's Apprentice", and Cooper played his role to near perfection. He had taken to that bullwhip like a duck to water. He had the makings of a real pro.

"That face," Derwent sighed, "and that body. Where did you find him? I look and look, but I never come up with anything like that."

"Where does one find boys like that?" Mick growled. "At the gym, of course. There's no mystery to it. That's what they have there. Lots of us go on regular shopping trips. You'd know that, you reeking cunt, if you ever bothered to darken the door of one."

"And that cock," Derwent rhapsodized. "Just big enough. Any larger and it would be grotesque. Just the right combination of length and girth. Too bad about that missing foreskin."

"He's Jewish," Sonny said.

"Pity."

"I know a doctor in Oakland," Mick said, "who surgically reconstructs them. It's extremely painful from what I've been told. But the results are remarkable. Better than natural, in fact."

"We can give you his card."

"I'll think about it," Sonny said.

"And while we're on the subject," Derwent said, "have you considered getting him a tattoo? Or a piercing? He'd look divine with some decoration. Those nipples. Think of those nipples. . ."

"I rather like him in his pristine state," Sonny said, shuddering inwardly.

"Yes, we all start out like that with our very special young men," Mick said, "but mark my words, sooner or later you'll want him to bear some stigmata. There's something so wondrous about a man who's given up his perfection for you. The more beautiful they are, the more profound a gift that is. Almost spiritual, really. On the part of the giver, at least. A man feels so bonded with you after an experience like that. And the gift keeps on giving. When he leaves you, it's such a comfort to know the mark you made on him will remain. You can't put a price on that. Believe me. It's astonishing how much depth a good piercing can bring to a relationship. I can't recommend it highly enough."

"Piercings close up," Sonny said.

"That's why I vote for a tattoo," Derwent exclaimed. "A tattoo is forever."

"Until it's covered over with another tattoo, you insufferable twat," Mick spat. "There are artistes all over the Bay Area who specialize in obliterating their competitors' work."

"Fuck you."

"So eloquent, Derwent. So very eloquent."

Sonny revered Mick but he certainly wished someone would push Derwent under a bus.

"Piercings do close up," Mick said, "but there's always a scar. Even if it's tiny, he'll always know it's there. For the rest of his life. And you'll know he knows."

Sonny hadn't thought of it that way. Obviously, it required further consideration. It was stirring watching Cooper follow Mick's instructions unquestioningly. He didn't flinch at even the most outrageous suggestions. It wasn't that heavy a scene, of course. But heavy enough to be convincing. Derwent's moans and screams hadn't been totally an act. If Cooper was squeamish, it would certainly have been apparent. But he never wavered. He was a real champ, and what had been established for certain was his capacity to inflict pain. His ability to look magnificent doing it wasn't a surprise, though it was certainly gratifying.

———

Sonny's next stop was at Tiffany. Derwent might be an idiot, but Mick certainly wasn't. Now that "The Torturer's Apprentice" had received his seal of approval, a reward was in order. Sonny would say that he'd had another glowing report from Cooper's instructor at real estate school, but Cooper would know the real reason.

He loved that Cooper would know that. He settled on a set of platinum shirt studs and cufflinks and had them gift wrapped so it was apparent to the clerk that he wasn't shopping for himself. As pleasant as shopping at Tiffany was, he couldn't get out of the store fast enough. The young man helping him had been extremely handsome but extremely effeminate. He actually lisped, and if his wrists had been any limper he'd hardly have been able to grasp the key to the display case. The idea of Cooper fucking a faggot like that turned Sonny's stomach. Watching Cooper fuck Stone had been hot as blazes. That was the kind of man Cooper should fuck if he had to fuck men at all. Guys as masculine as himself.

Stone had been an excellent prop the last few weeks. He showed up at the most opportune time and was easy to work into the plan. Sonny had to think of a very special way of rewarding him for his services. He had already arranged for Stone to meet his friend, Esteban Rabinowitz, who put him on contract almost immediately. Sonny thought the terms Esteban offered were far too generous, but Esteban was a slimy Argentine Jew and thought, apparently, that the opportunity Stone represented was too good to risk missing out on. Esteban obviously understood that though he had been exotically handsome in his youth and remained quite striking, beauty didn't last forever while being a slimy Argentine Jew did, and thus he had to be practical in a way that Sonny was never forced to contemplate. He thought of picking out something for Stone in Tiffany, but a present like that might make Esteban suspicious. Better just send the young man a check, but who should he write it to? He had no idea what Stone's real name was. Time to consult Ned. In the unlikely event Ned didn't know, he was fully capable of finding out.

———

Lance finally sent the proofs from Cooper's shoot. They were certainly worth waiting for. The man was a genius at glorifying the male body. Too bad he was such a prude. He did nudes, but only of the most "artistic" type. When it came time that Sonny required something more elemental, he'd have to use a different photographer. He knew of a man who'd shoot anything, but his pictures weren't this fine technically. Still, the idea of Cooper in chains, Cooper cuffed and gagged, Cooper in nipple clamps, Cooper undergoing extreme, if only simulated, torture—Sonny would take what he could get.

IV

"I'm going to miss you," Cooper said.

"Buenos Aires isn't the end of the world," Stone said.

"It almost is."

"It's just for three months."

"That's a long time," Cooper said, pulling out, "to go without this."

"That's certainly true," Stone said. "Just remember, it'll be worse for me than it will for you. You can always find another hole that loves you. You won't be as easy for me to replace."

"Am I driving you to the airport?"

"I think I'd better take a taxi."

"Don't be stupid," Cooper said. "It's no trouble."

"When have I worried about a thing like that?"

"Good," Cooper said. "I'm driving you."

"Please, Coop," Stone said. "I'd rather you didn't."

"Why not?"

"I might decide not to go," Stone said. "That would violate my contract."

"You'd violate your contract for me?"

"Maybe."

———

"I've been wanting to pair Nick with someone else ever since we finished shooting the folio of him and Big Steve," Lance said, "but I never found the right model."

"He shot you and Big Steve?" Cooper asked.

"Yes," Nick nodded.

"They were magnificient together," Lance said, "so I couldn't use just anyone in Nick's fourth volume."

"Fourth volume?" Cooper asked.

"There were two solo ones," Nick said.

"I'd rather not do it at all than pair him with a model who isn't up to his level. When Sonny brought you in, it got me thinking."

"I'm flattered," Cooper said.

"I'd seen you around the contests, of course," Lance continued, "but until I had a chance to shoot you I couldn't tell. I really wasn't sure until that shoot you and

Stone did. Just because a guy is a terrific model on his own doesn't mean he'll be able to work well with someone else."

"Straights," Nick snorted.

"Actually," Lance said, "it's not that simple. A lot of straight guys work out fine in duo shoots. It's just as likely to be a gay model who gets nervous about being naked with another guy. But you and Stone were a dream team. That's when I knew I could do something really special with you and Nick."

"Have you heard from him?" Nick asked.

"He just left a few days ago," Cooper said. "The mail from South America is probably slow."

"This shoot will be very different," Lance said. "It's going to be about contrast. Your luxuriant hair against Nick's military cut. His mustache and your smooth face. He's Nordic, you're kind of Mediterranean—yet at the same time you're not quite. And then the difference in your sizes. It'll all make for great visuals. Very dramatic. With Stone, the focus was on how similar the two of you were. Your hair texture and growth pattern. Your facial structure. You really could be brothers. The difference in hair color and skin tone just served to bring the similarity into clearer focus."

"Not to mention his foreskin," Cooper muttered.

"Nick's got that, too," Lance said. "We'll do the classic bodybuilding poses just like we did with Stone. And we'll do the wrestling sequences. But this time I'd like to add another component."

"What's that?" Cooper asked.

"Some light bondage and domination stuff. Not seedy, very stylized and artistic. But only if you're comfortable with it."

"Shouldn't you be asking Nick if he's comfortable with it?"

"I already know about Nick."

"I don't see any harm in it," Cooper said. "It's just for the camera. I'm more concerned about what Sonny's going to say about the whole thing."

"You don't need to worry about Sonny. He loved the folio with you and Stone."

"That was Stone," Cooper said. "Nick's going to be a harder sell. He's best friends with you know who."

"Sonny will be fine once he's seen the pictures," Lance smiled. "Trust me."

"Who is he anyway?" Cooper asked, squeezing lemon juice onto his fish. "Some big trust fund baby?"

"Lance?" Nick asked.

"Stone and I did a shoot at his apartment. You can't tell me that taking wedding photos pays for a place like that."

"You'd be surprised."

"And I get the feeling he and Sonny have a past."

"They do," Nick nodded. "A few years back Sonny tried to make Lance his protégé."

"That couldn't have worked out."

"Not for the reason you think," Nick said. "Sonny hadn't crossed over definitively yet. All he really wanted was permission to watch Lance screwing women. You must realize that Sonny's fundamentally a voyeur."

"Sure," Cooper said. "That's how he is with me a lot of the time."

"Interesting. Anyway, the sex thing wasn't the problem. It's the last time anyone can remember Sonny being outbid."

"Aha. So there is somebody."

"And that's all you're getting from me," Nick grinned. "I'm lots of things, but I'm not a gossip queen."

"You told me about him and Sonny."

"You're with Sonny. His past isn't off limits."

———

T.'s rose garden blazed in the late afternoon sunshine. The fragrance, as Cooper walked between the bushes to the front door, was intoxicating in a slightly sickening, feminine kind of way. He wondered if there was a blooming plant somewhere that smelled like a locker room.

T. and the Labradors met him at the door.

"Big Steve just called. He's going to be a little late."

"God, I hope he trusts me alone with his husband."

"And vice versa," Tristan said. "Come in the kitchen. I'll show you how to make cole slaw."

"Make cole slaw?" Cooper asked. "Doesn't that come from the deli?"

"New Yorkers," Tristan snorted.

———

"Great dinner, sweetheart," Big Steve said.

"I'll second that," Cooper said.

"Thank you, gentlemen."

"Just rinse the dishes," Big Steve said. "I'll load the dishwasher later."

"As you wish, m'lord."

"So, what's up?" Big Steve asked, turning to Cooper.

"T., would it be O.K. if you stepped out?" Cooper asked. "I don't mind Big Steve telling you all about it after I'm gone but I'd like to speak to him alone. If that's O.K."

"Certainly," Tristan said. "The dogs and I will be in the back yard."

"All right," Big Steve said.

"First of all, I'm not here to talk about Sonny."

"I didn't think you were."

"O.K." Cooper said. "The thing is, I want to compete. I took my licensing exam this morning, and I'm sure I passed it. And Sonny's offered me a job in his office when the results come back. So I've got all that out of the way and I'm ready to go."

"I see," Big Steve said. "Nothing's stopping you."

"You'll train me?"

"Why wouldn't I?" Big Steve asked.

"We haven't talked about it."

"We're talking about it now."

"Right. So what do you think?"

"It doesn't matter what I think," Big Steve said. "I'm not the one going to be competing."

"Sorry, I meant, what's your assessment of my chances?"

"Now you're talking," Big Steve smiled. "All right. I'm going to spare you the speech about how hard it is, because you work as hard in the gym as anybody I've ever trained."

"Thank you."

"And you'll either juggle going to college and starting a new career and preparing for contests or you won't, so we really don't need to talk about that."

"Right."

"For the record," Big Steve said, "you're the kind of workaholic who can probably do all that without breaking a sweat."

"Thanks."

"One thing bothers me, though."

"What's that?"

"I'm not sure Sonny's going to approve," Big Steve said.

"That's my problem."

"I know."

"So?"

"Way I see it, Big Steve," Cooper said, "if he can't support me in meeting my goals, maybe he's not the right guy for me."

"Really."

"I'm serious about this, Big Steve."

"As you say, it's your problem if Sonny decides he doesn't like it. Now, as for your chances, well, I could have you ready for a novice show in, say, seven to eight weeks. But you're probably not interested in that."

"You're right," Cooper said. "I'm not."

"So here's what we'll say. I can guarantee you a placing in the top three in any junior competition in Northern California between now and the first of the year."

"And open shows?"

"Have to be honest with you, Coop. You're at least a year out from being competitive on that level."

"Fair enough," Cooper said.

"Gentlemen," Tristan said, coming in through the back door, "I know I'm not supposed to be in here, but I think Calpurnia has just gone into labor."

———

At the gym, Cooper had learned how to maintain focus while surrounded by hot looking men. Pondering Lance's proposal, Cooper wasn't sure how it would turn out. But it was just the same as the gym, basically. It wasn't just any hot looking man of course. It was Nick, and that made it difficult. And they were going to be in such close proximity for such long periods of time during the shoot anything was possible. But still, by the third session he was able to relax into it. It wasn't that he became oblivious to the spectacle that was Nick Romanovsky. He just came to appreciate it on a more or less purely aesthetic basis. He assumed Nick was experiencing much the same thing. If he was experiencing anything at all. He gave no indication whatever.

———

Cooper had learned to read Sonny's signs very early. For all his purported caginess and cunning, Sonny was hopelessly transparent. He would have been a disaster at a poker table. But this was really a minor flaw compared to an inability to think strategically. A disaster at poker was one thing. A disaster at chess was something else entirely. No wonder he was paranoid. He was ridiculously easy to outmaneuver. He was easy pickings for manipulation. He was just lucky it was Cooper he was dealing with and not, say, Christopher. Christopher would rip him to shreds and never look back.

Sonny's demands weren't purely sexual. Cooper was certain of it. Each time, he had an unmistakable sense that he was being tested. That the tests grew more and more bizarre didn't alarm him. He wasn't sure where his limits were, but Sonny was nowhere near them. But it did make Cooper curious. There was the question of Sonny's motivation, which he hadn't quite worked out yet. And there was the more existential question of what Sonny would come up with next. This was intriguing both because of what Cooper might be about to experience and because each new scene provided another glimpse into Sonny's psyche. That was turning out to be a very unusual place.

———

"Gentlemen," Lance said, "that's a wrap. Thank you for all your hard work. I'll let you know when the proofs are ready."

———

When they got to Sonny's place after dinner, company was waiting for them.

"This is Mimi," Sonny said.

She was a large woman, Cooper's height and powerfully built. She reminded him of those female athletes you saw on television representing Eastern European countries in the shotput at the Olympic Games.

"Why don't we go into the playroom?" Sonny suggested.

Cooper followed them inside. Christopher was tied spread eagle to the bed. His genitals were caged inside some sort of wire and leather contraption. It couldn't be comfortable, and Cooper didn't want to imagine what it would feel like if the thing wasn't removed before Christopher became aroused.

———

Cooper kind of got what Sonny was up to—trying to see how far he'd go, obviously. He had no idea what was in it for Christopher. Stone had said that Sonny was exploiting Christopher's determination not to be relegated to Cooper's past. In other words, Christopher was obviously trying to win Cooper back just long enough to really screw him. The way he hadn't been able to the first time around. Cooper had committed the unpardonable sin. He'd broken things off before Christopher had a chance to do his worst. Even Nick Romanovsky hadn't been able to pull that off. As far as Cooper was concerned there was no unfinished business. Sonny could manipulate things all he wanted, but only because Cooper was willing to let him. If Sonny's plotting included Christopher, that was purely incidental. Christopher himself had no such leverage. What better way to demonstrate that than to treat him as if he were a complete stranger in any further encounters?

V

Sonny had to hand it to Jules. The man was a genius. Watching Cooper screw someone he so obviously despised was exquisite. There wasn't a moment of hesitation. He simply got down to business. He was like a perfectly programmed robot, unencumbered by emotion. Mimi, a seasoned professional, was impressed. And Christopher was absolutely convincing as a torture victim. Jules had a real prize there.

But it still wasn't enough. Sonny had to know for certain. There had to be one more test. Even Jules couldn't be allowed to know about this one.

———

"These ladies are Marthe and Belle," Sonny said. "Do what they say."

They were statuesque, bullwhip wielding, twin dominatrixes. Their leathers shone richly with freshly applied oil.

He sat and watched as they stripped Cooper and greased him up. They shaved Cooper's genitals, and Sonny nearly had an orgasm watching Cooper struggle not to. The women were experts, and Sonny had instructed them to try to force Cooper to finish early, but he managed to maintain control of himself. Just barely, by the look of it. They strapped Cooper into an elaborate harness of leather straps, chromium hoops, and lengths of chain. They buckled him into the sling.

Then the fun began. Sonny had requested six-tenths level torture and a slow pace. The restraints were set to be difficult but not impossible to escape from. Either Cooper would figure out that he was supposed to loose himself from them and turn the tables on the two women and then proceed to do it, or Sonny would have to begin disengaging himself. Marthe and Belle knew that being "conquered" by Cooper was the desired outcome but also that they mustn't let on or aid him in any way. That wouldn't prove anything. If Cooper didn't come through, it would be a real disappointment. Sonny had a lot invested, and it wasn't going to be easy starting over with someone new. It might be months or years before he could find another candidate of this caliber. That's what a prize Cooper was. But if he couldn't cut it, he couldn't. Unpleasant facts had to be faced if you ever hoped to achieve satisfaction.

It wouldn't be the first time Sonny had had to cut his losses. If you couldn't be a perfectionist about something this important, there was no point, really, in playing the game at all.

———

Sonny left a message with Jules' butler that he needed to know when the cinematographer would be back from Cartagena. It was time to book a photo shoot for Cooper. The man was notoriously difficult to schedule. It would be easier to cancel if things didn't go well than to wait until Sonny was certain.

———

This left him with one last matter to attend to. The lease on Renata's apartment was up for renewal. Renata had been a nag recently. She was obviously nearing her expiration date. Better call her landlord and give him notice of an impending vacancy.

VI

"What did you think of the pictures?" Nick asked, dismantling his hamburger.

"I can't believe you eat those," Cooper said.

"One per month. Without the bun," Nick said.

"Why not order them that way?"

"I happen to appreciate the traditional presentation."

"Suit yourself."

"I always do," Nick said. "Now about the pictures."

"Lance is a genius," Cooper said.

"Unquestionably," Nick nodded. "He showed me the folio he made of you and Stone. I practically had to wear oven mitts to handle it."

"Stone looked great," Cooper said. "Not so crazy about myself."

"Spoken like a true disciple of Big Steve," Nick laughed. "You looked terrific in them. You looked terrific in ours."

"I looked small," Cooper inisisted.

"No, you looked like the perfect complement to your fellow model."

"I looked small."

"Lance had no complaints."

"And he's the acknowledged genius," Cooper said.

"Right."

"And man of mystery."

"You've got the itch for him, all right," Nick grinned. "Looks like Sonny's in for a fight."

"No itch," Cooper insisted. "He's just one of the five hottest men in the city. That automatically makes him interesting."

"That's the fourth corollary to Big Steve's first law."

"What's that?"

"Anything a hot man does is hot," Nick said.

"Haven't heard that one."

"You will," Nick said. "Mind sharing your list?"

"Big Steve, Tristan, Lance," Cooper counted on his fingers, "you, of course."

"Glad I made the cut. That's four."

"Holding the other position open for Stone."

"You don't include yourself?" Nick asked.

"Honestly?"

"Sure."

"I'd put me at about number nine," Cooper said.

"Who are numbers six through eight?"

"Gotta leave room for new talent."

"I see."

"Just curious about Lance, is all," Cooper mused. "I mean, where does he go to the gym? Does he ever date? Just basic things like that. I never run into him anywhere except when there's a contest."

"Hire a private investigator if you're so determined to know all that stuff."

"You seem to know all about him."

"And you'll find out," Nick said, "when he's good and ready."

———

Monday morning Cooper stopped at the apartment just long enough to shave, shower, and dress for his first day at work. He hadn't been by since Friday, and there was mail waiting for him. He opened the letter.

August 24

Dear Cooper,

So in a few days you will be starting your new job. Dad and I are very proud of you. We know you will be successful. It will be difficult, of course, beginning this new career and continuing to take classes at the university, but we are so happy that you have decided to finish your degree.

We just got back from a few days in Boston. Your brother and Cherie are fine. Genikayte is a little monkey child, running and climbing like an acrobat. You should see her playing in the park. She reminds me of you. She is starting to talk now. Her first word was "no"—exacly like you at that age.

We are going to Josh's opening night on the seventh. Just think—his first starring role. He says the show isn't very good, but there are a few nice tunes. And some pretty girls in the chorus, so Dad is sure to have a good time.

Yakov and Naftali are doing well. They are hoping to come for a visit at Hanukkah. Naftali has relatives in Montreal he hasn't seen in a long time, so they will go up there as well. It will be wonderful if we can all be together.

Don't worry too much about Nanny. Her health is good, and I really believe that she is mostly pretending to be gaga. She's got some good years in her yet.

Dad and I are so fortunate to have such happy, successful sons!

Love,

Mom

P.S. The enclosed check is to help you buy some professional *clothing.*

———

The postcard showed a row of apartment houses, multistory structures in ornately sculpted white stucco. "*Greetings from Buenos Aires*" crawled across one corner of the card in moderne script. On the back, Cooper read

Thought you'd get a kick out of the architecture here. Three guesses what it reminds me of, and the first two don't count. Miss you, bud——like REALLY *miss you!*

———

There were messages on the answering machine. Nothing important, really, except one from Lance Garrison.

"*Hey, Cooper, just a call to confirm our shoot for Monday afternoon at 4:30. It would be great if you could make it to the gym right before you come by. That way you'll have a good pump for the photos. Anyway, see you then.*"

———

Nick had given Cooper the name of his tailor. The shirts and trousers fit him like a dream, but they were expensive. The check from Mom and Dad was going to come in handy. Even working part time, he really needed to have more made. Sonny had offered to set up an account for him with his own tailor, but Cooper wanted to maintain as much independence as possible.

Sonny had been certain that Mom and Dad would object to Cooper's plans, but Sonny didn't know them.

Cooper gave himself a last long look in the full length mirror he had just bought for his bedroom. He was about to meet Sonny's colleagues for the first time, and you only got one chance to make a first impression.

BUSINESS IS BUSINESS

I

When Sonny and Felicia filed for divorce, Cooper quietly rejoiced. Finally Sonny had figured it out. Sonny was getting serious about his life. Sonny was taking care of business. It was all going to work out. Impatient by nature, Cooper compelled himself to be patient. Outspoken to a fault, Cooper bit his tongue a thousand times a day. Normally implacable in pursuit of his aims, Cooper refrained from attempting to influence matters, reasoning that in the long run the victory would be even sweeter for his not having fought for it. Some things, he told himself—not many, it's true, but some—actually fall into our laps. Some things are simply meant to be. Our exertions merely impede or obstruct their natural progress. Though this was far from being a typical stance for him, Cooper adopted it with all his accustomed fervor. So he maintained what he liked to think of as an Olympian detachment from the events as they unfolded, though he was as attentive to Sonny as ever through the interminable wrangling about the division of property and the custody arrangements. Cooper was, he believed, in a position to be magnanimous.

When Sonny wrote an offer on a Hillsborough mansion even more ostentatious than the one he was signing over to Felicia in the settlement, Cooper silently congratulated himself, taking care to exhibit exactly the appropriate degree of enthusiasm. And when Sonny instructed his decorator, Joel Robbins, one of his closest friends from the old ice show days, that Cooper was to have a free hand in all matters regarding the renovations, it seemed as though he was finally home free. At last he could begin thinking of himself as the next Mrs. Sonny Dallas, though in truth he was far more inclined to think of Sonny as Mrs. Cooper Luxemberg. He didn't gloat. That would be beneath him. He took care not to be effusive. That was for sissies. But he couldn't keep himself from being a little bit smug. He couldn't think of a man his age in the whole city who could have pulled it off as well. It was a coup of historic proportions.

A few weeks later, with the escrow on the new house due to close and plans for the renovations nearly complete, they celebrated Cooper's birthday at his favorite restaurant. This, Cooper believed, would be the occasion for Sonny to declare his intentions. And so it proved. After opening the small blue box and exclaiming over the contents, Cooper turned his attention to the envelope.

"I've taken the liberty of renewing the lease on your flat," Sonny explained. "Pre-paid for the next year."

———

The scene a few nights later when he broke up with Sonny was remarkably civil, Cooper thought. He chalked it up to his refusal to lose his temper. His mother had taught him that one must control one's temper in inverse proportion to the gravity of the situation. Trivial annoyances could be greeted with limitless pyrotechnics, but serious matters had to be addressed with icy cool. This wasn't typical for Cooper, but the situation wasn't typical, either. At one point things threatened to go very badly. When he told Sonny he was tired of being a mistress rather than a genuine partner, Sonny laughed at him. Instead of pushing over the table, Cooper forced himself not to move or speak. Somehow realizing his mistake, Sonny quickly apologized. That had been the most dangerous moment. Still, though Cooper never totally regained his equanimity, there was no real chance of a scene after that.

Unfortunately, Sonny went on to orate boozily on the perfection of their relationship in its current state, expressing long windedly and with unmistakable conviction how unnecessary and even potentially detrimental he considered the notion of any alteration to what he referred to as "arrangements". Cooper listened quietly, sadly realizing that Sonny had never thought of him as anything more than a diversion. It was the bitter pill perennially prescribed by life to the "other woman", and he couldn't believe he'd been so stupid. It didn't matter that he was different from all those mistresses. The issue was, he finally understood, that Sonny wasn't different from any other married man with a mistress. Cooper had tragically overestimated him.

Finally, closer to tears than he could ever remember being, he simply walked out. Sonny didn't call the next morning, and Cooper took this as his signal to clear out. He left all the jewelry and credit cards. He left all the artwork and tchotchkes. He left every stitch of clothing he could recall Sonny having bought him. He left the Rolex and every last photograph. He didn't want anything he hadn't brought with him when he moved in. Eventually Sonny would stop by the flat and find it all.

———

In real life, Chanel Rococo was a boy named Johnny Miller. In men's clothing he was completely nondescript except for his extreme height, which was accentuated—one detractor said "exacerbated", and really that was closer to the truth—by the slenderness of his frame. But on stiletto heels and wearing her signature mane of titian hair, Chanel Rococo was prodigious. The proverbial force of nature, she reigned over her claque (or troupe, or coven, depending on the perspective of the observer) of subordinates with an iron fist, or, more usually, a razor sharp tongue. They inhabited a rackety, decaying house in Haight-Ashbury on the ambiguous terms which obtained in the neighborhood, where it was still "the summer of love" even though for the rest of the world 1967 was a fading memory. No one seemed to know for certain whether they were tenants or squatters, themselves least of all. Or, for that matter, which of them were more or less official residents and which ones were passing through, at least theoretically. Occasionally, rumors of a landlord would sweep the household, but no one claiming that status ever materialized.

The best Cooper could figure it out, the critical mass—and boy, were they critical—consisted of Chanel herself, her principal divas-in-waiting Holly Montezuma and Marina del Rey, and three or four acolytes whose identities either were still evolving or Cooper simply couldn't keep track of, such as with a litter of kittens lacking sufficient distinguishing characteristics to allow anyone to tell them apart. This crew had been Sonny's coterie when Cooper first met him, though for some reason he never bothered to explain, he kept them under wraps for the first several months. They were noisy, chaotic, dire even, but unflaggingly loyal and possessed of a limitless avidity. Their turbulent energy Chanel ruthlessly exploited in support of whatever agenda occurred to her on any given day.

Cooper approached the group with no small trepidation. The potential for catastrophe of a particularly histrionic nature was daunting. The one thing he had no doubt of was his reception. In their worldview youth and beauty trumped every-thing, and in this new state of affairs he didn't waste a second wondering whose side they would take. At least initially. In the longer term, as long as he slept with none of them but gave them all equally the impression that he eventually might, all should be well. But they were so damned unpredictable. That and his own near desperation made for a volatile mix.

Ultimately what tipped the scales wasn't their devotion to him but their devo-tion to the Labradors. That was something that could be depended on. On his own, Cooper could have lived just about anywhere. But finding a landlord who would allow three large dogs—well, Cooper didn't have time for the search that would entail. Leaving them with Sonny wasn't an option. The break would never be per-manent. But the fact was that Sonny couldn't be trusted with them. He'd end up hiring the canine equivalent of a nanny, and Cooper didn't want them cared for by strangers. They already knew the drag queens. And that overgrown back gar-den would be perfect for the dogs' roughhousing and minor domestic squabbles. Then there was the doting attentiveness he knew would be lavished on them. You couldn't put a price on that. He knew he could be certain that they would be spoiled as they were accustomed to being spoiled while he took on the role of sole provider.

Presuming on the hospitality of his hostesses as he was, Cooper still felt strong enough in his position to insist on a few conditions before moving in. Sharing a bathroom was going to be hard enough. But sharing sleeping accommodations was unthinkable. The unsuitability of this seemed apparent to everyone, and the first floor room that had originally been the maid's quarters was cleared out for him. He refinished the floor, painted the walls, hung new curtains. He bought a waterbed and a third hand armoire. The Labradors brought their familiar bedding with them.

———

Monday morning Cooper went to work as usual. No one paid him any special atten-tion. Sonny apparently hadn't spoken to anyone from the office over the weekend. It was even conceivable that Sonny hadn't yet realized Cooper had moved out of the apartment and was simply giving him time to cool off. Just before noon, as Cooper was reviewing some listings he planned to show a new client later in the day, Sonny stormed into his office, breathing fire and pawing the turf.

"What the fuck are you doing here?" he demanded.

"I work here," Cooper said.

"Like hell. Get out."

"Sonny, we're both professionals, and this is a business. There's no reason why our personal issues. . ."

"This is *my* business. I own it. And I may be a professional, but you're nothing but a cheap little gold digging tart. Get the hell out. Go peddle your slimy ass somewhere else."

"Sonny, what on earth?" Elizabeth Montefiore appeared in the doorway. Shadowy in the hall behind her loomed Ned Westerleigh, looking, Cooper thought, like the headmaster of a particularly spartan boys' school.

"Keep out of this, you two," Sonny barked. "And you. You've got five minutes to get your ass out the door. If you take so much as a ballpoint pen that doesn't belong to you, I'll call the police."

"Sonny," Ned said, "there are clients in the foyer listening to every word of this."

"Whose clients?" Sonny demanded.

"Cooper's, as a matter of fact," Elizabeth answered.

"He has no clients. And I thought I told you two to butt out."

"You two remember this," Cooper said as he passed Elizabeth and Ned on his way out. "He's the one who wanted it this way."

"By the way," Sonny called after him, "where are the dogs?"

"Hire a detective," Cooper snapped.

"Why, you little shit. I ought to beat the hell out of you."

As if he could.

"That would certainly show everyone what a class act you are," Cooper called over his shoulder.

———

"You told me so," Cooper said, standing under the showerhead. He'd heard the whispering the minute he got to the gym. Everywhere he went people had apparently heard some version or other of the breakup story. The only way he'd be able to save face with the few people whose opinion mattered was to take the bull by the horns. Throwing himself on Big Steve's mercy was the surest path, perhaps the only path. Grovel if you have to, Cooper reasoned, but only on your own terms, which meant in front of the right people.

"I didn't tell you anything," Big Steve said, lathering up next to him.

"Yes you did. You told me I'd never have the kind of relationship I wanted with a man like Sonny Dallas for a partner."

"I don't remember ever discussing him with you," Big Steve said. "Closest I came to it was once upon a time standing in my kitchen listening to Nick in the dining room telling you never to repeat a certain name in my presence. Still have no idea what he meant by that. Complete mystery, in fact."

But he couldn't completely stifle his grin, as Cooper noted out of the corner of his eye.

"Right," he said, blushing at the memory. "Thing is, Big Steve, you're the kind of guy who doesn't have to say a word to get his point across."

"I am, huh?"

"Damn right."

"How'd I do it then?" Big Steve asked.

"All kinds of ways."

"Name one," Big Steve grunted.

"Mostly you've kept me focused on Matt and Ashby," Cooper said.

"Not on T. and me?"

"You and T. are so spectacular together, nobody but an egomaniac would seriously consider you as role models. It would be like patterning your life on the Seven Labors of Hercules. That's what you and T. are. Mythic."

"Swear to God," Big Steve muttered. "College boys. So Matt and Ash. What about them?"

"You knew they were the best possible example of what I should have been looking for. So you went with it. Made sure I was around them enough to figure out that's what it looks like when two guys are really tight. You and T. both. Always with the 'meet us all for brunch' and 'you should come over Thursday night, we're playing Scrabble' so I couldn't possibly miss it. Even when I wasn't there, I thought about them."

"Uh huh," Big Steve said, with a crafty grin.

"Every time I saw them together I knew the thing with Sonny wasn't working. I knew it, and you knew I knew it. I know you did. I just couldn't bring myself to cut my losses. I thought he'd come around. I thought he'd do it for me."

"Sorry, kid."

"Don't be. I fucked up, is all. I'll do better next time."

"Good man."

———

"Sonny was sleeping around," Tristan said the next day, watching Cooper do curls. "Everybody knew about it."

"Except me," Cooper said, setting the bar back in the rack. He couldn't believe he'd been so stupid, playing by their rules while Sonny got up to God knew what.

"I mean, I don't know what your arrangement was."

"No sleeping around," Cooper said. "That's what we agreed to. But three ways were O.K."

"Matt says Sonny's been going through stewardesses like a house on fire," J.B. said.

This was the first complete sentence Cooper had ever heard J.B. utter. He noticed J.B.'s struggle to master his stammer, and appreciated it. Apparently J.B.'s new speech therapist knew what she was doing.

"Sonny does have a stewardess fetish," Cooper nodded, picking up the bar to start his next set. Lots of their three ways had actually been four ways, with Cooper screwing two stewardesses while Sonny watched and jerked off.

"You know that sling he had installed in your apartment?" Nick asked.

"You know about the sling?"

"Everybody in San Francisco knows about the sling," Tristan said.

"He wanted to hire J.B. and me to do a little scene. We were going to tie you up, shave you, flog you, put clamps on your nipples, strap you into the sling, and take turns fucking you."

"Cooper, if that was something the two of you agreed on. . ." Tristan suggested.

"It's not," Cooper grunted.

"Supposed to piss all over you when we finished," J.B. said.

"I'm not even going to tell you about what he was trying to organize for his New Year's Eve party," Nick said. "Just please promise me you won't go back to him."

———

"Elizabeth Montefiore will be joining me," Cooper told the *maitre d'*.

"Very good, Mr. Luxemberg."

He could tell what the man was thinking as he followed him to the table. Well, screw them all. Of course he didn't expect anything else from Sonny, who he'd always known could be a vindictive bitch. All the wells were poisoned. He'd heard it in the hostess' voice when he called to make the reservation. But no matter how exclusive this establishment wanted to be, it was still just a restaurant, not the Vatican. And unless he violated the dress code or caused a scene, the cardinal rule still applied. His money—that's right, *his* money, money he had *earned*—was as good as anybody's.

He ordered a Calistoga with lime, and it took just long enough to arrive to send the clear message that his business wasn't welcome. Obviously, they wanted him to complain so they could ask him to leave. To show that he didn't care, he didn't touch the drink. At the very least, he had to maintain that fiction.

Elizabeth arrived, tall as an Amazon, exotic as the princess of a mythical kingdom, serene as a goddess. Twenty years on from her heyday on the catwalks of Paris and Milan, she still turned every head in the place, gay, straight, or uncommitted. He stood, kissed the velvet cheek. They had grown up two decades and three blocks apart, and her perennial quip that Cooper and she were the only people in all San Francisco who didn't speak with an accent had always delighted Sonny, not least because it completely negated the existence of Stefano Fabiani.

"You don't appear to be naked and starving," she observed, taking her seat.

Cooper knew from experience not to help her with her chair.

"Is that the rumor of the week?"

"Last week, actually," Elizabeth said. "I won't tell you what this week's is."

"Thanks."

"So. Not naked and starving. Not noticeably drug addled. And ravishing as ever. Sonny will be furious when I tell him."

"I didn't invite you to lunch to send a message to Sonny," Cooper said.

"Didn't you? Good. But let's do get one thing out of the way."

"What's that?"

"He'll take you back," Elizabeth said. "Just say the word."

"Did he tell you that?"

"Rather the opposite."

"Huh?"

"That's how I know," she said, "and you know that when it comes to Sonny, I do know."

"All right."

"So?"

"So when you talk to him about this lunch," Cooper said, "make sure you tell him that I never asked that particular question."

"You're sure? You're not—I don't know—holding out on him? Because he'll take you back but he won't beg. He's too proud for that, even if nobody ever heard about it."

"I'm sure. I'm not going back," Cooper said.

"Funny, I wouldn't have thought of you as a bridge burner."

"Why not? Because I'm young? Because I'm not rich enough to call the shots?"

"Because, basically, you're too nice."

"I'm not nice at all."

"So you always insist on saying," Elizabeth nodded. "All right, because you're too smart to operate that way."

"That's more like it. But I didn't burn any bridges. You saw how Sonny was that day. Breathing fire."

"He's not a young man, Cooper. In spite of all the time and money he spends on looking it, he's barely even middle aged any more."

"All the more reason to act like a grown up."

The waiter arrived and took their order. Asparagus and prosciutto for Elizabeth and grilled sole for Cooper.

"How are the dogs?" Elizabeth asked.

"Flourishing."

"I don't know what made Sonny angrier. Your leaving the jewelry or taking the dogs."

"He hated the dogs."

"Not as much as he hates you having them," Elizabeth said.

"That's his problem."

"Right."

"Elizabeth, I need a job. It's been six weeks, and I can't get arrested."

"I know, dear."

"I've looked. I swear to God I have. I've had interviews. Plenty of them. I get there and it's obvious they just asked me in because they wanted a good look at Sonny's bad boy."

"I know," she said. "Everybody in the city knows."

"They can't all be friends of his."

"They're not. Some of them won't have anything to do with you because they're being loyal to him. Some of them are doing it because they're afraid of him. Others are afraid you'll cause some kind of scandal. And in some cases it's just because you're gay. They won't discriminate against gay men like Sonny who are wealthy and powerful, but it's safe enough to discriminate against someone like you."

"Honest to God, Elizabeth, I never thought he'd take it this far."

"He's hurt. He's hurt and he's angry."

"He's got no one to blame but himself."

"Do you think he doesn't know that?" she asked.

"What? You're not making sense."

"It just makes it worse for him," she explained, "knowing that he was in the wrong. He can't do the right thing because it would mean apologizing."

"I'd think realizing his mistake would make things easier."

"Please, Cooper, who are we talking about here?"

"Got it."

"So, no prospects at all?"

"Not unless I'll put out. I'd be better off going back to Sonny."

"Which you won't do."

"Would you?"

"This isn't about me," she said.

"Well, is it so wrong for a guy to want to be his boyfriend's equal? To stand on his own two feet?"

"Oh, darling, what you're suggesting is impossible. It would never do."

"Why the hell not?" Cooper asked.

"Because the minute they allow that, the queens of this town will have to resign themselves to dying alone. They can only tolerate the existence of young men like you to the extent that your dependence on them gives them all the power."

"In other words, there's no hope," Cooper said.

"I'm sorry, but that's about the size of it. Here in San Francisco at least. I can get you a job in L.A. or San Diego with one phone call. But not here, I'm afraid."

"You'd do that for me?"

"Of course. You're a hard worker. You're smart. You're good at anything you do. You've got a true gift for real estate. In a few years, you could be a spectacular success."

"Well, if that's how you feel, perhaps you'd consider something else," Cooper said.

"Keep talking."

"You have a broker's license. And I'm willing to work my tail off. We should start our own agency."

"Go up against Sonny?"

"Not really," Cooper said. "I think there's room for more players, that's all."

"It sounds like you're out for revenge."

"Some, I'll admit. But if nobody's going to give me a chance, it's my only alternative. Work for myself."

"I see that," Elizabeth said, "but I'm afraid you'll have to do it without me."

"What if I won't take no for an answer?"

"You are asking me to be terribly disloyal to one of my oldest and dearest friends," Elizabeth said. "You know that."

"Business is business."

"For you and me, perhaps, but not for Sonny. With him, everything is personal. And he's legendary for holding grudges."

"Maybe so. But do you know how I see him? I see him as someone who has repaid your loyalty and hard work by never offering you a partnership."

This, Cooper knew, had long been a sore point with Elizabeth.

"That's his affair," she said.

"But it's so unfair. You've put more into that agency than anyone. More than Sonny himself."

"It's his firm. He can do what he likes."

"And you just go along with it. Busting your ass so that Felicia can continue living in the manner to which she's become accustomed and he can pay for his new house. His life just got lots more expensive, and he's going to balance the books on your back. Yours and Ned's."

"Cooper!"

"Sorry, Elizabeth. But you know I'm right. And you know I don't bullshit."

"One of your less attractive qualities, I have to say."

"In a friend, maybe," Cooper said. "Not in a business partner."

"I repeat, the firm belongs to Sonny. He can run it however he pleases."

"Even if it's for all the wrong reasons."

"I don't think I want to hear any more of this," Elizabeth said.

"Suit yourself. I was only going to point out that it either has to be because you're a woman or you're a Jew."

"You know better."

"Do I? Do you?"

"Is there anything else you have to share?" she asked, "or shall we change the subject?"

"That's all."

Cooper knew he'd reached the safe limits of her exasperation.

"You're sure? You're completely finished?"

"What else do you want me to say?"

"Don't play innocent," she said. "You know I'm only Jewish by adoption."

"Not even Sonny is enough of a snob to hold that against you."

"Or that I'm mulatto."

"He never believed that rumor," Cooper said.

"Oh, no?"

"He said your features were obviously wrong for it."

"That may be what he told you, but he knows the truth."

"Elizabeth, you're not really. . ."

"Not technically, no."

"What does that mean?" Cooper asked. "Not technically?"

"Technically I'm not a mulatto. Technically I'm an octoroon."

"You're what?"

"An octoroon. It means. . ."

"I know what it means," Cooper said. "I'm sorry I laughed. I just always thought the whole thing was only a stupid rumor."

"I should never have told Sonny."

"It's a shitty reason not to make you a partner."

"It's not why he hasn't," Elizabeth said.

"You say that," Cooper said.

"I know it."

"Then why?"

"Because he's Sonny Dallas, and he can do what he wants."

This, Cooper recognized, was not a reason at all.

———

The concierge at Ned Westerleigh's building scowled but buzzed Cooper in. The lobby reminded him of the one at Ned's club in London, where Sonny and he had visited on what he thought of at the time as his honeymoon. Here there was the same dark paneling. Brass fittings gleamed everywhere you looked, and the smell of furniture polish and cigar smoke pervaded everything. Yes, the two spaces were virtually interchangeable. Every inch an Englishman, Ned would undoubtedly have found similar accommodations anywhere on the globe.

In the elevator Cooper pressed P for the penthouse, and the car refused to move. He hit the "door open" button, called "excuse me" to the concierge and received a sneering "sorry, sir" in return, and was finally on his way.

The elevator doors opened directly into Ned's flat, which was more of the same. Given the décor, it was a shock not to see Big Ben or the Tower Bridge outside the windows, where, instead, Alcatraz lurked in the fog. Flush and Fidget, Ned's superannuated Springers, sniffed at his ankles and wagged their stub tails lethargically. Tebaldi singing *Tosca* was loud enough, Cooper thought, to shatter some of the smaller Waterford pieces scattered around the room. Sonny had always been a Callas man. Cooper found Ned's preference for Tebaldi laudable, but what did he know about it, really? Perhaps he had a tin ear, as Sonny had insisted that time Cooper accused Callas of screeching.

"Ned," he shouted above the din.

The shriek of a tea kettle and the dogs' answering whoops were probably not Tebaldi's preferred response to her artistry, but to Cooper's thinking they lent just the right touch of surrealism to the scene.

"In here, Cooper." Ned's silvery mop of hair gleamed in the doorway to his study.

"The tea kettle, Ned."

"Oliver will get it."

"It's Thursday, Ned."

"It's not."

"It is."

"Bloody hell."

"You'd be at work if it weren't," Cooper pointed out.

"Bloody buggery hell on toast."

Ned sprinted into the kitchen and Cooper took the liberty of turning down Tebaldi.

"You must have put the kettle on yourself."

"I must've, musn't I?" Ned agreed, emerging from the kitchen. "We'll let it steep. Unless you'd like something stronger."

"Your act is wasted on me, you know."

"Whatever do you mean, my dear boy?"

"This dotty British aristo shtick of yours. I know better. You've got the sharpest mind in the city."

"It's a fair cop, m'lord," Ned whined in broad cockney.

"Please."

"Seriously, my dear: protective coloring. Just like a small, defenseless mammal in the jungle. If they didn't all think I was a gaga old poof they'd soon realize how dangerous I truly am. Let that be a lesson to you. Choose your camouflage wisely and cultivate it obsessively. Tea in the study, I think."

Cooper had visited this holy of holies only a handful of times. Ordinarily, Ned preferred to entertain guests in his living room, or, weather permitting, on his expansive roof garden overlooking the bay. It was a small room, cluttered with memorabilia. Cricket bats, straw boaters, loving cups and plaques engraved with honors, dates, and mottoes lined the walls interspersed with framed photographs. Ned at Winchester. Ned at Oxford. Ned in front of a World War II bomber plane, Ned at various colonial outposts, dressed in outfits ranging from tropical to arctic, from school uniform to paratrooper togs to high diplomatic drag. Sonny claimed that Ned was a fake and all these artifacts were fakes, but only when he was hopelessly drunk.

The youngest son of a Marquess and a distant cousin of both the Windsors and the Romanoffs, Ned was a walking, talking cliché. Everybody thought they knew him, but Cooper had figured out soon after meeting him that what they knew was not the man but the type. It was a type Americans generally underestimated or at the very least misunderstood, and Ned invariably turned this to his advantage. The lesson wasn't lost on Cooper, who'd been described as "just a pretty face" or "musclebound dummy" enough times to get the point.

Ned bustled into the room and set the tea tray on his desk.

"My dear boy," he said, busying himself with the arcane ritual of pouring, "how kind of you to drop by."

"It's always good to see you, Ned."

"You know, that's what people invariably tell me," Ned chuckled. "American sincerity is particularly transparent. It's as if inscrutability has been bred out of all of you."

"All right. I admit it. I'm dying of curiosity."

"Not of love, alas," Ned said.

"No."

"And presumably not dying at all, actually."

"Not any more than we all are," Cooper said.

"You've upset our dear Elizabeth, my boy."

"I didn't mean to."

"Oh, yes you did." Ned wagged a finger. "Naughty, naughty."

"I'd say I'm sorry, but. . ."

"Doesn't signify. And anyway, I don't mean upset in that sense."

"What other sense is there?" Cooper asked.

"You've got her thinking."

"Exactly what I intended."

"Indeed," Ned nodded. "You mustn't mind that she told me."

"I expected her to."

"I told her as much."

"Really."

"Let's be frank, shall we?"

"You be Frank, Ned. I'd rather be William."

"Now, now."

"Sorry," Cooper said. "All right, then. Frankly, what I want is a job. A real job. No minimum wage shit, no mopping out crappers. Something commensurate with my abilities. And experience."

"Oh, rot. A job's not such a difficult thing to acquire."

"A job here. In San Francisco," Cooper corrected himself. "I'm not going anywhere."

"Ah," Ned nodded. "Slightly more complicated, I agree. But really now, I'd think there would be any number of gentlemen clamoring to accommodate you."

"On my own terms. No strings attached. No conditions. Just a job."

"I see."

"All I need is the opportunity," Cooper said, "but that's not happening. So I came up with this other plan. The one I discussed with Elizabeth."

"Hm."

"You don't think I have what it takes," Cooper said.

"You don't know what I think."

"Sorry."

"Nobody knows what I think," Ned said. "Ever. I bloody well make certain of it."

"Understood," Cooper said.

"Now, don't sulk. You know that Ned's nothing if not a prima donna. So indulge me my aria, if you please."

"All right."

"What it takes, you say. Yes. What it takes to go after Sonny Dallas and all those other prune faced queens. Three things, I should think."

"Which are?" Cooper asked.

"So glad you asked. And do have one of Oliver's chutney tartlets."

"No thanks."

"Damn your abdominals, young Cooper. Have a tart, I tell you. Have two."

Cooper put three on his plate.

"Good boy, that's better. An army marches on its stomach, you know. Napoleon said so, and who would know better? Now, what it would take to dethrone Sonny Dallas?"

"Who's talking about dethroning anybody?" Cooper asked. "I just want a chance to earn my fair share, that's all."

"Liar."

"I'm not."

"Come, come, my boy. You know as well as I do that as far as Sonny and his ilk are concerned, one more little piggy at the trough is one little piggy too many. For them, too much is never enough. And they don't believe in share and share alike except with regard to their hustlers. So I stand by my term. Dethrone. By surviving at all you'll be taking food out of their houseboys' mouths, and they won't take kindly to that."

"I knew you would try to warn me off," Cooper said.

"It's my job."

"As Sonny's oldest friend."

"As *your* friend, Cooper," Ned corrected him. "And I prefer to be described as Sonny's *closest* friend."

"Sorry."

"Now as I see it," Ned said, "it will take three things. Intelligence first of all. You won't be able to beat them by brute force. Because brute force in this instance means money and influence. No, you'll have to outsmart them. And I'll be the first one to say that you're easily clever enough for that. Sonny likes to go around telling everyone you're no more than a gorgeous lunkhead, but that couldn't be further from the truth."

"Thank you."

"The second requirement is ruthlessness," Ned said. "And two months ago, if anyone had described you as ruthless, I would have answered 'balderdash!' But I'd have been wrong, wouldn't I?"

"Perhaps."

"Oh, you're ruthless enough. No one could doubt it at this point. Except at their peril. Not after you left all that jewelry behind. Talk about going for the jugular. You've got poor Sonny all at sixes and sevens, and you've barely even started."

"If you say so," Cooper said.

"Which leaves just one thing. Capital. Enterprises such as you propose don't materialize from thin air. They're ravening beasts, especially when they're new born. And they know one food only. Capital."

"Agreed."

"Now, as I understand it, you're asking Elizabeth to provide certain things. A proper professional credential, for one. Her good reputation in the profession for another."

"Not to mention expertise," Cooper nodded.

"No, my dear boy, you can't expect her to supply the capital as well."

"I don't."

"Not even part of it?"

"No."

"Very well," Ned said. "That being understood, it wouldn't greatly surprise me if she eventually agreed to your scheme."

"Really?"

"Indeed."

"Is that how you'll advise her?" Cooper asked.

"I? Advise Elizabeth? My dear boy, I wouldn't dream of it."

II

Cooper told no one about his plans. He only let Chanel and company know he was leaving at the very last minute. They were full of questions, to which he fabricated answers colorful enough to satisfy their hunger for drama. In response to what he considered a simple request, they ransacked the house for Bibles so they could erect a stack on which to swear faithfully that the Labradors would want for nothing in his absence. This candlelight ceremony caused him grave misgivings. Their intentions he didn't doubt, but their competence was questionable. He had visions of the Labradors vomiting unsuitable treats onto the rugs. No alternative for their care occurred to him, so he crossed his fingers and hoped for the best. At worst, the natural resourcefulness of the dogs themselves would probably be sufficient.

He wouldn't need much where he was going. Packing took all of ten minutes. He knew Chanel's crew would go through everything he left behind as soon as he was out the door. None of the clothing would fit them, but they'd undoubtedly find people it did and give it away. The underwear was even easier disposed of. He'd never see any of it again. He was resigned to this. So in addition to his meager wardrobe selections, he boxed up his family photos, the things from his Bar Mitzvah, and a handful of other treasures to take along. It wasn't so much a matter of sentiment as a reluctance to leave these objects to the mercy of strangers.

Holly Montezuma and Marina del Rey insisted on helping him pack, so he used the opportunity to feed them the misinformation he was counting on them to spread. He knew he couldn't simply disappear without giving rise to rumors. He hoped at least to influence what those rumors consisted of. No one over the age of ten would take seriously the baroque saga he trusted his hints would inspire, but engendering belief wasn't his goal. The more outrageous the fables, he reasoned, the more rapidly they would spread and the better a distraction they would provide. This tactic he had adopted from Ned, an unquestioned master of the art. If his plans worked out, it would be just one of the debts he owed that crafty Brit.

—

The first leg of his journey took him only as far as a barbershop in Daly City. There, a protesting Chinese grandfather finally agreed to cut his shoulder length luxuriance into a rakish flattop. The eventual result would have done justice to a fighter pilot in the Argentine air force, he thought, though it reduced the old man nearly to tears. He purchased a particularly redolent wax for its proper maintenance and left a tip equivalent to double the basic charge. He promised to come back the next time he was in the neighborhood.

He hadn't shaved in several days, and the shadow of his incipient van dyke already showed dark on his face. By the end of the week, his own mother would have to look twice to make sure it was him. Not that he expected to encounter her at his destination. He gave serious thought to stopping next door to the barbershop and getting a tattoo, but in the end his Jewish upbringing got the better of him.

He put the top down and headed south. The Jaguar purred along Highway One. Gradually the perpetual fog and chill of the region were replaced by the kind of warmth and sunshine people sang songs about on the radio. The gleaming car devoured the miles, while Cooper painstakingly invented the man he was going to be for the duration. This person had to be two things: a walking, talking cliché, and someone not easily traceable back to himself. The first was easy, almost laughably so. The second was a trickier problem but far from insurmountable. He wasn't trying to withstand all possible scrutiny. Law enforcers and private detectives held no terror for him. He simply aimed to bamboozle the casual busybodies he considered the main threat. There was also his family to consider. He didn't want them knowing. He would have to explain why he hadn't asked them for the money.

———

He rented a studio apartment in a small, nineteen-twenties building just off Sunset Boulevard, the cheapest one he could find in the 90069 zip code. The block was crawling with actor/model/waiters of various genders. He spent three whole days disinfecting and repainting the apartment before installing the minimal furniture he selected. A mattress set flat on the floor, a small table and single chair to eat at, a black and white portable television, a second hand recliner. This stage set had to aid him in maintaining his characterization whether he ever entertained a guest there or not.

He subsisted on protein shakes, eggs, skim milk, canned tuna, and fresh fruit. He drank nothing stronger than distilled water. He tended his flattop and van dyke meticulously. His body hair, left unshaven for the first time in years, grew in luxuriantly, further camouflaging him. He left the apartment only to tan or make trips on foot to the shops for necessities. The Jaguar slumbered under a dust cover in a dark corner of the basement garage. He made no phone calls except to his mother; sent no postcards.

——

He splurged on one thing only. His second week in the city he bought a membership at the most exclusive gym in West Hollywood. This was perhaps the most crucial part of his plan, and he knew he had made the right choice when men there began hitting on him immediately. He pretended not to understand their overtures at first, then to be shy. Most of all, he pretended to be straight. He volunteered no information but when asked he gave them a name. Paul. Paul Giannini. Yes, new in town. Yes, just out of the service. Originally from New Jersey. Yes, Italian, but only on his father's side. His mother was Finnish. People were remarkably stupid, he decided. They'd believe anything you told them, or at least pretend to if they thought it might help them get laid.

After Sonny fired him, every job interview Cooper had gone on ended in one of two ways. If the prospective employer was straight, there was a firm handshake and a promise, albeit one made with averted eyes, to call him if any suitable position came open. If the prospective employer was not straight, the interview ended with exactly the kind of proposition Cooper was now fielding at his gym. He had decided that if Sonny and his type were determined to make him a whore, he'd be a whore. But only on his own terms. The best whores, as history has demonstrated time and time again, either learned how to exploit the exploiters or circumvented them entirely. And they never sold themselves cheap. He simply had to adapt those cardinal rules to his own situation. It was an exercise in problem solving more than anything.

As he lay by the pool, wandered the palm lined streets, luxuriated in the balmy evenings, basked in the admiration of everyone who laid eyes on him, Cooper realized that Los Angeles had been his only possible choice for more than the purely utilitarian reason that it was the capital of the particular universe he aspired temporarily to conquer. He had always thought of San Francisco as the sexiest of cities, but a few days and nights in Los Angeles were enough to convince him of his error. This was the sexiest of cities and San Francisco the most romantic. It was the first time in his life that he understood the difference, or even that there was one.

———

Word got around that he was not available for dates, either gratis or paid, and the volume of men approaching him abated substantially. He was careful, however, not to lose people's attention, posing ostentatiously in the gym, taking far longer than necessary in the shower, responding to any and all glances with a boyish grin. "Look but don't touch" paid off quickly. A couple of guys introduced themselves as photographers, and slowly, ever so slowly, he allowed himself to be talked into posing for them, shirtless in jeans at first, eventually the way they had originally wanted him. He acted like it was all new to him.

Before long, friends of the photographers' friends suggested he appear in films. What kind of films? Oh, just posing, like in the gym? Sure, why not? And eventually—*all I have to do is jerk off? Guess I could give it a whirl.* He knew, of course, that this wasn't where the serious money was. But he didn't have long to wait. *Let you film me with some guy sucking my cock? Don't think so, sport. Make it a chick and we'll talk about it.* Once those words left his mouth, it was ridiculously easy, though he had to admit that the audition was a little unnerving. Still, before he knew it, "Paul Giannini" was a sensation.

———

He didn't go to any of their parties. He refused to take their drugs. He turned down all suggestions of extra curricular fucking among casts and crews. He made it absolutely clear that for him it was just a job.

He was utterly reliable, and so was his cock. When he wasn't on a shoot, he was at the gym, so his body never disappointed. In straight porn, of course, that wasn't supposed to matter. There were directors who wouldn't use him. *"Too pretty." "Too built." "Too much of a distraction from the girls." "I'm not making videos for queers."* But there was still more work than he could take on.

He saved his pay like the most responsible mechanic or plumber. It wasn't much, but he had known it wouldn't be. Even the girls didn't make that much. He and the other guys were practically furniture and were paid accordingly. The real money was in the side work as he had known it would be. The films were his entrée to that circuit. How else was a lunkhead just out of the service going to get access to the opportunity? He could have gotten himself into it in a more direct way if anonymity hadn't been the goal. He could have raised the money without ever leaving San Francisco, but he would have been Cooper Luxemberg doing it. Sonny and his friends would have howled with satisfaction. In L.A., it was Paul Giannini climbing in and out of those beds, sharing himself with those leathery faced society matrons, the bored wives of doctors and bankers, the has been movie queens and jaded heiresses. They kissed and told and passed him along to their friends. If he had been two Paul Gianninis or even three there still wouldn't have been enough of him to go around. They devoured him like cake. They mainlined him like a drug. They cackled over him like Macbeth's witches. But they paid. They paid and paid. They vied for the honor of showing their appreciation in more and more grandiose ways. They were as profligate with him as their husbands were with their women. One of his fellow thespians turned him on to a Beverly Hills pawn shop that gave good value for trinkets he wanted to liquidate. He lived on practically nothing. Most of what he made went into the bank. He noted with satisfaction how quickly it was adding up. His original estimates of how long it would take to reach his goal turned out to be conservative. He had padded Ned Westerleigh's estimate of funds required by fifty per cent, and he was still months ahead of schedule.

Filming was grueling work, and usually boring as well. He quickly grew to hate everything about it: the lights, the heat, the dozens of people fussing over the silliest details and ruining his concentration or at the very least his detachment, the whining and/or tantrums of the "actresses", the druggy lethargy of his fellow "actors", the sleazy arrogance of the directors. His ladies were grueling work, too. He hated their slack, wrinkled skin, the raspy sound of their voices, and the way they smelled. Most of all, he hated what he had to do with his cock and everyone he had to do it to. It wasn't anything like actually having sex, and occasionally he wondered if he would ever enjoy sex again.

When it was all over, he was filled with a sense of relief combined with satisfaction at a job well done.

III

"Look who's back in town," Nick leered, sliding into the booth across from him.

"Hey."

"I'm probably in the minority," Nick said, "but that haircut is so hot on you."

"Thanks," Cooper said. "Not particularly partial to it myself."

"I don't know,"Tristan said, sitting down next to Nick and doing a head feint to keep his own hair from being mussed by the giant paw reaching toward it. "I really couldn't say one way or the other. You just have sexy hair, no matter what. Damn you."

"But this," Nick said, reaching over and stroking his bristly face, "has got to go. Gotta stop camouflaging that gorgeous mug."

"Agreed,"Tristan nodded.

"Don't forget. Anything a really hot man does is hot," Big Steve growled, sauntering up to complete the foursome.

"By definition," Nick nodded.

"Anything," Cooper repeated, dubious.

"It's Big Steve's version of the Third Law of Thermodynamics," Tristan explained. "You know, the one he won the Nobel Peace Prize for."

"God, I missed you guys," Cooper said, laughing and coming perilously close to tearing up at the same time.

"So," Big Steve said, settling into the booth and staring at the menu, "mission accomplished."

It wasn't a question.

"Guess so," Cooper said.

"Where are you staying?" Nick asked. "Not with those drag queens, I hope."

"Rented a house just up the hill from Castro Street," Cooper said. "Picked up the dogs this afternoon."

"Caught one of your flicks," Big Steve said. "Glad to see you haven't slacked off on your workouts."

"How the hell?"

"It was playing one weekend at one of those sleazy theaters in the Tenderloin," Nick grinned, "so we went on a field trip among the breeders. You should have seen how nervous those guys were with the three of us in the house. By the way, whole lobby display dedicated to your career."

"God, no," Cooper protested.

"Anything a really hot man does is hot," Nick said, without a hint of irony.

"By definition," Tristan agreed.

———

The midnight blue Mercedes sedan slipped into the lone remaining available space at Coit tower and Cooper watched Elizabeth get out. Despite the stiff breeze off the bay whipping at her hair and clothing, she moved with extraordinary self-possession. You can take the girl off the catwalk, but you can't take the catwalk out of the girl, he thought a moment too soon. Catching sight of him, she broke into as much of a trot as her stiletto heels would allow and nearly toppled into a hedge.

"Darling," she gasped as she reached him, "is it really you?"

"Thanks for coming," he said, grasping her by the elbow to steady her.

"You made it sound so mysterious on the phone. I almost wore a fake mustache and a fedora."

"I'd have loved to see you in that getup," he laughed as they sank in unison onto the bench he had occupied overlooking the bay.

"I can't say I like your haircut."

"It'll grow out. And don't worry. The facial hair goes away tomorrow. Then I'll officially be back in town."

"Nine months without a word, you bastard. A woman could have a baby in that much time. I should have stood you up."

"Yes," Cooper agreed, "you probably should have."

"People have been frantic about you."

"People?"

"Sonny."

"That's nice of him. Anyone else? Have you been frantic, Lizzie?"

"Ned has been uncannily serene regarding your absence. He could have taught Confucius a thing or two, as a matter of fact. I took my cue from him."

"As you should."

"I must say, if you could tell Ned where you were, you could just as easily have told me."

"I didn't tell Ned anything."

"You expect me to believe that?"

"Don't you?"

"I suppose," Elizabeth said, "but he certainly gave the impression that he knew something."

"I'm sure he did."

"Did what? Know something? Or give the impression he did?"

"Take your pick," Cooper shrugged.

"And that odious Holly Montezuma, spreading those ridiculous rumors about you having been recruited by Israeli intelligence."

Good old Holly, just as he'd hoped.

"Not really."

"I swear, Cooper. She insisted to everyone who would listen that you were in training to become some kind of Jewish James Bond. Sonny bought it hook, line, and sinker. He nearly had a stroke."

"Isn't your brother. . . ?"

"Yossi is just a garden variety major in the IDF. It's my cousin Fern who's Mossad. We think."

"Oh."

"So where have you been?" she asked.

"Not telling. But I'm back now for good."

"So you say. Now about Sonny."

"What about him?"

"Well, I thought maybe. . .I mean nine months, Cooper. Surely that's long enough to prove a point."

"What point would that be?"

"Who knows? But certainly you've cooled off by now."

"I was never hot," Cooper said.

"Liar. You were furious. Not as furious as Sonny, admittedly. But still. Now seriously, is there no chance at all? Because he'll take you back."

"Darling Elizabeth, listen carefully. This is not a soap opera. There will be no tearful reunion. It's over."

"He's miserable without you."

"He'll find someone else."

"He already has," she smiled. "Several times."

"You see?"

"But not like you. You were so good for him, Cooper."

"His loss."

"I know you think he treated you badly, but there's no reason for you to hate him."

"I don't hate him. I understand him."

"What do you mean?"

"We don't want the same things," Cooper said. "We never did. I get that now. And as long as that's the case, there's really no future for us as a couple. If we got back together somebody would end up unhappy. So what's the point?"

"I just wish you'd give him another chance."

"The next time we break up would only be worse. But I didn't ask you to meet me here to talk about Sonny."

He pulled the envelope out of his jacket pocket and held it out to her.

"What's this?"

"Open it."

She fumbled with her gloves. The breeze almost whipped the envelope out of her grasp. She gripped it more tightly, opened it, looked inside, and gasped.

"Cooper?"

"I'm going to open a real estate agency in this city, Elizabeth. I need a licensed broker for a partner, and I'd rather it was you than anybody."

"But. . ."

"That's to get us up and running," Cooper said.

"I can't take your money."

"If you don't, someone else will. Deposit it in an escrow account while you make up your mind."

"I don't know what to say."

"Say you'll think about it at least," Cooper said.

"Can I tell Sonny I've seen you and you're alive and safe?"

"Not until you promise me you'll seriously consider this."

"What about Ned?"

"I'm sure he already knows. But sure. Tell Ned anything you want."

"Hey, stranger."

"Lance," Cooper said, racking the barbell. "Never seen you in this place."

"Heard a rumor you were back in town," Lance said. "Wanted to come have a look."

"Good to see you, man."

"Likewise," Lance smiled. "Listen, you're probably planning to grow your hair back, but I'd like to do some sessions with that flattop first. You game?"

"Really? Think it makes me look kind of dorky."

"You're wrong there, amigo. Hot as hell. Go see whoever it is you use and have it trimmed up, O.K?"

"I think you're crazy, but if you think you can get some good shots."

"I'm certain of it. Make sure it's good and shiny when you come over. After I've got the shots, you can do whatever you want with it. But I saw you in one of your movies and thought to myself, 'Lance, you've got to get that look on film'. I'll do you justice, I promise."

———

Cooper fed the parking meter and headed up Greenwich Street toward the address Ned had given him. It was one of those Victorians whose first floor had been converted into a storefront. Presumably the upper floors were rented out as apartments, but the whole place seemed deserted. The plate glass store windows were papered over. But Ned's wine colored Bentley gleamed at the curb, so Cooper tried the door.

"Ned," he called.

"This is the place, dear boy."

Inside, the space was in the process of a major renovation. In one corner someone had set up a card table and three folding chairs. A bottle of champagne sweated into an ice bucket. Ned must be showing the space to clients later. Clients who rated champagne at lunchtime.

"So good to see you," Ned grinned, coming down the stairs, "and I've invited our dear Elizabeth along. I hope you don't mind."

"Hi, Cooper."

"Hello, Lizzie. Ned, this is some place."

"Isn't it? And the suite of offices upstairs will be equally impressive when renovations are complete."

"Got a tenant lined up?" Cooper asked.

"I rather fancy I do," Ned twinkled.

"Good for you."

"I'm so glad you approve."

Something about the tableau, Ned in his sparkliest Old Boy mode and Elizabeth a little diffident in the background, gave an impression of High Kabuki theatricality. Cooper's guard went up.

"So what did you need to see me about? These new tenants need an office boy? Did you speak to them about me?"

"Why don't you and Elizabeth take a seat?" Ned said. "I'll just fetch the canapés from the kitchenette."

"Ned? What's going on?"

"Don't spoil it, Cooper," Elizabeth giggled a little nervously.

"Wouldn't dream of it," Cooper said, "but what the hell is 'it'?"

Ned bustled back in balancing a silver tray on one hand. In the other, he held three champagne flutes by their stems.

"You do the honors," he said, handing Cooper the champagne bottle.

"Aren't we spoiling the surprise?" Cooper asked.

"I don't believe so. Why do you ask?"

"Your clients, Ned. It will hardly do for them to show up to a half empty bottle of Bollinger."

"Not to worry, young sir. Elizabeth, why don't you pull out the paperwork and we'll all go over it together."

"Paperwork, Ned?"

"Paperwork. Articles of incorporation for the Luxemberg-Montefiore Realty."

"Lizzie?"

"Don't get too excited," she smiled. "You may not find the terms to your liking."

"Lizzie, this is fantastic."

"Just let me fill you in on the basic outline," Ned said. "Then you'll want to go over the details with your attorney."

"Go ahead."

"You, Cooper, will hold forty-eight percent interest in the firm. The remaining fifty-two percent will be split evenly between Elizabeth and me."

"You, Ned?"

"Your humble servant."

"I never dreamed you'd be interested in coming along."

"My dear boy, you have no idea."

"But what about Sonny?" Cooper asked.

"I've been waiting literally decades for such an opportunity."

"He'll be rabid."

"I certainly hope so."

"I wouldn't have thought betrayal was in your line."

"It's not," Ned said, "but it is in Sonny's. It was the worst thing anyone has ever done to me. And seeing as my history includes Nazis, Communists, and Irishmen, that's saying a great deal. I daresay he has forgotten all about it, but I never have."

"You know about this, Elizabeth?"

"He hasn't told me the story," she shook her head. "I only found out he was interested in our venture when I showed him your check two days ago."

"And that was that," Ned nodded. "Now, if you'd rather not have me. . ."

"You must be joking. Where do I sign?"

"Shouldn't you have your attorney go over all the papers with you?"

"Probably," Cooper said. "If I had one. Who's got a pen?"

"Cooper, are you sure about this?" Elizabeth asked.

"Never surer of anything."

Cooper signed the documents.

"We'll need to find office space," he said.

"Well, I was rather hoping you'd find these premises to your liking. Spacious reception area, as you see, with restrooms and a kitchenette attached. On the second floor are a conference room and a couple of workrooms. Offices on three and four. It meets all our conceivable needs for years to come."

"You approve, Elizabeth?"

"Yes. And the location is extremely advantageous."

"Can we afford it?" Cooper asked.

"A suitable arrangement has already been discussed with the landlord," Ned smiled.

"Ah, the landlord. It's not some friend of Sonny's who'll pull out of the deal the minute he gets a nasty phone call? Nothing like that?"

"The landlord," Ned said. "Is yours truly. The agreed lease payment, one dollar per year for the next three years."

"Ned, you old dog."

PART THREE: *TEMPS PERDU*

A Symphony

1977-1978

FIRST MOVEMENT: GRIFFIN IN LOVE

I

The first sound that Griffin hears is Brock's soft snoring in the upper bunk, reliable as sunrise and hypnotically rhythmic as Griffin's metronome. It is exactly as loud as the purring of one of Granny's cats curled in your lap. It is as comforting as a warm kitchen on a snowy day when you've just come in from milking the cows and as familiar as the beating of your own heart. And since it is Brock's snoring, it is a sound Griffin would give anything to lie in bed listening to until the end of time.

There was rain in the wee hours. Griffin is a light sleeper and woke to its patter on the roof slates. He listened for a time before going back to sleep. Now, hours later, he hears the dripping and trickling from eaves and gutters. There are also the familiar sounds of the ramshackle building. He mentally checks them off: a creaking stair tread, a gurgle of plumbing, a barely audible sibilance of air leaking into the room through the ill-fitting door, an occasional rattle from the radiator, which, due to the lateness of spring this year has not yet been turned off for the season. He hears the ticking of his alarm clock an arm's length away and the fainter hum of Brock's electric one over on the World War II army surplus dresser across the room.

Through the open windows he catches the last chirps and chitters as night insects settle themselves against the emerging daylight. These are accompanied by tentative warbles as waking birds tune up. Half a mile away, a truck groans up through the gears. The driver misses a shift, and Griffin winces at the sound of grinding metal. He knows what truck it is and who's behind the wheel. Even more distant, a dog barks the dispirited bark of a jaded farm canine barely roused from sleep, a bark of pure reflex which conveys neither curiosity nor intent. Far below their garret windows, Griffin hears the cryptic murmuring he knows is old groundskeeper Chet reciting Walt Whitman. This is Wednesday, which means that old Chet's chosen text is "Passage to India," and the phrases, indistinguishable at this distance, nevertheless unfurl themselves like gleaming banners in Griffin's consciousness. He, too, knows the poem by heart. He has stood beside old Chet on dozens of Wednesday mornings reciting it in unison with the grizzled campus eminence. The recollection brings a lump to his throat.

Old Chet once told Griffin he had known Whitman personally. This would make him nearly a hundred, which, despite his appearance, Griffin considers unlikely. He has concluded that old Chet's intimate familiarity with the poetry has transmogrified itself into this belief in a personal encounter with its creator. Indeed, isn't this the same mechanism by means of which Griffin's Presbyterian bretheren experience the presence of their deity? More plausible is Old Chet's claim to have known Griffin's father, correctly identifying him as an entering fresh-man in September of 1939, by which time Chet had already been campus ground-skeeper for almost twenty years. On their initial encounter Chet addressed Griffin by his father's name, and the ensuing confusion alarmed Griffin and embarrassed the old man, who soon took to narrating tales of Garrett MacDonald's undergradu-ate antics, some of which Malcolm Sunderland would later confirm. Old Chet also claimed to have known Griffin's grandfather in France in 1918, but Griffin has no way to corroborate these stories. All he's ever been able to establish with certainty is that both men did indeed serve in the American Expeditionary Force. Griffin's sketchiness as to the details of his grandfather's life prior to marrying Granny has always embarrassed him. Granny herself seemed surprisingly uninformed on the subject. And Griffin's father's journals offer little more than tantalizing hints.

The ticking of Griffin's alarm clock grows fractionally more intense in the last moments before it sounds. He believes this is an actual phenomenon and not merely his imagination working overtime, though it has a tendency to do just that. Something to do with increased tension in the mechanism as it struggles to over-come resistance in the components which trip the bell. He has trained himself to reach over and push down the plunger the instant before the clamor erupts so that Brock can sleep on undisturbed.

The last sound he hears as he shuts the door behind him and heads downstairs to the showers is Brock's soft, uninterrupted snoring in the cool semi-darkness of the garret room. Griffin will carry the memory of that sound with him all day.

"There is a balm in Gilead," he mutters.

———

It's a typical May morning, which in this part of Kentucky means cloudy and cool. The damp gloom will disperse before noon, giving way to humid, bright green brilliance. As Griffin trudges across the still soggy campus, the somnolent gothic revival buildings produce a decidedly English impression. This is undoubtedly the prospect originally envisioned by the coal baron who endowed the institution in those bleak, post Civil War years when the long term survival of a college dedicated to educating aspiring Presbyterian clergy and assorted other young gentlemen was anything but assured. The coal baron, with his bad teeth, apocalyptic temper, and third grade education hadn't known anything about higher education except what he believed a proper campus should look like and paid handsomely for appropriate architecture, no matter how impractical it might prove to be. Depression, war, and modernity in general have eroded the value of his original endowment to the extent that there is little remaining chance that the school will ever achieve his aspiration of "the Commonwealth of Kentucky's very own Oxford," but those same years and decades have bestowed on the campus a patina which lends authenticity to the outward appearance at least.

Griffin understands better than most of his classmates—true believers in the mythology of the institution almost to an individual—that the campus is more like a film set than a real, live, Olde Englishe Universytee, that the "spirit" of the school is about as ephemeral as flashing images against a theater screen, and finally, that the atmosphere of the place will be fatally exploded the moment anyone greets him in the local dialect. But then again, most days he makes it as far as the music building unaccosted and with the spell unbroken.

———

Elizaveta Fedorovna sets down her book. *Cousine Bette* has been a favorite of hers since girlhood. She remembers hiding the book from her governess, who considered novels indecent. She has never been without a copy of it since. She adores

Balzac. Whenever she tells the French professors on campus what she's reading, they look horrified. *"Balzac? So lowbrow, Madame Grammatikova. How is it possible that you can have such questionable taste?"* They never actually say this, but she reads disapproval in their expressions. Such snobs, these Americans. Of course Balzac is trash. It's literate trash but trash nonetheless. She knows that. It's the whole point. And she can't help loving it. She wonders if her colleagues would approve of her other reading material this morning, her beloved Dostoevksy. *Notes from Underground*. Do the communists in charge back home allow anyone to read Dostoevsky these days? If they do, she can hardly imagine that *Notes from Underground* is on the approved list. She rises from her chair, shelves both volumes, takes her teacup to the kitchen and rinses it, Sasha her spaniel at her heels.

One hour reading Dostoevsky in Russian, one hour reading Balzac in French. Two hours maintaining her grasp on her two native languages. This is her routine, seven days a week. She can't tell you the name of a single American author, which she knows is shameful, but she can recite long passages from French and Russian literature. How proud her long dead governess would be. Except for the Balzac. It really should be Corneille and Racine she spends the time with. They taunt her from the shelf.

She glances at the wall clock. Six-thirty. Griffin should just be arriving at his practice cubicle.

It is nearly sixty years now since she left Russia. They were on a concert tour in France that summer and fall. What they were doing touring France during the fourth summer of the Great War is a mystery she's never gotten to the bottom of. Whatever possessed her parents, braving that passage through the Baltic and North Sea to Calais—even on a vessel flying a Swedish flag? The older she becomes, the more that part of the story astonishes her. Papa was a violinist, Mama his accompanist. That was the year they were performing the Brahms and Faure sonatas. She and her sister Nadezhda, two years older, were a piano duo. Their repertoire that season was heavy on Arensky and Rachmaninoff. Ivan and Konstantin were still attending conservatory in St. Petersburg and stayed behind. There had been no thought, as the four of them boarded their train for Stockholm that morning that they might never return. But the tour went exceptionally well. Papa extended their stay and extended it, and then October came and the Bolsheviks took power, and everybody they knew at home said "no, don't come back, stay in the west." Ivan and Konstantin joined the revolution, which made Papa and Mama furious. Later the boys thought better of it and joined the White Army. And were never heard of again.

Paris filled up with Russians fleeing the cataclysm. Soon there were too many violinists and pianists chasing too little work. They nearly starved. They probably would have if Nadezhda hadn't found her comte. Mama ransacked all France looking for another young nobleman for Elizaveta, but the competition was too fierce. The war had taken its toll. She was far from being the only girl her age destined to become a spinster. They made an extended visit to England with the same objective in mind but unfortunately the same result. By then Papa had decided that their future was in America. The minute the armistice was signed they were on a ship heading west. But there were too many refugee musicians in New York, too. Papa and Mama took students. Elizaveta toured on her own. Not the large cities but what Papa referred to as the provinces. When she wasn't on a train she was in a hotel. Engagements got harder and harder to book. The towns got smaller and smaller. Finally, just when she couldn't stand it any more, the miracle happened, and here she still is.

She has her cottage and her garden and her Cocker Spaniel. She has her books. She has her position at the college. She has her hard won knowledge that happiness depends on whittling your expectations down to the smallest nub. Most of all, she has her students. They let her dream their dreams with them.

———

Brock steps out of the shower. He shakes his head like a dog and sends the water flying out of his hair. He dries himself energetically with the sandpaper-like terrycloth of the college issued towel.

Back in the dorm room he makes the beds, drinks the last of his morning protein shake, and dresses. Then he thunders off down the stairs to greet the day and bask in the adulation of his subjects.

———

The Jaguar sedan is Malcolm Sunderland's lone extravagance. He backs carefully out of the barn and then steers gingerly down the gravel drive to the county road. The house is really too big for a single man, but he likes it. It's far from a mansion.

It's just large. Farmers in the region tended to have large families and built big houses to shelter them. The man who built Malcolm's house was no exception. The builder's descendents don't farm any more. They don't even live in the county. They had no interest in the property after the farmer died, and that's why Malcolm was able to buy it so cheap. It's far enough out of town to afford him some privacy but close enough to the campus to be convenient. When the weather is fine and his schedule isn't too taxing, he often walks there.

He steers the shining car into his reserved parking space behind the administration building. The college president is out of town all week, which is a blessing. Malcolm has heard the same rumors as everyone else, that the president is being courted by a school in southern Ohio. He's a fine man but has been a less than perfect match for St. Gregory's, and it will be a relief if he does indeed move on to greener pastures. Once upon a time Malcolm would have considered that this presented him with an opportunity to advance that final step. After decades of disappointment he's finally put such aspirations behind him. The trustees will surely look for a younger man this time around. And age, as he knows, is far from being his most crucial disqualifying characteristic. He's prepared to hang on for one last decade as dean, though he does dread the prospect of appending "emeritus" to his title.

When he reaches his office, his secretary greets him with her usual churchly demeanor.

"Good morning, Dean Sunderland."

"Good morning, Mrs. Iverson."

"Lovely morning, Dean Sunderland."

"It is indeed."

"You have a conference with Professor Bancroft at nine. I believe it's about the review of the fall semester student evaluations in the Humanities Cluster. I've laid out that file on your desk. And your weekly meeting with the junior class president is at ten."

"It's not Friday."

"You rescheduled for today. Brock Van der Jagt won't be on campus this Friday."

"Right. I remember. Thanks, Mrs. Iverson."

"I'll just slip downstairs and prepare the tea things. For Professor Bancroft."

"Yes, Mrs. Iverson. Thank you so much."

"Not at all, Dean Sunderland."

———

Juliette squeezes another wedge of lemon into her lukewarm tea and gazes into the cup as if it were possible to read the future in the few specks which escaped the sodden bag now weeping disconsolately on her saucer.

Griffin sets his tray down across the table from her, and it's the usual fiasco. Five and a half semesters of their ministrations under his belt and he remains as skinny as a rail, so the cafeteria ladies continually intensify their efforts to fatten him up. Bacon, sausage patties the size of hockey pucks, biscuits drowning in gravy, scrambled eggs, cheese grits, sticky buns—it's easily enough to feed a family. Griffin will ingest every morsel and somehow manage to be famished by lunchtime. He has the runaway train metabolism of his dirt farmer ancestors, and it's exacerbated by his perennial anxiety.

Juliette watches him distractedly as he eats. The granddaughter, daughter, girlfriend, and currently fiancée of good old boy football heroes, she is unfazed by displays of male gastronomic excess that would horrify most girls her age. Griffin himself, however, continues to be endlessly fascinating. If Huck Finn had grown up to become Walt Whitman, this surely is how he would have appeared in late adolescence.

"How did practice go?" she asks, as Griffin mashes four pats of butter into his Matterhorn of cheese grits.

He frowns, not looking up from his labors. This morning, she notes, he has those dark blue smudges under his eyes which indicate that he is more than usually exhausted.

"The ballade is o.k.," he grunts. "The scherzo is almost o.k."

Juliet has known him since before either of them could speak. She can recall to the week when his voice changed yet still finds his deep, husky tone jarring; still expects, unaccountably, to hear him produce some vocalization more in keeping with his fragile appearance. She is far from alone in her bemusement at this phenomenon.

"The variations are a little better than o.k.," he continues, "but that damn Bach is giving me fits. And that's not the worst of it. I can't get the Prokofiev up to tempo. Last week I had no trouble with it, but now, when it really matters. . ."

Juliette waits for the inevitable climax of his lamentation.

"And it's thirty-four hours and counting," he says in a tone of despair appropriate to an intensive care ward or the deck of a sinking ocean liner. "Girl, you're so lucky you gave your recital last month."

Yes, she thinks, that was some good time all right. Performing her junior recital, holding her roommate's hand through a pregnancy scare, and getting herself unexpectedly proposed to. That was an absolute picnic.

"You'll do fine," she says by reflex and immediately regrets her lackadaisical tone.

"But maybe not fine enough," he sulks.

She nods. She knows as well as he does that there's way more at stake in his case.

Juliette suspects that looking back on them she will think of these few weeks of junior year as her golden age. Brock's proposal, on his knees in the sand under a newly risen Florida moon; her successful recital performance four weeks later, qualifying her for senior piano major status; the unrestrained outpouring of envy from the girls in the dorm—she's never felt more alive, more filled with a sense of all the richness her life will inevitably accrue: marriage, motherhood, maturity, the womanly wisdom she increasingly recognizes and appreciates in her mother, aunts, and grandmothers—all of it just beyond her reach, luscious, ripe, low hanging fruit, redolent and vivid with color, poised for its inevitable fall into her outstretched hands. Nothing more is required to bring it all to pass but patience.

Despite Griffin's pessimism, she knows he will be spectacular in performance. He will soar. People will see and hear and will finally comprehend what she long since learned to take for granted. They'll make their comparisons and quietly adjust their expectations of her and finally leave her alone. She can't wait. The relief. . .

Madame Grammatikova has always understood, of course, though God bless her she never said a word until Juliette raised the issue herself—"No, my dear, I'm very sorry, but you're right. Griffin, perhaps, but not you. . ."

It was surprisingly easy to make her peace with it. The old, familiar dreams of concert stages, histrionic conductors, thronging fans; those garish, turbulent images which had so stirred her, so vividly enlivened her girlhood, slunk away, vacating her awareness like banished phantoms. And there, waiting, smiling his crooked, sardonic smile, was Brock, who'd always believed as fervently as she in what she thought was her destiny even though her dreams had always meant that his own would never come true. There he was, solid and patient as her dreams had been ephemeral and clamorous. Once he sensed her change of heart he wasted no time. Her new found clarity of mind allowed her to value the opportunity for all it represented, and that was that.

They'll graduate next spring and get married. They'll move back home where Brock will go to work in his family's business. She'll bear his sons—sons because there hasn't been a girl born in his family in over a century so the deck seems stacked, but mostly because she can't imagine him except as the father of boys. She'll play the organ for services at Grace Presbyterian. She'll accompany the high school choir and the annual Gilbert and Sullivan production presented by the county light opera society under the direction of Brock's Aunt Olympia. She'll take a few beginning piano students, and if a Griffin MacDonald ever shows up in her studio she'll dream his dreams with him. And once she's taught him everything she has to teach, if that's still not enough she'll bring him to Madame Grammatikova, because Madame will go on forever. She has to.

———

From ten until eleven on Mondays, Wednesdays, and Fridays, normal activities on campus come to a halt so that everyone can attend chapel services. Attendance is required of all students and roll is checked. More than six cuts in a semester can result in disciplinary action. Only athletes on the road with their teams, students on college sponsored excursions, and individuals whose illnesses require a doctor's care are excused. Faculty and staff are "strongly encouraged" to attend. Campus lore tells of professors being denied tenure for failing to demonstrate sufficient commitment to "the ideals and values of the college" as evidenced by regular chapel attendance. Chapel on Friday is secular in nature, consisting of lectures by prominent faculty members, concerts and recitals, poetry readings, and the like. Mondays and Wednesdays, however, are unapologetically religious, services identical to Sunday morning worship in every detail except that communion is omitted. Today is Wednesday so Juliette is the scheduled organist, leaving Brock and Griffin on their own.

The opening hymn is one of Griffin's favorites, "Once to Every Man and Nation". He's a sucker for those grand old Welsh hymn tunes with their dour tonalities and insistent rhythms. The MacDonalds are resolutely Scottish and Presbyterian, but he's as much Welsh as Scots. His mother was a Williams, and he inherited his first name from Granny MacDonald's mother's people. He's never considered himself a singer, but the organ and congregation make enough racket to ease his inhibitions.

The college chaplain, Rev. MacAllister, presides this morning, deferring to Dean Sunderland for the reading of campus announcements. Some religion major Griffin doesn't recognize reads from the Psalms, and one of the English professors reads the Gospel lesson. Dwight Prentice performs the Eric Thiman setting of "Jesus the Very Thought of Thee". If Griffin was a singer, that's what he would want to sound like. The chaplain's sermon is mercifully brief. The topic is personal integrity. His remarks make Griffin faintly uncomfortable.

The service closes with the singing of the "Founder's Hymn". This number has nothing to do with the founder, actually, except for purportedly having been "inspired" by him. It consists of several alternate stanzas composed by a former president's wife to be sung to the Parry tune JERUSALEM, which are followed by the more familiar text by William Blake, "And Did Those Feet in Ancient Time?" That text is itself modified so as to make more sense in this setting. Each mention of "England" is replaced by "Kentucky", necessitating a slight alteration in the sung rhythm. The result is surreal, but Griffin is enthralled nevertheless.

Brock is a better singer than might be expected of a football star. Like everything else about him, his voice is oversized. Standing next to the heavenly creature, with the organ at full volume and the congregation densely packed around them, Griffin tingles in every fiber with something very close to ecstasy.

⸺

By early afternoon it's sunny enough for Brock to work on his tan. Sunbathing is not specifically prohibited on campus but is strongly discouraged. The only place young men are really supposed to appear bare chested is in the field house, but Brock has found a way around this. He clambers out the dormer window of the room onto the dormitory roof. He climbs to the peak and down the back side, where there's a flat—or nearly so—space large enough for two or three people to lie down. Noting the angle of the sun, he spreads his beach towel out just so. He steps out of his gym shorts leaving only his jockstrap, anoints himself liberally with tanning oil, and, checking the sun once more to make sure, lies down.

People, including many who believe they know him well, would be surprised at the extent to which Brock is enjoying college. He is generally considered to be the kind of young man for whom classes and studies are little more than annoying distractions from football. He very nearly believed that himself before he actually enrolled. The life of the mind was fine and good for his girlfriend and her best buddy but seemed irrelevant to him. Now, with five and a half semesters under his belt, he's convinced that reading Plato, studying the -ologies from anthropo- to zo-, and gazing at colored plates of Renoir and Rembrandt paintings in heavy volumes in the library have transformed him. He knows he will never be a man of the world, but he'll never lack for conversational material should he ever encounter the genuine article, and from now on whenever he's described as a jock he'll know that he's that and something more. Better than that, with a college diploma hanging on his office wall he'll never have to be embarrassed when he imagines Juliette's reaction to hearing it said of him.

Everyone he knew, his parents included, who were perfectly happy to pay his way through school but would have been just as happy had he stayed home and joined the family business, assumed that college was no more than a way of extending his football career by a few more years. That had been a motivation, of course, but not the primary one. In actuality, it ranked no higher than a distant third. First of all, there was Juliette. By the end of junior year in high school he had known that whatever their adult destinies might or might not entail, he was not yet ready for her to pass out of his life. There had to be more between them than there had already been. It couldn't be over yet. He knew he didn't want it to be over at all, ever, but was smart enough to realize that she had not yet been able to determine exactly how he might fit into her future. Buying time was the only answer. That meant college; her college, because she had already chosen St. Gregory's. She'd been a student of Madame Grammatikova's since grade school, so there was no serious thought about alternatives. Brock had been recruited by coaches at larger institutions with more prestigious football programs, but since he had no professional aspirations, signing on at St. Gregory's didn't represent a setback. Rather the opposite, actually. He wouldn't have made starting quarterback his freshman year anywhere else. It was a disappointing surprise to his high school coach but it delighted his father, who was a small college football hero himself and not at all anxious to have his own previous luminosity eclipsed by his son.

This much of the story was easily enough explained. It portrayed him as a more sensitive young man than most hearers would credit but following his girlfriend to college at least made sense, especially because Juliette was exactly the kind of girl a boy, even a boy as spectacular as Brock, would happily do that for. The part concerning Griffin was both harder to explain, which he never bothered to attempt considering it nobody's business anyway, and navigate. As far as Brock is concerned, since freshman year he and Griffin have been as inseparable as he and Juliette, but what did that mean? This was not a metaphysical question but a profoundly practical one. It had important implications for the future and thus required an answer. You could eventually marry your girl and raise a family, but what could you do with your best buddy? You could hardly keep him as a pet. You could conceivably become business partners, but Brock sensed that if Griffin were the kind of guy he could have been business partners with they wouldn't have had the kind of bond they did. It was a perplexing problem, and it has taken Brock since freshman year to work it out. At first, he addressed the problem literally. He knew he'd be returning to their hometown after graduation and taking his place in the family business. Try as he might, he couldn't see a role for a concert pianist in a Kentucky farm town. He could, he supposed, bring a grand piano into the Cadillac showroom and have Griffin entertain the customers and sales staff every day, introducing him as "Mr. Griffin MacDonald, dealership pianist", but the idea was obviously absurd. He couldn't have sold it to his grandfather with a gun in each hand. Or to Griffin himself, which was a more serious obstacle. But Brock was not accustomed to insoluble problems. Indeed, he couldn't remember ever having encountered one.

Then one evening, sitting between his two friends in the recital hall as they listened to Madame Grammatikova perform the *Goldberg Variations*, he realized that the solution was breathtakingly obvious and so simple a child could have figured it out. Madame Grammatikova was a concert pianist, yet here she was on the faculty of St. Gregory's. That was Griffin's future, right there. College professor of piano. This insight propelled Brock into action. Madame Grammatikova was already past the normal retirement age and surely wouldn't work forever. Griffin might conceivably be her successor. This would solve everything, but Brock required a plan B at the very least; better yet, plans C and D as well. A couple of hours in the campus library provided him with the information he needed. Within comfortable commuting distance of their hometown there are, in addition to St. Gregory's and the University of Kentucky, five colleges with piano professors who can reasonably be expected to retire within the next five to seven years. Brock isn't crazy about the idea of Griffin going off to one of those places Madame advocates for graduate school, but he has to study for his advanced degree somewhere. Brock would rather he stayed close at home for that. U.K. would provide both the opportunity and the crucial element of proximity. The minute a position came open, Griffin would be Johnny on the spot.

It is simple, it is elegant, and it gives everyone concerned exactly what they want and need. In other words, Brock's plan could not be more perfect. Despite this, he has not shared it with anyone. He's sure its perfection will reveal itself to all concerned in good time. Since he settled it in his own mind, he's been able to bask in the serenity that his dream of the three of them staying just as they are forever is on its inevitable path to becoming reality.

He shifts position on his towel, and settles back, eyes closed but nevertheless alert to all the possibilities of the universe, gleaming like a pagan god in the sunshine of his old Kentucky home.

———

Henry Purcell: "An Evening Hymn". Juliette takes the nod from Professor Galliard and begins to play. Exactly on cue, at perfectly calibrated volume and with rock steady pitch, Dwight Prentice begins to sing. Juliette loves accompanying Dwight. He never hesitates, never muffs his lyrics, never blames her when he makes a mistake. He is the finest student vocalist on campus. Tall, smooth haired, elegantly handsome, with that opulent, creamy baritone so warm it could melt an iceberg, he should be fending off coeds with a stick but isn't. This is because he is generally thought to be homosexual. He is too fastidious, too refined. When he sings, his facial expressions are too animated. He not only lacks athletic ability but any apparent interest in such pursuits. No more proof is needed, and no counter argument made on his behalf is taken seriously. It doesn't matter a bit that he's engaged to probably the most beautiful girl in the student body, Mary Alice Sterne. People on campus believe what they believe, and Juliette silently curses them for their ignorance.

Mary Alice is a great exponent of Purcell as well. Earlier this afternoon, in Professor Rainsford's studio, Juliette accompanied her in "Dido's Lament." Mary Alice is that rarest of vocal majors, a true mezzo soprano. Juliette has only known two in the past, and they, unlike Mary Alice, were determined to extend their vocal ranges, straining like the dickens to become coloraturas instead of being satisfied with what God had given them. Mary Alice's smooth, warm tone is as rare as her black haired, pale skinned, Pre-Raphaelite gorgeousness. She is as talented and conscientious as Dwight is. They make an almost unbearably beautiful couple. Or would, if anybody other than Juliette believed they are a couple in the first place.

All of Professor Galliard's students study and perform "An Evening Hymn." From what Juliette can tell, it's as challenging an aria as any in the repertoire. Those long, meandering melismas in the "Hallelujah" section, with their unexpected, almost jagged contours and switchbacks demand perfect intonation and breath control. She has seen vocalists nearly pass out trying to perform them. Not Dwight. He's note perfect, as always. And when he reaches the end of the aria, he's not even winded. He gives Juliette a devilish grin and they sit back and wait for Professor Galliard's notes.

———

What people don't understand about Madame Grammatikova is that she plays her students with even greater virtuosity than she plays her Bechstein. This is what makes her a virtuoso teacher rather than a virtuoso who teaches. Relatively simple to become a legendary performer if you have the talent and a reasonable amount of luck. She's known enough of them in her life. She's felt that very lightning coursing through her veins. She knows she could have done it. But a legendary teacher? Seventy-seven years old, and the next day and a half will determine whether she has achieved that elusive goal. There won't be another opportunity. Not at her age. Not here in what can only be described as a backwater. No, it's either Griffin or it's not to be.

"Now Griffin," she says, after all these decades still keenly aware of these treacherous English vowel and consonant sounds, "what must we always remember when we are playing Bach?"

He is slumped over the keyboard in a horrifyingly undignified posture that she would ordinarily correct. But the situation requires something beyond her normal repertoire of responses. And besides, doesn't everyone understand by now that it is only in films—bad films, at that—that geniuses look like gods? Even in the old days back in St. Petersburg they understood that. So let the boy slump there like a pile of dirty laundry. Let him pant. It doesn't matter that he looks like the bedraggled juvenile hero of some lost novel by Dickens; like a truant schoolboy fated to be forever overlooked by the muses, presided over instead by the fates. Etiquette, for these few, crucial moments, be damned.

Brock, Juliette's Brock, will make certain Griffin is presentable tomorrow night. Nothing to worry about on that score. Brock is undoubtedly the man for the job. No question about it, Griffin will look the part at least to the extent that anyone present in the recital hall could possibly tell the difference. The rest of it, the hard part, the crucial part, is up to her. That's as it should be.

"Madame," Griffin mumbles in that incongruous growl, "we always remember that we are playing the piano."

"Exactly, child. The piano. Not an overgrown harpsichord. We do not waste a moment considering how we might realize an authentic baroque performance for the simple reason that such a thing is not possible given the essential nature of our instrument, which, let it not be forgotten, had yet to be invented at the time Bach composed this work. Instead, we concentrate on maintaining exemplary pianistic technique with each and every note we strike. We play Bach as we would play any other repertoire, so that it sounds as if Bach himself played on a Bechstein, nothing more or less. And if our musicologist friends object, we remind them that Bach himself didn't specify what instrument his keyboard works were intended for. So basically, the question is as meaningless from their perspective as it is from ours."

"But I did, Madame."

His t-shirt is so flimsy he might as well be bare-chested. She can see every twitch. She could be looking at an anatomy chart. So frail. Such a fragile boy to be fighting such a mighty adversary. Is it always like this? Yes, she thinks. Nearly always. Such are the ironic caprices of the gods. The stalwart ones, Juliette's Brock, for instance, perfectly adapted as they are to their sports and games, are invariably hopeless in a struggle such as this. On these birdlike shoulders rides the weight of all Griffin's dreams; yes, rides his fate.

"Of course, little one, you did. It was fine. It was nearly perfect, in fact." She knows exactly what agony she inflicts with this muted praise but drives on, implacable. No purpose at this point in anything but complete honesty. It is too important. She has too much respect for what he may become. It will either be or it won't, but it can't be if she doesn't force him toward it. Only she can do this. It rests on his shoulders, but still at this late date on her heart. His remains too faint. That is the problem. That is what must change. Until it does, she must fight on in the only way available to her because he can't or won't or most likely still doesn't know how.

"Now the Chopin. What do we do when we play the Chopin?"

"No matter the tempo marking, we don't rush, Madame," he speaks like an automaton, one whose springs and clockwork are running dangerously low. Like a 45 rpm recording played at 33. "We play phrases, not notes. And above all, we don't overdo the rubato."

"Correct."

A robot. When what the situation calls for is a Prometheus. She has stolen fire from the gods herself. She knows the courage and resourcefulness—yes, even the desperation—it requires to perform that particular miracle and emerge unscathed. She knows this is the one thing that she cannot teach him.

"But, Madame."

"But nothing. A reminder only, not a criticism. Yes, Griffin, nearly perfect."

Her second most devastating criticism. She sees him gulp frantically. As if choking, starving for air. She's never seen him weep and won't have it now. She pulls them back from the impending crescendo.

"My dear, this time next year you will be about to graduate. You will be preparing to perform your senior recital. We have always dreamed, you and I, of being able to announce at your senior recital that you will be continuing your studies at Julliard, or Eastman, or Curtiss, or the New England Conservatory, yes?"

She sees his eyes on her as she counts the names off on her fingers, which are plump and nondescript. They appear no more out of the ordinary than some washerwoman's fingers, or Griffin's own farmboy ones for that matter, totally incapable of wizardry.

"You could be ready by then, you know. You nearly are now—oh, so very close. In my years of teaching you are head and shoulders above all the others. Every single one of them. But still you are not ready. Because? Because? Oh, you know what I am going to say."

"Play the music, not the notes," he mutters.

"Yes. Yes, exactly. You play the notes perfectly. Sometimes, even, you play the notes divinely. But still and always you play notes, only notes."

"But, Madame."

Even more than in his throaty voice, she reads the protest in his eyes, those deep blue eyes. Too large for his face, and really the darkest blue eyes she can ever recall seeing. It was those eyes, ancient and enormous in his tiny, pale face the afternoon his grandmother first brought him to her studio, that told her there was nothing ordinary about Griffin regardless of any and all other indications.

"I know. You will say once more that you do not understand. But you must understand. You must learn what it means. Do you think I am playing a game with you? That I would not teach you the secret if it could be taught? It can only be discovered, and for every musician the discovery is different. The results of that discovery are always the same. Music not notes. Now take a moment to compose yourself and then I will hear the *Corelli Variations*."

———

Juliette. His Juliette. Miss Grant County and fourth runner up for the title of Miss Commonwealth of Kentucky last year. She played Debussy's "Claire de Lune" in the talent round at those pageants. She's a shoe-in for Homecoming Queen next fall. She's the all-American princess, and everybody loves her.

But also Juliette with her IQ of 150, her devastating ability for punning, her encyclopedic knowledge of the periodic table, the laws of thermodynamics, the Articles of Confederation, Luther's Ninety-Five Theses, and the complete works of William Shakespeare—not to mention loads of other things Brock doesn't even know the names of; the girl who can correctly conjugate the irregular verbs of four languages on the fly while charming the local taxi drivers, shopkeepers, chambermaids, waiters, and customs officials—he'll never forget that spectacle in Europe last summer with her family; that Juliette, his Juliette, the Juliette he has adored since before kindergarten, the Juliette he chose long ago to be his bride and the mother of his sons; that very one and only Juliette, who takes his breath away every time he sees her. . .

Is stitting. Alone. At their regular table. Visibly upset. And he knows what she's upset about like he knows which direction the sun is shining from this early Kentucky evening.

"Where is he?" he asks, setting his tray down across the table from her. She hasn't eaten a thing that he can tell. "Why isn't he here having dinner with us?"

"He's barricaded himself inside his practice room and won't come out."

"When?"

"Right after his lesson this afternoon. Damn that old woman."

"Doing her Sphinx imitation again?" Brock asks.

"I'm afraid he's going to crack."

"He's not going to crack."

"But I've never seen him like this," Juliette says. "Not even when his grandparents died."

"Jules, he won't crack. You didn't."

"That was different."

"How?"

"There's more at stake," Juliette says.

"So what? We've always known that."

"Have we?"

"Of course we have. It's not news, Jules. It just is."

"All right."

"So why the terrors?" Brock asks.

"The program that old witch has him performing makes mine look like talent night at the orphanage."

"Exaggerating as always," Brock says. "I know it's only for—what do you call it? Rhetorical effect?—so I'm not impressed. Besides, that old witch, and you surely don't mean to call her that, would never have set him a program like the one he's playing if she didn't know down to her toes that he's up to it."

Juliette doesn't answer. Brock watches her working out the logic of all this. Of course she and Griffin are artists, so logic rarely applies, but it's all he has. He doesn't speak their language so he has to improvise. During this pause he drinks in her ethereal beauty. Ethereal is a word he recently added to his vocabulary. He savors it like a newly discovered, exotic condiment—*ethereal: of or belonging to the ether*. Which had led, in turn, to *ether: the rarified element formerly believed to fill the upper regions of space*. Thank you, Merriam-Webster.

"Come on, Julie girl, you know I'm right."

"Maybe." She wrinkles up her nose and he falls in love all over again. He never feels stupider than when he tries to put into words how much he loves her.

"Maybe, nonsense," Brock says. "Of course I'm right. I know him better than anyone on this campus. Even better than the old witch does."

"But."

"No buts. It's true, like it or not. I know you like to think that the two of you have this special, mystic bond because you're musicians, but there are some things a girl just can't know about a guy, and that's what I know about Griffin. Everybody's always talking about him like he's a space alien or a freak of nature and if you look at him wrong he'll evaporate. Like he's made of chips of five thousand year old

Chinese porcelain held together with spider webs. What bullshit. That boy's about as fragile as your granny's cast iron skillet."

"Maybe," Juliette concedes, "but he doesn't know it."

"Sure he does. He might not know he knows it but somewhere deep down it's in there. And when he needs to know it, he'll figure it out."

"I just worry about him."

"I know," Brock says, "but how the hell is he going to go off and wow the crowned heads of Europe if he can't put on a little show for us yokels? Ever think of that?"

"Oh, Brock."

"Don't go getting exasperated, girl," Brock grins, having talked her down once again. "And yes, I will make sure he has his dinner."

———

Griffin stares at the score. Densely clustered notes clot the page. The phrase markings sweep sinuously among them. The accidentals and rests float like black stars. The thin lines of the staves struggle ineffectually to contain the chaos. He knows this page of music by heart. He sees it in his dreams. Tomorrow night when he performs it from memory, he will be note perfect. Nevertheless, Madame Grammatikova insists that he has missed something. The one thing that matters, ironically enough. In his hours, days, months of living and breathing this music, something essential has concealed itself from his obsessive scrutiny.

It is beyond belief but believe it he must; must accept that Madame knows what she is talking about. She knew the composer personally. His children were her playmates. She could not possibly be mistaken about this. He has never known her to be mistaken about anything. So with less than twenty-four hours to go before he walks alone onto the stage he wrestles with the riddle, frantic for the faintest clue.

He suspects his efforts will prove futile. He might as well stare down into the cryptic spaces between the piano keys or yank open the lid and attempt to read the bass strings like tea leaves. He is, he understands, being too literal. What Madame is alluding to has nothing to do with redoubled efforts to decode musical scores or deconstruct complex pieces of acoustic machinery. It transcends all physical artifacts and it apparently rests somewhere within him.

He has never allowed himself the sort of introspection which might lead to the enlightenment Madame insists is necessary. He doesn't even acknowledge the fear which prevents him. He has always been satisfied being scrawny, funny looking Griffin MacDonald, who loves his friends to distraction and, oh, by the way, plays a little piano. This has always been enough. It always will be because it has to. He cannot conceive of an alternative to that Griffin.

A tap at the window interrupts his ruminations. Or maybe he has only imagined it. He's jumpy as a cat these days. A second tap resolves the question, and he's thrilled for the interruption. He moves to the window, shoves upward on the sash, and there in the twilight beyond the panes smiles Brock.

"Hey, buddy, how's it going?"

"Going," Griffin shrugs.

"Missed you at dinner," Brock says. "Thought you might be hungry."

He holds out a greasestained pasteboard carton about the size of a shoebox. "Went to Estelle's. Picked you up an eight piece box. There's cole slaw, too. And biscuits and honey."

"Thanks," Griffin says. "Not really hungry."

"You just think you're not hungry. Now dig in, because I'm not leaving until you're finished."

"You'll have to help me with the chicken."

———

The third floor of the library is probably the quietest place on campus at 8:00 p.m. on a Wednesday. For the past hour and a half Juliette has been going back over all the party scenes in *The Great Gatsby*, scribbling furiously in the margins of her disastrously thumbed and dog eared copy. More notes fill pages of the legal pad on the table in front of her. Her paper for Professor Mountjoy is due in ten days, and she's still groping for an approach.

"Juliette, is that yaw'll?"

She looks up. It's Betty Sue Higginbottom, freshman, three doors down from Amanda and her in the dormitory.

"Hi," she smiles, dreading what she knows is coming next.

"Yaw'll're always so serious," Betty Sue says, sitting down across from her.

"Just trying to keep my grades up."

"Oh, foot. Everybody knows yaw'll're the smartest girl on campus. Bet yaw'll could get straight A's without studyin' a lick."

"Don't know," Juliette says. "I've never tried."

"Now, now. All work and no play."

"They were talking about a boy named Jack."

"Sure, but yaw'll know." Betty Sue squirms a little. "Listen, I'm glad I ran into yaw'll 'cause I was thinkin' it's about time for the four of us to go on that double date we talked about. What with Griffin's recital tomorrow night and all. Actually kind of surprised yaw'll hadn't said anything about it."

"Must have slipped my mind."

"Well, how about Friday?"

"Brock and I are going home for the weekend."

"Next week then."

"Talk to me on Monday," Juliette says. *If you can find me, stupid girl.*

"All right," Betty Sue agrees. "Yaw'll don't forget now."

Juliette watches her flounce away. It's always the same with these girls. All hot and bothered over Griffin. She used to warn them off. Any more she doesn't bother. They lose interest quickly enough. Griffin's too tough a nut even for a love-sick freshman girl to crack. They all seem to think of him as a cute, shy boy who just happens to be a musician, whereas he's actually a musician who just happens to be a cute, shy boy. This profound misunderstanding means that he's a completely different animal and puts him totally out of their reach. It will take more than an empty headed church girl like Betty Sue to make a mate for him. It will require somebody strong willed, clearheaded, fearless, ferociously loyal.

Juliette realizes that she's describing herself. She sees no contradiction in this. She's Griffin's sister, for all practical purposes, and what girl doesn't want her brother to marry someone just like her?

———

Madame Grammatikova rarely receives telephone calls this time of night and her immediate thought, as she crosses the room to answer it, is of some distant misfortune.

"Hello."

"Madame Grammatikova, it's Malcolm Sunderland."

"Oh, hello, Dean Sunderland."

"I'm sorry to disturb you at this time of night, but I was wondering about Griffin."

"Of course. Well, you can rest easy, because we're all going to be very proud of him tomorrow evening."

"So he's all right?"

"Nothing more than a few jitters, I'm sure. He'll be fine once the time comes."

"Oh, well, I won't keep you then. Thanks so much."

"Anytime, Dean Sunderland. Good night."

Dean Sunderland is Griffin's godfather, and, since the death of Griffin's grandmother, the nearest thing he has left to family. She's not surprised at his concern. She remembers the dean as a freshman piano student back before the war. Not really very talented, but oh, so diligent. He was Garrett MacDonald's roommate back then. That's how it all started.

———

The chapel bell is tolling the eleven o'clock men's curfew as Griffin climbs the steps in front of the dormitory. Joey O'Dowd is waiting to lock up and gives him the slightest of nods as he steps inside. He's almost always the last one in on weeknights. The women's dorms close an hour earlier than the men's, so most of the young men are already home. A few night owls sprawl in the TV lounge staring at the ancient black and white set. Joey returns to his station behind the reception counter, where he remains on duty until midnight, unlocking the door for late arrivals and noting their names for the daily report to the dean's office, though in practice the young men of the college are adept at using windows and fire escapes for after hours entrances and exits.

Griffin heads upstairs belching the fried chicken Brock brought him. He'd been toying with the idea of fasting as an aid to the enlightenment Madame Grammatikova is demanding of him, but he'd no sooner have rejected Brock's offering of food than he'd have walked on water. From the very first, he's obeyed Brock's orders immediately, automatically as a reflex. He's never questioned this. It has never occurred to him that he might. When Brock itches, Griffin scratches.

This is not for what some of their classmates might consider the obvious reason. Although Brock outweighs him by a good eighty pounds of solid muscle and goes around looking and sounding like some latter day Viking warrior, Griffin has never experienced the slightest fear of his roommate. Off the gridiron Brock is, in actuality, the gentlest of creatures, exemplary in the patience and tolerance he extends to everyone he encounters and the most benevolent of dictators imaginable. Nor is Griffin's obedience due to social pressure or even mere custom, though a visitor to the college might form that impression.

On every college campus, there is one individual universally deferred to. This is a fundamental truth of academic life, as reliable as the cycles of nature. It might be anyone. Dean, revered professor, librarian of legendary eccentricity, coach of uncanny charisma, or superannuated maintenance worker. Here at St. Gregory's, even though it's highly unusual for a student to enjoy this position of pre-eminence, that individual is Brock. His athletic ability, charm, and amazing looks make it more than possible. It's absolutely necessary.

Ironically, it was Griffin's godfather, Dean of Students Malcolm Sunderland, who set in motion the events which resulted in the current state of affairs. What originally prompted the Dean to assign Brock and Griffin as roommates no one has ever been able to fathom. Pondering it, and people did and still do, obsessively, most observers have ascribed the mistake either to a simple clerical error or to the dean's absent mindedness. The dean's absent mindedness is a campus legend, but like many such legends is a more or less complete fiction. Dean Sunderland finds it convenient for all sorts of reasons to be thought of as absent minded and does nothing to disprove the general belief. Every now and then, some pundit or other points out the boys' long association back home in Grant County as the explanation. These individuals are always shouted down on the grounds that though obvious, this makes no sense. Everybody knows that at St. Gregory's, freshman football players are segregated from the rest of the student body. They inhabit "the dungeon", a catacomb situated underneath the stadium bleachers, from where unimaginable sounds and smells emanate more or less perpetually. That, by all rights, is where Brock ought to have been assigned housing, and as for Griffin, well, nobody much cared.

Coach Falmouth had been livid, but it wasn't Dean Sunderland who stared him down. No, that was Brock himself. Coach Falmouth had every imaginable reason to call Brock's bluff but unaccountably didn't. Which was a good thing, really, because Brock wasn't bluffing at all, and college history might have been profoundly altered. People assumed that Brock hadn't been willing to endure the privations of "the dungeon". Knowing him better, Griffin credited it to Brock's aversion to having anyone decide anything on his behalf. This was undoubtedly closer to the truth than anyone else had come, even Juliette, who was as baffled as everyone else.

The one thing the whole campus agreed on was that Griffin had been no more than a pawn in the affair. That Brock might actually prefer Griffin to one of his teammates as a roomie was out of the question. The universe simply couldn't have tolerated such a motivation. And the whole thing quickly assumed the status of major campus mystery. Regardless of that, the community had received the clear message that Brock called his own shots, thank you very much. But none of this explained Griffin's perennial, uncomplaining acquiescence. Nor could he have explained it to himself. It seemed obvious that he should do as Brock told him simply because it was Brock doing the telling. So when Griffin reaches their room and Brock says, "come down to the showers and talk to me while I shave," tired as he is he sets his things on his desk and follows Brock out of the room he has just entered, trooping downstairs to the third floor showers.

In a few weeks, Brock will compete in the Kentucky bodybuilding championships. Last year he placed third. This year he means to win. He works out religiously, his diet is stringent, and he has recently instituted this new ritual, unwilling to leave shaving his body until the last night before the contest, a rookie mistake he blames partially for last year's placing. So once a week, invariably late at night with most of the dormies sleeping, here he is. And since Brock prefers never to be unaccompanied, here's Griffin watching as he strips off and lathers up.

It's a bizarre scene indeed by St. Gregory's standards; the kind of thing, for instance, which could prompt the villagers to storm the castle by torchlight and batter down the doors. Bodybuilding is generally disapproved of; appearing in competitions still more so. Male physical display, except of the most casual sort, is highly suspect. And shaving the God ordained hair off all but the scantiest few unmentionable square inches of your body? While your roomie looks on? The transgressiveness of the activity weighs heavily on Griffin, though of course Brock is exempt from all possibility of censure and this lends him a kind of immunity by association.

Potential social disapproval isn't the most troubling aspect of the scene for Griffin. He doesn't actually remember meeting Brock, their initial encounters having taken place in the cradle room at Grace Presbyterian back home. That's how far back they go. Even farther, in fact, two of Brock's uncles having graduated from high school with Griffin's father. But even though this history permits him to take a lot about Brock for granted, somehow he's never been able to think of the two of them as members of the same species. And the spectacle of blond, floppy haired, deeply tanned Brock making businesslike strokes of the razor across his massively muscled chest reinforces this skepticism to a nearly impenetrable degree.

For as long as Griffin can remember, Brock's physical person has been a source of fascination. Not just for Griffin. Apparently for everyone. Always the tallest, always the strongest, always the handsomest. The first boy their age whose voice changed, the first to sprout hair in certain places, the first to seriously kiss a girl as opposed to doing it as part of some juvenile game. Though come to think of it that had been Brock as well. Always a focus of attention due as much as anything to his physical attributes. Griffin knows as well as anyone that boys aren't supposed to be fascinated with each other's bodies, but they are, inevitably. After all, what is another boy's body but a sort of imperfect mirror of your own, about which you are endlessly curious and with which you are helplessly obsessed? What secrets that your own body has not yet disclosed to you might you uncover from diligent observation of someone else's? This fascination, universal but unspoken, seems as elemental as the chemical formula for water.

And finally, when the contrasts between bodies are so pronounced, so impossible to ignore, how can you escape the resulting feelings of awe and wonder? How can shoulders be that broad, muscles that full? What must it feel like to see from that height or have your chest swell that far into the expanses stretching in front of you? What is it like to have hair that blond, that smoothly perfect, so that people, your classmates as well as complete strangers, are constantly staring at it and you never have to wonder if it looks all right? Or skin which has never been marred by the least blemish and uncomplainingly tolerates any degree of sun exposure, so that you never, not even for a moment, have to concern yourself with the possibility of dire consequences?

Faced with such a paragon, how can you fail to ponder such matters if you are any boy other than Brock? Though of course admitting as much to anyone would be unthinkably disruptive to the order of things. For Griffin, then, Brock's unassailable masculinity and supernatural beauty—yes, beauty, that's the only appropriate word, and damn the connotations—has only one possible explanation. If God truly exists, something Griffin has not yet begun to question seriously, then his buddy Brock is what He must have intended all men to look like when He created the universe. Griffin and everyone else he knows, with their varying degrees of inferiority to this ideal, are, conversely, living, breathing evidence of the fall of man.

That's what Griffin is thinking about as he perches on the shower room counter and stares at the marvel that is his roommate and best friend, listening with half an ear to Brock's commentary; so accustomed, indeed, to staring like this that he can unconsciously formulate and verbalize appropriate responses to things he doesn't actually hear should such be required. Paradoxically, it has never occurred to Griffin that the same divine origin might be ascribed to Juliette's astonishing intellect or his own musical gifts. It is Brock's physicality alone which Griffin apprehends in such theological terms.

II

As soon as Griffin wakes, he senses something out of the ordinary. He mentally catalogues all his accustomed sensations, methodical and detail obsessed as Sherlock Holmes, until he identifies it. Old Chet. Those aren't the irregular rhythms and line lengths of Whitman. He listens more intently, not to distinguish words, which would be impossible here on the mere cusp of audibility, but for something, anything he can recognize. And soon enough he's got it. That heartbeat of iambs, those longwinded pentameters.

Old Chet only recites from *Paradise Lost* in times of grave emergency or to honor auspicious moments. Wondering which this morning brings, Griffin presses down on the plunger of his alarm clock and crawls out of his lower bunk. It is a lengthy work, *Paradise Lost*. The great English epic according to Professor Beck, whom Griffin studied it with. Nevertheless, Old Chet has the entire work memorized. He's still reciting as Griffin emerges from the dorm.

"Chet," he calls, breathless from the stairs. "Chet, what is it? What's the matter?"

"Why good day." Chet regards him from the shadow of his broad hat brim, his eyes glinting like chips of mica. "A momentous day it is indeed."

"How so? What's special about it?"

"Why, what else? Tonight, young sir, you take the stage and become the sensation of the college. All are in anticipation of the event. All, I tell you. And many years ago, your revered grandfather foresaw the success you will have."

"Oh?"

"Oh, yes," Chet affirms, "I remember it well. A morning much like this. France that spring—so strange. The budding trees, the wildflowers, the carnage, the blue skies, the gas clouds, the singing birds, the whistling artillery shells. . ."

Chet at his most oracular.

"And Papa?" Griffin prompts.

"And your grandfather, yes. Gordon MacDonald. You're his spit and image, young sir. Every time I see you, I feel like I'm looking at him."

"Yes?"

"He foresaw this day, I tell you. Your achievement. The sensation you'll cause. He knew it was coming."

Griffin waits.

"I can recall his exact words, you understand."

Griffin waits.

"He knew. About all this. About your daddy. About you. About today. And about you and me standing here."

Griffin can't remember Old Chet ever quite this transported.

"Ah, if he could only be there to hear it. But of course, he will. He will. As I will. Yes, I'll be there, young friend Griffin MacDonald."

Not inside the recital hall, Griffin knows. But lurking in some shadowy corner of the lobby or haunting the wings.

"Yes, yes, I shall indeed. Alongside Gordon MacDonald. And alongside Garrett MacDonald as well. And the very best of good fortune to you, friend Griffin and son and grandson of my friends. And may all the gods of Olympus smile with favor on your quest."

"Thanks, Chet," Griffin stammers. He heads off toward the music building, toward his practice cubicle, his fingers clamoring, famished for the cool smoothness of the black and white keys.

———

Brock squeezes a small dab of pomade into his palm. Setting the tube on the counter, he rubs his hands together, then smooths them through Griffin's hair until the substance is evenly distributed and the hair is uniformly shining and fragrant. After rinsing his hands, he sets to work with a comb. Deftly forming the part, he scrupulously observes the two R's, ruler straight and razor sharp, just as Big Jim taught him. A few more expert swipes and Griffin's fox red hair is in a perfect state of glistening immobility.

In the Van der Jagt household, the style Griffin sports this evening is designated the winter cut. The summer cut entails being assaulted with a #2 clipper exactly as sheep are sheared. It was performed once just before Memorial Day and again for the Fourth of July each year. After that, the hair was allowed to grow out until just before school started on the Tuesday after Labor Day. Then the Van der Jagt boys were herded downtown to the barber for a trim and cleanup about the neck and ears, their style gradually evolving into this floppy on top, trim back and sides configuration—the winter cut, which falls in what Brock always thinks of as an English schoolboy flop, not that he's aware of ever having encountered a real live English schoolboy. Such is the nature of the Van der Jagt hair texture that six days a week the winter cut requires no serious maintenance. On Sundays, pomade and a comb are employed to achieve this neat, masculine look, giving rise to the spectacle of Brock and his seven brothers, identically, redolently coifed, sitting in perfect stairstep formation in their family pew at Grace Presbyterian.

By the time he was eleven, Brock had been deputized, put in charge of this Sunday ritual so Big Jim could sleep in. He presided over that line of younger, smaller replicas of himself like a master sergeant prepping his troops for dress parade. Thatcher, Mick, twins Tim and Tom, Andrew, Rob, and baby Jeffie, each in his turn stood at attention for Brock's ministrations, which transformed them from rackety tearaways into serious young Van der Jagt menfolk.

Before leaving home for college, Brock hadn't anticipated how badly he would miss his brothers. But that last glimpse in the rear view mirror of Jeffie waving goodbye from the front yard—waving so hard, in fact, that it made him bounce up and down—well, a couple of blocks away Brock had to steer the Corvette to the curb and cry a little. What was he thinking of, leaving them all behind? By the time he saw them again at Thanksgiving, they wouldn't be like that any more. Would eighteen month old Jeffie even recognize him?

His profound funk only lifted later that afternoon when Griffin stumbled into the dorm room they'd been assigned to share, wrestling with a footlocker way too heavy for him. Brock had known Griffin for as long as he could remember, of course, but except for a couple of occasions he hadn't paid much attention to him, their acquaintance having been so thoroughly mediated by Sunday School ladies, teachers, friends, and most of all Juliette, that they'd never exchanged more than a few perfunctory syllables. But there Griffin was, panting slightly, sweaty and disheveled, all too clearly an answer to prayer. It was the first time Brock had ever looked at him at all carefully. That fall, Griffin was about the same size as Tim and Tom, who were just entering seventh grade.

His eyes were several shades too dark to be Van der Jagt blue, his freckled skin would never achieve that satiny Van der Jagt summer tan, and he wasn't blond by any stretch of the imagination, but his winter cut was already recognizably emergent, and Brock finally realized who he was supposed to be.

"Come on," he says. "I'll drive you over to Polk Hall. Then I'll go pick up Juliette."

"I can walk over," Griffin says.

"You will not walk. You'll spoil your shoes that way and get dust on your trousers. I'll drive you."

"All right."

"Don't worry about your tie. I'll come backstage and fix it before you go on."

———

The last seconds before Griffin steps onto the stage are a kaleidoscope of impressions: Brock touching up his hair one last time, then straightening his bow tie; Madame at his left shoulder, murmuring barely audible final instructions as if they're incantations; Juliette, stony faced, attacking his jacket with a lint roller. Then the sudden, desolate silence of the green room as they desert him, a silence as profound and unnerving as that of a burial vault in some pyramid.

Eventually the stage manager's single tap on the door and her hushed "Madame has taken her seat".

Down the short but nevertheless endless corridor to the wings, the lofty, shadowed expanses looming above and behind the stage, the emptinesses he must somehow fill with music. He takes his place just at the edge of one of the blank legs, its dark fabric concealing the audience from him but not deadening their sound. They might well be standing next to him. He can hear their muttering, the rustle and crackle of programs in their hands, the soft squeaking of seat cushions as they unconsciously, minutely shift positions. One step into the light. Polite applause, and the Gobi Desert, frozen tundra, storm wracked ocean of polished wooden flooring between him and safety, the gleaming ebony surfaces both tantalizing and taunting.

Another step.

And another.

He sees them out there. Malcolm Sunderland, fifth row on the aisle. Funny little Professor Altschuler, Madame's dear friend from New York, fourth row center, seated next to Professor Catherwood, Chairman of the music department. A few friends from the dorm—there must not be anything on television tonight. A handful of professors. Classmates, a surprising number of them, a much bigger turnout than he'd expected. There must be two hundred people out there at least, and he can't imagine that none of them have anything better to do.

Front row center. Sweet, lovely Juliette. How did we get here? How? That afternoon. Rain outside. Madame's cocker spaniel Barrett snoring in the corner. The enormous grandfather clock ticking, ticking, ticking. Granny turning the pages of her book so, so slowly. The door to Madame's studio opens, and out steps Juliette. Graceful, pretty, self possessed Juliette. A girl from a storybook. A girl too wonderful to inhabit the real world.

Granny recognizes her.

"*Griffin, that's Juliette Simpson. You know her from Sunday School.*"

Only then does he recognize her himself.

Juliette. How did we get here?

And Madame. That rainy afternoon her hair had already been the exact shade of silver he sees shining at Juliette's shoulder. But that afternoon she had seemed terrifying and at least seven feet tall. Madame, dear formidable Madame. She has given him life as surely as his mother did, but, it has to be acknowledged, in a way his mother never could have done.

And Brock. The handsomest boy in the world. The strongest, the bravest, the most magnificent. The truest friend imaginable.

How did this happen? How did those amazing creatures make room for him, *him* in the epic of their lives?

They stare up as though they are villagers spellbound by some miracle unfolding in the sky.

But at what? At *him*?

"*Look at the audience,*" Madame always told them. "*Look out and smile. Smile, but do not make eye contact.*"

He smiles. He takes a bow.

———

Malcolm Sunderland has known Griffin since infancy. And during Griffin's time as a student here at St. Gregory's, hardly a day has gone by without him seeing the boy on campus. Over the years he has come to take Griffin's physical resemblance to his father Garrett for granted. In spite of all that, he has never anticipated how complete the illusion might become.

He's unprepared. But as Griffin moves onto the stage, striding with Garrett's easy, confident gait, resplendent in his rented tuxedo and slicked down hair, for a moment Malcolm isn't sure he's not having a heart attack or stroke. He grips the arms of his seat and forces himself to take slow, deep breaths.

Reluctantly, he remembers. Griffin is still an inch or so shorter than Garrett's five foot ten, and he's more slender than Garrett ever was. But he's got his father's face, coloring, and most importantly, manner. And that hair, woefully unfashionable nowadays, is exactly the way they were all wearing their hair that fall, 1939, when Garrett and Malcolm first met.

Yes, he thinks. That tilt of the head. That tension in the jaw. That posture.

And in that tuxedo. . .

Malcolm remembers Garrett and Amelia's wedding day like it was yesterday. He considers standing up as Garrett's best man one of his life's proudest moments. He had just finished his first year as associate professor of English here at St. Gregory's. And Professor Bullworth had announced a week earlier that his retirement from the history department would take place in another year. People on campus were already speaking of Garrett as Bullworth's likely successor. Their undergraduate dreams seemed on the point of coming true. Their lives stretched into the future as if possessed with a kind of inevitability.

By now Garrett should have been head of his department, if not a vice president of the college. By now Amelia should have produced a whole brood of robust sons, whom he, Malcolm, would have helped to raise. On that sweltering Mississippi afternoon there had been no way to predict how completely everything would go wrong. Or how quickly.

———

On the bench, eyes closed. Deep breath. Concentrate. Another deep breath. Concentrate and relax. Eyes open. Hands. That feeling that those hands, they're—they're not attached somehow. They're not him. They have a conscious-ness separate from his. Wasn't there a cheesy movie about a pianist who strangled his unfaithful wife? It was his hands, acting independently of his conscious will, that com-mitted the crime. Why in the world is Griffin thinking about that? At a time like this?

He pulls himself back into the moment.

Bach. Yes, Bach. That miraculous balance of perfect legato and crisp, precise, even articulation, every single note clear and distinct but the whole smooth. The lines and the phrases twining themselves, spinning webs out of the tips of his fin-gers. Suddenly he realizes what he should already have known. The sections of the suite—they're not just named after dances, they are dances. Yes, it's true. The notes dance. His fingers dance. His hands dance. His forearms dance. And along with them the keys dance, the hammers and strings dance.

Everything dances.

———

By the time Griffin has played a few bars of the Bach English Suite, Juliette knows that he has finally gone somewhere she can't follow. He's experienced some sort of epiphany, and the difference between them as musicians is no longer merely his superior technique but something beyond that, something she recognizes but has no name for, shining, transcendent, hard as diamonds, insubstantial as dreams. Damn him, damn, damn, double damn him. Tears well up in her eyes. She can live without fame and glamor, but without this insight? Trapped here on the ground watching him soar? She's not sure she even knows him now. One thing's certain. He's not funny old Griffin any more.

She feels Madame's hand close around hers. So she's not imagining this. Yes, well, Madame of all people would sense it. It was going to happen sooner or later, and what better time than tonight? Especially with Professor Altschuler, Madame's old friend and colleague, here from New York. It's what they've all hoped for, dreamed of, for all these years. It's coming true before her eyes. She should be joyful.

———

The Chopin ballades and scherzos are among the most demanding works in the solo piano repertoire. And here we have one of each. The F Major Ballade and the

Scherzo in C sharp minor. How audacious. Professor Itzak Altschuler, Professor Emeritus, the Julliard School, settles lower into his seat. He has heard these pieces performed countless times, from his studio to fashionable salons to renowned music halls. He has performed them himself, in recital, on radio, once even from the back of a flatbed truck for several thousand cheering troops pursuing the Nazis deeper back into Germany. Priests know the mass, cantors the psalms, chemists the periodic table. Professor Altschuler knows piano repertoire.

The boy does well. The professor's dread slowly dissipates. How many old friends over the decades have sought his approval of their protégés? What evasions he has been forced to devise, what feats of diplomacy he has had to execute. None of that will be necessary tonight. Trust dear Elizaveta Fedorovna. Half a lifetime here in this backwater has not dulled her faculties. "A diamond in the rough" is how she described the boy to him. To be fair, this is too modest an appraisal. Yes, he has to admit it. The boy does very well indeed. Another year of study with Elizaveta Fedorovna may well turn him into something special. As it is, the least that can be said about him is that he's a very pleasant surprise. It has been well worth the professor's trip. And not just because of the pleasure of seeing his old friend.

———

Back in the green room for the interval. Brock massages Griffin's neck and shoulders like he's an Olympic athlete between heats. Juliette dabs at an invisible smudge on his jacket with a moistened handkerchief. Madame, barely present, silent and inscrutable as an Alpine glacier shrouded by fog, says nothing, does nothing. Only the faintest glint in her averted eyes tells him she's pleased. The ten minutes flash past like sunshine off the surface of a lake.

———

The Bach English Suite: scenes from an 18th Century ballroom. The Chopin Ballade in F Major: a dramatic anecdote. The Scherzo in C sharp minor: an especially rambunctious practical joke. Now, gazing at those alien fingers poised above the gleaming keys: the *Corelli Variations*—what? Madame had known Rachmaninoff personally. Griffin asked her this very question. *"Child, if Sergei Vasilievich were here, he would say to you that you are not a stenographer taking dictation. Now play!"*

So—yes. A manifesto. Not political. Not even philosophical. And here's where the danger lies. Griffin can't transform this music into metaphors or associations. It is, it seems to him, terrifyingly literal. He has lived his life up until this point safely cocooned in the figurative and symbolic. He tiptoes through his daily existence shielded by metaphor, allusion, analogy. But inadvertently he has painted himself into this corner. There is no way out except to assume, once and for all, his identity in honest to God flesh and blood. This performance will be nothing less than his testimony and confession.

Or he can rise from the piano bench, make an excuse—a strained forearm, a complete lapse of memory, and submerge himself back in his past.

Tentative at first, the succeeding variations grow ever more forthright and emphatic. He might as well strip naked in front of them all. But now that he's begun there's no turning back.

———

Whenever people ask him, Brock always claims to know nothing about music, as befits a lunkhead jock good old boy. He can't remember anyone ever questioning this denial. But you can't spend as much time as he has over the years with classical pianists for his girl and his buddy without learning anything at all. How many hours has he spent lurking in hallways outside practice cubicles? How many lessons with Madame Grammatikova has he eavesdropped on? How many mealtime or late night discussions of technique or repertoire has he silently sat through? How many recordings listened to and heard dissected? He'd have had to be deaf or unusually stupid not to have picked up a few things.

So he is aware. He can tell as well as anybody in the hall and probably better than most that something remarkable is taking place. The kid is brilliant. He's never played like this before. As an athlete, Brock understands it. Something similar has happened to him. On more than one occasion, on more than one playing field. You work. You study. You practice. You concentrate. You dedicate yourself. And then, just at the right moment it all pays off. It feels like being struck by lightning. But it's really just the inevitable result of preparation. What the audience is witnessing is another version of something Brock knows as well as anyone living, the big game.

He knew Griffin had this in him. He's never understood why everyone else underestimates him. He can hear it now, the way they'll all be talking about this tomorrow, like it was completely unexpected. Like it was some miracle. O.K., sure. Griffin is small. Though in real terms, he's not that far off average. He seems smaller than he is. And Griffin is quiet. Griffin is shy. Truth to tell, Griffin often gives the impression that he's afraid of his shadow. Brock has spent his entire life listening to the mythology of Poor Little Griffin MacDonald. The last few years, he's known that it's nothing but bullshit. Why won't people bother to look past the surface? Brock knows the kid better than anyone except maybe Madame Grammatikova. Certainly better than Juliette, who, he believes, identifies with Griffin too closely to be objective.

He knows how tough Griffin is. How tenacious. He has the heart of a warrior. He just chooses his battles according to criteria nobody but Brock has ever been able to decipher. How else could he be up there on the stage doing what he's doing?

If you don't get that, Brock thinks, you're just not listening.

———

Every piano major who has ever performed a recital on this stage, literally every single one, no matter how ill-prepared, untalented, ham handed; no matter how inauspicious the occasion has turned out to be; no matter how exhausted he or she is by this point in the evening or how bored and restless the audience; every last one has performed an encore.

So.

Griffin has taken six or seven bows—he's lost count. But he sees Madame nodding slightly at him and he knows it's time.

He sits on the bench. Closes his eyes. Thinks. Which he shouldn't need to do because this is as carefully rehearsed as every other part of the performance.

Prokofiev. "Toccata." Yes.

Machine guns. Jackhammers. Production machinery in a factory. Fast, loud, expressionless. Devoid of everything but velocity and rhythm and volume.

Yes. Exactly.

And. He's. Done.

———

Betty Sue Higginbottom leaps to her feat the minute the last chords crash down. She's not about to let anyone in the audience see her exhibiting insufficient enthusiasm. This is how she stakes her claim—leading the ovation. Griffin. Her Griffin. Well, he's just a sensation, and she wants to make sure everybody knows she knows it, especially that snooty Juliette Simpson.

To be absolutely honest, Betty Sue isn't too sure about the musical selections themselves. She wishes Griffin had played something more dreamy and romantic. Like "Fur Elise," or "Moonlight Sonata," or that other one with the French name, what is it? Every beauty pageant she's ever attended, and that's lots of them—it must be dozens, really—some girl or other has played it for the talent competition. Even that cow, Juliette Simpson. Then it comes to her. "Clair Daloon." Yes, that's it. Griffin should have played that instead of all these loud, agitated pieces she can't imagine being able to hum on her way between classes.

Still, it's been a lovely recital. Griffin looks so handsome in his tuxedo. And so romantic banging away on that huge piano, ugly and deafening as so much of the music was. He'll look just that handsome standing at the altar as daddy escorts her down the aisle.

———

The cookies and punch have all been consumed. The programs have been discarded in the trashcans. The gossips have pretty much run out of scandal. Only a few audience members remain in the foyer where the reception was held. Malcolm Sunderland recognizes them, freshman and sophomore music majors mostly, required to attend a certain number of evening performances on the campus each semester. They're always the first to arrive and the last to leave. They'll be there laughing and flirting until the custodian locks up.

He attends many of these events. He was a freshman music major himself so, so long ago. He dreamed of an evening like this, when he would take to the stage, master the instrument, reap the applause. He was not one of Madame Grammatikova's success stories. The dream flickered out early in the spring with remarkably little drama. But he still remembers it and he knows Madame does, too. As Dean of the College, he's technically her superior. But he knows that in her eyes he'll never be anybody but that nervous young man who couldn't quite get the better of Beethoven's "Pathetique."

And now Griffin.

He watched the three of them leave the building, Griffin flanked by Juliette and Brock. They seemed so young. They were beautiful; they were laughing; they were perfect. And he so badly wishes he could believe in the perfection of that image. As if that faith might somehow redeem him.

———

Madame Grammatikova sits sipping tea at her kitchen table. At her feet, Sasha, the latest in a long line of black Cocker Spaniels, gnaws on a rawhide bone. In the living room, the grandfather clock has just finished striking eleven. She should be on her way to bed. She has a full schedule of classes and private lessons tomorrow, and God knows she's not as young as she used to be. At the last meeting of the music department faculty they were hinting—ever so subtly, but hinting nonetheless—that it might be time for her to think about retirement. After tonight, she's certain, there won't be any more of that. They'll give her the one more year to see Griffin safely to graduation. After that nobody will need to hint. She'll be all too ready.

What a shame that her homeland and her adopted country are still sworn enemies. How she would love to see St. Petersburg one last time. That's really all she can think of that she hasn't done.

Now that Griffin has come through. Itzak Altschuler's estimate is the same as her own. The boy has the talent and intellect required. His work ethic is up to the task. The remaining challenges are external. Time, opportunity, luck. Together, she and Itzak will see to the first two. Nothing can be done with regard to the last except to keep faith with the dream.

III

It is and always has been Brock. Griffin can't remember a time when it wasn't Brock. He has always believed that it always will be Brock in the same way that he believes the sun will continue to rise and set and the tides will continue to flow and ebb. His belief is as constant as the cycling of the seasons and as elemental. As Griffin perceives the universe, Brock is its center. If Brock is Jupiter, Griffin is Ganymede. If Brock is the sun, Griffin is Pluto. Over a lifetime, Griffin has assembled an extensive catalogue of relevant analogies.

As far back as Griffin can remember, there hasn't been a conscious moment when this wasn't so. It apparently goes back even beyond his earliest recollections. Last Thanksgiving as he sat at the Van der Jagt holiday table, Brock's mother, a former Miss Kentucky as well as Miss America third runner up, reminisced at embarrassing though gratifying length about Brock and Griffin in their side by side cribs in the church nursery every Sunday morning. She had known even then, she insisted, that they would always be friends.

Of course no one can know such a thing, not even a southern beauty queen. Griffin understood well enough that Regina Van der Jagt's sherry fueled musings reflected her current prejudices and aspirations far more accurately than they did any objective reality, past or present. Nevertheless, she had hit, albeit obliquely, on a crucial fact. Griffin has never been able to imagine a life lived in any condition other than his perennial proximity to Brock. For years, before Brock addressed a single word to him, Griffin recognized his allegiance to that schoolyard luminary. Try to imagine the moon torn by some inconceivable cataclysm out of earth's orbit, mindlessly wandering the dark, empty vastnesses. Griffin can't. He won't try.

All the brave talk about far off graduate schools, extensive concert tours, an international career, has been, as far as he's concerned, purely hypothetical. Pipe dreams. Elaborate and grandiose fantasies and perhaps not even his own. All devoted to the future fortunes of some other boy named Griffin MacDonald, who, strangely, was just like him but at the same time emphatically not him.

Now, suddenly, he is conscious that everything has changed. And it is this that has made sleep impossible and brought him into the damp chill of the wee hours, to this stone bench across the weathered, brick paved roadway from the dormitory, where he sits and shivers and stares up at their window.

Finally he has to admit that the life he has taken for granted is the flimsiest of illusions, far less substantial than gossamer lit by moonlight; that the Griffin MacDonald he has always recognized as himself is as mythical as a chimera. There is, it turns out, another Griffin. The real Griffin? He's not certain. But this Griffin differs from the familiar one in that he is resolutely, defiantly a creature of skin, bone, muscle, gushing blood, and pulsating organs. He inhabits a world where sunshine means heat against his skin and ground means a hard surface beneath his feet. He acknowledges things like hunger and thirst as more than mere inconveniences. They are essential realities, as valid as the formula of a parabola, the boiling point of water, the array of electrons in an atom of cesium—any and all of those things the human mind constructs to explain the world it observes. This Griffin utterly rejects all of the familiar Griffin's comforting and evasive definitions—admiration, aesthetic appreciation, friendship, even brotherly love—not because they are inaccurate or timid but merely because they are incomplete and there is a larger, more profound truth which must at last be acknowledged. *It is and always has been Brock* includes a component which up to now has been conveniently ignored, and this new Griffin will not tolerate the continuation of these evasions. How, this newly emergent being demands, can you continue having the dreams you have and insist that they are metaphorical in nature? How can you continue to ignore the reality that the slightest, most casual touch from Brock moves you so profoundly? How long will you lie to yourself about what you feel most clearly and deeply?

The truth is that the original Griffin's obliviousness was fragile enough at the crucial instant that the merest whisper was sufficient to explode it. The admission was to all intents and purposes reflexive. Once you acknowledge such a truth to yourself, you can't go back. Once Adam and Eve tasted the fruit they couldn't return to their previous ignorance even if they had never eaten another bite. In that instant, the swords guarding the gates of paradise burst into flame.

The moment occurred during the opening passage of the Chopin F Major Ballade. The shock of it was so astounding that Griffin very nearly stopped playing. But he knew instinctively that no path of return existed. That as with the passing of time, there was only one direction. The new awareness ramified itself in every direction with such force that for the life of him he's not sure how he ever played the piano before.

He has no idea what his life will be like without Brock in it, or even if it can continue. But he knows that the willfully unconscious waif dogging Brock's footsteps like a devoted puppy has absolutely vanished from the face of the earth.

IV

Griffin arrives back at the dorm moments before midnight curfew on Saturday to find a note from Dean Sunderland waiting for him at the front desk. He feels Jerry O'Dowd's not entirely friendly eyes on him as he scans it. The neat, architectural printing reveals nothing.

"He wants to see me."

"He's been calling every half hour to check if you've come in," Jerry grunts. "Last time was twenty minutes ago. Best head on over to his place. I'll let him know you're on your way."

The last time Griffin received a summons like this from Malcolm Sunderland, Granny had died. What now? He prays that nothing terrible has happened to Juliette or Brock. Or Madame Grammatikova. Some additional catastrophe would be the cherry on top of this ghastly escapade, his punishment from God, he supposes. Nothing he experienced or witnessed during the last two nights was one tiny bit edifying. The best that can be said is that he now knows with certainty who he is. The knowledge raises still more questions, but at last the central riddle of his existence has an answer.

Malcolm Sunderland's place is not actually in town but it's not real country, either. There are neighbors in both directions along the narrow, hedge lined road. The old farmhouse, two stories, white clapboard, set among huge, ancient beech trees, is dark except for the porch light. Malcolm's note suggested that he shouldn't park out front, so he steers the Volkswagen down the dirt track past the side of the house toward the barn. Malcolm has left the barn doors open, and he pulls inside, parking beside Malcolm's Jaguar.

The back door of the house is unlocked. Griffin knows the house like it's his own home. He moves through the dimly lighted kitchen following the aroma of pipe smoke to Malcolm's study.

"They told me at the dorm that you were on your way."

"What is it?" Griffin stammers. "What's happened? What's wrong?"

Malcolm is in a faded flannel shirt and the overalls he wears for yardwork. He looks more like a tobacco farmer than a college administrator. He runs a hand through his salt and pepper hair.

"I'd give anything not to have this conversation with you. You'd better sit down."

Griffin sits.

"It seems there's a night club over in Lexington."

Griffin's heart plummets.

"A certain night club. A very particular kind of night club."

"'The Green Light,'" Griffin says, barely audible even to himself.

"I believe that is the name of the establishment."

Until a little over forty-eight hours ago, Griffin had always thought of himself as a fundamentally honest person. Now he knows better. But still, though his life up to now has been a charade, he won't lie to his godfather.

"I've been there. The last two nights."

"So I'm to understand."

"Someone followed me?"

"No. You weren't followed. It seems that certain concerned individuals from the college stake that place out. They're there several nights almost every week. They sit in a car parked out front just in case somebody from the college turns up. Every year or so, some poor unfortunate soul does."

"Oh."

"Like you," Malcolm continues, "though what they're really hoping for is a faculty member, I suppose. Or somebody in the administration."

"I'm sorry."

"I didn't ask you here for an apology," Malcolm grunts.

"I'm sorry anyway."

"All right. You're sorry, though I'm not sure what that even means. The point is, you can't possibly continue in the college. It's all in the Compact of Student Ethics. Entering a bar, any bar, is grounds for discipline. A bar frequented by homosexuals—well that means expulsion. The parties who saw you have already informed me, you see. The written complaint will be on my desk Monday morning."

"Expulsion."

"Expulsion. Loss of all credits for the semester, and you can never return to the campus except as an invited guest—say fifty years from now. Also, a notation of expulsion on your transcript. So that if you attempt to transfer to another institution; well, there are some, I suppose, that might admit you with a thing like that on your record, but not many, I wouldn't think."

"I guess it's what I deserve," Griffin said.

"Really? Is that what you think?"

"I don't know."

"You'd best figure it out quickly."

"I mean, no," Griffin says after a long silence. "No, that's not what I think. To have my entire future ruined? For going into a bar? For that? I mean, even if I was—or, uh, am—aren't I still the same person? I think I am. No, I'm sure I am."

"Good," Malcolm says. "You are your father's son, still. All right. What I have here is your form withdrawing from school. You'll see it's dated Friday."

"I don't understand."

"You came to my office Friday afternoon to withdraw from school for personal reasons. I tried my best to dissuade you, but you insisted. Go ahead, sign it."

"How does this solve anything?"

"It's very simple. If you weren't a St. Gregory's student Friday night when you entered that establishment then you weren't in violation of the Compact. Your presence there has no possible significance for anyone in the college community. I can ignore any complaints I receive, and there will be no question of any negative notation on your transcript. You simply disappear from campus, and eventually the rumors die out. I'm quite confident that all your professors will grant you credit for the semester based on the work you've already completed. And there's enough money left in the trust to get you through your senior year of school somewhere else."

"Madame Grammatikova will be devastated."

"She's tougher than you think. She's already made some suggestions about your future."

"She knows?"

"I thought I should speak with her immediately. She can't see you, I'm afraid. It might compromise her position."

"What about your position?"

"I'm your godfather. I administer your trust fund. That gives me a little latitude. Not much, but it should be enough. Besides, you'll be gone before first light."

"I will?"

"I got your things out of the dorm. You don't need to go back for anything. In fact, you can't."

"You've thought of everything," Griffin says, "except. . ."

"Brock and Juliette."

Griffin nods, unable to speak.

"Madame Grammatikova will speak to Juliette, and I'll handle Brock."

"I'd give anything if they didn't have to know."

"Madame Grammatikova and I don't work miracles," Malcolm said. "We'll do the best we can."

———

It is not yet dawn when Malcolm hears Griffin creep downstairs. He doesn't get out of bed. There is to be no farewell scene. Griffin won't have it, and he doesn't possess the strength to insist. He saw the walls come up last night, saw Griffin's look grow guarded. By the time he refused Malcolm's help loading his belongings into the Volkswagen, it seemed they were strangers. Moments earlier he had shown no interest in suggestions as to where he might go or how to contact friends of Malcolm's who might be of help.

Malcolm can't face those empty, alien eyes, set as they are in that beloved face. He cowers in his bed with his regrets and inadequacies and decades-old secrets. He hears Griffin's car rattle and wheeze down the drive. He listens as its asthmatic buzzing fades into the sounds of the dying night.

He should try, finally, to sleep. But there are things to do.

———

Somewhere west of St. Louis, Griffin finishes his dinner of Vienna sausages and baked beans out of cans and beds down in the Volkswagen. It's after midnight, he's been on the road since before dawn, and he can't remember the last time he actually slept. The last sound he hears is the growl of trucks thundering by on the road west.

SECOND MOVEMENT: THE KINDNESS OF STRANGERS

It was a slow morning at the shop. Kip sat on his stool at the register reading *The Man Without Qualities*. Or trying to. Butch had been running the vacuum cleaner for a good twenty minutes and the racket was about to drive him batty. To the point that Kip couldn't even remember what paragraph he was supposed to be on. Honestly, if he could get through Proust—in the original French, yet—why can't he get through this, in a perfectly serviceable English translation? Even with that infernal vacuum cleaner going? Every time he criticized any aspect of Butch's job performance, out came the vacuum cleaner. He should know better by now. He had always been a slow learner. Slower than Butch, apparently. Or Robbie, who was the one before Butch. Or Wayne, the one before that. Or all the other letters of the alphabet, because there had, indeed, been at least one of each. Ugo, Valentine, Zachariah. . .

Slow learner indeed.

When the kid stepped into the shop, Kip figured him for a high schooler playing hookie. Really, it was getting so bad in the neighborhood lately that the cops had starting making truancy sweeps. About time, too. He was tired of listening to Butch complain about the mess they made in the restroom and the petty vandalism to the shop inventory. Just because their schools taught them to hate all books didn't mean Kip should have to foot the bill. He idly considered getting up and ushering the kid back outside.

The vacuum cleaner shut off, and the next thing he knew Butch had the kid by the collar. Good. That was what Butch was here for. Anybody could run a vacuum cleaner and give attitude, but a guy with shoulders that big could pull things off that normal people couldn't.

Trouble was, however, that for all of Butch's muscle and growl and glower, he was a big softie. That's what Kip thought half a minute later when he saw the big lug, arm around the kid's shoulders in a suspiciously tender manner, approaching the register.

"He says he's here about the job next door," Butch announced. "At the Classical Music Annex."

"Oh?"

"Don't worry, kid," Butch said to the youngster, "he doesn't bite."

"Who says I don't?"

"Seriously," Butch insisted. "He just looks mean. Those fangs are ornamental."

He sounded, Kip thought, like a defense attorney giving a pep talk while escorting his client to address the bench.

"I'm Kip Truman," he said, offering his hand.

"Griffin MacDonald."

"You're interested in the job next door?"

Griffin nodded and gulped.

"Perhaps we should have a talk in my office."

———

Up close, Griffin wasn't that much of a kid. He looked like he was at least safely out of high school. He was medium height but slightly built. It wasn't his actual size that made him seem smaller and younger than he was, it was his manner. He looked like he'd vanish in a puff of smoke if you said boo. He had delicate, boyish features, enormous eyes of a surprisingly dark blue, and floppy, fox red hair cut unfashionably short at the back and sides.

"Now about the job next door," Kip said. "I really have to have somebody who knows classical music."

"I just finished my junior year of college as a piano major."

"Really? Berkeley? State? The conservatory?"

"Out of state."

"Out of state is a very big place," Kip pointed out.

"St. Gregory's College. It's in Kentucky."

"I'll have to take your word for that."

"Honest."

"You know, Griffin," Kip said, playing a hunch. Or maybe it was just that he was a sucker for southern accents. "I'm thinking you're a very bad poker player. I'm just guessing about that, but. . ."

"Awful," Griffin blushed.

"How many symphonies did Shostakovich write?"

"Fifteen."

"String quartets?"

"Fifteen."

"If I give you the job, you have to know about Shostakovich because he's my favorite composer."

Now why did I say that? Kip wondered. *I'm not even supposed to think that.*

"All right," Griffin said.

"Name four composers other than Beethoven, Mozart, and Haydn who wrote at least nine symphonies."

"Vaughan Williams, Dvorak, Bruckner, Mahler."

Griffin didn't have to think about it, just blurted out the names. Like they were his pals from the chess club.

"Five operatic sopranos. Callas doesn't count."

That didn't slow Griffin down, either.

"Tebaldi, Schwartzkopf, Nilssen, Price, Flagstad."

"Three contraltos."

"Galli-Curci, Schumann-Heink, Forrester."

"Two operas by Rossini. *William Tell* doesn't count."

"*La Donna del Lago* and *Semiramide*," Griffin said.

"Five violinists."

"Heifetz, Kreisler, Menhuin, Oistrakh, and Stern."

"You say you're a junior piano major."

"Yes."

"Repertoire you prepared for your juries this semester."

"Junior recital, actually," Griffin said. "A couple of weeks ago. Bach, English Suite, BWV 807; Chopin, Ballade in F Major and Scherzo in C sharp minor; Rachmaninoff, *Corelli Variations*; Prokofiev, "Toccata". That was my encore."

"So if we go next door and pull the dust cover off the Baldwin, you can play any one of those numbers? Right this minute?"

"Whenever you say," Griffin nodded.

———

When Kip called about the basement apartment, Millicent thought *not again*. And when he said that this boy was different, she thought *that's what you always say*. Because she'd known him since his first week in San Francisco, and there had been plenty of them. But when the boy showed up, she saw what Kip meant. He was neat as a pin, even though he'd apparently been living in his car. His fingernails, those windows to the soul, were immaculate. And his manners couldn't have been more pleasing. She left him in the parlor while she fetched the lemonade and short-bread, because she had the refreshments ready in spite of her misgivings and lo and behold, that little Griffin MacDonald was exactly the kind of well brought up boy you served homemade lemonade and homemade shortbread to. There was no mistaking it. She finished loading the tray and stepped back into the parlor.

"I see you're looking at my photos," she said, setting the tray down on the coffee table.

"Is this you?" he asked, eyes wide.

"Millicent Peabody, Women's Army Air Corps, at your service," she said, tossing him a snappy salute. "Wouldn't think so to look at me now."

"No," he shook his head. "That's not true. You haven't changed that much. I recognized you immediately. What I mean is you were a pilot? In World War II?"

"The forces couldn't spare any of the men pilots. The young ones were all needed for combat missions, and the older ones manned the flight schools. So some of us girls who had learned to fly before the war helped out. We ferried aircraft across the Atlantic."

"You're kidding."

"They didn't fly themselves."

"I just always thought," he said, then stopped.

His confusion was adorable. She wanted to hug him. Just wrap him up in a blanket or something and protect him, like he was a lost toddler. Only thing was, he wasn't Kip's usual type. What could that mean?

"I guess I never thought about it at all," he said, "but how were you able to do it? Those planes look tiny."

"Well, we didn't fly those Mustangs straight across the Atlantic, you know," she explained. "We picked them up from the factory. They'd all been checked out by the factory test pilots, because you couldn't just send them off on a trip like that right off the production line."

"Of course."

"Don't be shy, dear. Have all the shortbread you want. There's plenty more in the pantry."

"It's really good. It reminds me of the shortbread my granny made."

"Does it? That's very sweet of you to say. Anyway, we picked the planes up from the factory, and we made refueling stops in Newfoundland, and Greenland, and Iceland, and sometimes Scotland as well if the tailwinds weren't strong enough, and that's how we got those crates to Jolly Olde England."

"It sounds terribly dangerous."

"Oh, it was, dear, it was. Sometimes girls didn't make it. I lost several friends that way. But the return trip was even worse."

"Oh?"

"No, we didn't swim back. We weren't out there dodging sharks and icebergs in our tank suits. We sailed in those old freighters. You lay awake night after night wondering if the U-boats were going to get you. Just shoo that cat off your lap if she's bothering you, dear."

"I like cats," Griffin said. "Granny always had cats back home on the farm."

"Did she, dear?"

"They kept the rats down. Just housecats, you know. Not Siamese."

"I wish Chang and Eng were that useful. They have no initiative at all. If a mouse looked 'em dead in the eye, they wouldn't move a muscle. They don't do anything around here but eat and poop."

"They certainly seem well fed."

"That's a laugh," Millicent said, slapping her knee. "Now, my friend Kip Truman says you need a place. After our snack, why don't we step downstairs and have a look at my garden flat. I think it would be perfect for you, but I wouldn't want to pressure you or anything."

⸺

Butch checked the balance of the pizza box on his right hand, set the shopping bag on the step, and knocked. When he opened the door, Griffin looked surprised and actually a little bit frightened.

"Butch."

"Hey, buddy. Hope you like pizza."

"Huh?"

"Invite me in, doofus. This is your housewarming party."

———

The kid working the cash register matched the description Butch had given him. Small, cute, afraid of his own shadow. No wonder Butch had warned him to go easy.

"You Griffin?" he asked, sauntering over.

"Yes."

"I'm Pete. Butch's friend. You've got a VW you're thinking of selling."

"Oh, yeah," Griffin said. "Butch told me you might come by. The car's in the alley."

"Already checked it out. Does it run as nice as it looks?"

"Like a top," Griffin said with a shy little grin of pride. "Got me all the way here from Kentucky a couple of weeks ago. I change the oil myself. Every two thousand miles."

"Cool."

"And the tires are almost new."

"Michelins," Pete nodded, "I noticed. Why are you looking to sell?"

"Don't really need it here in the city. Parking's always a hassle, and I can get anywhere I need to go on the bus."

"How much you lookin' to get for it?"

"I'd like nine hundred."

"I'd have to drive it first. What time do you get off shift?"

"You can take it out now, if you want," Griffin said. "Since you're Butch's friend."

"You sure?"

"It'll be fine," Griffin said, handing him the key.

"I won't be gone more than twenty minutes."

———

The one thing Kip hadn't said about the kid he was sending over was how ador-able he was. One glance at that smooth, smooth hair and that pretty little face and Harry wanted to take him into the back room and tickle him silly. And that was just for starters. Perhaps Kip's omission wasn't surprising, though. He was such an aficionado of rough trade these days it was possible that he genuinely hadn't noticed.

"Kip says I have to hear you play piano. Very insistent about it, he was."

"Sure, Mr. Gordini."

"Call me Harry. I know I'm old enough to be your grandfather, but my pa is even older. He's the real Mr. Gordini."

"O.K."

Shit. That usually loosened them up a little, but this one didn't so much as crack a grin.

"I'll just take the cover off the Steinway."

"What would you like to hear?" Griffin asked, taking his place on the piano bench.

"Anything by Gershwin."

Kip must have coached the kid, because what Harry got was a nice, easy, lyrical rendition of the first eight bars of "Summertime", not too histrionic, and easy on the rubato.

"Just going to stop you there," Harry said.

"What's wrong?"

"Not a God damned thing, youngster," Harry said, turning on the charm full blast. "Gotta ask, though. Is that a key people can sing in? We do a lot of sing alongs around here. Kind of the point of the place."

"Should be fine," Griffin said. "Maybe a little low for a real soprano or tenor, but just right for an alto or baritone."

"Great. How about some Cole Porter?"

"Sure."

Not a second of hesitation. Some of these classically trained types made faces at Harry's requests.

"Nice. Now let's have something by Jerome Kern. With a segue into one of Coward's patter songs."

It went like a dream. Whatever Harry asked for, the kid delivered. Note perfect, with confidence and decent expression. Whether he could do as well in front of a live audience was another question.

"Very, very nice," Harry said, after twenty minutes or so of asking for anything he could think of. "Now, we're not hopelessly lowbrow around here. Don't want you thinking that. We do appreciate the classics. Every now and then somebody will ask for an aria. You do arias, I guess?"

"Unless it's something really obscure," Griffin said.

"Don't worry. Ninety-nine per cent of the time it's Puccini or Verdi. Oh, and the famous Mozart ones. Rossini, too."

"Fine," Griffin nodded.

"You can throw in a little something at the end of your set, if you like. Chopin goes over pretty well. As long as it's not too quiet."

Griffin tossed off the "Minute Waltz" like it was child's play.

"Like that," Harry said, "exactly. Now just for me, how about that Prelude by Rachmaninoff? You know the one I mean. Everybody knows that one."

Griffin seemed happy to oblige. He played the piece like David taking down Goliath.

"O.K." Harry said. "I'd like you to come in Tuesday night and play a set. Forty-five minutes, and you'll need to do as many audience requests as you can squeeze in. If that goes all right, we'll talk about making you a regular."

"Thanks."

"Don't thank me yet. I pay one half minimum wage, and you keep all the tips in the jar at the end of your set. You have a suit?"

"Navy blue," Griffin said. "Medium weight wool."

"Wear it. Eight o' clock slot on Tuesday, so be here by seven-thirty."

———

"What's that?" Griffin asked, peering out his front door at Butch.

"Atomic powered dust mop," Butch growled, "what's it look like?"

"A television."

"Bingo. Found it sittin' by a dumpster. Color TV. What people won't toss out. Unbelievable. Took it home and checked it out. Little crackle in the speaker, but nothin' serious. Otherwise it's mint. I ain't bringin' you over no more pizza and lemonade on Sunday nights unless you've got a set we can watch, so now you do."

"Thanks, Butch," Griffin said.

"Just get it set up for you."

———

"Have a seat, Griffin," Kip said.

"Thanks."

"How's things? You getting settled all right?"

"Everybody's been really helpful," Griffin said.

He sounded like he thought maybe he didn't deserve it. Kip's usual boys never thought they didn't deserve anything.

"I hear Harry's making you a Tuesday night regular."

"He seems really pleased," Griffin nodded.

"He's a good man. You'll want to stick with him. He takes good care of his acts."

"That's what everybody says."

"And speaking of that, just want to let you know I'm giving you a raise. Forty cents an hour, retroactive to the start of your second week. You'll see it in your next check."

"I don't know what to say."

———

"Hey, faggot! Yeah, you."

Butch stopped in his tracks. Ahead of him, Griffin was frozen, standing stock still in the pool of glare from a streetlight. He was a sitting duck.

"Over here, faggot. Get your faggot ass over here and suck my dick."

"Now, faggot."

So there were two of them. At least.

"No, don't run, you fucking pansy. We'll catch you anyway, and it'll just hurt worse."

"Hey," Butch called. "Leave him alone."

"Sure we will. Fuck off. Or we'll fuck you up, too."

"I said, leave him alone."

"Who the fuck are you?"

"You bastards know who I am," Butch roared. "You know exactly who I am. You remember last time? Huh? So you gonna leave him alone, or do you bastards want another trip to the emergency room?"

There was silence. Griffin was looking back over his shoulder in the direction Butch's voice had come from.

"You assholes listen to me. You can have anybody you want to go after, but you leave this guy alone. Or I'll come find you. Got it?"

Still no answer.

"Wait right there, Griffin," he called. "I'll come to you."

———

"God, Butch," Griffin said, shaking. "I'm so lucky you were following me home."

"Wasn't luck," Butch said. "I follow you home every night."

"What?"

"I know they're out there. Have to get you a can of mace to carry."

"Mace? Is that what you used on them? That time you were talking about?"

"I used this," Butch pulled the pistol out of his jacket pocket.

"My God."

"Forty-five," Butch said, "police special. Didn't shoot 'em. Just roughed 'em up a little. Let 'em get a good look at it, see? Get you one if you want it."

"I couldn't."

"Somethin' smaller maybe. Thirty-eight. Listen, let's get you home. Can't stand here all night."

———

"Take those clothes off and jump in the shower," Butch said. "I'm goin' upstairs. Miss Peabody has this special tea. Herbs and stuff. Calm you right down. I'll go up and get a few bags. You got something to heat water in? Coupla mugs, maybe?"

"Uh huh."

"O.K. I'll be right back."

———

"You about done in there?" Butch called. "Tea's ready."

"O.K. Be right out."

He heard the water stop running. Griffin pulled back the curtain.

"Hand me a towel."

"Stand still," Butch said, "I'll dry you off."

———

"There," Butch said. "All tucked in. Nice and cozy."

He started unbuttoning his shirt.

"What are you doing?"

"Don't worry. Not up to any funny business. Scoot over. You need a good cuddle. Help you sleep."

———

Jean-Pierre had no idea what to expect. Madame Grammatikova had given him a comprehensive description of the young man as a pianist, but on the subject of the young man as a person, she had been, he thought, extremely cryptic. He had scheduled this meeting at his apartment rather than his office. Meeting Mr. MacDonald at his office might give the impression that his admission to the conservatory was already settled, and it was far from that despite what he had heard from Madame Grammatikova and what he thought he heard when he listened to the recital tape she had sent.

At five minutes before ten, the doorman called from downstairs to say he was sending the young man up. Jean-Pierre appreciated punctuality. As far as he was concerned, too many music students underestimated its importance. The knock on his front door, a single, forthright rap, was another clue. He waited for a long three count before opening it. Curious he might be, but he certainly wasn't anxious.

The young man standing there in the shadowy corridor was almost exactly Jean-Pierre's size, small by American standards, perfectly average by European ones. His hair was carefully combed and he had worn a suit. Jean-Pierre found most students unacceptably casual in their dress, and this was another important clue.

"Professor Schein?"

"You must be Griffin," Jean-Pierre said, extending his hand. "Please, come in."

"Your apartment is beautiful," Griffin said.

That accent. Jean-Pierre didn't know whether to laugh or cry. The English speaking people of the world had such a haphazard way with their language.

"Very kind of you," he said. "Let's go into my studio."

The boy moved well. Jean-Pierre had to give him that. Show him a musician not at home in his body and Jean-Pierre would show you a failure. You didn't play piano with your hands alone. You played piano all the way to your toes.

"Now, I've spoken several times with Madame Grammatikova," he said.

"You know her?" Griffin asked.

"Not really," he said. "I had heard of her. One hears of so many people. I contacted one or two of my old teachers and they filled me in. Gave me quite an earful, actually."

"She's a character," Griffin grinned.

It was a fond grin. A grin that didn't often appear on that smooth young face, Jean-Pierre sensed. Really, had anyone asked him to judge the boy's age he would have said sixteen; perhaps seventeen, but not a day more, certainly. Jean-Pierre had been that way himself, always looking younger than he really was. To hear his friends tell it, he was still ridiculously boyish at thirty-two.

"A character, yes," Jean-Pierre said, "but also a true virtuoso, from what one has heard. You were very lucky to have such a teacher."

"I know."

"Now before we go any further, we must speak of practicalities. Art is all well and good, but it is a hungry child. Ravenous, in fact. Starving artists only exist in operas, I'm afraid. Successful students are invariably well fed. And I must tell you that the conservatory has no scholarships available for transfer students. What we are talking about here is two years. If you are admitted, it will only be with the understanding that you will repeat your junior year. There are substantial course deficiencies in your records, and in addition to that, we can't give you credit for a recital you prepared and performed at another institution. Two years before you will graduate—you understand?"

"Madame Grammatikova explained all that," Griffin nodded.

"So. Is that possible? Do you have the resources?"

"My godfather says there's enough money left from my grandparents' estate, as long as I'm willing to work part time."

"I see," Jean-Pierre nodded. "I have to tell you, at the conservatory we discourage part time work. But almost all of our students have jobs anyway. Still, it won't be anything like your college was. Our program is extremely demanding."

"I'm not afraid of hard work," Griffin said.

His expression when he said it was so serious it nearly made Jean-Pierre laugh.

"Very well," he said. "I've listened to your recital tape several times, but we never make a final decision until we've heard a student perform live. Why don't you go to the piano and warm up for a moment? Then I would like to hear you play the *Corelli Variations*."

—

"Griffin, honey," Millicent Peabody said, motioning him through her front door. "What a lovely suit."

"Thanks."

"You didn't really have to dress up, dear. It's just the two of us. Sunday dinner at home."

He shrugged.

"I don't know what your background is, but you'd be welcome to attend Grace Cathedral with me any Sunday you like," she said. "Especially if you promise to wear that suit. Chang, stop rubbing on that pant leg. Those cats. They leave their hair everywhere. I was always told Siamese don't shed."

"I have to take it to the cleaner soon anyway," Griffin said.

"It's just a cold lunch, I'm afraid," she said, motioning him to his seat. "I don't cook much in the summer months."

"It looks delicious," he said, taking off his jacket and laying it over the back of an unoccupied chair at the table.

"Now tell me, what have you heard from Professor Schein?" Millicent asked, passing him the platter of sliced ham. "Any news?"

"I'm supposed to call him tomorrow," Griffin said. "He promised me a definite answer then."

"I'm sure they'll accept you, dear. I prayed about it during service this morning. Jean-Pierre Schein. I make a point of attending all of his recitals at the conservatory, you know. Those Frenchmen are outrageously handsome. That jet black hair. One night I took my friend Gertie along. She nearly fainted in the receiving line."

———

"Good flick," Butch said, getting up from the sofa and stretching. "Guess I ought to be on my way. Don't forget to wrap up the rest of the pizza and put it in the fridge. Makes a good breakfast."

"Butch?"

"Yup?"

For some reason the kid looked as serious as a heart attack. The movie had been a comedy, so—what?

"I, um, I need you to do me a favor," Griffin said.

"What's that, little buddy?"

"It's just. . ."

"Yeah?"

"Oh, God, Butch, I feel so stupid asking you this."

"Stop right there. You know you can ask Ol' Butch anything."

"I just—I don't want to be a virgin any more," Griffin gulped.

He was staring at the floor so hard Butch almost thought he'd burn a hole in it.

"Came to the right place then," he muttered. "Kind of an expert at poppin' cherries."

Griffin didn't speak.

"Come here, you," Butch said. "Here's how we start."

He brushed the floppy hair off Griffin's forehead and softly planted a kiss there. Then he kissed the eyes before moving on to the mouth. The kid was trembling. Really trembling, like he'd just been fished out of a frozen lake or something. Butch wrapped his arms around the frail shoulders and squeezed just hard enough to settle him, to make him feel *located*. He was a full head taller and outweighed Griffin by about a hundred pounds. He'd have to go slow and easy.

"Come on," he said softly. "Let's go in the bedroom. Get you out of those clothes."

THIRD MOVEMENT: LOST TIME

The first sound that Griffin hears is the thunder of his neighbors' footsteps on the wooden stairs outside his bedroom window. The top floor of Miss Peabody's house is a separate apartment which she rents out to Scott and Jared, a brawny pair of demigods to whom Griffin has never spoken, either individually or as a couple, except to say "good morning" or "here's some mail the postman delivered to me by mistake".

They are early risers, or at least their twin cairn terriers are. Every morning Scott and Jared—always both of them—stomp down the wooden staircase leading from their back door to the garden. They carry the dogs down from the third floor, the stairs apparently being judged too treacherous for canines, and the racket of their descent wakes Griffin just a moment or two before his alarm clock sounds. It is as unvarying as sunrise, seven days a week.

Also unvarying, except in the most inclement weather when the dogs apparently prefer to finish their business quickly and be carried back upstairs, is twenty minutes or so of rough housing which ensues involving dogs and men and occasionally an outraged Siamese or two, depending on what time of night Millicent's pets have demanded exit from her quarters. Scott's accustomed attire for this ritual is an athletic shirt and gym shorts even in the chilliest of weathers. Jared prefers to make his appearance bare-chested, and wears sweatpants exclusively. Griffin knows this because he stares out his bedroom window at them. He can't help himself. He's as discreet as he can be, peering out through the tiniest of cracks in the blinds, but he is as powerless against the spectacle as Lot's wife staring back at Sodom in flames. Jared is astonishing. Griffin would never have imagined a human body could be that massively muscled. He is not exactly handsome but rugged and masculine looking.

He wears his hair very short, a silvery mat that looks like he combs it with a wash-rag. The silver is apparently premature. His face, rugged as it is, is quite youthful.

But it is Scott that Griffin worships. The first time Griffin saw Scott he thought a miracle had taken place and a certain boy from his past had come to San Francisco to track him down and carry him away. His heart stood still. He stopped breathing. The vision moved closer along the crowded sidewalk toward where he stood, rooted. And the illusion only dissipated at the distance of a few paces. It wasn't Brock at all, just some stranger. An incredibly perfect stranger, handsome and blond and muscular in the same manner as Brock, but still unmistakably a stranger. The few seconds of that fantasy were enough to break Griffin's heart all over again.

Scott is only slightly less massive than Jared. His smooth hair, blonder actu-ally than Griffin remembers Brock's being, is the stuff of dreams. His face is that of a matinee idol. When he speaks, his voice is pitched only two steps higher than Jared's. Neither of them has a perceptible accent. Griffin tries his best to ignore their existence, particularly Scott's, but this is pretty much impossible.

Millicent Peabody adores them. She insists that except for Griffin himself they're the best tenants she's ever had. Indeed, she sings their praises more or less constantly. If Griffin wasn't infatuated with them he's sure he'd think it's really obnoxious.

———

It's going to be a long day. Griffin probably won't make it home before bedtime. He loads his backpack. Textbooks. Musical scores. His metronome. Two spare pairs of undershorts in case of bowel distress, a constant threat which he blames on his more or less perpetual anxiety. A t-shirt to change into if it gets warm enough, though in San Francisco this time of year that's no sure thing. He has a change of clothes waiting in the dressing room at Harry Gordini's for tonight's gig but needs to bring socks and a belt. Peanut butter sandwiches and an apple for lunch. More peanut butter sandwiches and a pear for dinner. A baggie of almonds, another of cashews, a third of dried apricots for in between. Then, because he has to keep his morale up for the next day and a half, two Hershey bars. Any more and his face will break out. He's perilously close to it already.

That done, he heats a saucepan of water for his morning oatmeal and slices a banana to go on top.

———

Millicent is sweeping the front steps as he emerges into the fog filtered sunlight. The cats watch her like disapproving foremen. If their paws were capable of grasping tiny little bullwhips, their expressions say they'd crack them at her.

"Good morning, dear."

"Good morning, Millicent."

"Sleep well?"

"Like a log," he lies. He is determined to match her cheery demeanor. This is a woman who flew Mustang fighters across the North Atlantic in wartime. And who, faced with the end of her flying career after the war when pilots—nice male ones, as God intended—were suddenly a dime a dozen, went back to school and became a surgical nurse. She's an object lesson in survival despite the disappointment of shattered dreams, and he wishes he had the fortitude to emulate her. But if he can't actually do that, he can at least pretend to. He feels like he'd be letting both of them down admitting that his mood is more a match for the perpetual gloom of the San Francisco mornings.

"It's going to be a beautiful day," she says.

He's quite certain she's wrong, but senses that her prediction is more existential than meteorological.

———

Griffin has timed his departure perfectly. Down the block, just out of earshot, he catches sight of the fog dimmed gleam of Scott's glorious hair. Two monumental pairs of shoulders recede down the sidewalk toward the corner of the block. Jared's silver hair is nearly invisible in the gloom; Scott's golden locks are nearly the only color visible in the scene. If Griffin followed them any closer he'd be afraid they might somehow sense his presence, his famished eyes drinking in Scott's magnificence with an intensity he knows they couldn't help but find creepy.

Jared is magnificent, too. But Griffin's heart belongs to Scott.

Jared is the kind of man to tie you up and do unimaginable things to you against your will until you beg him never to stop. Scott, on the other hand, is perfection on two exquisite legs. He's the man you worship with every breath you take as long as you continue taking them.

They round the corner. He increases his pace in order to close the distance. Once he reaches the busier street it will be safer. Should either of them look back for any reason, there's an excellent chance he won't be noticed among all the other people on the sidewalk.

A few blocks up, they'll part at the entrance to the MUNI station. Scott will take the BART out to Berkeley, where according to Millicent he teaches part time. Jared will catch a bus to his office. Griffin will wait until Scott has disappeared down the steps before he approaches the bus stop. He'll get on the bus behind Jared, who will either notice him or not depending on how long the wait for the bus has been and how engrossed he has become in his reading material. He generally reads magazines about architecture. Registering Griffin's presence is about a one day in three occurence. If Jared does look up, he'll flash a piratical grin that will be the stuff of bedtime fantasies for the next week or so despite Griffin's undying love for Jared's husband.

Griffin will get off the bus a couple of stops before Jared does. He knows this because he stayed on once—just one time—to see where Jared got off.

———

Griffin isn't in love with Scott. Obviously. That would be ridiculous. He knows nothing about Scott that can't be discerned by continual, though he hopes discreet, observation. In other words, nothing but the surface appearance. They've never exchanged more than a few words, and those have been of the most casual nature. He doubts that Scott even remembers his name. But it's more than mere infatuation he feels. It's obsession. The resemblance to Brock, though superficial, transfixes him.

Scott, truth to tell, is broader in the shoulder and more massively muscled than Brock was. Back at St. Gregory's, Griffin would hardly have imagined such a thing was possible, but living in San Francisco has been a revelation in that regard. Given what he knows now, Scott's physical superiority to Brock isn't surprising. Scott is older and has apparently spent more time in the gym. His physique is, if anything, emblematic of what Brock might someday become. In addition to that, Scott's hair is a shade and a half lighter than Brock's, and has a finer, silker texture. Scott's face has more refined, almost pretty, features than Brock's boyish ones, and Scott either isn't capable of it or chooses not to tan to as dark a shade as Brock always did. He is, in other words, unmistakably not Brock. But he is sufficiently like Brock to be a constant reminder of Griffin's loss, and that's still the ultimate tragedy of his life.

———

The bus, as always at this time of day, is packed. Jared has found a seat in the back. Griffin stands, hanging on by a wrist he really shouldn't be subjecting to such exertions as may occur due to the bouncing and sudden stops. His wrists, as far as he knows, are his future.

———

"Good morning, Griffin," Mrs. Porcelli, the Administrative Secretary, greets him. "You must be here to review the proof."

"If you're not too busy."

"Not at all. I'll just be a moment."

She bustles off to fetch it. Around him it's just another day in the conservatory offices. Copying machines go thunka-thunka, secretaries murmur, telephones ring. All offices are alike, Griffin decides. Whatever the enterprise, selling insurance, administering hospital care, educating virtuosi, the basic infrastructure, the staffing and machinery concerned with generating paper with markings on it and routing that paper in myriad directions to shadowy faced readers in unimaginable destinations, seems somehow constant. Griffin tries and fails to imagine what it feels like to spend one's life as part of that unending task.

"Here you are, Griffin."

"Thanks."

"Are you excited?"

"I know I'm supposed to be," he says, shocking himself with his candor.

"That's the spirit," she laughs.

The pages she has handed him are the proof copy of his recital program. The titles of the works he will perform are listed. Accompanying them are the program notes he so diligently researched and composed. Appropriate program notes are required. Their preparation is considered part of the recital assignment.

He is scheduled to play Beethoven's Sonata in C minor, popularly known as the "Pathetique." Following that, he'll perform the Chopin Scherzo in C sharp minor from his program last year at St. Gregory's. Then, to give himself a little relief, two Rhapsodies by Dohnanyi, flashy, highly accessible pieces which present somewhat less challenging technical demands. By that point in the program, he'll be starting to tire slightly. He'll finish with the piece he played as an encore back at St. Gregory's last year, Prokofiev's "Toccata". He has prepared an encore as well, Liszt's *Allegro agitato molto* in F minor from the *Transcendental Etudes*. But of course encores are never listed in the printed program. This, it is considered, would be presumptuous, the assumption being that encores are invariably impromptu, though of course they aren't.

He finds two typos in the program notes and circles them with the red pencil Mrs. Porcelli has provided. Then he signs the proper form and hands it all back to her.

"Good luck tomorrow evening, dear."

"Thank you," he smiles. "My old teacher always said you can never have enough of that."

———

The second he gets out of his first class of the morning he heads for his practice cubicle. If he's as little as five minutes late getting there, the cubicle is up for grabs. That's the unwritten rule here at the conservatory. Competition for the tiny, airless spaces is fierce. Back at St. Gregory's things were much more casual. There, nobody would have dreamed of trying to poach his cubicle. They'd have had Juliette to contend with, for one thing. But more than that, he was important enough there that nobody would have dreamed of trying it. If the last year has taught him anything, it's the meaning of the phrase "big fish in a small pond". Here at the conservatory he's barely even a hatchling. He makes it to his cubicle with seconds to spare. When he arrives, Joey Ferelli glowers at him and taps his wristwatch as if to say he has only refrained from taking possession out of the goodness of his cold Italian heart.

———

When Griffin emerges an hour later, it's like rush hour on the MUNI. Late Wednesday morning is the peak time of the week. Lots of students have their private lessons on Wednesday afternoon. Students who haven't practiced all week are desperately playing catch up. You can hardly move. Looking down the corridor he sees a flash of golden hair in the crowd ahead of him. His heart stands still. From behind it's impossible to tell, but it's the right height at least. Perhaps there has been some kind of miracle.

Then he hears Annabelle Janklowitz's cackle and his heart starts beating again. It's that Swedish violinist from over at Berkeley who comes to rehearse with her a couple of times a week.

——

It's exam day in his composition class. They have to write thirty-two bars to a specific set of parameters. Ever since he left Kentucky, Griffin has had a tune in his head that he finally realized is not a quotation he can't identify but, honest to God, the creation of his own brain. He thinks of it as "Brock's tune", and he has used it over and over again as a subject in this class. He's certain professor Schoenstein recognizes all this recycling, but since it's a beginning composition course has chosen to ignore it. They're not being graded on creativity anyway, just adherence to theoretical precepts.

Over the months a countermelody has evolved, closely related but different, a plaintive, tentative response to the statement made by the original tune. Today, he mentally places them end to end, then writes them out on the staff in retrograde inversion. He casts this in 5/4 meter. It's spring in Kentucky, and the rhythm he has created evokes Brock's loping gait as he makes his rounds of the campus. Griffin harmonizes this line with a series of diminished chords, doubling the roots in the upper register to create a descant. This, he decides, calls to mind Juliette watching Brock from a top floor window of the library. He's got only a few minutes left, but what he has already done is the hard part. He fills in the bass with a simple, arpeggiated accompaniment, and he's done.

When he thinks of Brock and Juliette this way, abstracted beyond recognizability, contemplating them is almost painless. They could be characters in a play he saw once upon a time, vivid but unreal.

——

"You have to hold something in reserve," Jean-Pierre says. "The sonata is referred to as '*Pathetique*', not '*Apocalyptique*'. You're playing a very ambitious program. You can't give everything you have right off the bat. You'll never make it to the end."

"I don't know how to do what you're saying."

"Relax and focus," Jean-Pierre says. "Play the music itself, not what you think people are expecting the music to sound like. It's not a race. It's not a wrestling match. You're not in competition with anyone. Perform the music, but don't make a performance of it."

It's just more words. Madame used to do the same thing—talk in riddles. Griffin would wake up from dreams where he repeated her mantra endlessly, but he'd be none the wiser for it. It nearly drove him crazy. And when he finally figured out what she meant, the price of the knowledge was having to walk away from his life. It's happening again with Jean-Pierre. His riddles are different, but the idea is the same. All he gets are more words he knows the definitions of well enough but can't grasp the concept behind.

"You'll figure it out," Jean-Pierre says. "You'll be fine."

He'll figure it out—right. He has just over thirty hours left and he has no idea where to start. But Jean-Pierre's correct. There's no alternative. He'll crash and burn otherwise.

"Let's hear the Prokofiev next," Jean-Pierre says. "On that one, you have my permission to go balls to the wall."

"Do what?" Griffin can't believe the things that sometimes come out of the mouth of this oh, so urbane Frenchman.

"A new expression I learned last weekend. You like it?"

———

Griffin isn't the only one around here who has a crush on Jean-Pierre. The females of the institution, every last one, adore him, from the newest student to the ancient assistant librarian, and including everyone from full professors to the wives of major donors to the little Mexican women who perform janitorial duties. Even a couple of lesbians who hate men on principle have made an exception in the case of the dapper, charming, insanely handsome Frenchman with the courtly manners and spellbinding keyboard technique.

His appeal crosses over the scary boundary into the territory Griffin uneasily inhabits. For unlike at St. Gregory's, here Griffin is not the only example of his type. He recognized that his first day on the campus. Gays aren't exactly numerous here, but they're an unquestioned presence. He took comfort in this at first. But he soon realized that he had little more in common with the gay boys of the conservatory than he did with anyone else. They're a breed he's only imagined before, flamboyant, theatrical, prone to emotional displays that make him cringe. They gossip in whispers loud enough to echo down the hallways. They don't wear clothes but costumes. Their haircuts seem calculated to elicit outrage. They call attention to themselves in every imaginable way, something Griffin has spent so much time and effort avoiding that he can't conceive what their motivation is.

Jean Pierre's status is a matter of constant speculation all over the conservatory. He's often seen in the company of a tall, elegant, exotically beautiful woman named Elizabeth, but the gay boys, and more than a few of the straight girls, insist that she's merely a friend. Even if Jean-Pierre were gay, Griffin can't imagine that he'd be interested in any of those chattering young things, yet they worship him. More than that, they compete for his attention in such transparent ways that Griffin is embarrassed for them. He can't imagine humiliating himself that way.

———

From the bus window, he catches a glimpse of a blond head above heroic shoulders. His heart skips a beat. The vision is there on a street corner and then gone. It might have been Scott. It might not have been Scott. It's too late to reach up and pull the cord to signal for a stop. Griffin wouldn't dare, and in any case, the man has already been swallowed up in the crowds.

———

Griffin's in the dressing room munching on his fourth peanut butter sandwich of the day when Harry Gordini steps in.

"Griffin," he smiles. "Didn't notice you come in. Just wanted to make sure you were here. Jordan's about to finish his set."

"Present and accounted for," Griffin mumbles through the sticky mouthful.

"Wish you'd let me send you in a hamburger," Harry says. "You eat way too much peanut butter. It can't be good for you."

"Hasn't killed me yet."

"Can't imagine how you stand the stuff. Well, I'm taking you out for a real meal," Harry says. "Sometime soon. Celebrate this recital of yours, which I can't wait to see. Or hear. Whatever."

"It's really cool that you'll be there."

———

It's a quiet evening at the club, even for a Wednesday. The tip jar is practically empty, and even the bartender looks bored. There are hardly any requests during his first set, so Griffin plays mostly Gershwin, throws in some Rachmaninoff just before his break.

———

When he comes out for his second set, the place is even emptier. But one of the regulars has come in, Jason, a tall, blond, athletic looking young man with a dangerous jawline and a devastating smile. The first couple of times he introduced the gentleman he was with as his uncle, Griffin believed him. He'd grown up with lots of boys who had uncles that numerous, though generally not so well dressed. Butch, who moonlights here as a bouncer, had to clue him in. Since then, Griffin has made a special effort not to stare. Jason always makes sure his "friends" leave Griffin a generous tip. Griffin's finances are strained enough that he can't help appreciating the gesture, but at the same time it seems to emphasize how inferior he is to a being like Jason. He wonders how full the tip jar would have to get for him to afford Jason's services. He wonders if he'd ever get over the mortification of having to pay a guy like that to spend a night with him. But he can't help thinking that it might be worth it. Just once.

———

When Griffin emerges into the alley behind the club, Butch is out there taking a cigarette break, which, since he no longer smokes, Griffin finds baffling. What does

Butch do out there for fifteen minutes at a time? He's far too embarrassed to ask Butch about it. Which seems silly, considering that he has actually had Butch's cock in his mouth—more than once—not to mention in his ass, and you wouldn't think that after that there would be any secrets between two people.

"Big day for you tomorrow," Butch growls. His face is in shadow, but his slicked hair glints seductively in the dimness. His deep, gravelly voice invariably gives Griffin chills.

Why aren't they in love?

Mostly it has to do with Butch being sensible enough to keep sufficient distance, apparently understanding that Griffin is so desperate he'll fall for the first man who gives him any real encouragement. Even Griffin, scrambled as he is, gets that much. Still, it would be so nice to have a guy like this to go home with. Big, strong, gentle. They should put Butch's picture in the dictionary. They wouldn't need to provide any further definition for the word "man".

This, of course, is not sufficient basis for an actual relationship. Grifffin gets that. It's not like Butch and Griffin have anything in common other than occasional, haphazard proximity. When they're together they have little or nothing to talk about. If Butch wasn't addicted to pizza and television, there wouldn't be any point at all. Griffin is sure Butch would get bored with him pretty quickly if they never did anything but have sex. Of course, the real reason, he believes, though he knows Butch would deny it if asked, is that Griffin's just not cute enough. Griffin would give anything for the whole thing not to be so damned complicated. In feeling this way, he knows he's a member of a very large club.

"Yes," he says, heart breaking a little over the all too obvious futility of his life. "Big day tomorrow."

"I'll be there," Butch says, "at your. . .whatever it's called."

"Recital."

"Yeah. Harry said I can have the night off. I'd go even if he didn't. Couldn't miss that."

Griffin finds this last declaration overwhelming, and can't respond.

"Got your mace handy?"

"In my pocket."

"Shouldn't need it," Butch grunts. "Pretty quiet tonight. But you never know. Better safe than sorry."

"Uh huh."

"Wish you'd have let me get you that gun."

"I'd shoot myself by accident."

"C'mere a minute," Butch says.

He gives Griffin a hug that leaves him breathless. Then, before releasing him, a long, slow kiss. The feel of stubble against his face makes Griffin want to weep.

"For good luck," he mutters, stroking Griffin's hair. "Now get home. And straight to bed."

But he doesn't let Griffin go without another kiss.

———

Trudging the last few yards up the sidewalk, he can hear Millicent's television blasting away in her living room. Sounds like it's a war movie on the late show. She swears her hearing is just fine, but he can't believe how loud she plays her set. He hears it clearly in his downstairs apartment. She never stays up late enough that it keeps him awake, but he worries about her. The cats yowl at him from the porch as he opens the gate.

"Same to you," he mutters.

———

Butch is right to caution him, Griffin knows. Hardly a week goes by without a gay bashing in the neighborhood. But he finds that threat abstract compared to the things that have him nearly in tears by the time he steps through his front door each night. There's more than plenty to make him anxious. There's his recital tomorrow night, which is rather a sink or swim proposition. There's Madame Grammatikova's health, which he has heard is not good. There are Malcolm Sunderland's perpetual concerns about him, unspoken but unmistakable between the lines of his weekly letters. There are his own unanswered and unanswerable questions about Brock and Juliette. He can't bring himself to ask Malcolm about them, and Malcolm offers nothing. They must be planning their wedding, here with graduation just weeks away. What have they heard or been told about him? Do they ever think about him at all? If so, what? Does he even want to know? If he knew the truth, could he face it? He's supposed to be starting his new life, but he can't seem to let go of his old one. If that's not enough to make you anxious, what is?

But it's not the anxiety that reduces him to this state, not really. It's the loneliness. Since arriving in the city, he has experienced amazing kindnesses. He depends on an astonishing array of people to get him through his days. He wouldn't trade their solicitude for anything. It means survival to him. He'd die rather than seem ungrateful. But it is all assistance of a practical nature, vital, but only peripheral to his needs. He's still not connected to anyone. That's what really mattered to him back at St. Gregory's, back in Eden before the flaming swords barred his re-entry to the garden. He needs to belong to someone. He needs to feel like someone belongs to him. As tenuous as those relationships were, they seemed real enough at the time. He feels their absence like a physical pain.

⸺

All this heartache and agonizing effort, he thinks, lying in bed belching peanut butter and praying for sleep. All of it, just to get himself back to the point he had reached this time last year. Tomorrow night, if all goes well, he'll be eligible to call himself a senior piano major. Again. He thinks of his situation as an existential treadmill.

⸺

In the wake of Griffin's piano bench epiphany that night at St. Gregory's— though to be accurate about it it was more like waking up from a dream than making a discovery—he came to think of his tragedy as having been born the wrong sex to earn the love of someone like Brock. A simple accident of birth, in other words. A question of genetics. Nothing to be done about it. Just fate.

But the months since that night have taught a far bitterer lesson. Unimaginably so, though when he thinks of it nothing about it should have been surprising. His predicament is much worse than having been born with the wrong set of parts for the role he aspired to. He's never wanted to be a woman and still doesn't. Really, he can't begin to imagine himself as a female. But that's not the only way of thinking about the matter. Still, if it were as simple as *Brock will never love me because he's straight,* the solution would be simple as well. Brock's avatars are everywhere in San Francisco. And at least some of them share Griffin's orientation. Just grab one of them—problem solved.

Not Scott, of course. He's taken. But there are others. Griffin sees them everywhere he goes.

But no. It's not the gay/straight thing that has Griffin trapped. It's way bigger than that. It's. . .

All right. The thing is. . .

Out there on some street, on a bus, sitting alone at a table in a restaurant, jogging down a hill in the fog, playing rugby on the Marina Green, waiting to check out at the supermarket, laughing with a friend who actually is just a friend, toiling away mightily in a gym, slumbering in the shadows of a tiny room overlooking a bus stop, street corner, schoolyard, parking lot, whatever, a lone paragon waits for the arrival of someone who will change his life. In his deepest hopes, Olympian dreams, twilight musings—all of them unspoken—the man he awaits is—well, look. It's obvious. It's as close as Griffin's upstairs neighbors.

Demigods don't rampage across the landscape—meadows, hillsides, prairies, deserts, and desolate crags—in search of fieldmice. The man Griffin's looking for is most definitely not looking for him.

Obviously, he should learn to settle. Grannie used to talk about eating what was on the plate and being thankful for it. Don't cry over absent caviar or *foie gras*; eat the God damned turnip greens and cornbread sitting in front of you. Making do and getting by was the way life worked for all but the most fortunate. Learning to accept it was as obligatory as breathing. It was a lesson Griffin thought he understood until Brock was suddenly out of reach, or rather until he woke to the reality that Brock had never been within reach and the hole in Griffin's heart remained, bleeding and jagged edged.

But what, exactly, is on Griffin's plate? The chattering gayboys at the conservatory? Even if he could acquire that taste, they're impossible, too. He's as invisible and insignificant to them as he is to the musclehunks in their locker rooms. When they register his existence at all, it's to snicker at his accent behind his back. Their clothes come from the same thrift shops as his and are equally as shabby, but they wear them with panache. They manage to look cute in them, not just down at the heel. They know the lingo. They have the moves. They inhabit their sexual identities like natives, while he's the equivalent of an immigrant just off the boat, totally unassimilated.

Leaving? Those shy young men, socially awkward as he is, who spend hours poring over the opera recordings along the back wall of Kip's shop before leaving empty handed just before closing time because it's not payday for three days yet?

The famished-eyed, balding, nondescript gentlemen sitting alone in the corners at Harry Gordini's club hoping Griffin will get around to playing their requests before they have to head home because they've got an early day tomorrow at the office? The young priest who despite his stutter engages Griffin in conversation on the bus from time to time, whose observance of his vows of chastity is as much a matter of shyness and circumstance as conviction? One of them might, just might, come to love Griffin given time and opportunity.

Or how about someone like himself? Isn't that what they always say? The secret to a happy relationship is when two people have lots in common? Griffin can't imagine a worse idea than that.

Losing Brock taught him one final lesson that makes all those alternatives impossible. For Griffin, being loved isn't the issue, because, frankly, that's impossible. What he needs, if his life is to have any meaning, is someone to worship. Settling for less than that would be like agreeing to turn his back on Chopin and Liszt and play "Moon River", "Lara's Theme," and "Danny Boy" for the rest of his life.

———

Every night, unless it's blowing a gale or bucketing down rain outside, Scott and Jared descend the stairs from their apartment to the back garden. Griffin listens as they converse too quietly for their words to be intelligible while their terriers frolic and perform their nightly duties. He can easily distinguish Scott's musical tone from Jared's guttural one. Then, while one of them takes the dogs back upstairs, the other fires up the hot tub.

Tonight the weather cooperates.

Griffin listens to the roar of the pump and the multiplicity of gurglings and splooshings and finally begins to feel soothed.

Before long the two men are in the tub together, and now there are other noises. Griffin can only imagine which one is doing what. Or what what is. It doesn't matter, really. They inhabit a parallel universe where amazing men do astonishing things together. Where everyone is beautiful and courageous and friendly and kind and they all get what they deserve. Griffin lives at edge of that world. His world abuts it without actually connecting to it. He can see inside but has no idea how to go there. Or what he'd do there if he ever found his way inside.

The last thing he hears before drifting to sleep is the sound of gods at play.

FOURTH MOVEMENT: *QUASI UN' RONDO*

I

Hot moonlight blazes from a cloudless sky. The trees cast shadows as clearly defined as images on a photographic negative. The hood of the Sting Ray gleams. Brock sits behind the wheel staring at the light in Juliette's bedroom window. This is his last night as a single man and he plans to sit there until that light goes out. They graduated two weeks go. Juliette was salutatorian. She had more stoles and ribbons and medals hanging off her than a five star general attending a tea party in the White House rose garden. Brock managed to squeak into a 2.5 GPA. His father, Big Jim, was not impressed. Anything over 2.0 was wasted effort in his book. Actually, in his book, the last four years had been wasted effort. Brock could have been working in the business and learning the ropes. Big Jim dropped out of college at the end of the football season his senior year and never looked back. All he cared about in college was staying eligible. That was his story. But Juliette is thrilled with Brock's accomplishment, and she's the one he cares about pleasing.

When they get back from their honeymoon, he'll start work at the dealership. He'll sell Buicks, Oldsmobiles and Cadillacs, because, junior in the firm as he is, Papa Charlie, the patriarch of the Van der Jagts, says he's too valuable to have to start out at the Chevrolet-Pontiac-GMC store. That's where non-family members learn the ropes. Brock has been assured that customers all over the county are postponing their automotive purchases in anticipation of his arrival on the showroom floor. If true, this is ridiculous, but he'll gladly accept any commission draws that materialize as a result.

This is what small town notoriety means. Brock was a superstar at Williamstown High, and four winning seasons as starting quarterback of the St. Gregory Cougars have only burnished his reputation among the locals. These accomplishments weren't enough to attract the notice of pro recruiters. The league St. Gregory's played in was too obscure for that. But that doesn't matter to his fellow citizens any more than it does to Brock himself. A football hero is a football hero on whatever scale, and nothing can compare to it. He's their own, home-grown golden boy, and if that means they want to spend their hard earned coin buying flashy cars they don't need from him instead of some other salesman, that's the way America works. Whatever gives you an edge is what you go with.

Working the sales floor will only be temporary. Brock is meant for grander things. He's been groomed for management since birth. Papa Charlie will retire soon. Big Jim will succeed him as captain of the ship. That means Uncle Walter will move up to general manager of the Buick-Oldsmobile-Cadillac store and, through the falling of subsequent dominoes, Brock will become one of the sales managers at Chevrolet-Pontiac-GMC. It's all as predictable, indeed obligatory, as the primogeniture practices of European royalty that Brock found so fascinating when Juliette explained them to him. At the time, that knowledge seemed to legitimize much of his boyhood experience. As the senior Van der Jagt of his generation, Brock will one day rule the entire empire, from motorcycles to farm implements, including its offshoot enterprises dealing with boats, riding lawnmowers, and private aircraft. An empire to be sure, but on the smallest of scales. If it weren't for the heavily wooded stretches of the county, he'd be able to see past the borders of his domain from the gothic revival belfry of Grace Presbyterian.

Late tomorrow afternoon, in the sanctuary there, he'll promise to have and hold the girl just now getting ready for bed behind those curtains glowing across the yard. He can't remember a time when he didn't dream of the day she would become his wife. But it's not really a dream come true. You can't describe something that way when you've planned it as painstakingly as he has his marriage. Men may dream, but heroes plan.

II

Juliette wakes before dawn. The cool breeze coming through the open window is like an invocation. She is wide awake and invigorated. She slept soundly, undisturbed by dreams. And without recourse to the pill her mother offered her. She has heard horror story after horror story from friends, cousins, and various and sundry women of her mother's generation about sleeplessness and jittery misery the night before their weddings. She assumed she would be no different. She expected to toss and turn through the night just like a princess in a children's story. But perhaps she shouldn't be surprised it didn't turn out that way. She invariably travels her own path. There has always been something a little bit off about her. Her mother and sisters recognized it eons ago. So did her friends. Somehow she's not like other girls. Something in her temperament. She's not sure what it is, exactly. Nothing that anyone could label tomboyishness, though she certainly seems to lack a measure of what people refer to as "girlishness". It's just a cerebral, no-nonsense approach to the world around her. It's a reliance on intellect rather than intuition, or perhaps a case of intuition informed by intellectualism. She's never clearly defined it. She couldn't begin to identify its cause. But she sensed long ago that it's somehow the aspect of her personality that Brock prizes most. He seems to believe that only a weak man could value a weak woman as a partner in life. She thanks God daily for not making her like everyone else. She nearly goes out of her mind watching the girls around her stumble through their lives like heavily disguised zombies.

She stares up at the ceiling, savoring these last moments she'll ever spend alone in her old bedroom, this cozy little space that has always seemed to confine rather than shelter her. This monument to feminine kitsch. All her life, she realized recently, she's been looking forward to escaping this room, this house, this family, everything her childhood and adolescence have represented. She was born for something else. She has always known it. She's no longer certain what it is but knows it's out there waiting. Whether she'll actually find it living just a few blocks away with a football hero husband is another question altogether, and one she doesn't allow herself to dwell on.

She feels magnificent this morning. Like she's more powerful than a diesel locomotive and capable of jumping tall buildings in a single bound. Like nothing and no one can stop her. She'd better enjoy it while it lasts. If the last week has been any indication, her morning sickness will kick in in less than an hour. She'll be miserable at least until early afternoon, perhaps longer. She's been hiding out here in her room during these "spells" all week, but today she won't have the luxury. She'll have to pretend to be bright and cheerful for her mother, her sisters, her aunts, Mrs. Godfrey from the beauty shop who will come to do her hair, Mrs. Patterson her mother's dressmaker who will come to put her into the gown. If she pulls it off it will be a performance worthy of an Oscar. She only hopes that the symptoms will clear before she starts the long march up the aisle. Or maybe she doesn't. Maybe a pause halfway up to vomit all over one of Brock's aunts is exactly what she's hoping for.

———

Morning sickness. Dr. Andrews confirmed it last week. What she was suffering from wasn't an intestinal virus, some nervous condition, food poisoning, or any of the causes her mother might have proposed had she been consulted. Juliette wasn't surprised at the news. She knew pretty much the moment it happened that she had conceived. She knew and she was exultant. She's supposed to be guilty and mortified, of course. Unable to look herself in the mirror. Prostrate with shame. But what a silly reaction that would be. Let them all talk about her behind her back. Let them all speculate. Let them count on their fingers like kindergarten children. Let them congratulate themselves on their astuteness when the baby arrives less than eight months after the wedding. Let her mother be mortified and let her mother-in-law breathe fire like the dragon she is. Juliette imagines that particular fury and can't help but smile. She plans to stoke the furnaces of Regina Van der Jagt's ire for the next several decades in every way she can think of. They can all go to hell. Her only allegiance since hearing Dr. Andrews' news is to the child she's carrying and the man who is that child's father.

She hasn't told Brock yet. She hasn't told anyone. Dr. Andrews knows. Mr. Padmore the pharmacist knows because he filled the prescription for pre-natal vitamins. But they're old hands, reliable as stone and down to earth as the Kentucky soil they walk on. They won't talk. She doesn't need to beg or threaten them. It might be different if she were someone else, some other girl less brilliant in the local heavens; if she weren't getting married today. But she is who she is and the whole town is buzzing about the wedding, and she knows she can depend on the discretion of those two pillars of the community. Dr. Andrews told her there's no need to change the honeymoon plans. It's perfectly safe to go to Europe for fifteen days as long as she doesn't take any silly chances. No water skiing, for instance. Easy on the alcohol—which won't matter a bit once she's choked down that single glass of wedding champagne at the reception. And no raw shellfish, as if that's what people go to Paris craving.

She'll tell Brock about his child when they get to Paris.

—

If it were a question of blame, she'd have no one to blame but herself. Football hero that he is, Brock has nevertheless always been a perfect gentleman about sex. Respectful as a Presbyterian bishop, contrary to what she knows everyone thinks he must be like. She knows the people of the town assume that monumental struggles have been required on her part to maintain her prenuptial purity. But the truth of the matter is absolutely contrary to their simple, uninformed belief. She'd be a virgin right this minute if she hadn't thrown herself at her husband to be. Repeatedly, over a period of weeks. He resisted, like the knight in shining armor she knows he fancies himself. But she insisted. It took longer than she expected but she finally wore him down. She doesn't regret it one bit. Why does any girl insist on being a virgin on her wedding night? What girl needs that kind of stress added to everything else she's going through? What possible harm can there be in a test drive? If she'd had any concerns about becoming pregnant, she knows what kind of precautions she could have taken. This is the late twentieth century, yet in this one respect people insist on continuing to live in the sixteenth. She's actually quite proud of herself. Now she can enjoy the wedding. Now the honeymoon doesn't loom mysterious as a fog wreathed iceberg by moonlight. Now they can just get on with their lives.

But boy is her wedding gown going to feel tight.

III

Brock rose early as well. He had things to do, and the wedding meant that his routine had to be accelerated somewhat in order to squeeze it all in. Leaving anything out was unthinkable. It would take more than a mere wedding to justify that kind of lapse in discipline. He chugged down his first protein shake of the morning and then drove the Sting Ray through the silent streets of the town to the Y. It wasn't open that early in the day, but he has a key. He's the local prince. No door is closed to him. He may be getting married later today, but he isn't about to skip his workout.

Three weeks ago, the weekend before graduation, he won the Mr. Kentucky Bodybuilding Championship. It was his third attempt at the title. He hadn't expected the quest to be that prolonged. He couldn't remember ever having to attempt anything three times before succeeding at it. He had planned on winning last year. He gave it his best shot but came in second to a guy from Louisville. He knows people ascribe the loss to certain events that took place not long before the competition, but that's ridiculous. He hadn't been distracted, deflected, depressed. He hadn't lost focus or skimped on his preparations. He simply underestimated the difficulty of the enterprise. He'd have been runner-up to that guy regardless. He knew it the moment he arrived at the weigh-in and saw the monster warming up. Unaccustomed to defeat in any form, he took the setback hard. He knew he had no one to blame but himself, so he redoubled his efforts. Not just at the gym. He was much more careful about diet as well. And most of all, he worked on his mental focus. That was the key. He won't forget the lesson.

He has to decide soon whether or not to enter one of the big regional contests later in the year. By the time Juliette and he get back from France, he has to have his plan in place. Because he's not interested in entering a competition like that only to be an also ran. Those days are through.

IV

Elizaveta Fedorovna rinses out her teacup. At long last everything has been unpacked and put away in her new kitchen and now she's not sure where anything is. That's what happens when you move to a new place after living somewhere for over half a century. The college bought her old cottage. It will be the new home of the Creative Writing program. It's hard to imagine anyone wanting to live in it without doing extensive renovations, and even then everyone seems to want larger residences these days. Not to mention places farther from the campus, which is enjoying unexpected growth and the resulting noise and confusion. When she announced back at Christmas that she'd be retiring at the end of the academic year, the Board of Governors voted to name her Professor Emerita and offer her this apartment on the campus rent free for the remainder of her life. It seemed a ridiculous proposition at first, giving up her beloved home. But on further reflection, she could see the point of it. The cottage's roof needed extensive repairs. The gutters were a constant cause for concern. The plumbing, though effective enough, might give up the ghost at any time. And she didn't even want to think about the condition of the furnace. Why not let someone else worry about all that? Why not take her choice of the apartments they had made available to her and leave behind such considerations forever? She moved in the week after graduation. She already regrets it but supposes she'll get used to the comfort and convenience of her new quarters.

The Board of Governors even went so far as granting her a small stipend to supplement her Social Security, her pension, and her savings. They were more generous than she could have hoped for. They treated her as well as they treated Dean Sunderland badly just months earlier. She can't help feeling embarrassed by it.

———

Last night she listened once again to Griffin's most recent recital tape. Dear Professor Schein sent it to her the morning after the performance. They have spoken by telephone weekly since Griffin became his student, long conversations in French, which they both prefer to English. She considers these consultations a supreme gesture of kindness on Professor Schein's part and attempts to return it in kind. She defers to Professor Schein in all matters, listening to his reports of Griffin's progress and speculations as to Griffin's future, asking a question now and then to clarify a point, offering suggestions only sparingly and only (she's been very careful about this) with regard to extra-musical matters. This is where Professor Schein sometimes seems out of his depth. She has made herself the consultant on the care and feeding of Griffin the young man, never Griffin the musician. Professor Schein gives every indication of appreciating her diplomacy.

The young Frenchman seems to have been just what Griffin needed. The recital tape tells the tale. Griffin, still officially a junior, has shown noticeable development both technically and artistically under his tutelage. He'll be a senior at the conservatory this fall, and Professor Schein assures her that indeed, they are discussing Griffin's prospects and plans for graduate school. There has been, as far as she's concerned, no loss of time resulting from Griffin's misadventure—if it can even be described as such. Time is never wasted in an artist's life as long as the work remains the center of his efforts. It's absurd, really, to speak of an artist's progress in terms of school rankings and degree programs. These are artificial and arbitrary measurements, almost totally irrelevant. An artist continues to progress or an artist is no longer an artist. Griffin has passed that test with flying colors. Although he has done it in a distant place and with the help of this charming stranger, she regards it the crowning achievement of her career. The development of a musician is always a collaboration.

———

Griffin has passed his test, yes. But her former colleagues at St. Gregory's, all but a handful of them, failed their test miserably. Regardless of how Griffin may be flourishing in his new life, the whole matter should have been handled differently. It should never have been a "matter" at all. Griffin is who he is. Everyone ever born has been the person fate decreed, no more, no less. Each and every person in the history of the species—individual and different, as nature has made them. Some are left handed. Some have kinky hair. Some are tall, some are broad. Some are smart, some are good, some are kind, some are greedy. If nature had intended otherwise, nature could have made them identical creatures. And if it had, the race of men would never have left their homes in the trees. Or caves or wherever. As Madame sees it, their differences from one another are the prime engine of all human progress.

But this one difference is, for some incomprehensible reason, anathema. People's irrationality over it calls the whole notion of civilization into question as far as she's concerned. The reality, as she knows it, is this. Tchaikovsky was that way. So was his brother, Modest. Nabokov's brother as well. There were dozens of them in St. Petersburg when she was a girl. Their number had probably included her own brother, Kostya. Her parents were certainly of that opinion, speaking of it quite frankly in front of her sister Nadezhda and her. Then there are all those English ones she has read about. Carpenter, Wilde, Forster, Isherwood. And the French. Proust, Saint-Saens, Poulenc. Not to mention countless others. In every nation, in every race, and, as far as she knows, in every period of history, men who loved other men. Yet despite what the people of her adopted country insist about it, civilization has continued to advance, often with the help of the very men they demonize. The race has continued to multiply. Any contention that such men are the vanguard of doom and decay is on its face absurd.

They should have left the boy alone to develop as he must. And they should have left his poor godfather alone as well. She lives for the day they realize their mistake, but she knows all too well she may not see its dawn.

V

By the time Brock has returned from the gym, downed another protein shake, and thrown a load of workout clothes into the washing machine, the sun has risen high enough in the sky that he can lie out in the back yard for a while. It's far too early in the day for prime tanning conditions but he's in maintenance phase right now, just keeping the base dark enough that he won't look like a ghost by the time he gets back from France. He shaved his body last night before going to bed. He's satiny smooth. He won't be stubbly on his wedding night. When he practiced his posing in front of the full length mirrors at the gym this morning, he looked like a gleaming statue. He only does this when he has the place to himself. He knows he's close to the boundary of what his fellow citizens consider acceptable behavior, knows he runs the risk of being considered a narcissist or worse if he's not careful about how he displays himself.

Juliette considers the shaving component of his regimen unspeakably bizarre. How can he voluntarily shave all but a few square inches of himself every few days when she can barely bring herself to shave her legs once a week? She complains about it regularly, seeing in it the most sinister evidence of the double standard between the sexes. He's assured her she doesn't need to continue shaving her legs to please him, but it's a habit she won't consider breaking, as if doing so would constitute an inexcusable breach of the social contract. What would her mother and sisters say? Not to mention the rest of the townsfolk? He hasn't even been able to budge her by speaking of his mother's certain reaction, and more and more that's becoming his trump card. He hasn't been able so far to convince her that the two of them are different from everyone else in their situation. That whatever they decide to do is all right simply because of who they are.

He's found a new product he likes much better than his tanning oil of old. He anoints himself liberally, adjusts his position in accordance with the angle of the light, and reclines on the beach towel spread out on the green velvet of the lawn he mowed yesterday afternoon.

VI

Regina Van der Jagt always felt sorry for Marguerite Colfax Simpson. Literally always. Since before grade school: the girls' families had known each other for generations. Regina and Marguerite were friendly, and sometimes not so friendly, rivals all those years. They were always neck and neck if not actually tooth and nail. There was very little between them in terms of looks, charm, or popularity, though Marguerite always held the higher GPA. But there was just enough of an edge that everyone recognized Regina's pre-eminence. There really was no disput-ing it. Co-captains of the cheerleading squad, sure. But she was the one who always dated the first string quarterback leaving Marguerite to choose among everyone else. And whatever club you mentioned, Regina was always the president while Marguerite was the vice president or sometimes only the secretary. Regina was always the pageant winner, never the runner up. It was in her name, God damn it—Regina. Queen. It was who she was. Marguerite always bore the grave misfortune of second rateness with grace and dignity and that dry sense of humor people seemed to set such store by, but Regina suspected, not to say actually hoped, that there were tears on Marguerite's pillow over it. As would only be proper. There can only be one queen in any generation, and it was only fitting for everyone else to mourn their disappointed aspirations. In Marguerite's instance, the closer one came to grasping the crown, the bitterer the disappointment must be. It was like the law of gravity, really. It wouldn't have surprised Regina in the least to learn that Marguerite dreamed about and perhaps even plotted her demise. Indeed, she'd have been disappointed, not to mention thunderstruck, if she had learned this wasn't the case. To crown it all, Regina had been the first to marry, and had married more successfully than Marguerite. Certainly, Jeffrey Simpson, Marguerite's husband, was from one of the best local families, had been handsome and charming as a young man and was now becoming quite distinguished. And it increasingly looked like he'd be a shoe-in for County Attorney if and when old Dickie Tilford gave up the office or the ghost, whichever came first. But Jeffrey Simpson, for all his good looks and lovely manners and professional prestige, had never been and still was no Van der Jagt. And in Grant County, a girl who didn't manage to marry a Van der Jagt was settling for second best. That's all there was to it.

Except, it seemed, it wasn't. The rules had changed when Regina wasn't looking. She couldn't believe she missed it.

Regina finally had to admit defeat. James David, aka Big Jim, had given her all those sons. All those handsome, athletic, charismatic sons. Spectacular boys by any reckoning, and she had thought, well, here I am, still and forever on top of the heap. Nobody can match this. Not in my generation at least. She lived happily in her illusion from the day of Brock's birth until this very morning. Every touchdown scored, every merit badge earned, every accolade amassed by every one of her regiment of sons had accrued to her own greater glory. The mother of athletes among athletes, the mother of heroes among heroes, the mother of the boys every girl in the county set her cap at or at the very least dreamed of. Motherhood as apotheosis had been her hallmark. It literally made her a legend. But then, sitting at the kitchen table and sipping the tea that Mrs. Murchison had finally figured out how to brew to her satisfaction, Regina realized she couldn't maintain her illusion any longer. She might convince others but she could no longer convince herself, and the buttery flakes of warm from the oven sticky bun suddenly began to taste like ashes in her mouth. Eight magnificent sons but no daughter. She'd always considered those boys the brightest jewels in her crown. But what it meant, really, was that she would never, ever, be the mother of the bride. All those weddings to look forward to, or, as she had now come to understand it, dread, and there she'd be, forever relegated to the background. It was worse than being, as her sister Olympia had been in their youth, a perpetual bridesmaid. This afternoon Regina will be all but a non-entity. Marguerite Simpson will be the real queen and Regina will be, well, an aging Cinderella who missed out on that fateful encounter with her fairy godmother.

Marguerite Colfax Simpson, of all people. Upstaging Regina with those three daughters of hers.

Regina will have to put her foot down. It's too late to do anything about Brock, of course. But she won't lose another son of hers to one of Marguerite's daughters. That can't be allowed to happen.

VII

Brock has been sleeping in the guest room since he moved into the house. He's keeping the master bedroom brand new and immaculate for their return from France, though he has moved his clothes from his parents' house into the smaller of the two closets. He dusts the room daily. His mother's maid, Roberta Murchison, won't have much to do when she comes to touch it up just before they get home.

Brock's parents gave them the down payment on the house as a wedding present. Juliette's Uncle Warren Colfax arranged for the mortgage at very advantageous terms. It's more house than newlyweds really need. He knows the size of the place embarrasses his bride to be, but appearances have to be preserved. A Van der Jagt can't just go live in a chicken coop. He's heard that over and over again. And he can't possibly bring Juliette to live in a house smaller than he knows his brother, Thatcher, is shopping for for his own fiancée. Thatcher is actually a little ahead of Brock on his assigned trajectory due to having dropped out of community college and gone to work. This has occasioned more than a little consternation on the part of Grandmother Van der Jagt. It's apparently a matter of family honor that Brock can't allow himself to be upstaged, even by his own brother. Particularly since

Thatcher's fiancée is widely considered to be no more than half a step up from White Trash. He could hardly do worse if he married a "colored" girl, by which Grannie really means someone of Italian or Portuguese extraction.

Brock wonders if he can ever free himself from the insane prejudices of his family without having to emigrate.

He stands dripping gently onto the hardwood flooring fresh from his swim after the tanning session. He gazes into the pristine room. He's already arranged for flowers to be delivered the day before they get back. He's already instructed Mrs. Murchison as to how they're to be displayed.

VIII

Malcolm Sunderland really didn't expect to be invited to the wedding. Juliette and Brock would want him there, he understood, but he couldn't imagine their parents agreeing to it. The scandal was still too fresh. And the particulars of it had made him a marked man. So when the invitation unexpectedly arrived, he chalked it up to youthful optimism or obliviousness and RSVP'd immediately in the negative. He was sorry, but he wouldn't be able to attend. Then he put it out of his mind.

Malcolm didn't dwell on the discussions which must have taken place. He didn't like to think about what must have been said. Imagining it was excruciating. All he knew was that someone had refused to take no for an answer. And somehow Madame Grammatikova was deputized to ensure his attendance. Someone knew that of all the people in the universe it was Madame he wouldn't be able to say no to. Someone knew him that well.

He examines himself in the mirror. Or, more specifically, he examines his new haircut in the mirror. A rather severe crew cut, it makes him look like photographs of Sergei Rachmaninoff in middle age. He wonders if Madame will notice and remark on the resemblance. She knew Rachmaninoff back in Russia. She visited him in California after he immigrated. He wonders if it's truly the new haircut or if the resemblance has always been there and she's never mentioned it. Or he could just as easily be imagining the whole thing.

Malcolm has always doubted his perceptions, but it's been worse than ever this last year.

There was a price to pay for saving his godson, and he paid it. He paid it with the loss of his position at St. Gregory's. He hadn't been fired. There hadn't been anything specific to fire him for. They'd known it and he'd known it. Still, protecting a homosexual student from college discipline, even if the duplicity involved remained unproven and even though the individual concerned was incidentally his own godson, was too much for the board of governors to put up with. The situation was untenable. He had to go. Even so, he had to grant that they'd gone about it like gentlemen. There were no confrontations. On the surface he was treated as cordially as always. He wasn't even encouraged to resign. He was simply made vaguely uncomfortable. He knew how it all worked, and that was enough. He knew that the light touch they were applying was because they trusted him to do the right thing, particularly after that one terrible error, so he did what was expected of him. The president of the college had the good grace to act surprised and saddened at his resignation, and prior to his departure at the end of that term there had even been a chapel service paying tribute to his decades of service to the school. But he isn't stupid. They were happy to see the last of him. Happy and relieved. He'd never be able to embarrass them again. They always had their suspicions about him, but helping Griffin as he had—they couldn't pretend to ignore it after that. And suddenly there he was, a fifty-five year old homosexual without prospects. There was no question of staying on in the town. It would never be over, and he needed the place and everything about it behind him. He sold the house to the wife of the college president, who wanted it as a headquarters and showroom for her business selling antiques. He was shocked at the price she offered. It paid for his new place in Lexington, small, modern, convenient. It has no character, but it has no drafts. He's old enough to consider that a fair exchange.

At church one Sunday a few weeks after he moved to Lexington, someone called his name. He turned to look and there was Newell Throckmorton, an old friend from graduate school and, as it turned out, newly installed vice president of something or other at the university. They went to lunch after the service, and before the coffee and dessert had been cleared, Malcolm had an interview scheduled with the head of the history department. He spent last year as an adjunct lecturer. For this fall, he's been advanced to Assistant Professor. He might even manage to get tenure before time to retire. His dusty, cobweb festooned Ph.D. out of retirement, he still can't believe his luck.

He hasn't told Griffin the real story. Just about the new job, the new house, his exciting new life. Someday perhaps, when he's sure Griffin's emotionally strong enough not to be devastated by knowledge of the causes behind those effects, he'll tell all.

He finishes adjusting the bow tie. He can't stand here forever messing with his clothing. It's a good forty-five minute drive over to St. Gregory's to pick up Madame and then a similar distance on to Williamstown for the wedding.

IX

Brock surveys himself in the mirror. He had his hair cut three days ago so it wouldn't look too freshly trimmed this afternoon. He had his tuxedo custom tailored in Lexington. A rented one couldn't possibly have fit him well enough. He has taken similar care with each aspect of his appearance. And the result is this perfection grinning back at him. He has never looked better. His picture could go in the dictionary to illustrate the definition of "groom". Yet despite his transformation into a Platonic ideal, his efforts are ultimately meaningless. Weddings are about the bride. The groom is basically an accessory. It has always been that way and Brock assumes it always will be. Nevertheless, he insists on looking his best. He has been to enough weddings of exquisitely beautiful brides to awkward, doofusy grooms with questionable haircuts and ill fitting tuxes to know that no man in that position is ever truly invisible. He won't do that to Juliette and he won't do it to himself. It's a question of respect. It's about the photographs his children will look at someday. It's about knowing he did everything he could. There was no length he wouldn't go to to make the day perfect for the woman he plans to spend the rest of his life with. No matter what happens, he'll always know what he did for her.

More than his father did for his mother. More than he can imagine either of his grandfathers having done for their brides. More, really, than any man he knows of personally.

It's a message to all of them. This is how you marry a woman.

X

Olympia Morgan DeFrancesco—she always insists on this billing, though she's been a widow for over twenty years—takes her place just off the bow of the piano. For a generation now she has been wowing local audiences with her coloratura pyrotechnics, but weddings, some of her most frequent appearances as a performer, substantially inhibit her amplitude. They require a level of decorum which limits her inspiration. She has to consciously tone herself down. And the repertoire generally lacks imagination. Juliette turned up her nose at traditional wedding numbers like "Because" and "O Promise Me," opting instead for just one vocal selection, a plain little aria from the second notebook for Anna Magdalena Bach, "*Bist du bei mir*". Olympia can't imagine anyone in the audience will ever have heard of it. And since she's singing it in German, they won't understand a word of the lyrics. A translation of the text appears in the program, but who'll bother to read it? And if they do read it as they listen they'll be distracted from her performance. They'll miss the nuances she finds in the work. Her artistry will be lost to them. It's maddening. It's pointless. The diva inside her wants to rip off her clothing and burn down the building. But it's not her wedding, so she can't complain. At least not out loud. The aria itself is simple, lovely, and unaffected. Tasteful in the extreme, not that anyone here will know or care about that. But Olympia considers it crashingly anticlimactic for a wedding such as this one, which by all rights should be positively Wagnerian. The groom, her nephew Siegfried—er, Brock—is downright incandescent this afternoon. He looks like he's about to ready to step into a phone booth (she knows she's mixing her metaphors, but her nephew embodies them all, somehow), shed that tuxedo, and reappear a moment later authentic and swaggering, smiling and pugnacious, bent on rape and pillage, not bucolic village nuptials.

Olympia remembers "*Bist du bei mir*" from her days as a voice major. Her teacher assigned it to her freshman year. She performed it during first semester juries and then promptly dropped it from her repertoire, intent as she was on her quest to become the Soprano of the Western World. "*Bist du bei mir*", for all its eloquent sincerity, was insufficiently histrionic to inspire a girl who considered Callas inexcusably demure and subdued and Tebaldi downright soporific. Yes, she dropped it from her repertoire and never looked back. She required Puccini. Or Verdi at least. She needed *verismo* like fish need water. She was already on her way to becoming a legend—that crazy freshman girl who considered herself halfway to superstardom already. Olympia met her match later that year in the form of Dino DeFrancesco, Adonis-cum-wide receiver, who won her over with his improbably shiny hair, ridiculous shoulders, vocabulary consisting of monosyllables and grunts, and a sneer that would have done justice to any one of the bad boys populating the Italian operas she was addicted to. She had always dreamed of a man capable of bruising her heart if not actually breaking it, who could scorch her with a glance;

who could, in short, make her cry "uncle", and here he was. The unmistakably Italian surname was a bonus, as were the eyes he undressed her with every day in psych 101 until she finally quit playing hard to get and answered him when he said hi. To top it off, she found her older sister Regina's horrified disapproval of everything about Dino powerfully aphrodisiac.

Olympia barely managed to graduate from college. Dino didn't get a degree at all, just bigger muscles. They eloped, running off to Los Angeles, where Dino expected his looks and physique to bring him instant fame and glory. The sex never stopped being cataclysmic, but the rest of the time she swung back and forth between boredom and misery. Suffering turned out not to be as picturesque as she'd expected. It didn't inspire her to greater feats of artistry. It didn't inspire her at all. Perhaps it simply didn't read in the shadow of palm trees. In any case it got old. She was on the point of filing for divorce when Dino crashed his Pontiac on the Hollywood Freeway one night with fatal consequences to himself and the three starlets accompanying him. The presence in the scene of the starlets didn't surprise Olympia. She knew Dino was incapable of keeping his cock put away. It was how she had initially stolen him from his fiancée and two other simultaneous girlfriends. The shocker was the check she got in the mail. Olympia didn't know Dino even had life insurance. It seemed totally out of character. But the tragedy and its unexpected payoff meant she didn't have to sneak home to Kentucky with her tail between her legs. She wasn't the girl done wrong. She was the glamorous young widow with a gleam in her eye.

The money didn't make her rich. But it was enough that she could buy the old Teegarden place and set herself up breeding Newfoundlands. With their huge size and shaggy coats, they didn't seem particularly suited to the Kentucky climate. This apparently made them obligatory fashion accessories among a certain young set in the Bluegrass Region, and Olympia's business took off like a rocket, or Dino's flame decorated Pontiac, eventually propelling her to repeated Bests in Breed at Westminster.

And in the process making her the eccentric of the county.

There never was another man. Every time she felt the urge, a quick survey of the local talent dissuaded her. No one in that whole part of Kentucky was man enough to make her feel the way Dino had. Essentially he'd been a pig, but a transcendently attractive one who had known instinctively how to make her feel like a woman. Certain of Regina's in-laws might have given him a run for the money in that regard, but Olympia didn't dare give her sister the satisfaction. And anyway, better no love life at all than a mediocre one. As in opera, so in life.

It hardly signifies. Her first love will always be music, just as her nemesis will always be her sister Regina. She has spent her entire life refusing to let Regina get the better of her. Let Regina swan around like some fancy pants French duchess lording it over the whole Commonwealth just because she managed to marry into the Van der Jagts, that ridiculous tribe of testosterone inflated egos just one half step up the evolutionary ladder from the apes. What a gang of meatheads. Though Olympia does have to admit she approves of Brock unreservedly. He somehow escaped the worst of the family traits and comes close to redeeming the whole loud, obnoxious bunch with their incomprehensible tastes and neanderthal opinions. Regina may receive a brand new Cadillac convertible every fall when the model year changes, she may have a matched pair of prize Arabians stabled out back of that barn of a house she inhabits with that pack of wolves she gave birth to, she may spend every January in Curacao and every July in Maine. But the single most important fact about Regina is that she couldn't carry a tune in a washtub. She's absolutely tone deaf and she doesn't know Frederic Chopin from Charlie Chaplin.

In contrast, Olympia still has her glorious voice, most of her figure, a remarkably close approximation of her girlhood hair color, her faithful dogs, and her new best friend. Though to be accurate about it, Juliette Simpson-about-to-be-Van der Jagt doesn't yet know she's been cast in that role. This is because the selection has only now been made. Olympia knows a pregnant female when she sees one, so Juliette's about to need an ally against her mother-in-law. And who better than dear, charming Auntie Olympia, who knows where every single one of Regina's bodies is buried?

She gives a slight nod, and the girl at the keyboard begins to play. Stephanie somebody or other, a friend of Juliette's from college. Surprisingly pleasant to work with. Surprisingly adequate from a musical standpoint. Most of Olympia's accompanists are either duds technically or think the performance is about them, not her. She takes a breath and lifts her serene gaze toward the great rose window at the rear of the sanctuary.

XI

The trumpeters play a final flourish and the organ swells to engulf their silvery notes, segueing artfully into the triumphal theme which announces that Brock's bride is approaching. Juliette and her father appear at the end of the long aisle. Brock straightens his back, squares his chin, and stares in her direction as if willing her to his side. She seems to move without effort, as if floating just an inch or two above the surface of the sanctuary floor. She is a princess. A sublime vision. She glows. She sparkles. She is the supreme prize, the ultimate symbol representing this, his current apotheosis. She comes to him propelled by all the celestial magnetism of the universe. He feels her eyes on him from behind the folds of her veil. He feels her adoration radiating toward him in waves. He welcomes and absorbs it, sending out his own in answer. In the blink of an eye that is also an eon she is standing before him, her father grinning genially as he places her hand in Brock's and the music reaches its crescendo.

XII

The last time O.B. Simpson had seen his great-niece she was being christened. He only came to her wedding because his sister, her great-aunt Portia, lied to him. She was deathly ill, Portia said in her letter, and would like to see him one last time before she died. He arrived in Williamstown to find her healthy as one of his Charolais yearlings, spry and full of piss and vinegar. She refused to apologize for her deceit. She laughed at him when he complained about it, so he laughed, too. What else was there to do? She was the last of his siblings living, and if any of them had a right to expect anything from him, he guessed it would be her. She'd always been the least objectionable of the bunch.

It was more pleasant than he would have imagined seeing all these unfamiliar relatives. The ceremony, as much as he silently decried it, was lovely in its primitive, almost barbaric way. The reception was worth attending for its anthropological implications alone. He could hardly wait to write about it in his journal. Everyone he had encountered since his arrival was as charming as could be to this near stranger who was as close as the Simpson tribe came to a living, breathing patriarch. His nephew Jeffrey had matured into handsome prosperity. He had no idea what the cost of that had been to Jeffrey's integrity, but that was none of his business. Jeffrey's career as an attorney was sufficient testimony in that regard, he believed. O.B. considered the laws of mankind to be comprehensively obscene and the men who administered them the worst of soundrels, but Jeffrey was amiable enough. His father, O.B.'s brother P.P., had been a mean son of a bitch, and O.B. had never had much faith in Jeffrey's resilience. He'd apparently been wrong on that score. Middle aged Jeffrey didn't seem to have any trouble meeting his gaze. That hadn't always been the case. All in all, his one disappointment with Jeffrey, though one could hardly deem it Jeffrey's fault, was that Jeffrey had no sons. The girls were charming, smart, and beautiful, but they were girls. After he and Jeffrey passed on there would be still be Simpsons in the world, but none of them would be related to O.B. that he knew of. Served him right after all these years of ignoring his family to witness the end of the line looming. Served him right never to have had children of his own. Particularly after L.M. died in that plane crash still a single man. Their own father and his father before him had been only sons. And then there had been Jeffrey's older brothers, dead in the Second War. Nature must have found something wanting in their branch of the Simpsons to allow them to be cut off so totally in just a few generations.

Kentucky was greener than O.B. remembered it. He supposed that decades living in the desert had altered his perceptions beyond any possible remedy. After all that time, mesquite, manzanita, and ocotillo denoted normality. All this flourishing greenery threatened to suffocate him. It was more than his eyes could bear, like unpleasantly bright sunshine. Kentucky was greener and the people whiter than he remembered. Whiter, but less argumentative, apparently. They were unnervingly polite. They seemed quite determined about avoiding any appearance of conflict. His final argument with his older brother P.P. had been the day before he shipped out for France. He had known, as P.P. snarled out his full name, Osric Benvolio, at him, that he wouldn't return any time soon. "Fuck you, Prospero Puck," he yelled back, as angry at his mother's obsession with characters from Shakespeare as he was at his brother. It made fighting like men impossible. He thought about that every day while he was in France.

In 1919, ranch land in Southern Arizona was selling for pennies per acre. O.B. took his army savings and bought a place. He invested heavily in the best breeding stock. By the sweat of his brow and the toil of his brain he made himself a successful rancher. Ranching wasn't an obvious choice for a man who didn't eat red meat. But it had become necessary due to his peculiar vision. Cattle, he had come to believe, were creatures of enormous innate nobility whose unfortunate position as a source of protein for human consumption ruled their evolution to the expense of any other potential they might possess. He dreamed of finding a way to reacquaint them with their original perfection as nature had created them. The land he bought on the banks of the capricious, mercurial San Pedro River was the only place he felt at home. The people he employed there, Mexicans one and all, became his family. Over his decades on the land, he went years at a time without traveling to town, entering a building he didn't own, encountering an Anglo face or hearing any English spoken but a broken and heavily accented variety, and he found that he preferred things that way. His minions dealt with the world outside the boundaries of his property and did an admirable job of it. While they were minding his business for him, he rode the fence rows from morning until nightfall on a succession of bay colored quarter horses, accompanied by generation after generation of tailless sheep dogs, and kept his own counsel. Mostly he thought about the improvement of his herds. The Mexican women raised chickens and turkeys for his meat. They kept extensive vegetable gardens. And their husbands tended the fruit orchards he planted. With the help of those same Mexican laborers he excavated ponds where he raised catfish as a supplement to the poultry. For dairy goods, he kept a herd of goats. The Mexican women milked them. They figured out how to make butter and cheeses from this unlikely source. He kept this herd in balance by selling off individuals to the Serbs and Croats who worked in the copper mines of Bisbee, twenty or so miles away, who were great fanciers of the meat.

His plans for cattle didn't include raising animals for slaughter. His plan was to utilize the principles of selective breeding to create a race of super cattle that he would sell to the world as breeding stock. Only individuals inferior to breeding requirements were to be killed for meat, and only his workers would consume it. In this way, his cattle would eventually ennoble the entire species. It might have proven to be a fool's errand, but the devastation resulting from the Second War left the much of the world bereft of its herds. The health of what remained was questionable. Meanwhile, through showing his cattle at strategically chosen livestock exhibitions, O.B. gained a reputation as a kind of wizard at raising huge, majestic cattle of tractable temperament, robust health, and great climate tolerance. In the aftermath of the conflagration, the world beat a path to his door. The Russians came to observe his practices. The Argentines followed in their tracks. The Europeans and Japanese purchased breeding stock from him. The Canadians as well. Eventually, he was a prophet who lacked honor only in his own country. He believed that the Texans conspired against him. They couldn't beat him by breeding better cattle, so they manufactured a political dispute and convinced themselves they'd gotten the better of him. But politics was beside the point. The Germans had taken eugenics and made it political with their idiotic racial policies. The Stalinists had declared war on the whole science of biology with their inexcusably stupid but politically expedient Lysenkoism. History chronicled the errors of both groups. But O.B. knew better. Nobody ever prevailed in a scientific dispute by ignoring objective reality. What mattered in this instance was genetics. All that mattered was genetics. What he did with his cattle was a form of applied genetics, taking carefully selected individuals and breeding them to one another generation after generation until the species was altered for the better. It was about working with individuals based on objective criteria, nothing else. Politics would never trump science. It might co-opt science for its own purposes, but such arrangements never lasted because scientific principles meant certain outcomes were inevitable and others were impossible however much the politicians might decry or attempt to evade facts. So the Texans would get their comeuppance sooner or later and O.B. would be vindicated among his countrymen. That was inevitable. While they yet blustered and pontificated, his small, painstakingly bred and meticulously maintained herds made him rich. Not that money meant anything to him beyond the validation it represented. He couldn't imagine what he might spend it on that would make his contentment more perfect than it already was.

Meanwhile, his family back in Kentucky left him alone, and he returned the favor. Beyond the people he employed, the horses he rode, and the dogs who were his constant companions, he recognized only his cattle as his kindred. They were as they were because he had created them that way. In a very real way, he considered himself their father.

Now, decades later save for that one visit home to greet the arrival of the first of her generation of Simpsons, this homecoming. The absurdity of the scenes O.B. found himself participating in was almost more than he could apprehend. All these pale skinned people jabbering incomprehensibly at him as if he could understand not only their speech but everything about them. Their strange habits and bizarre preoccupations. Their cryptic customs. Their unfathomable beliefs. It was like being transported to an alien planet like the man in those novels by Edgar Rice Burroughs that were his preferred reading. None of what his kinfolk said made any sense to him. Worst of all was the wedding itself. It implied a set of assumptions about the world that he simply couldn't imagine any sane individual accepting. They prayed to their God, but their faith seemed ill chosen. Their holy book portrayed Him as the "Good Shepherd", but looking around O.B. saw nothing admirable in that purported deity's husbandry of his flocks.

That young man of Juliette's: O.B. knew the finest breeding stock when he saw it. With his handsome looks and magnificent physique, his true purpose should have been obvious to anyone setting eyes on him. Yet, with the possible exception of that aunt of the groom who was a breeder of prize Newfoundland dogs, these people considered it appropriate for him to be married off for life to a girl like Juliette and father no more than a handful of children when untold good could be done for the species by ensuring that he father as many children as possible by as many prime females as could be supplied to him. He truly was a remarkable specimen. One in a million. A race of men fathered by a creature like that could change the world. Fifteen years from now, when his fertility began to flag, there would be plenty of time for marriage. He'd still be a young enough man, a desirable husband, a pillar of domesticity if that's what the community thought they wanted from him. Until then, let him make his most valuable contribution. But instead, his potential was being almost completely ignored and thus wasted. It was downright criminal. A deity who truly intended the best for the human race wouldn't tolerate it, would always have had selective breeding top and center on his agenda.

O.B. couldn't wait to get back to the ranch. There, everything made sense.

XIII

Brock lies awake, pleasantly satiated. Beside him, Juliette snores softly. That snore is one of the things he loves most about her, but he's not sure he'll ever tell her that. He's afraid she'd either deny that she snores, be angry with him for mentioning it, or be hurt and embarrassed that he's aware of the habit. Any of those prospects would be enough to make him hold his tongue. But the real reason he'll keep the secret is because it's something delicate and special close to his heart. A minor imperfection against which her more sublime qualities shine even brighter, making it in his mind a profound treasure.

His body feels like it would after a workout, after the big game. It is a comfortable, familiar sensation. It is the way his body would like to feel always, alive but profoundly relaxed. Only when he achieves this physical state can he allow his brain to go off duty. But before he drifts away tonight after a day filled with incident and impression there is one last matter to ponder. He has left it until now in order to address it undistracted, unhurried by the day's hectic timetable. It deserves the singlemindedness he can only now give it. Now that he's reached this finish line of sorts, there's nothing more to keep him from looking back, on thinking through the whole thing one last time before moving into his new life. All those months since Griffin left. All those months leading to this day, this night, this moment lying next to his bride.

People—everybody he knows with the possible exception of Juliette, that is— have blamed his funk of the past fourteen months on Griffin's betrayal. Unspeakably vile little Griffin, concealing his true nature, exploiting Brock's friendship and good faith, taking advantage of him in the most sickening manner possible. Thinking God only knew what perverted thoughts as someone of that kind would have to living in such close proximity to a young man of Brock's qualities. What could be more intimate, really, than two young men living in that isolated dormitory room up under the eaves of the building? What an opportunity for voyeurism, unspeakable imaginings, concealed lust. Culminating in Griffin's unmasking. The stories which circulated on the campus afterward were full of sensational detail and gruesome innuendo. Brock ignored as much as he could of what he overheard. The story Malcolm Sunderland told wasn't titillating in the least, merely sad, and it was the version Brock chose to believe. But he was apparently alone in that. The collective imagination had been inflamed. The murmurings were sickening. And his reaction to the events was interpreted in the light of what everyone on campus thought they knew. What clean living young athlete wouldn't be angry, wouldn't feel humiliated and dishonored, by his unwitting association with such a creature as that? Only Brock understands that this isn't the case. He doesn't feel betrayed by Griffin. He is not shamed by their friendship all those years. He isn't shocked and repulsed by the revelation. That is not the reason for his moodiness.

———

His initial reaction to the fiasco was two fold. First had been an urge to chase Griffin down. To stop him in his flight and bring him home where he belonged. It had been all Dean Sunderland could do to stop him. He's still not sure the Dean actually did or whether the deciding factor was that silent glance of warning from Madame Grammatikova. Brock might have continued to argue with Dean Sunderland, might simply have ignored him and followed his impulse, but there was no arguing with her. From long observation Brock knew her as formidable but never understood the extent of her power. It was the first time in his life that he had been forced to acknowledge a will as strong as his own.

Behind that impulse—or reflex to use a better word—for pursuit and rescue was a perception he never would have expected but nevertheless embraced wholeheartedly and instantaneously the moment it made itself apparent to him. He hadn't given much thought to homosexuals in the past. He knew they existed of course, but mythologically rather than pragmatically. What little he knew about them was received wisdom only, the rumors all young men heard as they grew up, which were the most conventional and unpleasant sort of lore. In less than a heartbeat, all that had to change. Brock could no longer entertain the concept as he had previously once it attached itself to his friend. From that moment any consideration of the phenomenon could only take place within the context of his deep affection for Griffin, a feeling almost as passionate, he readily admitted to himself, as his feelings for Juliette. Another young man in his situation might have found this confusing, perhaps even to the extent that it induced some unpredictable psychological state. But confusion was not a condition Brock ever accepted in himself. Other people might be confused, but Brock was always clear-headed and certain. He took extreme pride in it. So this could be figured out. He only had to keep a cool head, which of course was his specialty, and give it time and calm consideration. As he saw it, either he had misjudged Griffin all these years, which hardly seemed possible, or everything he, and by extension everyone around him, knew about homosexuals was wrong. It was time to investigate.

———

The task was surprisingly difficult. There was almost nothing helpful in the college library. What little relevant material Brock found listed in the card catalogue wasn't shelved in the stacks. It was kept in the special collection, and to access any of it he'd have to fill out a request slip, present it at the circulation counter, wait for the items to be located and brought out to him, read them immediately in the special reading room and then return them to the counter before he left the building. It would be as conspicuous an endeavor as detonating a bomb in Founder's Quad. By breakfast time the next day the whole campus would know what he was researching. He couldn't go through with it. Not because he was afraid of the consequences, but because it wouldn't accomplish anything but to further stir things up.

———

Brock had to wait for the semester to end for an opportunity to make a trip by himself into Lexington. He chafed at the delay, and his impatience reinforced his classmates' impression of his mood. Meanwhile, he came across, almost by accident though he thought of it as fate, a copy of a book by a man named Kinsey. He recognized the name. Juliette had read the book, or perhaps another one by the same author, for one of her psychology classes. He pored over it at every opportunity. In the book, he read that nearly forty per cent of American men had had at least one sexual experience with another man.

———

It wasn't the number itself that stopped Brock in his tracks, though that was certainly eye opening. It was the reference to experiences. Statistics were statistics: comfortable abstractions. Yet abstract as they were, they had practical implications. For instance, if forty per cent of American men had such experiences at some point in their lives, how abnormal could those experiences be? Really? And if such activities truly were that common, then at least some of the people speaking so disapprovingly of Griffin must have had such experiences themselves. Some of the uproar Brock was hearing on the subject could only be hypocrisy. He couldn't help but be heartened by that. It was a kind of vindication. But at the same time, he found thinking about it troubling. Because regardless of how common they might be, experiences in this instance could only be understood as actual people doing actual things. He'd been thinking of homosexuals as men who possessed certain qualities. Which was true as far as it went. But it was only part of the story. What he'd been ignoring in all that contemplation of numbers was the fact that possessing those qualities implied an interest in certain acts.

———

Brock understood, roughly at least, what those acts were. They weren't especially difficult to imagine. But he certainly had never considered the possibility of someone he knew doing anything like that. Now he had to acknowledge the connections linking all those dots. It was no longer as simple a matter as Griffin possessing certain characteristics, unusual as they might be. Once he had made that connection, Brock couldn't keep himself from imagining Griffin doing such things. But there was one reality that made this particularly difficult to deal with. The acts in question didn't take place in solitude. They required the participation of at least one other person. That's where he found himself on shaky ground.

———

As the initial sensation caused by the events abated, Brock's focus shifted from what he had felt to what he was supposed to have done. How could he not have known Griffin's secret? That's what everybody on the campus was wondering. He should have been able to tell, either instinctively, as they all claimed they had, or at the very least through prolonged proximity and observation. In all that time as Griffin's roommate, in all the years back home even before coming to college, shouldn't he have been aware of the signs? Shouldn't their long association and deep friendship have precipitated some tearful dorm room confession? It strained the credibility of Brock's classmates and professors to the breaking point that he claimed to be completely surprised at the revelation. They had known. Why hadn't he? Oblivious Brock, with his girlfriend and buddy—how could he possibly have had no inkling? Nobody could have been that dense. Of course it was easy for onlookers to make that kind of criticism. It was completely different when you were in the situation yourself, as others presumably had been or still were whether they acknowledged it or not. Brock believed this complaint against him was at least partially hypocritial. But it also contained a grain of truth. He had to admit it to himself. How good a friend had he truly been to Griffin if he'd been so insensitive?

But ignorance was just the beginning of his failure. That ignorance had resulted in a failure to act. He should have known about Griffin and he should have done something. His classmates thought he should have hustled Griffin off to the college chaplain for prayer and counseling. Who knew? Perhaps it was even a case for exorcism, though Presbyterians didn't generally go in for that kind of thing. He should have consulted the psychologist on staff at the student health center. He should have teamed up with Dean Sunderland to make sure Griffin saw a psychiatrist. There were all kinds of things he could have and should have done. Because Griffin could have been helped, could have been deflected from his self destructive path, could have been saved and cured of his unholy affliction. Homosexuality was a character flaw just like alcoholism or drug addition, though undoubtedly far worse than either of those. Will power and the support and encouragement of close friends, along with prayer and diligent study of the scriptures, would surely have been sufficient to lead Griffin back to safety and purity out of that almost unspeakable abyss. And given all that, Brock's most crucial failure had been that of not using his enormous influence over Griffin to convince him that his deliverance was possible. Now, with Griffin on the loose and God only knew where, that possibility was incalculably remote. That's what everyone had expected of Brock, and for the first time anyone was aware of he had let them down, leaving them outraged and skeptical.

Brock didn't buy any of it. He still believed that he had known Griffin better than anyone else, and he sensed that none of the remedies proposed by the campus experts would have worked. One morning at the gym, practicing his poses in front of the mirror, he met the eyes of that smiling creature in the glass and finally had to acknowledge the reason why. That image constituted an unassailable counterargument to all of the community's clamor. Brock could never have played a credible role in Griffin's "salvation", emblem as he was of all that Griffin must desire.

———

Brock finally made his trip to Lexington. By then he had moved home for the summer. He had been hoping to sneak off for a day but soon realized that his mother's constant surveillance made it difficult. Eventually he hit on a plausible excuse. He told Juliette and his family that he was going to consult a trainer there about his bodybuilding. This was true when he said it, but only because his desperation for a pretext had led him to arrange the appointment at the last minute. The meeting lasted less than an hour, leaving him most of the day to explore the university library. To his relief, there was no shortage of relevant information. It was far more than he could get through in one sitting. He quickly realized he'd have to make a second trip.

———

The second trip led to a third, a fourth, and finally a fifth. He read, he took notes, he spent what seemed like a fortune photocopying. Lots of what he read surprised him. None of it changed his mind. Rather, much of it reinforced his initial, instinctive reaction in Griffin's favor. There was nothing wrong with him, nothing that

needed to be fixed. What Griffin had needed in addition to a friend who understood him, and what Brock had tragically failed to provide, was sufficient protection from a world apparently full of idiots and loonies. The information Brock
read on the subject was far from unanimous in its findings, but that in itself was
both a surprise and a validation. Everyone back at school talked as if the issue was
settled, leaving no room for argument. The world, they implied, condemned men
like Griffin with one voice. Now Brock knew better. There was no clear answer
to the question. There never had been, really. And the views of the scientific community were changing rapidly. Even some religious scholars were questioning the
traditional teachings. The possibility that Brock's instinctual acceptance of Griffin
was in line with the thinking of world renowned experts was dizzying. In one way
he could hardly believe it, but at the same time it made perfect sense. One thing
became absolutely plain to him. Straights and gays was by no means as simple a
proposition as Cowboys and Indians or Cops and Robbers. There were apparently
plenty of good and bad guys on either side of the dispute. The rules as he had been
taught them simply didn't coincide with reality. There was nothing concrete that
the various authorities agreed on beyond their acknowledgement that homosexuals
existed. But lack of consensus didn't seem like a very good basis for the way gay
men—not "homosexual" because Brock's vocabulary had changed as a result of
all that reading—were treated. As he had done so often in the past when experts
proved themselves no smarter than he was, Brock turned back to his own instincts
as his principal guide.

—

Meanwhile, he still hadn't answered the initial question. It continued to tantalize
him. What should he have done and when should he have done it? What could he
have done for Griffin that would have prevented those sad events?

—

His final expedition to Lexington didn't take him anywhere near the university
library. He was past the point where further academic research could help him.
In order to understand what had brought things to their climax, he had to see the
place. He hadn't been able to imagine it. From the shocked mutterings on campus

he'd only been able to form the sketchiest of impressions. But when he got there, there was nothing exotic or depraved to observe. To all appearances it was just a working class tavern in a nondescript neighborhood. Its only distinguishing characteristic was the almost complete absence of women in the room. The sole exception was an individual perched on a stool next to the jukebox. She sported an outfit both provocative and garish, a prominent adam's apple, and an unmistakable five o'clock shadow. Brock couldn't decide whether the individual was bored or on barbiturates. One of his uncles had encountered such a figure years back. He'd made it sound like an outtake from a particularly unfortunate Halloween misadventure.

The barroom itself was dim and dingy. Brock couldn't see the least sign of the rampant hedonism he'd been led to expect. If anything, it was a scene of unrelieved drabness. The men there seemed too dispirited to aspire to even the most mundane of immoralities. He had disguised himself with a baseball cap, a pair of sunglasses, and a baggy sweatshirt. Still, he reasoned, no one who gave him a second look should have been able to miss seeing the Adonis below the surface. Yet no one took any particular notice of him. He had tried to prepare himself to react calmly to any possible attention he received, but he needn't have bothered. He was a stranger, and he was large, and he guessed that made him too intimidating to risk approaching. For something to have in his hands, he bought a beer he had no intention of drinking out of consideration for his abdominals. His eyes swept the room for some detail he might have missed or a sign that something interesting might be imminent. But nothing whatever caught his attention. And even as unhabituated as he was, his instincts insisted that as long as he might choose to wait for it, nothing worthy of note would take place there that night. The entire establishment might as well be an exhibit in a museum for all the life he could discern. He'd never witnessed anything as futile as those sad men drinking and ignoring him.

This was the place where Griffin had come in search of companionship. Perhaps even romance, or at least the promise of it. It was enough to make a grown man cry. And, Brock thought, trudging back to his car, the room had reeked of cigarette smoke. He couldn't recall anything Griffin had hated more than cigarette smoke.

———

It was that last detail that overwhelmed him. The smell of smoke clung to his clothing. When he got back to the Sting Ray he put down the top and rolled down the windows so the slipstream as he drove home could strip away that smell. The true smell of Kentucky, his grandmother had once said, and he wasn't able to tell whether she was making a joke or registering a complaint. He imagined Griffin entering that room, looking at those men, smelling that smell, crushed by the reality confronting him. This was his future. This was what he had to look forward to. What wouldn't Brock have done to spare Griffin that?

———

It was too late to worry about it, but the question continued to haunt him. What wouldn't he have done? He tried, but failed, to banish the images from his mind. Griffin in that place, Griffin in the arms of a man he met there. The images disturbed Brock. They hurt his heart. Not because there was anything inherently objectionable about them. He had come that far. But because they represented something so much less than Griffin deserved from life. Brock fought those images and fought them, but they wouldn't go away. There was only one way, he finally decided, he could fend them off. Those images had to be replaced by others. But the new images couldn't be cliché images of Griffin happy with some girl, Griffin inhabiting some quaint cottage, Griffin existing behind lace curtains and a white picket fence. Images like that, comforting though they might appear, were no fit replacement for the ones that gave Brock such distress. They weren't real. There was no authenticity to them. At least the images of the barroom and the men there were true to the facts. That's what made them so hard to dislodge. The only image that would be powerful enough to dispel them could only be the one image Brock hadn't allowed himself to contemplate: Griffin in the arms of a man worthy of him.

———

Brock's family, friends, classmates, and admirers thought of him principally as an athlete. It was in sports that he had primarily distinguished himself. Any other noteworthy accomplishments had followed from his triumphs as quarterback, as wrestler, as discus thrower and shot putter, as the reigning archetype of the playing field and the stadium. But even in earliest boyhood he had sensed that such successes were fleeting and, worse than that, shallow, and came instead to aspire to some greater significance he couldn't describe and was only able to imagine dimly. In his mind, sports were not worthy of being taken seriously as an end in themselves. And an athlete, magnificent as he might be, was ultimately just a guy who played games. Games were for children. They were an imitation of other things, things that mattered, but they were still an imitation. But an athlete who understood athleticism as preparation for those larger and more important struggles was on the road to a truly worthwhile existence. Thus, an athlete, no matter how successful and impressive, was, despite what people might think or say, no hero. But an athlete who went about it properly might be considered a hero in training. That was the philosophy Brock formulated over years of practices, games, and lockerroom post mortems. Genuine heroism, as he defined it, was what he aspired to, and by junior high school he realized that it was not a gift received but a condition that one worked toward and, with perseverance, eventually achieved.

So the question he was now forced to consider was, could a man dedicated to true heroism turn away from the one thing, the crucial thing, a dangerous or challenging situation required of him? Obviously not. The question itself was absurd. To refuse to do what circumstances called for would be to consciously choose not to act heroically. And once a man made that choice, whether from fear, discomfort, inconvenience, or conventionality, could he really call himself a hero? There were, Brock knew, all kinds of failures in the lives of men, but that failure was the only one that mattered in the life of a hero. So now he had to consider the one thing he hadn't allowed himself to admit as a possibility. Because it was, he was finally ready to admit to himself, the only thing he could have done that would have made a difference to Griffin.

———

So he forced himself to imagine doing those things with Griffin. Forced himself repeatedly and in detail. He forced himself to visualize himself doing them until his distaste for them abated and he could accept doing them as a genuine possibility. He forced himself to envision the acts until he knew he could perform them wholeheartedly and without reservation. Not through any genuine desire on his part, but because Griffin's need compelled it. Until he was able to convince himself that a true hero could do even those things if life made that his duty.

And it was not his mind only that he forced into these new acceptances and awarenesses. He did everything necessary to train his body, to prepare it, to bring it to readiness for whatever might be required of it. He wasn't training himself to be gay. He couldn't imagine touching any other man the way he was preparing himself to touch Griffin. No other man could ever need him the way Griffin had. And that need of Griffin's had as much to do with their long association and deep friendship as with the specific details of Griffin's sexual identity. There was no confusion on that point. Each day Brock grew more and more confident in his ability to meet whatever challenge his pursuit of true heroism might bring his way. Even though none of this had any practical application, since any possible role he might have played in Griffin's crisis was already in the past, he at least had the satisfaction of knowing what he might have done if he had only recognised the need and in it his opportunity.

———

It would only have been a temporary solution. Through the sexual attentions he would have bestowed on Griffin he could have kept his friend satisfied and safe long enough to get the three of them to graduation the next May. That was probably all that he could have accomplished. But it would have been worth doing. Brock wouldn't have failed either his friend or his heroic ideal. But realistically speaking, Griffin needed more than just that few months. And soon enough Griffin's needs and Juliette's needs would have collided. Griffin would have understood this even if Juliette never knew anything about what Brock had done.

This meant that Brock's duty would have entailed an additional requirement. Somehow Griffin's future happiness would have had to be assured. And there was only one answer for that. Somewhere in the world there had to be a man, someone like Griffin in that one crucial respect but possessing enough of Brock's own characteristics that Griffin could accept him as a worthy successor. A man like that had to be out there somewhere. Life couldn't be so cruel as to have created a boy like Griffin without also creating his match. Brock wouldn't accept that such a thing was possible. So the second part of his duty was as clear as the first. Brock would find that man, handsome, athletic, brave, kind, serious-minded and gay. He was pretty sure such a person wouldn't be found in an establishment like "The Green Light". The man his imagination conceived of as Griffin's ideal match wouldn't dream of setting foot in a place like that. Brock would be far more likely to find him in a gym or on a playing field. An athlete like himself. Or perhaps a young coach.

But find him he would, a man exactly like Griffin needed. Griffin was too shy and uncertain to go on that quest. He would find it too daunting. Brock would have to do it on his behalf.

———

Of course all this was hypothetical. It was hypothetical and, more important, retrospective. The horses had already stampeded out of the barn. Griffin was who knew where, and there was no indication he would ever return. But Brock had come to a certainty as to what he would have done to make everything work out if he'd only had the awareness of what was required, and that was his comfort. That's what he was thinking of all those months when people were blaming Griffin for his moody silence.

———

Summer drew to a close. Brock decided he didn't want to move back into the dorm room with Griffin not there. He knew the head of campus maintenance had been wanting to close the top floor of the building for at least a year rather than spend money on needed renovations, so why not make him happy and give the room up? He didn't want a new roomie, either. In fact, he thought it would be better all around if he didn't live on campus at all. Hardly any senior men did. He went to see his father at work to ask for more money so he could afford to rent an apartment. Big Jim's snide grin said he thought Brock wanted a convenient place to have sex with Juliette. Brock knew that one of his father's greatest pleasures was thinking the worst of his oldest son, so he didn't try to convince him otherwise. Big Jim's grin only grew sunnier as he wrote out the check.

———

When he got back to St. Gregory's it was no homecoming. Everything had changed. It was all different in a way that made him wonder if he still belonged there. It truly was like having transferred to a new school. At first he thought perhaps he had changed rather than the place, but it didn't take him long to figure out that wasn't the whole explanation. There was a new dean, a woman the president had brought in to replace Dean Sunderland. The idea of a female dean at a school like St. Gregory's should have been astonishing, but Brock's new outlook barely registered it. He met her his first afternoon on campus. He took her for the mother of an incoming freshman and asked her if she needed directions. She laughed as she introduced herself. She had heard all about him, she said, and he wondered what that meant.

———

It didn't take him long to realize that Dean Sherwood was the only change he approved of. The other alterations to the college were more sinister. Looking around campus, he saw campaign signs everywhere. Gene Baxter was running for senior class president. Brock had been president of their class the year before. Gene should have asked him if he planned to run again this year before declaring his own candidacy. It was a traditional courtesy of the college. Seeing the signs didn't make Brock angry. He was just surprised. He hadn't decided whether he actually wanted to run for the office or not, but Gene should have waited. Gene knew how things were supposed to be done. He should have spoken to Brock first. Alongside Gene's campaign signs, Brock saw notices promoting a new organization on campus. They called themselves Students for Traditional Values. Brock couldn't imagine what they meant by that.

———

"Is it true?" Brock asked.

"Is what true?" Madame Grammatikova's flinty eyes revealed nothing.

"Dean Sunderland was forced to resign?"

The first time Brock heard this rumor he laughed. But within two days on campus he'd heard it enough times to become genuinely concerned.

"I didn't hear anything about him being forced," Madame Grammatikova said.

"Well, maybe not forced," Brock said. "Maybe strongly encouraged."

"Encouragement can take many forms," Madame said, looking and sounding particularly sphinxlike.

"So it's true," Brock said. "He didn't leave voluntarily."

"Here's what I know," she said, and he got ready for the revelation.

"Uh huh?"

"In a case such as this one, the truth and the facts aren't necessarily the same thing."

"It's these damned 'traditional values' guys," Brock muttered. "That's who must have been behind it."

———

They had come to see him his second afternoon back on campus. They wanted him to join their group. They seemed to have in mind his becoming some kind of spokesman. By then he'd heard enough about them to understand that by "traditional" they meant anti-gay. They apparently had some kind of witch hunt in mind. He told them, politely as he could, that he wasn't interested. They didn't seem to like his answer. They came to see him again a few days later, and this time they brought reinforcements. Their pitches sounded to him like a set of thinly disguised threats. He fought off his anger as he listened and then told them that as far as he was concerned they were entitled to any opinion under the sun but that his philosophy had always been live and let live. When they left, he was sure he hadn't heard the last of it.

———

By the end of the first half the Cougars were down 35-0. The defensive squad had basically checked out of the game right after kickoff. The offense had done little better. It was unbelievable. Late in the season, or during a difficult road trip, a collapse like this might have happened through fatigue. But this was the season opener in front of their home crowd. It didn't make any sense. Brock had thrown pass after pass to receivers who apparently had no intention of laying a hand on the football. And the linemen hadn't tried any harder. Brock had been sacked over a dozen times. He had never experienced anything like it. Since becoming the Cougars' starting quarterback his freshman year, he'd played in only two losing games, both by the narrowest possible margins. This was unprecedented. He expected equally unprecedented fireworks from Coach Falmouth in the locker room during halftime, but was shocked nearly senseless when he turned out to be the sole target of the ire. Trudging back onto the field to a chorus of boos for the beginning of the second half, he had to face facts. He was being set up. Somebody had decided he needed to be taught a lesson. He had to do something.

Brock didn't throw a single pass during the second half of the game. No matter what play the coach called, he ran the ball. Coach yelled at him like a lunatic, but coach couldn't bench him without forfeiting the game. The second string quarterback had his left wrist in a cast, and the morning before, the third stringer had landed on administrative suspension for cutting chapel services. He wasn't even at the stadium. There was nothing anybody could do but keep playing and hope their opponents would stop him. Which they did, but not completely. He ran for nine touchdowns. Dal Turner missed every single extra point kick, but the Cougars still won 54-52. Afterward, Brock limped off the field to the loudest boos of the afternoon. The minute he got to the locker room, Coach Falmouth screamed at him that he was cut from the team.

———

When Brock opened his front door on Monday morning, Casey Donaldson, the chief of campus security, frowned in at him and handed him an envelope. It was a note from the college president, asking Brock to come by his office. He had spent the weekend licking his wounds, listening to Juliette cry and wondering how things could get worse. This, apparently, was the answer to that question.

———

"Good morning, Brock," Dr. Hotchkiss said. "Please sit down."

"Good morning."

"Thanks for coming in so early. I wanted to speak with you before you went to any of your classes."

"No problem."

"Ah," Dr. Hotchkiss said, "but there is, I'm afraid. Saturday's game. That was the most ridiculous display I think I've ever witnessed."

"I'm sorry, sir, I . . ."

"I don't mean you. You were truly heroic. The last time I saw anything like it was in France in 1944. I can't tell you how impressed I was. I mean it.

No, I'm speaking of your teammates. And Coach Falmouth, who, if he isn't guilty of instigating their behavior at least didn't stop them. It was disgraceful. Differences of opinion should never be worked out on the playing field. It's too dangerous. You might have been badly injured. Your athletic career might have been ended. You could even have been crippled for life. I've seen such things happen in sports. As college president, the safety of our students—all of them—is ultimately my responsibility. And it's a responsibility I take very seriously. That's why I've called you in. To let you know that I'm taking steps to make sure it doesn't happen again. I won't have vigilante activity on this campus. There will be no witch hunts."

"I appreciate that, sir."

"I'll be making an important announcement in regard to all this in chapel service this morning. And I'll be visiting your practice this afternoon to speak directly to the team. I don't think you'll have any more trouble."

—

"I do not know for certain when Coach Falmouth will be able to return to his duties," Dr. Hotchkiss said, "but unfortunately it will not be in time for this Saturday's game against Centre. For that game, the Cougars will be under the direction of Assistant Coach Bolton."

Brock looked around the chapel. It was clear that his fellow students were skeptical of Dr. Hotchkiss' story that Coach Falmouth's sudden leave had been the result of "personal issues". Brock didn't feel any safer. The college president might think he was taking control of the situation, but Brock was pretty sure he was mistaken.

"I know all of you, like I, will keep Coach Falmouth in your thoughts and prayers," Dr. Hotchkiss said.

—

The team obviously wasn't taking Dr. Hotckiss' threats seriously. They beat Brock up but good in practice that afternoon.

—

When he opened his apartment door that evening, a dozen or so Students for Traditional Values were out there.

"I said live and let live," he told them before closing the door again.

They didn't go away immediately. He heard them muttering out there for several minutes.

———

It wasn't that Charlie Puckett didn't catch Brock's first pass Saturday afternoon, it was the way he didn't catch it—hands limp at his sides and the ball bouncing off his chest. Nothing had changed since last week's game. As Brock expected, they were all ignoring the president's instructions. Brock was going to have to run the ball again. At least this time he wasn't taken by surprise.

———

At halftime the Cougars were down by ten points, which at least was better than the week before. Brock's teammates were playing just hard enough to make it look like they were trying, but he knew they had no intention of winning. After the week he'd had in practice, he wasn't sure he could pull off the same miracle again. But that didn't mean he wasn't going to try. If he was going to lose, he'd at least go down fighting.

"Killing yourself out there, man," Todd Gentry muttered, falling into step with him as he trudged toward the locker room at halftime.

"Not getting much help," Brock grunted.

"I know I'm only a lineman," Todd said, "but I do know how to catch a ball. You see me open out there, maybe you should give me a try."

"Huh?"

"Found out that freshman who killed himself in the dorm Thursday night was my third cousin. I didn't know him, but those traditional values guys shouldn't have treated him the way they did."

———

It turned out that Todd actually could catch a pass. He caught four in the second half. The Cougars won the game by two points.

———

It didn't solve anything, however. After a couple of bad hits during Tuesday's scrimmage, Todd took himself to the infirmary. The doctor there diagnosed three broken ribs and a collapsed lung. He'd be out of action for the rest of the season.

———

Dr. Hotchkiss put Coach Bolton on leave along with Coach Falmouth. He threatened to cancel the rest of the season and pull players' scholarships. But Brock was skeptical that it would make any difference. The Students for Traditional Values seemed to believe that they were calling all the shots. Brock didn't have any reason to doubt it.

———

The next Saturday, against Cumberland, Brock ran out of gas. With just over a minute to go and two points behind, at third down and long yardage he had no choice but to hand the game over to the kicker, Dal Turner. Dal hadn't scored a single point in three games so far, so Brock didn't bother watching the field goal attempt. He just slumped on the bench, finally beaten. He didn't see the ball perfectly split the space between the goal posts.

———

"You're a stubborn bastard," Dal told him on their way to the locker room, "but everyone else on this team is an idiot. Do they really want to lose every game this season?"

———

Coach Falmouth and Coach Bolton came back from leave the next Monday. Brock didn't know if they had backed down or if Dr. Hotchkiss had, but practices gradually got better. And the next Saturday, against Pikeville, the Cougars played like a real football team and won by three touchdowns. They finished the season undefeated, but it was never again the way it had been Brock's first three years on the team.

———

He sent notes to the wrestling and track coaches asking them to take his name off their rosters. He was through with college sports. He had learned everything he could from that form of competition. He decided to focus full-time on his preparations for the Kentucky bodybuilding championships right before graduation. And he'd been neglecting Juliette. She had her senior recital coming up in April. And their wedding to plan.

———

His grades that semester were the best he had ever gotten. He only had one C. The two A's were the first ones, except in P.E. classes, he'd gotten in his life.

———

Brock thought about Griffin a lot. He wondered where he was, what he was doing, if he was all right. He wondered if where Griffin was was better than where he had escaped from. Because more and more that was how Brock thought of it. Griffin hadn't run away. Griffin had escaped. Griffin wasn't a victim. Griffin had taken charge of his life. Faced with an impossible situation, Griffin had done the only thing he could. The lesson this implied was the bitterest one Brock had ever had to learn. He had suffered defeat before. It was always a possibility on the playing field. When it came, you picked yourself up and prepared to play another day. Those defeats, painful as they were, were temporary. And because they occurred in games, they had no significance whatever. This defeat couldn't have been more different. What was at stake, at least potentially, had been nothing less than his best friend's survival. There was significance for you. And the violence of the opposition was almost beyond reckoning. They'd been prepared to squash Brock completely for offering nothing more than the most ambiguous of resistance. God help him if he'd been gay himself, or if he'd stood up to them as forthrightly as his temperament had inclined him to. "Live and let live" seemed as innocuous and conciliatory a stance as could be taken, but his opposition had been implacable. He might as well have tried to hold back the advance of a glacier. His quandary, as he now understood it, wasn't how he might have protected Griffin. It was how to continue to think of himself as heroic in a situation of such complete powerlessness. He was like an ancient warrior in winter quarters, wondering if his recovery from his wounds would ever be complete enough to allow him to fight another day. No, it was worse than that. He couldn't help wondering if there was any point to fighting at all. Was his concept of heroism anything more than an illusion?

That was the nature of the dark, impenetrable cloud he felt settling around him. It wasn't disappointment at who Griffin was or anything Griffin had done. It was the world's hate and belligerence that oppressed him. How could any man, no matter what his qualities and his ideals, make the tiniest difference against forces like those? How could he go on, heartbroken as he was by this terrible new knowledge?

———

One day a few weeks before graduation, Juliette emerged from her piano lesson flushed and agitated.

"What's wrong?" Brock asked.

"Not here," she said, looking around the crowded corridor.

They went outside to the quadrangle, to their customary bench in the corner opposite the chapel.

"What is it?"

"Madame has a tape of Griffin's recital two weeks ago. She let me listen to it."

"Where is he?" Brock asked.

"San Francisco. Studying at the conservatory."

"I didn't know there was one."

"It's one of the best in the country. Brock, that tape was amazing. He's playing better than ever."

He couldn't remember the last time he had seen her eyes sparkle like that. He hoped it was a sign.

———

He went to see Madame Grammatikova. She didn't tell him much. Yes, it was true. Griffin was in San Francisco. The conservatory had insisted that he repeat his junior year, but that couldn't really be considered a setback. It simply meant further opportunities to develop as an artist. She heard weekly from his piano teacher, a Professor Schein. His recital had been a triumph. He was making great progress. And as for everything else, he was as well as could be expected.

A few days later, Brock made a clandestine visit to Malcolm Sunderland in Lexington and heard pretty much the same thing.

None of their news answered his deepest questions, but it was at least something to help him keep going, to fight off that dark cloud. It was the final boost that brought his victory at the Kentucky championships.

———

How Brock wishes Griffin could have seen them today, resplendent and joyful, the young hero and his bride. How he wishes the world could have allowed Griffin even a glimpse. But some things simply can't be.

He knows the truth now. Griffin loved him. Griffin still loves him. Griffin will always love him. Griffin in love would have matched passion with steadfastness. That's the only way Griffin would have loved. It has taken Brock until this moment, lying next to his bride, to totally comprehend and accept this truth. Griffin will never let him go. But at the same time Griffin must move on. Griffin must live his life just as Brock and Juliette must live theirs. Brock recognizes the exquisite difficulty of the predicament. Only time, distance, and circumstance can free Griffin sufficiently to enable him to build that life. Only those things and Brock's own prayers, which are all he has left to offer his friend. Madame Grammatikova and Malcolm Sunderland were correct in their insistence on a clean, complete break. They have not obstructed like the heartless elders he considered them many times over the last months. They have insisted like Olympian deities. It is the only way forward for Brock's friend. Now he can only hope that Griffin's love for him will not prevent Griffin from loving another man. Perhaps Griffin already does. How Brock prays for that. But if not, he prays that Griffin will find another love soon, a love to carry him into his new life.

———

Juliette stirs in her sleep, then settles again. Brock reaches for her. He gently rear-ranges the two of them, draping his arm over her. The top of her head is silken against his chin. Her back is against his chest. She feels as fragile nestled there as a child. Brock matches his breathing to the rhythm of hers. He will hold her all night like this, sleepless if necessary. If real danger comes, he has no illusions. His thinks of his arms shielding her as a prayer if nothing else. This feeble gesture of his might be completely unavailing. Still it is something he can do.

Whose arms protect Griffin tonight? Whose keen eyes stare unblinking into the shadows surrounding them, on guard against all threats? Whose broad shoul-ders and strong back constitute Griffin's bulwark? Please God, let there be some hero strong and fearless, Brock's surrogate and brother in arms, holding Griffin there in that distant, unknown darkness.

Please, God. Please.

PART FOUR:
THE PAST IS PROLOGUE

The current rushing so swiftly...
The others that are to follow me, the ties between me and them
The certainty of others—the life, love, sight, hearing of others
Walt Whitman, "Crossing Brooklyn Ferry"

EAST OF CHATTANOOGA: 1901

The day after his father's wedding, Gordon MacDonald left home. He told no one of his plans, making his farewells silently. Mostly those had to do with livestock anyway. At the wedding and afterward he had been careful to do nothing that would draw attention to his preparations, which, in any case, were simple and few. The morning of his departure he rose at the usual time. He did nothing to call attention to himself. He went about all his usual business in his usual manner. He did the milking, slopped the hogs, cut the firewood, brought extra buckets of water into the kitchen from the well. After breakfast he slipped upstairs to his attic bedroom. He had saved a burlap feedsack and fashioned it into a makeshift valise. Into this went his clothing, his shoes, his Bible, and his dead mother's beloved copy of *Pilgrim's Progress*. In the pantry, he wrapped a hunk of left over cornbread in brown paper. He cut a small wedge of cheese and slipped it into the parcel as well. On his way through the orchard he picked half a dozen apples. In his pocket jingled his life savings—thirty-two cents.

———

Thomas Jefferson MacDonald farmed a small place outside Chattanooga. His father had died in the Battle of Lookout Mountain, killed by a Yankee artillery shell shot from a gunboat on the Tennessee River. His wealth amounted to his land, the ramshackle structures on it, and some livestock. There was a pair of heifers for milk and a pen full of hogs for ham, bacon, and sausage. A flock of chickens supplied the family with eggs and ultimately their flesh. His crops were corn for grinding into meal and tobacco which brought in what little cash the family subsisted on. His mother and his mother-in-law (the mother of his late wife, not his new one) lived with him, raising the children and running the household. They tended the extensive vegetable garden, cooked, canned, sewed, mended, laundered, cleaned, and nursed children and livestock alike. His new bride was seventeen years old. There would almost certainly be more children. There were seven on the place already. Several older ones had previously set off on their own.

His prize possession was the team of mules he used for farm work during the week and hitched to the wagon on Sundays to take the family to the local Presbyterian Church, where he served as elder.

—

The first leg of Gordon's odyssey was a short one. The family graveyard was in a grove just over the rise west of the house. He had spent most of his free time there the last eleven months. That morning, as on all his previous visits, he knelt by her gravestone and traced the letters of her name with trembling fingers.

Mollie Augusta Crawford MacDonald

"It ain't right, Ma," he sobbed. "It ain't right. You not dead a year yet. He shouldn'a done it. It ain't right that the younguns is already fergettin' ya and Baby Jonah never knew ya at all."

Baby Jonah, whose birth occasioned her death.

"It ain't right, Ma. And I ain't standin' fer it."

Eventually, his tears spent, he rose and moved off through the trees. He could tell from the sounds behind him that his absence had not yet been noticed. This didn't surprise him. Gradually the sounds faded. At the crossing a couple of miles down the county road, the trains slowed down enough that he'd be able to swing himself up through the open door of an empty boxcar.

He was twelve years old the morning he went off to discover America.

NEW YORK HARBOR: 1913

I t was the most amazing thing Leah had ever seen. Who could have imagined that buildings could be so tall? They seemed to rise right out of the water. And even nearer stood the amazing statue of a woman with spikes growing out of her head. What in the world could that signify? She was holding a torch in one hand and cradling something that might be a book in her other arm. She wasn't like any statue Leah had ever seen. Papa told them America was the land of opportunity, but to Leah it seemed like a land of miracles. Miracles and magic. If someone had described all this to her she would have called them crazy. If they had shown her a picture she would have accused them of tearing it out of a book of fairy tales.

What a place Papa had brought them to.

———

It was a longer journey than Leah thought it was possible for a journey to be. First they rode in the wagons Papa hired to bring them from their village to Lemberg, the biggest city she had ever seen. Then they rode those slow, noisy, stinking trains all the way across Austria and on across Germany to Hamburg. Leah was astonished at how big the world was. And Papa said they had barely started. Then there was the huge ship. When she saw it she was terrified. They would all surely die if they boarded it. A thing that size. How could it possibly float? But it did float, and it took them on this voyage she thought would never end. The world was supposed to be round. Why was it taking so long? Shouldn't they have gotten back to where they started from already? And just when she despaired of ever seeing land again—this vision. No wonder they called it the New World.

—

There were hundreds of children on the ship. Leah wondered what stories their papas had told them before they left their homes. There were the rich children in first class, of whom Leah had only fleeting glances as the Goldstein tribe boarded. There were the children in second class, with whom she was only slightly more familiar. Then there were hundreds and hundreds—all the remaining children of the world, it seemed—crammed into steerage with the Goldsteins. Children of all sizes, shapes, descriptions. Leah's grandmother forbade her to have anything to do with the Gentile children, but it wasn't so easy. It was so crowded; how could you avoid anyone? And besides, you couldn't always tell. Whoever they were, they ran around the corridors frantic at their confinement. They couldn't wait to be back on land. They longed to see grass, trees, open space. They ached to stretch their legs. They jabbered away at each other in what sounded to Leah like a hundred dozen strange tongues. After a few days, Leah noticed that their varied and confused languages all had one word in common—America. To her, this seemed like a sign from the Almighty.

—

Leah was not supposed to notice that her mother and grandmother were terrified. She was supposed to ignore it when, several times a day, they burst into tears and clung to each other weeping bitterly. Her older siblings explained it to her. Once they reached New York, each member of the family would be examined by an American doctor. Anyone who was found to be unfit—whatever that meant—would be turned away. Family members might be split apart. Some would have to go back home.

She had always known that Papa was crazy. What a fine adventure he had brought them on.

—

Somewhere in the middle of the Atlantic, the steerage children began, through some weird, unconsciously shared alchemical powers, reversing the story of the Tower of Babel. Out of a cognate here, there a word communally adopted because they found it somehow edifying to the heart and tongue, and glued together by means of good will and extensive pantomime, a new dialect started to evolve. By this means Leah was able to confirm the awful truth. All over steerage mothers and grandmothers were huddling together and weeping over their terrifying futures. All the adults, it seemed, cowered in the shadows of the terror. America might refuse them entry.

Only the children were immune. They seemed incapable of any emotion but optimism. Leah took her cue not from her family but from her generation.

———

Any lingering doubts she might have had were banished by her first glimpses of the city. She was captivated. Enthralled. To see it close up! To walk those streets, enter those buildings! To be the kind of person who lived there!

———

The man sitting behind the table called out "Goldstein," and as if waking from a dream the family rose from the bench where they had been waiting. The man handed Papa a sheaf of important looking papers. Mama and Granny began weeping again, but it sounded different this time. Leah watched, breathless. Papa turned and motioned them all to follow him as he strode toward the barrier.

U.S.S. LEVIATHAN: 1919

The great ship, one of the world's largest passenger liners, sliced through the pristine waters of the North Atlantic under a brilliant July sun. In all but forgotten days before the war, the cream of the German bourgeoisie promenaded on her decks. Now, under a different flag and carrying a different name than the one she'd been christened with, she sailed a world transformed, her decks teeming with American doughboys headed home.

Home from the adventure of a lifetime or the nightmare of all nightmares. The perspectives were as varied as her cargo. It largely depended on the individual experiences of the men. What had they witnessed, who had they lost, what had been the nature of their sufferings? Raw recruits from the farms, villages, factory floors, and construction sites two scant years ago, by now they regarded themselves as men of the world. They had danced in the avenues of Paris, hoisted drinks in the *ratskellers* of Berlin and Munich, courted women in half a dozen haltingly stammered languages. Back home nothing has changed but they are not the same boys they were when they left. They will never be the same.

The America they were returning to had been burnished almost to incandescence by their fond memories of it and by its contrasts with the places they visited on this grotesque parody of the grand tour their wealthy compatriots used to enjoy in a Europe then unspoiled, now hardly recognizable. Back home they will encounter no ruins, witness no famines, march in no revolutions, only parades of victory. And no matter how beautiful they found the women of Europe, they will be even more enthralled by the simple, unspoiled girls they left behind.

Home, home. The twelve thousand hearts on board the steaming liner beat as one. Home!

But was this all as unanimous as it appeared, mused Gordon MacDonald as he basked in the sun and luxuriated in the sharp slipstream of their passing? He sat staring into the distance unconsciously fondling his copy of *Leaves of Grass*, his constant companion on those foreign shores. Or was it some grand fiction they have all silently agreed to subscribe to, some bastard cousin of "the war to end all wars" or "making the world safe for democracy"?

Anyway, what did the word even mean, that elusive word "home"? Nearing his thirtieth birthday, he had spent his last eighteen years homeless for all practical purposes. Yet to his mind it had been the homelessness of a sparrow, a bobcat, an otter. Could any of the Good Lord's creatures ever truly lack a home? Still, the word exerted its solemn power over him just as surely as it did over his shipmates. A man couldn't help but want, at least sometimes, to settle down. To find a place, one place in all the universe, and people to think of as particularly his own.

Since leaving his boyhood home he had pulled rickshaws through the streets of Seattle, worked on fishing schooners out of Monterey, panned for gold in Alaska, rangered in Yellowstone, herded goats in West Texas, baled hay in Kansas, clerked in a grocery store in Whittier, California, harvested wheat in Cut Bank, Montana, washed dishes in San Francisco, tended hospital grounds in Denver, made bricks in Portland, Oregon, dug for copper in Bisbee, Arizona, riding the rails from place to place as carefree as a hobo. A roof over his head, a full belly, a few coins jingling in his pocket were all he ever had to show for these labors. Most recently, Uncle Sam rewarded his efforts somewhat more lavishly, but then again the risks, discomforts, and inconveniences of the work had been commensurately greater.

All men were brothers, Whitman loudly, confidently asserted, and everywhere Gordon had been he saw it was so. To a point. Brotherhood with limits was how he had learned to think of it. For all those men, every one of them, had real, flesh and blood brothers, sisters, mothers, fathers, aunts, uncles, cousins, grandparents, who, inevitably it seemed, took precedence over the more universal relations the poet/prophet celebrated.

Gordon had them too. His ghosts, he called them. He had left them behind more than half his lifetime ago yet they followed him wherever he went. They sought him out. Even in his homelessness they found him. They wouldn't leave him alone. They haunted him. More than their remembered faces or the echoes of their voices, their betrayals haunted him. Not even war and the passing of time diminished their insistence. His efforts to elude and escape had proven futile at every turn. He had decided, finally, that what he needed to do was find a way to replace them.

Perhaps he should settle down. Pledge allegiance to some plot of land or other, cast his lot with some community, commit himself to an occupation. Perhaps doing all that would finally silence their clamor. And even if it didn't, how long could a man go on following the crops and the seasons and the gold strikes and the migrations of the livestock, everything he owned in one ever shabbier valise, his entire library consisting of his Bible, his mother's *Pilgrim's Progress,* his *Paradise Lost*, his complete Shakespeare, his beloved Whitman?

I must choose one place, he thought to himself, staring out into the radiant emptiness ahead of the ship. *I must find new people and hold and cherish them as my other people did not hold and cherish one another or me. There must be more books, additional wisdom. I must build my library.*

The great liner steamed on, its funnels tracing the path from past to future—a straight line across the pale, empty sky.

GRANT COUNTY, KENTUCKY: 1920

There was nothing out of the ordinary about the man standing at the kitchen door when Mary Ellen opened it that morning. She opened her kitchen door to strangers at least once a day. Though they came in all shapes and sizes, they all had the same look in their eyes. Times were never easy, but some times were harder than others, and this was one of the bad ones. Lots of men out looking for work lately. This one was not young but not yet middle aged, medium height, wiry of build, with roughened working man's hands and worn and mended working man's clothing.

"Good morning, missus," he said, snatching the broad brimmed hat off his head. His matted down hair was an unusual shade of dark red, his eyes an equally vivid dark blue, and his freckle dusted face was windburned and freshly shaven.

"Good morning. The name's Douglas."

"Good morning, Missus Douglas. They said in town you might be looking for help here on your place."

They would have said that, all right. Due to her father's parsimoniousness and ill temper they were pretty much always looking for help. Nobody Pa hired stayed around for very long, no matter how bad the times got. Not with Pa's sharp tongue.

"It'll be my Pa you need to talk to about that," Mary Ellen said. "He'll be comin' in in a few minutes for his dinner, if you care to wait."

"Much obliged, Missus."

"I'm Miss."

"Miss Douglas. I helped myself to a drink from your well. I hope you don't mind."

"Of course you did," she said, liking his manners now that she thought about it. "And right welcome to it you were."

"I'll just wait out here on the stoop for Mr. Douglas."

"Fine." She shut the door on him. Not too hard, not too soft. Not so as to give him any impression one way or another but mostly because she was by nature a creature of moderation. She shut the kitchen door and didn't give him another thought. She had Pa's dinner to get ready.

———

A while later, Pa stomped into the kitchen, the man trailing behind him.

"Mary Ellen, this here is Gordon MacAllister. . ."

"MacDonald, ma'am," the man quietly corrected him.

"MacDonald. He's our new hired man. Be a good girl now and set another place at the table for dinner."

———

Isaiah Douglas had one great disappointment in life. He had no son. His daughter Mary Ellen was a good girl. As good as a girl could be, really. But a girl wasn't a boy and that was that. He was a simple man and his life had been full of hardships. His farm wasn't the largest, most fertile, or best located in the county, but its produce fed, sheltered, and clothed them. His wife hadn't been the prettiest, smartest, or most charming of the local girls, but she worked hard, did her best to please him, and had a better than average sense of humor. He married later in life than he had planned and his wife died earlier than he expected, and though he never spoke of it to anyone he missed her more than he would have thought, sometimes terribly. The weather was bad more often than it was good, and the crops never came in as bountifully as he hoped for, and the God he worshipped faithfully each Sunday seemed to hear his prayers with only half an ear if at all. Livestock ran away or took sick and died. Outbuildings burned, crops failed, neighbors threatened suit. Hired hands stole from him, or were lazy, or were merely stupid and accident prone. All these and other misfortunes he bore with an equanimity verging on fatalism.

The one thing he could not bear was that he had no son.

———

Mary Ellen was surprised one morning when, absent mindedly looking at a wall calendar from the feed store in town, she realized that Gordon MacDonald's employment on the Douglas place had entered its second month. Usually, men left before the end of the second week.

———

Mary Ellen was surprised one evening when, washing dishes dexterously while she dried, Gordon MacDonald addressed her as "Miss Mary Ellen" rather than "Miss Douglas."

———

Mary Ellen was surprised when, upon the birth of yet another litter of farm pups, Gordon MacDonald insisted on adopting the runt instead of drowning it as her father had instructed. It was the first time she knew of that Gordon hadn't done as he was told. And in such a cause. She hardly knew what to make of it.

———

In spite of himself, Isaiah Douglas found that he approved of the new hand. Gordon never complained of the work no matter how unpleasant the task, how long the hours, or how inclement the weather. He never talked back, never cursed, never had to be told a thing twice. He always did things right the first time. He never rushed through a job, preferring to go slowly, be careful, be thorough. He was never found daydreaming, never caught unawares. He never quoted scripture in conversation—a pet peeve of Isaiah's, who considered it irreverent—though he rode to services at the Presbyterian Church in the back of his employer's wagon every Sunday and sang out the hymns as fervently as anyone present. He never spoke unless spoken to.

One day, to Isaiah's immense surprise, he realized that he had come to think of Gordon MacDonald as the son he never had. ·

———

The first time Gordon proposed to her, Mary Ellen thought she hadn't heard him correctly and went right on butchering a chicken for dinner.

———

The second time he proposed to her, she assumed he was joking. He was generally as sober as a deacon on Sunday morning, but he must have gotten into Pa's medicinal supply and, unaccustomed to imbibing, made himself a little silly. Really, he had no knack for humor, she thought, and shouldn't attempt it.

———

The third time, she was sure Pa had put him up to proposing to her and said as much in no uncertain terms. She was prepared to marry him if her father insisted on it but would really prefer it to be at least as much Gordon's idea as Pa's. She didn't tell Gordon this, however. A girl, even an old maid like her, had some pride. She felt bad afterward when he moped around the place for two weeks straight.

———

The fourth time Gordon proposed to her, she thought to herself, well, why not? She was not getting any younger. All the other girls her age had half a dozen children apiece, some of them half grown. If it were ever to happen, now was probably the time. To be honest about it, now was probably the only time. She had never had any other suitor, and with her plain looks and—she believed—her complete lack of charm, she had no reason to expect one. Nor was the Douglas place itself enough of a prize to entice even a moderately picky gentleman. Yet Gordon MacDonald mysteriously refused to give up on the idea. So yes, why not? What did she have to lose?

MANHATTAN: 1934

"Class," Miss Finkelstein called out, "class, attention please."

Standing next to her was a pretty black haired girl. Rosie thought she looked like a child star from the movies.

"Class, this morning we have a new student. Her name is Shoshonnah Freitag. Say good morning to Shoshonnah, boys and girls."

"Good morning, Shoshonnah," the class chanted.

"Rosie Stern,"

"Yes, Miss Finkelstein," Rosie stammered, rising from her seat as Miss Finkelstein expected of her students when she addressed them.

"Shoshonnah will sit next to you. Make sure to explain everything she needs to know about our class."

"Yes, Miss Finkelstein."

———

Rosie was a shy, anxious little girl, and charming and beautiful Shoshonnah terrified her. But Shoshonnah turned out to be as nice as she was pretty, and before she knew it Rosie had her first ever best friend.

———

Shoshonnah had an older sister, Rivka, who was in third grade and wouldn't play with them unless Shoshonnah's Nanny Goldstein made her. Every morning, Rosie's mother walked her over to the Freitag's apartment. From there, Nanny Goldstein would escort the three of them to school. One morning it was raining, and instead of meeting the Freitag girls on the front steps they went inside. Rosie had never been inside the Freitag apartment before. She was a little disappointed that it was so much like the Sterns'. She was also nervous about introducing her shy, anxious mother, Miriam, to Mrs. Freitag, who was funny and charming.

Then an amazing thing happened.

"Leah?" Rosie's mother shrieked the minute Mrs. Freitag came in from the kitchen. "Leah Goldstein?"

"Miriam? Miriam Silbermann?"

"Is it really you?"

The girls never got to school that morning. They spent all day listening to their mothers tell stories about coming to America on the big ship.

AMSTERDAM: 1938

The two young Dutchmen waited outside the customs hall. With their expensive suits and sleek, brilliantined hair, they had an unmistakably American air that might have fooled onlookers, but the language of their conversation was as Dutch as windmills, canals, and wooden shoes. Despite the ambiguity of their appearance, one thing was certain. They were obviously brothers, perhaps even twins. The indolence of their postures vanished with the emergence of the first transatlantic passengers from behind the barriers. They peered intently as the trickle became a stream and eventually a torrent. Finally, the slightly taller, slightly broader of the two waved.

"Uncle Shmuel, over here."

—

The sleek, low-slung car glinted with raindrops.

"It's a Citroen, Uncle," Robbie explained, swinging open the rear door for him.

"The newest model," Marcus said, in exactly the same voice.

"You won't believe how fast. We'll make it from Rotterdam to Amsterdam in a flash."

"Boys, boys," Shmuel Luxemberg chuckled, settling himself into the comfortable seat, "not too fast, all right? Better to arrive late than never."

"How was the crossing?" Robbie inquired, shifting gears like a racing driver.

"We heard there were storms," Marcus said, bolt upright next to his brother.

"Not too bad," Shmuel assured them. "Not too bad."

In truth, however, it had been a terrible crossing. The weeks before Shmuel's departure were worse still, constantly on the run from one office to another and including several overnight journeys all the way to Washington. Really, he couldn't remember ever being this exhausted. But seeing his two nephews like this, imagining them back in New York and safe, made the nightmare of his quest seem insignificant. The thick sheaf of precious documents nestled in the briefcase at his side. These boys will take to America like a duck takes to the water, he thought. Really, it was a good thing his nephews had recognized him in the customs hall. They had changed so much since his last visit four years ago for Robbie's Bar Mitzvah that he surely would have walked right past them.

———

The narrow house facing the canal was exactly as he remembered it. Every day back in New York, he regretted leaving this house, this city. New York was the capital of the world, of course, and his business there had made him rich, but he lived in a state of perpetual regret. Only recently had he finally come to comprehend the prescient fate that led him away. "Like Joseph in Egypt," he muttered, as Robbie shut off the engine and Marcus busied himself hauling the luggage out of the trunk.

———

It wasn't the house or even Amsterdam itself that Shmuel longed for most in his self-imposed exile. It was this woman, this magnificent woman his sister-in-law Eva, who haunted him. He could only curse the ill fortune that had chosen her for his brother, Reuven. He stood in the foyer watching as she floated down the staircase to greet him. It seemed impossible that she could be the mother of a seventeen year old son, though her beauty had left its indelible stamp on his nephews.

"Shmuel." Her delicate voice was like the sound of a flute in its lowest register. "Darling, how wonderful. Now our celebration is complete. Marcus, Robbie, take his things up. Shmuel, I've ordered tea for us in the salon. Boys, hurry. You'll be late picking up Rachael and Helene from school."

"How are you, my dear?" Shmuel asked, alarmed at the tremor in his voice.

"Frazzled," she giggled. "Some days, five children seem like a dozen."

"And my brother?"

"Well," she giggled again. "Well and fat and successful. Oh yes, and happy, I hope."

"If he's not," Shmuel growled, "he's insane. Or impossible to please."

Footsteps in the hall distracted her.

"Ah, Mr. Pinsky, how is our pupil today?"

"Doing very well, Mrs. Luxemberg."

"Mr. Pinsky, this is my brother-in-law Shmuel, just arrived from America."

"Greetings, sir."

"A pleasure to meet you," Shmuel said.

"Mr. Pinsky is tutoring our Villem for his big day."

"A most pleasant task, I assure you."

"I'm glad to hear it," Shmuel said.

"Is this your last session with him, Mr. Pinsky?"

"I believe so."

"We're forever in your debt. All three boys now. You have such patience."

"Thank you, Mrs. Luxemberg."

"See you at temple, then."

———

A fire burned in the grate in Reuven's study. After dinner, the family scattered to their various pursuits. Robbie and Marcus went to see a movie. Eva and her mother were in the sitting room reading. The three younger children, Rachael, Helene, and Villem were upstairs doing homework. Shmuel and his brother were finally alone together.

In contrast with Eva, Reuven had aged badly. Remembering his volatile temperament, Shmuel resolved to tread lightly. He might only have one chance. His plan to rescue the family, which had seemed so pressing as he made the preparations, appeared, in this comfortable room, among these contented, prosperous people, if not superfluous at least premature. Outside these walls, he had to remind himself, all Europe was at risk. Bourgeois Jews, for all their prosperity and assimilation, were horribly vulnerable. But he found himself at a loss as to how to approach the subject.

"In America, all anyone talks of these days is war," he finally stammered.

"Is that so?" Reuven asked, cutting the end off one of his Havana cigars.

"Constantly," Shmuel assured him. "The newspapers are full of it as well."

"Even after Czechoslovakia?"

"More than ever, since Czechoslovakia."

"Well, what do Americans know, really, of Europe?"

"Most of them are from here."

"Generations ago," Reuven said.

"Still, it's not like the old days. Now we have radio and motion pictures. People over there are better informed than you think."

"Perhaps," Reuven said.

"The general opinion in New York is that the man is a lunatic."

"Hitler? Oh, no question about it. We have many German refugees here. They tell the most pitiable stories."

"I'm sure they've had horrible experiences," Shmuel said.

"Horrible, yes."

"Do they think there will be war, these refugees?"

"They thought there would be war," Reuven said. "Then came Munich. Now it seems unlikely that the Allies will do anything to interfere with his plans."

"You don't think their weakness will egg him on?" Shmuel asked.

"I suppose it could happen. But I don't concern myself with it. Hitler seems concerned only with his eastern neighbors. Too bad for the Poles, I suppose. But really, we in the west have little to fear."

"What if he went into Poland and the British and French finally had enough and decided to stop him?" Shmuel asked.

"I'm sure they'd be successful. With the French army and British navy ranged against him, Hitler would have a very difficult time. Of course here in Holland there's no reason to be fearful. Even if war broke out between Germany and the Allies, we know that we can depend on both sides to respect Dutch neutrality, just as in 1914."

"But what if Germany didn't?"

"Why wouldn't they?" Reuven asked. "Hitler calls the Dutch his Aryan brothers. He would have no reason."

"The Austrians are his Aryan brothers, too. That didn't stop him from occupying their country."

"Somehow, you begin to sound like our refugee friends."

"I'm worried," Shmuel said. "I'm concerned about you and Eva and the children."

"Worried? But why?"

"I think if there is war," Shmuel said, "it could be very bad for the Jews of Europe. I'm so worried about it that I've made arrangements for you all to come to America. I have all the necessary documents, enough for everyone."

"Go to America? Are you insane?"

"Not that I know of."

"You must be," Reuven said, "to suggest such a thing. Just leave? What about the business?"

"Sell it. The building and inventory alone are worth a great deal."

"Just like that."

"Yes," Shmuel said.

"And how are we to live in America?"

"You'll work with me," Shmuel said. "I'll make you a full partner."

"How generous."

"Reuven, listen to me, please. Even if you are right and the Germans don't come here, think what a war will do to your business."

"I'll tell you what it will do to business," Reuven said. "Everyone will want gold. And gemstones. In dangerous times there's not a better investment than precious metals and gems. I'll make a killing."

"That's monstrous."

"No, not monstrous, just absurd. And there's often great opportunity to be found in absurdity. We'll talk no more about this. I appreciate your efforts assembling all the paperwork, but you needn't have bothered. There is no danger. I'm absolutely certain of it. Now, I have to ask you, please, not a word of this in front of Eva and the children. I don't want you alarming them with this crazy talk."

———

The ornate sanctuary. The ancient, timeless words of the Torah. His youngest nephew at the great table, dwarfed by the rabbi. Of all the children, Villem most resembled Eva. The boy's beauty made Shmuel's heart ache.

Evil people want to hurt them, he thought, but I am powerless. And only because my brother refuses my help. Reuven always believed he was smarter than I, and unless I find another way to approach him that pride of his will kill them all.

———

"Something is bothering you, dear Shmuel." Eva's smile was perfectly bright, but he saw in her eyes a truer feeling. She had never been able to lie to him, and it had always been her eyes that betrayed her.

"Indigestion," he said. "All the rich food you keep shoving at me."

"Poor you," she giggled. "But seriously now, won't you tell me what is wrong? Is there a woman perhaps, back in New York?"

"No woman," he said.

"You say it like it's a relief."

"I have enough to worry about, thank you. I don't need a woman complicating my life."

"Is that what we do? Complicate men's lives?"

"Inevitably," Shmuel said.

"Well then, if there is no woman, I don't understand why you look so. . ."

"I worry about you, Eva. And the children. And Reuven, of course."

"Oh, you needn't worry about us. Things could not be better for us."

"I almost think you mean that."

"I do," she said, mouth suddenly set firm. And her eyes said that Reuven had told her.

"I wish I could be as sure as you are."

"Reuven takes good care of us. He always will. That is what I believe. It is what I think of when. . ."

"When what?"

"Never mind. There are the Shapiros. I must say hello to them."

———

During the days following Villem's Bar Mitzvah, the house quickly fell back into its normal routine. Robbie and Marcus accompanied Reuven to the store every morning, and the younger children went to school. Eva's mother, Mrs. Feldman, spent most of the day in her room reading. This left Eva and Shmuel alone together for hours on end.

Each day he said to himself he must do it, go back on his promise to Reuven and discuss the whole matter with her. But every time he opened his mouth to speak something stopped him. And it wasn't loyalty to his brother, but a shadowy something in her eyes begging him to remain silent on the matter. She knew everything and she had made her decision. He could only hope that she and Reuven were right and he was wrong and all his careful and expensive preparations had been a fool's errand. But he knew in his heart that it was a false hope. Whatever the people in this house believed, they had no influence outside its walls. What was coming to them would come. There was nothing they could do to prevent it.

Eva and Shmuel whiled away their lazy mornings and afternoons walking the streets of the city, visiting the parks and museums, drinking coffee in cafes, sitting beside the placid canals. Over and over his thought was that if he should ever return, the city would have survived but his loved ones would not be here.

—

The night before he was to embark on his return journey, Reuven came to his room. He brought a bottle of wine and two glasses, and as Shmuel finished packing and the two talked it was almost as if they were boys again. Just as Shmuel was consciously adding those few moments to the catalogue of things he absolutely must remember, Reuven surprised him.

"Eva has asked me to speak to you about Villem."

"Yes? What about Villem?"

"She would like—we both would like, actually, for him to return to America with you."

"Of course."

"Eva is thinking about his future. Business is very good for us these days. But soon Robbie and Marcus will marry and start families of their own, and she is worried that there may not be enough to provide for everyone. She hopes that you will not just make a home for Villem but also a place in your business."

"I understand," Shmuel said, heart soaring and breaking simultaneously. "Please tell her that I will do everything in my power for my nephew."

"That will make her very happy. And don't worry. You won't have to delay your departure. We'll have him up and ready to go first thing."

"I wasn't worried about it."

"You understand, of course, that this has nothing to do with—that other matter."

"All right," Shmuel said, "but I do have to make one condition."

"What is that?"

"I am leaving the rest of the immigration documents with you. Just in case you are able to find a use for them."

"Fine," Reuven said, accepting the packet Shmuel held out to him. "If it will make you happy."

ST. GREGORY'S COLLEGE: 1939

In high school, Garrett MacDonald was valedictorian and president of everything that a boy could join. He was first string quarterback and starting pitcher. Though he was only average height, his agility and tenacity on the court made him the natural leader of the basketball team, which he captained. If there had been other sports at his school he would have lettered in them as well. His junior year, he won statewide awards for debate and Latin Oratory, and he repeated these accomplishments as a senior. He was a noted actor and writer of short stories. He was as close to a renaissance man as could be found in any high school in the Commonwealth of Kentucky, and he saw no reason why the brilliance of his career to that point should diminish in the least when he enrolled at St. Gregory's College as a freshman.

This was not arrogance on his part, but rather a supreme confidence in his abilities and an indefatigable optimism. The only child of parents who never actually expected to have one, he benefited from an unusually diligent upbringing. From his mother he learned that thinking too highly of oneself was one of the gravest of all sins, a crucial lesson for a child so ostentatiously gifted. From his father he learned to love books, and more importantly, that a man's first responsibility in life was the welfare of others. The MacDonalds were devout people, regular churchgoers but somewhat unconventional in their beliefs. His mother's mother had been a Quaker in girlhood. His father's Presbyterianism was heavily diluted by an obsession with New England Transcendentalism and most of all with Whitman, whose poetry he spent hours reciting each day as he went about his labors on the family farm. Garrett himself, though scrupulous in all aspects of religious observance, considered himself a free thinker. He found Christian Humanism a congenial enough philosophy but increasingly felt drawn to agnosticism, though this was something he kept to himself.

If you had asked him to sum up his accomplishments so far, particularly as they related to his aspirations, he would have admitted to one deficiency only. Though he had myriad pals, adherents, and fans, true friendship, the kind of deep affection and meeting of minds he read about so avidly in books, had so far eluded him. He had made certain resolutions in this regard which he intended to be guided by at college. Surely what he sought was available in the same way his other accomplishments had been. Through diligence and purity of spirit.

———

Malcolm Sunderland trudged up the last flight of stairs, footlocker teetering on his left shoulder, enveloped in a cloud of anticipated doom. College, that oasis of intellectualism and culture toward which he'd been questing all his conscious life, nevertheless threatened to be a little less than utopia. Everything he dreamed of was undoubtedly to be found here. His obsessive studies of the college catalogue left no possible doubt as to that. But gaining access to all those splendors necessitated living here. And that, given the restrictions of his budget, necessitated in its turn that most dreaded species, a roommate. The threat posed by this hypothetical nemesis had grown more terrifying during the long weeks of summer as its reality grew daily more concrete.

It wasn't that Malcolm cared, really, about what sort of roommate he ended up with. Fat, thin, tall, short, smooth or unruly haired, clear skinned or acne ravaged, quiet or bellicose—none of those signified. It would be beneath him to let them. His anxiety stemmed from his absolute certainty that no matter how hard he tried not to he would nevertheless manage to give deep offense to this person in some unimaginable, unpredictable way. People's disapproval, though he almost never actually experienced it, was his greatest fear. And who is more likely to disapprove than the person one exists in the greatest proximity to?

So he found it almost impossible to take those last few steps through the open door of the tiny room. Inside, a radio was playing quietly enough that he could also hear the sounds of someone moving around. A few paces back from the doorway, partially concealed in the shadows of the landing, he peered in but received no clue. Finally his load grew too heavy. He would have to set it down, either inside or outside the room. In any case the sound would lead to his discovery.

"The jig is up," he muttered under his breath.

He stepped into the room. Standing in the exact center was the most dazzling person he had ever encountered. He set his footlocker down rather clumsily and winced at the thump. Then, straightening up, he stood, mouth open but speechless, staring.

"You must be my roomie," the vision smiled.

Still mute, Malcolm managed to shrug.

"I'm Garrett MacDonald."

"Malcolm Sunderland," he said, finding a voice.

"You don't look like a Malcolm. What's your middle name?"

"David."

"David," Garrett said, peering intently at him. "Yes, that fits you much better. I think I'll call you Davy. In fact, I believe it would be a good idea if everyone around here calls you Davy."

Malcolm considered this.

"With your permission, of course."

"All right," Malcolm said.

———

Lying in his bunk that night, Malcolm pondered that giddy instant when he had first glimpsed Garrett. His heart had raced. He had thought he was about to faint. He had, he recalled, failed to breathe for a moment. It was the most extraordinary experience of his life thus far, and he couldn't begin to fathom it. Except for the obvious: he was captivated by the young man now lightly snoring in the bunk above him.

He couldn't have known it and wouldn't have believed it had he been told, but Garrett was very nearly as fascinated with him. His Latin was as good as Garrett's, and he had the additional advantage of having been tutored in Classical Greek by a retired professor back home. And while Garrett's schoolboy French was just passable, Malcolm's was near fluent and his accent far better. He had brought a portable record player to school with him along with his collection of 78's: Beethoven, Brahms, Wagner. He had read Chekov and Ibsen, knew what Shaw had said about both of them, comprehended that *Ghosts* was about congenital syphilis. He had traveled to Chicago several times and once as far as New York. He had seen Shakespeare performed live. He had brought with him poster prints of a Picasso and a Van Gogh which Garrett insisted that they hang in their room. He was tall, with dark hair and eyes and a somewhat brooding aspect. The girls in his high school had nicknamed him Heathcliff as a result, though he would have died of mortification had anyone at college learned of it. Garrett thought of him as Byronic. Garrett also thought of him as the intellectual he had always aspired to be. For Malcolm, now Davy, lying sleepless in the lower bunk, Garrett was Adonis masquerading as a grownup Huckleberry Finn.

———

They were nearly inseparable over the next few days, exhilarated by each other's company. They never ran out of things to talk about. The similarity of their opinions and tastes seemed uncanny. Each secretly began to view their friendship as no mere happenstance but something ordained by divine providence. Then, late on the Friday afternoon before classes were to begin, they had a visitor in their room. The head football coach, hearing of Garrett's spectacular play in the impromptu touch football games the students organized in Founder's Quad each afternoon, decided to investigate. The dean's office gave him particulars. A telephone call to Garrett's high school coach filled in the picture. So Coach Roberts came recruiting. Garrett's euphoria couldn't have been more apparent.

Davy's heart sank at this. Despite his tall, robust appearance, he was no athlete. Naturally blessed with both strength and stamina, he lacked coordination, and, perhaps more importantly, a competitive outlook. His early failures at sport had poisoned them for him. And in a culture which viewed athletic endeavor as very nearly the sole criterion by which a young man's worth was measured, his subsequent refusals to participate had marked him as different and suspect. Had he suffered from some physical condition which prevented him this would have been pitied and excused, but absent any such mitigating circumstance his position merely appeared perverse. It seemed inevitable that Garrett's sudden notoriety as second string quarterback would bring this failing into sharp focus among their classmates and professors, and Davy dreaded the erosion of their intimacy that he felt certain would result. But whatever the college in general made of this eccentricity of his,

Garrett appeared oblivious to it. And though his practice schedule took up much of his time outside of classes, the intensity with which he maintained their friendship gratified Davy beyond words.

———

Women did not attend St. Gregory's College in those days. There were only a very few on the campus in any capacity, a handful of junior faculty members who taught art or music, the nurses in the infirmary, and the cafeteria workers were the extent of the female presence. All the emotions of young men in that baffling transition from adolescence to adulthood, all the longing for companionship and connection, all the youthful vulnerabilities and intensities of feeling played themselves out in this exclusively masculine atmosphere. And it must be understood that not only were they womanless. For all practical purposes sex was considered not to exist except hypothetically, something men experienced later in life and with their lawfully wedded wives exclusively, since this was a deeply and conventionally religious institution. Indeed, the local mores held that it hardly need be discussed, and it was surprisingly little mentioned in the day to day conversations of the students.

Young men may be trained to sublimate, may become accustomed to it, may even accept it. The body can be disciplined to almost any regime. The heart is far harder to control. No surprise then that the students formed deep attachments, and no suspicion was attached to it. Davy and Garrett's friendship was not considered in any way exceptional by their peers or the college establishment. All over the campus, pairs of men could be seen going about their business in each other's company. It was the happiest Davy could ever remember being. Then one night several weeks into the semester, as they lay in their bunks in the dark hush of the old building, Garrett said quietly but with what Davy sensed was absolute conviction "you're the best friend I've ever had. This feeling between us is something so special that we must hold onto it all our lives."

Hearing this, Davy believed that he had finally discovered his destiny.

MANHATTAN: 1946

The main showroom at Luxemberg Jewelers was the nearest thing to heaven Rosie Stern could imagine. The long glass display counters full of shining, glittering, gleaming treasures entranced her. The deep, plush carpeting caressed her feet. Every square inch of the store oozed elegance. Someday she would marry a rich man. She would make him bring her here and buy her one of everything.

For years, she and her best friend, Shoshonna Freitag, had gazed in at all that opulence through the deeply tinted plate glass of the front windows every time they happened to pass the store. They had convinced themselves that Luxemberg Jewelers was on the way to everywhere, though the adults escorting them usually disputed this proposition.

Since entering high school and being allowed to navigate the city largely unescorted—at least in daylight hours—the girls had taken to planning their itineraries with the store as a necessary stop, if often only a brief one. Finally one afternoon early in their senior year, Shoshonnah pushed open the magical front door, which interestingly didn't look magical at all, just expensive, and strode resolutely inside. Rosie, terrified but unwilling to remain behind on the sidewalk, followed her. Shoshonnah somehow knew exactly what to do and say to keep from being pegged as a nuisance by the shop employees. Rosie supposed this must have been instinctual, and in this, as in so many other matters since their earliest days together as first graders, took her cue from her friend. Before long the two of them were discreetly but warmly acknowledged as regulars. But regular what? Certainly not customers. The girls' families were far from poor, but their allowances, even combined, didn't run to such luxuries as were on display. Not even close.

Until today. Because last week Shoshonnah had become "unofficially semi-engaged" to Jerry Fugelsang, though nobody knew this except Rosie herself and Shoshonnah's older sister, Rivka, who had been in Jerry's graduating class two years earlier. This new, rarified status promoted Shoshonnah from the ranks of hypothetical customers beyond even the aspirations of potential ones. She and Rosie agreed that she was now an imminent one, which was what had brought them in today, to shop for an "unofficial, semi-" engagement ring. It went without saying that this had to be of identical quality and magnitude to an official and fully fledged one.

———

If Rivka had her way, her sister Shoshonnah would not exist. How much nicer her life would have been if she had a younger brother instead. She thought about him a lot. She called him Dov, and he was all the things Shoshonnah was not, patient, kind, considerate, and, unfortunately, a bit slow. In compensation for this, Rivka's imagination allowed him to be exceptionally good looking, because, really, though an exceptionally good looking sister was a disaster for a girl, an exceptionally good looking brother could actually be an asset. And she should know, because everyone used to say her brother Ari was as handsome as a movie star. Young Dov might prove useful by helping her mother not miss Ari so much, and he would never compete with her for boyfriends. Shoshonnah had snatched more than one of them from her in the past.

Which, after all, was why they had come to Luxemberg's this afternoon. Because after her years and years of getting to know Jerry Fugelsang and even going on several double and triple dates as Jerry's designated girl and learning all about Jerry's interests and preferences and co-editing the yearbook with him and co-directing the senior show with him and generally making herself indispensable to him, all it took was one wink from her younger sister and he was lost to her forever. She really ought to spill the beans about the "unofficial semi-engagement" to their parents. That would fix Shoshonnah's wagon but good.

———

While Rivka stewed, Rosie watched intently as the point became moot. That afternoon they were being waited on by a young man she didn't remember ever seeing there before. And boy, would she have remembered such a dreamboat, with his smooth, blond, goyish hair and his exotic cat green eyes. Not to mention those shoulders. Oy!

When she heard Shoshonnah giggle that special giggle of hers, Rosie knew that Jerry Fugelsang's days were numbered.

———

Rivka's overheated musings were interrupted by the sound of her younger sister giggling at the young man behind the counter. "Officially semi-engaged" indeed, flirting like that. Poor Jerry. Somebody really should warn him about how fickle her sister could be. She couldn't do it, of course, because she "officially" wasn't speaking to him, though he was so besotted with Shoshonnah he hadn't yet realized it. But really, it was impossible because he simply wouldn't believe in her as a properly disinterested party. And Rosie Stern, poor, easily manipulated Rosie, wouldn't serve because of her fierce loyalty to Shoshonnah. It was hard to see who could be trusted on such a delicate mission.

She would find somebody, though. She had to. And to lend the story the required degree of credibility, she'd better find out as much as she could about "blondie". A name was always better than a mere description. It wasn't just that movie star hair. He had such broad shoulders.

———

"Who was that on the phone, Sol?" Mama Leah asked Papa while Rivka scrubbed out the kugel dish.

"Shmuel Luxemberg."

"Who?"

"Shmuel Luxemberg. You know, Luxemberg Jewelers."

"What on earth?" Mama gasped. "Rivka, you come in here."

"What, Ma?" Rivka asked, not moving.

"What do you know about Mr. Shmuel Luxemberg of Luxemberg Jewelers calling Papa on the phone? What has that sister of yours been up to now?"

"Ask Papa. He talked to the man."

"Now just you wait a minute, young lady. If you think you can talk to your mother like that because you're a college girl now. . ."

"Leah, calm down," Papa shouted. "It's not what you're thinking."

"You know what I'm thinking, do you? You're a mind reader these days, Solly?"

"Mr. Shmuel Luxemberg was merely making a polite inquiry."

"A polite inquiry? About Shoshonnah?"

"His nephew Villem has just come home from the army. And apparently he met Shoshonnah in the store recently."

"Thursday afternoon," Rivka confirmed.

"And Mr. Luxemberg was wondering. . ."

"Oh, Solly, really?"

Rivka didn't know whether to laugh or cry. True, she might get her beloved Jerry Fugelsang back. But the idea of Shoshonnah as wife of the heir to Luxemberg Jewelers—it was all she could do not to start smashing dishes.

BAXTER'S CROSSING,
MISSISSIPPI: 1953

D ear Davy:
   "The time has come, the walrus said, to talk of many things."

Remember that first night back at St. Gregory's? Stupid question. I know you do. Two silly freshman boys, standing in the middle of Founder's Quad in the rain, declaiming "Jabberwocky" at the top of their lungs. So many memories, but somehow I always go back to that one. Your wavy black hair plastered to your skull, your basso profundo pounding out those iambs in that comic opera Scottish accent. I knew I had found my true friend, my missing half.

I have no memories of those days that don't involve you in some fashion. Everything significant and a whole lot of insignificant as well. All that happened happened with you beside me. Or in that lower bunk. The pranks, the triumphs, the obstacles overcome or undermined, and most of all the epiphanies. My God, young men and their epiphanies. How naive we were. How thrilled we were at each new insight. And how deflated we were later on when we realized how mundane those insights were. And you, my friend, always you on that wobbling teeter totter with me.

Always—I see it now, though I didn't then—a little behind me. Always in my shadow. Always the sidekick, never the hero. Always. Why was that? I always saw us as equals. I believed in our equality like I believed in gravity or the goodness of God. Looking back, though, I wonder. Did I ever admire you, idolize you, the way I know you admired and idolized me? I'm afraid I didn't, and if you realized it, I hope you've forgiven me. More seriously, I wonder, was I truly worthy of your adulation? God knows, nothing was more important to me than your regard. I'd have died a dozen times over rather than be less than the man you believed I was. Becoming that man you thought so highly of turned into my life's quest. How much you taught me about friendship.

Five semesters of that perfection. Not quite five semesters and then Pearl Harbor. You practically had to chain me up in our dorm room, I was so determined to enlist. You persuaded me to wait until the end of term only by promising to enlist with me as soon as we had taken our exams. You with your pacifist principles. You, a sixth generation Quaker. What passion, what commitment, to turn your back on all that for the sake of a friend.

Those long years of war, separated for far longer than we had ever been together, with only the occasional letter passing between us. But no matter where I was and what horrors I witnessed, you were the one I missed most, most deeply longed to share my thoughts and impressions with. The war, which cost so many so much, seemed to steal us from one another.

And that blessed day when I heard your footsteps on the stairs once more. Back in our old dormitory room at St. Gregory's. They had relocated two sophomores so we could have our old room. Everyone on campus thought we were heroes. But we knew better. We had watched the true heroes die. We were just returning soldiers, no longer boys but men. It could never have been the same, of course. Too much had happened. Too much time had passed. Your black hair was already turning gray. My wounded left leg had ruined me for sports. And the school itself had changed.

For the first time there were female students among us.

Those girls, Davy? Prim church girls. Girls off the farms. They were wild about us. They swooned over you, with your smoky eyes and Byronic aspect. How many of them I tried and failed to explain you to. And that spring dawn when I stood beside you in Founder's Quad and watched as you burned all your pre-war sonnets. I was too much of a coward to stop you. The work of a self indulgent juvenile, you called them. You wept as you watched the flames consume them. It wasn't the poems themselves you cried for, it was our lost youth. How I wish I had kept copies of them. I know they were better than you thought. You have always been a far finer man than you realize.

Then, the worst day of my life. That sultry afternoon in Lexington. There we were with our newly minted Ph.D.'s. You had been offered a faculty position at St. Gregory's, but there was nothing there for me. There was no alternative. I accepted my position here. I do not exaggerate this, Davy. That was the worst day of my life. We were to be separated again. That separation has only been redeemed by your wonderful letters every week.

I know you are wondering. Why all this nostalgia? Why this oppressively elegiac tone? What misfortune am I skirting around, unable or unwilling to commit to paper? None, honestly. Unless one counts time and change as misfortunes, but you are far too wise for that.

No, no misfortune, but news. Important news, which I have as yet shared with no one, and which I refuse to share with you without first acknowledging all you are and all you have been to me. I am truly the most fortunate of men, to have had as magnificent a friend as you.

And so, on to the "cabbages and kings".

Her name is Amelia Williams. Welsh on her father's side, but her mother is a Stewart, so that's all right. She is a county judge's daughter and a student here at Anglesea College. She graduates next spring, when we are to be married. Her degree will be in French Literature with a second major in piano performance. She plays divinely. I can't wait for you to hear her play Chopin. I can't wait for the two of you to meet. I know she will love you as I do.

I suppose you will be annoyed and disappointed that I have left our entire courtship out of my correspondence. I can only plead this: I didn't want to mention her at all until I was sure. I hope and trust you will understand and forgive.

I know you will be happy for us. I know this because I know how joyful I will be on the day I receive a similar letter from you. Our dreams all come true eventually. We just have to endure until they do. I know now that someday a faculty position will open for me at St. Gregory's. We will teach there together, you and I. Our wives will be like sisters, and we will raise our sons side by side.

"*Grow old along with me / The best is yet to be / The last of life / For which the first was made.*"

With deep, abiding affection, Garrett

GRANT COUNTY, KENTUCKY: 1956

The storm was a very bad one by the standards of the region. In the larger towns the snow was cleared fairly quickly, but in the countryside the roads remained impassible well into the third day. Davy Sunderland, who had postponed his journey until the beginning of the Christmas holiday due to his extended absence from campus earlier that term, became nearly frantic at this latest delay. A Quaker educated by Presbyterians, he found the ancient Greeks helpful at such times. He resorted to cursing the fates until at last he was able to set out across the winter landscape in his pre-war Packard.

Concerned about conditions on the farm, he called Miss Mary Ellen before he left to ask if there was anything he should bring. They were doing fine, she assured him. They wanted for nothing but his safe arrival. Then, in the subdued and offhand manner with which southern women express their gravest misgivings, she allowed that they might—just might, mind you—be running a little low on infant formula. Not trusting that supplies would be available in the smaller villages along his route, Davy detoured clear into Lexington, where he acquired infant formula sufficient, Miss Mary Ellen assured him later, to feed a regiment of the most ravenous babies for upwards of a week, but what did he know of such things?

This detour further extended the delay in his arrival at the MacDonald farm. It was nightfall when he got there. The drive up to the house was hopeless. He was forced to leave the Packard at the side of the county road and go on foot, his bag in one hand and as much infant formula as he could carry in the other. He was prepared for this eventuality, however. The first time he had worn these boots, during that horrible winter in Belgium, January of 1945, they had kept out the wet and cold admirably. The passing of years had left them no less efficacious.

The terrible, unthinkable events had taken place while he was on a steamer in the North Atlantic, chaperoning a group of English majors on a trip to Great Britain paid for by one of the college's most eccentric benefactors. Their return voyage Thanksgiving week had been rough and stormy, harrowing for the poor students, who had never been at sea before. Then there was the long train and bus journey back to St. Gregory's, where Davy finally learned of the tragedy. It was all over by then, and there was nothing he could do except telegraph his condolences to Gordon and Miss Mary Ellen.

The accounts he heard on campus were disjointed and partial. He knew only that there had been an accidental shooting, a slightly premature birth, medical complications, two dead, an orphaned infant boy. Since hearing the news he had been more or less numb, and as he toiled up the snow clogged drive through the frigid, silent twilight, he realized that part of him still expected to step inside the house atop the hill and find his friend waiting there as always.

———

"It was a lynch mob," Miss Mary Ellen said, clearing the supper dishes. Gordon had gone to check something in the barn, Davy's offer to accompany him declined with a sad little smile that was Garrett's smile. "He interfered with a lynch mob. Nothing else to call it. He wasn't trying to set that negro free, just wanted them to leave him in jail to stand trial. That's what their pastor said. God only knows the truth of it. When poor Amelia heard he had been shot and killed, the shock sent her into labor. She went into a coma about as soon as the child was born. The doctor said there was no way to be sure she even knew the baby had come. Now her folks are calling Garrett a horrible word I won't repeat and refusing to have anything to do with the boy. So Gordon and I went down to Mississippi and fetched him back with us soon as he was strong enough to make the trip."

"What have you named him?" Davy asked.

"Griffin," Miss Mary Ellen said. "Griffin for his great-great-grandpa. My mama's father. They were Welshmen. Griffin David."

"Griffin David," Davy repeated, his heart finally, completely broken.

"He always said, my Garrett, that he was the luckiest man in the world, having you for his special friend. Seemed only right."

"I want to help out," Davy choked.

"Of course you do, dear."

———

"There you are, baby," Miss Mary Ellen crooned. "All nice and dry now."

Davy watched as she slipped the child into a fresh pair of sleepers.

"You sit with him," she said, laying the child in his arms. "I'll go warm his bottle."

"I. . ."

"Don't worry," Miss Mary Ellen laughed. "These little ones are tougher than they look. You can't hardly hurt them."

"He's so tiny."

"Tiny? I'll give you tiny. You should have seen him the night we got to Mississippi. That was tiny. He's growing like a weed. He'll be three weeks old on Christmas Day."

"He looks just like Garrett," Davy said, voice trembling.

"Doesn't he though? Takes me right back, it does."

———

"I feel terrible, leaving so soon," Davy said the next morning after breakfast.

"Your mama will be wanting you home for Christmas."

"I'd rather be here."

"We'd all rather a whole lot of things, now wouldn't we, son?" Gordon smiled. "They tell me it's all part of God's plan, but sometimes a man can't help but wonder if they know what they're talking about."

"You'll be back soon," Miss Mary Ellen said.

"If there's anything," Davy said, "anything at all you or the boy need, you must promise to call on me. I truly mean to help."

"We know, dear," Miss Mary Ellen said.

"You've always been a good friend to our family," Gordon smiled, eyes brimming.

"You sure you won't let me fix you a lunch to carry with you?"

———

On the endless, solitary drive to Richmond, Davy made several resolutions. Principally these had to do with services he could and must perform on behalf of Garrett's tiny son. This would give his life meaning now that Garrett was lost to him forever. The last resolution, however, bore solely on Davy himself. That nick-name Garrett had granted him as an eighteen year old must now be laid to rest as permanently as Garrett himself. Time to take up once again the lonely burden of the name his parents had given him. Time to be Malcolm now that the dream was dead.

MANHATTAN: 1957

"It's bad, Shoshonnah," Willi said.

"What does that mean, it's bad?" Shoshonnah asked, stubbing out her Kent in a Steuben ashtray.

"We're broke," Willi said. "Worse than broke. We're heavily in debt. We're so far in debt I don't see how we can keep the business open."

"How is this possible?" Shoshonnah asked. "Uncle Shmuel was a rich man. The business has been successful for years. How can there not be any money?"

"If you spend more than you take in, eventually you end up like this."

"I don't understand."

"It went on for years, Meyer says. You know that when the war ended Uncle Shmuel spent a lot of money trying to find out what happened to the family. Then when he finally located Marcus and Robbie, he gave them thousands to help them start over. Then there were large donations to the State of Israel. And recently it seems there's been a woman who. . ."

"A woman?" Shoshonnah cried. "Uncle Shmuel had a woman? Unbelievable."

"No, Shoshonnah, not like that. It seems that there was a woman over in New Jersey. A Polish refugee woman who somehow convinced him that she had helped Mama and the girls escape from the camp."

"My God."

"Oh, it gets worse," Willi said. "Her story was they're still trapped in Poland. But this woman knows where they're hiding. She could get help to them. She might even know someone who could get them out."

"And he believed her?"

"Yes."

"He gave her money?"

"Thousands," Willi shrugged. "Tens of thousands. It went on for several years."

"I can't believe that Meyer Schoenbaum let him do it."

"Meyer didn't know," Willi said.

"Meyer's the best accountant there is. How could he not know?"

"Uncle Shmuel paid her in cash. He told Meyer he had a gambling problem and swore that he was getting help for it."

"But Meyer found out eventually," Shoshonnah said.

"The woman was pulling the same scam on another of his clients. Someone who wasn't as good at covering his tracks. Meyer finally got the truth out of Uncle Shmuel before he died."

"Oh, Shmuel," Shoshonnah moaned. "You poor, stupid schmuck."

———

The next morning Shoshonnah went with Willi to the store. She was no accountant, but she had always had a head for figures and she wanted to see the books for herself. Her task couldn't have been more straightforward. No attempt had been made to hide anything. Uncle Shmuel had simply plundered the business. She wondered if there might be some grounds to sue. Shouldn't Meyer Schoenbaum have warned Willi? But she sensed that this horse wouldn't run. Uncle Shmuel had never made Willi a partner, though everyone recognized him as the heir. You couldn't go to court on verbal promises. She knew that much.

The cold figures stared back at her, smug in the inevitability they expressed. It was the Nazis reaching out of the past to manipulate an old man's grief and empty hopes. The Nazis, still not content with the destruction they'd already achieved. Total annihilation—she finally understood what that meant.

Shoshonnah could hardly blame Uncle Shmuel. She had known for years that it was more than just the loss of his family, as if that weren't horrible enough. Something in the way he spoke his sister-in-law's name, something in his eyes when he spoke it, convinced Shoshonnah that Eva had been the love of his life. Over and over again he told anyone who would listen the story of his failed attempt to rescue them all. But it was always the loss of Eva which seemed to weigh on him most heavily.

It was all too easy to imagine herself in his position. If somehow Willi's life were threatened, or one of the boys, what wouldn't she be willing to do? Was there any length, no matter how extreme, she wouldn't go to?

———

Willi met with Meyer Schoenbaum again and came back shaking his head. Shoshonnah thought he looked suddenly ten years older. He spoke of bankruptcy as if it were a foregone conclusion. They would lose the business but keep the apartment. With his experience and his connections he'd get a job easily enough with one or the other of their competitors. It wouldn't be the end of the world. But it would for all practical purposes be the end of the Luxembergs as they had always thought of themselves. For what is any family but the sum total of its aspirations over time? The name would survive, but without the dream which had invigorated them generation after generation they'd be just like everyone else. Those Nazis had been geniuses, Shoshonnah thought. They'd had more ways of destroying people than you could count. They could reach into the future to do it.

Willi met with an attorney Meyer Schoenbaum recommended. A preliminary meeting about filing bankruptcy. He promised he wouldn't make a decision without consulting her. Each day he looked older, more tired, more hopeless. This is how they must have looked in the ghettos waiting to be transported, she thought.

———

Shoshonnah wouldn't have hesitated a second to call on her parents for help if she'd thought it would do any good. But the amount of money involved was staggering. Anything her parents offered would be a drop in the bucket. Their entire net worth would barely make a dent. Nor could she remedy their predicament by instituting even the most radical of household economies. She began to feel as helpless as Willi looked. But she was damned if she'd let him see it. She sensed it would be the last straw for him.

———

The morning Willi was due to meet with the attorney to file the papers, Shoshonnah made him call the man's office and cancel the appointment.

"I want to look at the books again," she insisted.

"What good will that do?"

She had no answer for him, but her father had always said that a good offense made the best defense.

"Give me a week, Willi," she pled. "One week only. What harm can it do to wait seven days?"

"God made the world in seven days," Willi said.

"Willi, please. Seven days. What harm?"

"You're right, dear," he said. He'd never been able to say no to her. "When things can't get any worse, there's no need to rush."

———

She couldn't stand it. Willi seemed to be dying by inches in front of her eyes. And every time she visited the store the employees seemed more demoralized. Willi insisted that he had said nothing to them, but somehow they knew. They had seen fate in the clouds that morning on their way to work, or perhaps they read the future in their cups of tea. The store itself seemed to sense doom. The fixtures still gleamed, but not as brightly. The jewels sparkled, but as if with only half a heart.

She had to do something.

———

Two years on from her divorce, Rivka still insisted that she hadn't known the truth about Jerry Fugelsang until the very end. Never had the slightest inkling, she claimed. And then, the second she realized—bang, out the door taking the boys with her. As far as Shoshonnah was concerned this was just Rivka's usual bluster. Rivka was the kind of perfectionist who couldn't admit her mistakes. Shoshonnah was the other kind. She knew she should never have gotten involved with Jerry in the first place. Even in high school he had looked like trouble. But he had also looked like a movie star. That tipped the balance. Just because a boy talked and dressed and acted like Bugsy Siegel didn't mean he was a gangster. And just because he hinted that his aspirations lay in that direction—well really, who could take that kind of talk seriously? He just went to too many movies.

Still, somewhere in her gut Shoshonnah had known. Her first glimpse of Willi Luxemberg had not merely encompassed a handsome young man just back from the service, or a whole new form of elegance so far removed from the tawdry glamour Jerry represented as to practically make the two young men members of different species, but indeed, an entire alternative future for herself and the children she planned one day to have. She never looked back. But Rivka, like Lot's wife, had. And once Jerry had been convinced to let her console him for his loss, Rivka truly turned into a pillar—of something, though perhaps not salt exactly. Something solid and unmoveable at least. No amount of *geschrei* from their parents could dissuade her. For her part, Shoshonnah held her tongue. Adding her protests to those of her parents would, she knew, only stiffen Rivka's resolve. That's the way it had always been between the two sisters. "You say 'potato' and I say 'you're nutso'".

She had to admit that while Jerry's choice of career never surprised her, his sudden eminence did. "I never thought he had it in him," she often found herself thinking, as rumors of his meteoric rise through the ranks meandered in and out of her consciousness. The evidence was unmistakable, however. The house in Riverdale. Rivka's Lincoln convertible, furs, jewelry. The family's exotic travels. The boys' private schooling. Shoshonnah would have been jealous of all this, but she knew what she knew.

———

She wore the gas blue dress that everybody said made her look like Liz Taylor. It wasn't exactly appropriate for daytime errands, but when the fish you have to fry are sharks you don't do business as usual. She went evening with her hair and makeup as well, because this was not just her best shot but her only one. Then, on her way out the door, she grabbed Cooper out of his playpen. You should never go to meet the Mafia unarmed, she reasoned. And what better weapon could a beautiful young woman have with her than an adorably squirmy fourteen month old?

———

Jerry was, as always, happy to see her. Over the years, his effusiveness at family gatherings had been an embarrassment. No wonder Rivka was always jealous. Rivka would have killed herself rather than admit this, but a sister knows. That morning, Jerry reeked of his usual cocktail of brylcreem, Old Spice, and cigar smoke. His clothing was as flashy as a new Cadillac on a showroom floor. Shoshonnah had heard that since the divorce he was drinking more than ever. His face confirmed this, but the glint in his fishy eyes warned her that this particular morning he was sober enough.

Ordinarily Cooper didn't like to be held, preferring instead to explore floors and furniture, but he clambered over Jerry like a mountaineer, loosening his necktie and tousling his hair, generally distracting him with a dazzling grin and his broad repertoire of vocal noises that were not quite words. Jerry was entranced. He must be missing his own boys terribly, Shoshonnah decided. Rivka wouldn't let him anywhere near them, as if being a Mafioso were something contagious.

With Jerry thus disarmed, Shoshonnah got down to business quickly and efficiently. It was ridiculously easy for them to come to terms, though she understood clearly that the stated terms weren't the actual terms at all. She left Jerry's office with his handshake burning her palm. The next morning, with Willi safely off to work and Ike and the twins at school, she accepted the briefcase full of cash the well dressed young Italian gentleman delivered with no more ceremony than if it had been a dozen eggs, but with rather greater qualms.

———

Shoshonnah was no fool. She had known better than to ask for the entire amount they needed to get themselves out of debt. Jerry Fugelsang might still be crazy for her, but he wasn't stupid and he didn't yet rank high enough to be totally his own man. An amount that large would have been impossible for him. What she wanted and what she got was a sort of down payment on survival. Enough to take care of their most pressing debts, keep their vendors willing to ship inventory, keep the lights on and the help paid. She was buying the time they needed to see some benefits of the cuts they'd have to make if they wanted to survive in business long term. Jerry's money was enough to pay down their debts sufficiently that their cash flow would meet their immediate obligations. The cuts she envisioned would allow them to pay off the rest of their creditors over time. It wouldn't be easy and it wouldn't be pleasant. The only thing you could say in favor of her scheme was that it beat the alternatives.

She swept into the store the next day with Cooper in tow and her briefcase full of cash. She marched into Willi's office and announced that from that moment she was in charge of the financial side of the business, and further, that he should leave her alone and ask no questions. This, in its own way, was as big a gamble as the one with Jerry.

She worked longer hours than anyone, and because her mother complained that Cooper was a difficult child to handle she brought him along with her most days. While she slaved away in her office, he occupied himself entertaining the staff and customers. Her mother complained about this, too, but listening to these complaints beat the alternative.

———

Shoshonnah knew from the start that six months was pushing it. As far as the Mafia was concerned, that was a long term loan. Still, she asked for six months and Jerry agreed, though the look in his eyes told her exactly how far out on a limb he was going. She couldn't imagine six months being enough, but it was all the time she had to turn things around. As the deadline approached, she realized with mounting dismay how naive she'd been. After economizing ruthlessly, renegotiating contracts with vendors tenaciously, doing everything she could think of to put their financial house in order, she still found herself with less than half of what she needed to repay Jerry.

She'd accepted this possibility from the beginning. She had understood clearly the risk she was taking. She knew exactly what was at stake. She looked around at what she had accomplished. Though still under serious financial stress, the business was nevertheless in no immediate danger. Another eighteen months to two years and their debts would largely be retired. They'd be able to dispense with the most burdensome economies even sooner than that. Already Willi seemed more optimistic than she'd seen him since before Uncle Shmuel's death.

So what she would have to do next was worth it, she supposed. She kept reminding herself that as she dressed to go meet Jerry, but her hands shook anyway. She tried not to think about how she would face Willi when he came home from work that evening.

———

She was running late and almost didn't answer the phone. She recognized Rivka's voice on the other end, but Rivka's sobs made her unintelligible.

"Rivka," she shouted. "Slow down. Take a deep breath already. What is it?"

"They killed Jerry," Rivka blurted. "Somebody planted a bomb in his car."

GRANT COUNTY, KENTUCKY: 1961

The new pastor's wife, Mrs. Della Jenkins, was the kind of young woman Mary Ellen Douglas MacDonald would have been proud to call her daughter. Pretty, but not too pretty; sweet, but not too sweet; forthright, but smart enough to know when to hold her tongue; soft spoken, but with the kind of backbone which made her difficult if not impossible to intimidate. Yes, Mary Ellen thoroughly approved of Mrs. Jenkins.

Still, in her day to day comings and goings it would never have occurred to her to seek Mrs. Jenkins' advice. Mary Ellen took enormous pride in her self reliance. She liked to think of herself as unusually well equipped to stand on her own two feet, to meet any and all challenges head on. With the Good Lord's help, of course. That hardly needed to be said. As the wife of a not particularly successful farmer, the challenges she faced were, she realized, fairly limited in scope. But no one could dispute how elemental, how profound, they could be. And in all her years, Mary Ellen had never flinched. With her Bible in one hand and one or another kitchen implement in the other, she faced fire, famine, flood, illness—both human and animal—death; whatever, indeed, the world dispensed with equanimity and good common sense. And, God bless her, she hadn't felt the need for anyone's advice since the death of her mother. Mary Ellen was twelve years old at the time, and had without a second's hesitation taken on all the duties her mother had left behind.

But if somehow the day finally came when advice indeed was required—this was a possibility that her advancing years increasingly forced her to ponder—she had come after much consideration to the decision that Mrs. Della Jenkins was the person she would turn to. There was no question in her mind about it. This was problematic, since she knew that by all rights she should turn to her husband first. She knew, as well, that the best she could hope for from him was a mildly exasperated request not to be bothered. Then there was the pastor himself, Brother James Jenkins, who should be approached. Or any one of the elders of the church or their wives. But she knew instinctively that none of these would do. She knew all of them well, except Brother Jenkins of course, and recognized that despite their exalted stations they were truly no wiser than she was, and she doubted that when that day came that she needed, really needed, the advice of another human being any one of them was capable of offering her more than she could offer herself. Every fiber of her being insisted that she could depend on Mrs. Della Jenkins, and she was thus convinced to flout convention and seek out a woman so much younger than herself, a woman so far down the hierarchy of wisdom and experience, and without children of her own.

For that matter, Mary Ellen's own experience of child rearing was limited. Garrett had been her only child. And Garrett for all practical purposes raised himself. He never needed anything more from her than to be fed, sheltered, and clothed. Little Griffin, the grandson she was now raising, was much the same. Or had been. But now? It was just possible, she supposed, that there might be something slightly—no, not wrong with Griffin. Not so serious as to be described as wrong. But. Something unusual enough that specialist knowledge seemed to be called for. Something she couldn't imagine mentioning to Gordon, who would just look at her with confusion, or Elder Dickinson, for instance, who would exhort her to lay it at Jesus' feet. This advice, though she understood the theologial imperative well enough, left her without any aid of a practical nature. That was the crux of the matter. Aid of a practical nature. If anyone could offer that, it had to be Mrs. Della Jenkins. Her piano solo at worship service just two Sundays earlier clinched it. It could almost be seen as a sign from God. It certainly could be portrayed in that way, should Elder Dickinson's wife Shirleen (one of the Cooper girls from the southern part of the county she was, and an incurable busybody and critic) make inquiries at some unspecified time in the future.

Still, Mary Ellen scarcely knew how to approach the young woman. She thought about it a lot. No idea came to her. Two Sundays passed and her perplexity about the boy only grew. Finally, on her way out of the sanctuary on the third

Sunday, she walked up to Mrs. Della Jenkins and just blurted it out: "There's a small matter I'd like to discuss with you. Would it be convenient for me to come by the parsonage some afternoon? This week?"

"Why certainly, Mrs. MacDonald." Mrs. Della Jenkins' smile was warm and seemed completely sincere. "What day would suit you?"

"Thursday," Mary Ellen said. "I believe Thursday would be best."

"I'll look forward to it, Mrs. MacDonald."

———

Mrs. Della Jenkins greeted Mary Ellen with the affection due to an aunt and the deference appropriate to an elder's wife, though Gordon had never actually served in that office. Mrs. Della Jenkins offered her iced tea which was made exactly as Mary Ellen liked it. Sweet, but not too sweet. Mrs. Della Jenkins served a plate of cookies to go with the tea, and the cookies were not store bought but made, it turned out, from Mrs. Della Jenkins' mother-in-law's own recipe. Mrs. Della Jenkins behaved as though Mary Ellen's visit were a purely social call. Mary Ellen judged that this showed a degree of tact which verged on full-on diplomacy and decided that she approved of the young woman quite unreservedly. And that she had been absolutely correct in her choice of confidant.

"It's the boy, Mrs. Jenkins," she began, the delicate flavors of the Russian Communist Tea Cookie lingering comfortingly in her mouth. "My grandson Griffin, that is."

"Such an adorable little boy," Mrs. Jenkins smiled. "That gorgeous dark red hair. Such an unusual shade."

"Griffin has his daddy's hair."

"It's lovely."

"Griffin is four and a half."

"I see."

"Small for his age," Mary Ellen nodded. "His grandfather's not a large man. His Daddy wasn't either. And his poor mother was delicate."

"Of course."

"It's just this," Mary Ellen stammered, feeling undone now that the moment of truth had arrived. "He plays the piano."

Mary Ellen was not sure why they even still had the piano. Her mother had been a very fine musician, but Mary Ellen, despite diligent effort, never showed any aptitude for it.

"He does? How sweet."

Obviously the young woman hadn't understood her. Best start from the beginning.

"I was in my kitchen a while back getting dinner ready to put on the table, and I heard him at it in the front parlor. He's not really allowed to touch the piano, but just as I was about to head in there to correct him I noticed it was an actual tune he was playing. It was 'Amazing Grace' just as sure as anything."

"Really."

"And after that it was 'O God Our Help in Ages Past.' He sat there at the piano and he played every hymn from that morning's service. From memory. We have a hymnal right there on the piano, of course, but it wasn't open. And even if it had been, Mrs. Jenkins, he's just four and a half. He doesn't go to school yet. He can't read."

"This is very interesting, Mrs. MacDonald."

"Interesting? Strange is what I'd call it. Very, very strange, and I'm worried sick about the boy. He's at it all the time now. Dozens of hymns. His grandpa thinks it's harmless, but it scares me, I have to tell you."

"Oh, Mrs. MacDonald, I don't think it's anything to be alarmed about. He's probably just a musical child. Now when you say he plays the hymns, exactly what does he do?"

"Plays them, is all. At first it was just picking out the tune, with one finger like. But a couple of weeks back, he started using both hands. It was like he knew all the notes, not just the melody. That's when I got rattled. No little kid ought to be able to do that."

"But sometimes they do," Mrs. Della Jenkins said. "Sometimes they do. Mozart did, for instance."

"You're joking."

"No, no. It's true. Now I really don't think there's a thing for you to worry about, but why don't you bring little Griffin to see me one afternoon soon and let me talk to him about it. Would that be all right?"

—

Mary Ellen was reluctant to keep her appointment with Mrs. Della Jenkins because it meant once again having to ask Gordon to drive her to the parsonage, this time with the boy along, and that risked piquing his interest. All in all, things went better around the house the more oblivious to domestic matters Gordon remained. He was not an unpleasant man in any way, but he was sometimes too curious about things. In addition, he had a tendency not to interfere, exactly, but to be underfoot which she found exasperating. She preferred to mind her own business and let him mind his. That's when she was happiest. When it came to the boy, their businesses overlapped uncomfortably sometimes. It had been this way with Garrett as well. It would be better if Gordon would agree to ignore the boy until he was eleven or twelve. Then they would switch off. Gordon could take over and she would go off duty.

In the event, however, the problem never arose. Gordon was addicted to reading biographies. He read them constantly, acquiring new ones from used book dealers as far away as Philadelphia, Boston, Chicago, a parade of exotic postmarks and return addresses. It was his one and only extravagance. And by a good fortune Mary Ellen had neglected to pray for in her anxiety, one such parcel arrived the day before she was to take Griffin to see Mrs. Della Jenkins. It was as if the Lord were keeping a special eye on the enterprise. Gordon happily agreed to drive them into town and sat outside in the pickup reading the whole time.

Mary Ellen soon had reason to question the role of providence in the matter, however, because immediately upon hearing Griffin play on her living room spinet, Mrs. Della Jenkins began to insist quite strenuously that the boy be taken as soon as possible for an interview with her old piano professor all the way over at St. Gregory's College. Yes, as far as that. A good thirty miles. It might as well be Mars. Gordon was certain to become involved. Why, if they left one day right after lunch, it would be nightfall before they returned. This would necessitate a cold supper. Gordon enjoyed a cold supper well enough. That wasn't a problem. He would *notice* a cold supper on a weekday evening. Ordinarily she served them only on Saturdays and Sundays. Yes, he would notice it. Just as he would notice driving on a journey that crossed county lines. No, it was too much. Too much by far.

As the impossibility of Mrs. Della Jenkins' proposal crashed down onto Mary Ellen's fragile shoulders, the young woman proved her infinite value as a friend and confidant.

"I'd hate to pull Mr. MacDonald away from his work on the farm," she said. "Wouldn't it be best if I drive us over there myself? In my Rambler?"

Nearly prostrate with relief, Mary Ellen nevertheless managed to preserve her decorum. Quickly, but not too quickly, she assented to this suggestion.

———

Mary Ellen had rarely been so far away from home. The campus of St. Gregory's College, in full summer foliage and somnolence that afternoon, appeared to her like a strange combination of institution for the mentally disturbed and quaint old world village. The professor's cottage looked like it had been modeled from the pages of a storybook. It was neat as a pin, and the profuse, homey flowers in low beds along the walk and fronting the porch comforted her enormously.

A Negro woman in a housekeeper's uniform opened the door to them and showed them into the front parlor. An old black spaniel shuffled over to sniff them and then shuffled back to its corner and went to sleep, snoring softly. The Negro woman, who knew Mrs. Della Jenkins and whose name was Eulalie, served them iced tea, which was sweet but not too sweet, just as Mary Ellen liked it. Eulalie brought out a little glass of lemonade with a maraschino cherry floating in it for Griffin. Mary Ellen was familiar with maraschino cherries only from her fruitcake recipe and found this vaguely disturbing. She had resolved, however, to take her cues from Mrs. Della Jenkins, who evinced no concern whatever at the sight, so Mary Ellen held her tongue.

Eulalie brought in a plate of cookies. They were homemade instead of store bought. Seeing this, Mary Ellen at last began to relax. Thank goodness Griffin was on his best behavior. But then, Griffin was always on his best behavior.

———

The woman who joined them a short while later was dressed like a duchess and spoke English with a nearly incomprehensible accent. Mary Ellen watched as she and Mrs. Della Jenkins embraced each other and listened intently to their expressions of greeting.

Then Mrs. Della Jenkins introduced her to Madame, who was beautifully polite but somehow terrifying. Finally, there was Griffin, grasping his glass of lemonade and looking warily curious.

"And this must be the boy," Madame Grammatikova said.

MANHATTAN: 1965

Marcus Luxemberg caught a taxi at Pennsylvania Station. His sister-in-law had offered to pick him up, but the last time he visited New York her driving had been enough to give him a heart attack. That pink and white Buick convertible might as well have been a Maserati racer the way she carved up the city buses and the cabs. It was far scarier than anything the Arabs had ever thrown at him and that was saying a lot.

Marcus was intrigued by the way Villem's life—he had never gotten used to that American nickname, Willi—paralleled his own. They had both married women who looked like movie stars. From any distance at all, Shoshonnah could easily be mistaken for Elizabeth Taylor, and the last time Marcus and Yael had been in Rome, there was a near riot when a rumor swept the crowds outside their hotel that Sophia Loren was staying there. Of course their mother, Eva, had been a great beauty. Perhaps Marcus and Villem had inherited an eye for beauty from their father.

———

"So you've been promoted," Shoshonnah said, wrestling with the corkscrew in what Marcus thought was a particularly seductive fashion. Not that she meant anything by it. He had never met a woman so overtly yet unconsciously sexual in everything she did. She was almost a parody of the frisky housewife. If her business acumen hadn't been so notorious, he might have taken her coquettishness seriously enough to cause trouble—who knew?

"Yes, well, it's just for as long as I'm attached to the embassy," he said. "The minute I'm sent back to Israel I'm busted to Major. It's a courtesy promotion.

Can't have the Military Attache's staff members being outranked by everyone else's in the whole diplomatic community. Makes us look bad."

"How typical," Shoshonnah said, pouring the wine. "Wouldn't it be much simpler just to promote you permanently? You Israelis seem determined to overcomplicate everything."

"Perhaps it just seems that way because of you Americans and your penchant for oversimplification."

"We have this argument every time you visit."

"We do," he smiled.

"And we never solve it."

"The one good thing about it," Marcus said, sipping his wine, which was surprisingly good for an American product, "is I'm now eligible for a higher level of housing assistance. I can afford a place big enough for Yael and the boys to come over."

"Marcus, that's wonderful. I can't wait to meet her—them."

———

Shoshonnah made no pretense to culinary skills. This was one more thing she had in common with Yael. Dinner that night was Chinese takeout. It was excellent Chinese takeout from what Marcus could tell, though he was hardly a connoisseur. Yael was the expert on Chinese food. She loved it. He wondered how difficult it would be to find kosher takeout in Washington D.C. It was of absolutely no consequence to him as a Zionist of the Marxist school. If there was a dietary law he hadn't broken it was an oversight. But it would be of critical importance to his in-laws, the Weinsteins, should they ever visit from Montreal.

Willi was aging beautifully. He looked like old photographs of their grandfather, Itzak Luxemberg, who had been a very distinguished gentleman. The boys were intriguing. The older three, Ike, Jake, and Josh, were perfect blond, green eyed Luxembergs, but were tall and willowy like the Freitags. Cooper, the youngest, promised to be broad shouldered and powerfully built like the Luxembergs but had the raven hair and unusual ice blue eyes of his mother. All four of them were intelligent, and they had beautiful manners. A little too beautiful for Marcus' taste. He hadn't raised Rafi and Gil to be so refined, but things like that mattered here in the States. Israelis were, he judged, more down to earth.

———

After dinner, Shoshonnah exempted the boys from their usual chores and shooed them into the living room to keep their uncle company. Knowing what would come next, Willi excused himself to his study—he couldn't bear to hear such things talked about.

The boys settled themselves in for one of Marcus' stories. He had all kinds of stories: escaping from the Nazis, joining the Resistance, traveling overland through the ruins of Europe to Palestine, executing acts of sabotage against the British before independence, fighting the Arabs periodically since then. It was interesting to observe the boys as they listened. Ike all too obviously was bored and couldn't wait to be allowed to turn on the television. Jake was intent, often interrupting to ask for clarification of some detail or other. Josh, the sensitive one, looked like he might burst into tears at any moment.

Cooper looked like he wanted to kill somebody.

ST. GREGORY'S COLLEGE: 1966

Sasha, Madame Grammatikova's cocker spaniel, nuzzled her and wagged his tail, but it didn't cheer Juliette up the way it usually did.

"Anything I can play, he can play better," she sighed.

"Don't say that, dear," her mother cautioned and went back to reading her book.

But it was true. The walls of Madame's cottage might as well be made of paper. Juliette could hear every note being played in the studio next door. Spring recital was just two weeks away. Juliette and Griffin had both begged to be allowed to study the Rachmaninoff Prelude in C sharp minor. The famous one. Madame permitted this but decreed that only one of them would be allowed to perform it in the recital—the one who played it best, of course. Juliette could play the A section as well as Griffin, but then everything went wrong. She couldn't get the B section up to tempo no matter how hard she tried, and sitting here listening to him sail through it effortlessly made her want to cry. The return of the A section, A', with its denser chords and heavier chromaticism, was an even direr challenge. Maybe she should just give it all up and concentrate on making the cheerleading squad next fall.

When she burst into tears of frustration over it during her lesson last week, Madame counseled her not to be discouraged. In a year or two, with sufficient application, she'd be up to mastering the piece. She mustn't compare herself to Griffin, or anyone for that matter. Every musician was unique and developed at a different rate. She must simply relax and enjoy herself more. She was a very talented young lady, and nature would eventually take its course.

Her mother said everyone knew that Griffin was a savant, a genius at one thing only and useless at everything else. Juliette should be thankful she was so well rounded. It was individuals with a variety of skills who made the world go around. Juliette was pretty sure it was the laws of physics that made the world go around, but she had learned a long time ago that no good ever came of arguing with her mother.

The grandfather clock across the room chimed the half hour, and Sasha nuzzled her more insistently.

"Anything I can play, he can play better," Juliette whispered to herself.

WILLIAMSTOWN,
KENTUCKY: 1973

B rock Van der Jagt checked his necktie and hair in the mirror next to the light booth. This was unnecessary. His tie wouldn't dare loosen or shift out of alignment, and his ruthlessly pomaded hair was as immovable as that object in that law by Newton that his Uncle Rex was always quoting incorrectly. Grinning at his reflection with profound contentment, he checked his watch. The performers on-stage, baton twirling identical twins Susie and Sally Rutherford, had approximately seventy seconds left in their act.

As president of the junior class, it was Brock's duty to emcee the annual Williamstown High School talent night. It was the biggest fundraiser the junior class put on each year, crucial to the success of the senior prom. The class officers and sponsors organized the event as diligently as the Joint Chiefs of Staff planning the invasion of a tropical island ruled by a corrupt dictator. The cast performed with the zeal of a platoon of Marines assigned the duty of liberating the island. And Brock was at the center of it all.

The twins' recorded music ended with a brassy flourish. The sellout crowd erupted into applause. Brock gave the twins a generous amount of time to take their bows then bounded out of the wings, grabbing the mike stand on his way to center stage. He knew exactly how good he looked in his navy blue suit, purchased specially for the occasion in an exclusive men's shop in Lexington. He could prac-tically hear the hearts fluttering all the way up on stage. He imagined the follow spot's gleam off his perfect blond hair.

"Thank you, Susie and Sally Rutherford!" he boomed into the almost super-fluous microphone. "Weren't they terrific, ladies and gentlemen? How about one more round of applause for Susie and Sally?"

The crowd obliged enthusiastically.

"And now for a brief pause while we set the stage for our final act of the evening."

Brock moved downstage left taking the mike stand with him. It required the entire stage crew, wearing black turtlenecks and trousers, to wheel the giant Steinways out to their tape marks at center stage, where they sat bow to bow, the keyboards opposite each other so that the performers faced one another across acres of sounding board.

"And now we proudly present," Brock said, "our final act of the evening. George Gershwin's *Rhapsody in Blue* performed by junior class vice president and co-captain of the varsity cheerleading squad Miss Juliette Simpson and Mr. Griffin David MacDonald."

Brock stepped offstage into the deep shadows of the wings. Polite applause greeted the performers as they approached their instruments. With a sinking heart, Brock realized the one mistake he had made all evening. From his concealed van-tage point he could only see Juliette, his beloved, the girl of his dreams, from behind. He looked instead directly at Griffin, halfway across the stage from him. Scrawny Griffin, who didn't look much like a junior in high school. More like a sixth grader, Brock thought.

Brock was vaguely aware of classical music. Occasionally his mother would play *Bolero* on the stereo until his father yelled at her to turn it off. And his Aunt Olympia had attained a certain notoriety around Grant County for her perfor-mances of the "Flower Song" from *Carmen*. And of course, every kid in America knew the first four notes of Beethoven's Fifth. But this stuff that Juliette and her buddy Griffin got up to, their esoteric discussions, their long hours of practice, their weekly journeys way over to St. Gregory's College for lessons. To Brock it was all as incomprehensible as particle physics or epistemology. And tonight's per-formance was all the more of a mystery to him because during rehearsals the two of them absolutely refused to perform their piece, pounding out "Chopsticks" instead as they laughed.

He has heard Juliette play many times, of course. As substitute organist at church or accompanying soloists or the youth choir. She played for choirs and ensembles here at school as well. But Griffin was a blank, even though Juliette claimed that of the two of them he was the better musician. Griffin had been around more or less forever, but Brock couldn't call to mind the sound of his voice, his preference in soft drinks, anything about him really but his physical appearance, which was nondescript except for that hair color. The fact that Juliette was absolutely devoted to him would have given Brock pause except that it was so transparently a brother-sister thing, or for that matter a girl-puppy thing.

So as the audience hushed and the follow spot lit them at their twin instruments, Brock was prepared for anything but what actually happened. They began to play and he was dumbfounded.

MANHATTAN: 1973

W hen Cooper came in from the graduation party, Shoshonnah was sitting on the balcony relaxing with a Benson and Hedges. She listened as he rummaged around in the kitchen. Eventually the blender went on. Another protein shake. Everyone she knew was dubious about his muscle building, but she saw no problem with anything that focused him so seriously on proper nutrition. He had given her fits as a child with his dietary whims. Nowadays she didn't have to worry. She was tired to death of worrying. When people said to her "don't worry", she invariably retorted "I never worry", but of course she did. All mothers did, regardless of what they claimed.

But now Cooper had gotten home from his graduation party in once piece, and she could mark a big one off her list.

She listened as Cooper rinsed out the carafe and put it into the dishwasher. Her biggest worry about the protein shakes always had been that he'd give himself food poisoning mixing them in a blender carafe that wasn't sufficiently sanitized. She bought extra carafes for the blender, and sure enough he never used one twice without cleaning it. The minute it was empty, poof—into the dishwasher.

It was the end of one phase of her life. She knew that. The boys were raised now. Sure, there were girlfriends to interrogate, intimidate, or make disappear, prospective in-laws to vet, career plans to critique. Sure. All those things. But it wouldn't be the same. Ever. Thank God. Cooper graduated from high school was the last apron string cut.

She sat and lit another cigarette and didn't go inside to ask him if he'd had a good time at the party. A boy who had just graduated from high school didn't want his last conversation of that hallowed night to be with his mother. A boy who had just graduated didn't want to be confronted by the possibility that his mother had waited up for him. Boys' mothers waited up. Young men's mothers didn't. She'd have loved to walk in there and see him with that protein shake mustache on his gorgeous mug and his hair a little tousled and his necktie loosened. But she wouldn't do that. No. Leave him undisturbed with whatever impressions the night had left. That was his real graduation present and he'd never know it.

She didn't have to see him like that to know she'd been the best mother possible. She didn't have to see him at all.

The lights went out in the kitchen and a few moments later she heard the shower go on in the bathroom the boys all used.

———

She hadn't been the most typical of mothers. She readily admitted that. She never cooked worth a damn, for instance, except for those legendary roast potatoes—her mother's recipe. She never stayed home with the boys when they were sick. Nanny did that. Sometimes Nanny and Willi both. She'd always gone to work at the store knowing that everything was under control. She never did a lot of things all the other mothers did. She knew some people actually accused her of neglect from time to time. Not in the legal sense, of course, and not to her face. But that didn't mean she never heard about it. Well, screw them. They didn't know. They didn't know shit.

They knew all about what she hadn't done for her sons, but they didn't know what she had. That wasn't something she talked about. She never called attention to it at all. But it was as real as wiping any two year old's butt.

When all her friends were driving Lincolns, she stayed with her faithful Buick. When all her friends were making their husbands buy them minks, she stuck to her shearling lamb and her faithful fox. When they were all moving their broods to Westchester, she insisted on staying in Manhattan. When they were scrambling to get their kids into private schools, she kept the boys in public ones. When they were buying Dior and Chanel, she was taking stacks of magazines to Mrs. Feigenbaum, her dressmaker, and hoping for the best. When they were jetting off to Europe to see Paris and Rome, she and Willi were packing the boys into the station wagon and heading for the Adirondacks. When her friends were all sending their kids to Bennington and Brown and complaining about the cost, her sons won scholarships to perfectly good but less prestigious institutions and she kept her checkbook closed.

She willingly subjected herself to all the jokes about tightwads. Cheapskates. Penny pinchers.

It was atonement, she knew, for a life made possible by ill gotten gains. It was the equivalent of all those things you did to ward off bad luck, like not walking under a ladder or on cracks in the sidewalk. But it was more than that. Her thrift was a prayer that she might never find herself and her family in need. Every cent that she saved she used to ensure that. She read, she researched, she experimented. She even gambled on a small scale. Eventually, it paid off. Her friends collected antique porcelain, played tennis, painted water colors, bred terriers, arranged flowers, learned French cooking. Bibi Mandel even took up belly dancing. Shoshonnah played the stocks for all she was worth, and it made her a rich woman. Daily she imagined how the *New York Times* would profile her, if she ever went public, as the "Housewife Wizard of Wall Street." When people snickered behind her back about her lack of extravagance, she pondered what outfit to wear when the photographer from the *Wall Street Journal* came to shoot her in her kitchen.

Really, it was astonishing how much a woman like herself could accumulate without anyone but the IRS being any the wiser. All you had to do was avoid conspicuous displays. She could have retired Willi and taken them both off to a private island in the Caribbean. She could have leapfrogged the Lincoln in favor of a Bentley. She could have bought her own couturier in Paris. She could have played for high stakes at Monte Carlo and lost without remorse. She could have made Issac a millionaire on his twenty-first birthday with enough left over to do the same for the others as they reached that milestone. She was no Rothschild, but she could have done all that and more.

Instead, she kept her secret. Secrets were something she'd always been good at. Someday they'd need the money a lot worse than they had needed any of the things she made them do without. And let's face it. They'd still been pretty spoiled compared to their cousins in California and Tel Aviv. When the time came it would be waiting for them. And if they never needed it, their children might.

ST. GREGORY'S COLLEGE: 1974

From the windows of his office on the fourth floor—the turret, actually—of Memorial Hall, Malcolm Sunderland had the best view on campus. His windows faced the chapel across the velvet expanse of the Founder's Quadrangle. The chapel had been envisioned by the school's founder as a replica of Westminster Abbey, but budgetary constraints—as well as engineering ones primarily regarding scale—had resulted in a rather impressionistic homage to that edifice instead. Still, the chapel was authentic looking enough and grandiose enough to be impressive. It was easily the largest structure in the county. You had to go clear into Lexington to encounter anything more imposing. Malcolm loved the way it anchored his view. At right angles to the chapel sat All Angels Hall, the college's oldest classroom building. Opposite it was the student commons. These had been modeled on buildings at Cambridge University. The founder never actually visited Cambridge, but he had seen pictures. To him Cambridge represented everything a university should be, and in copying the architecture he had been expressing his fervent hope that the institution he was endowing with for all practical purposes his entire fortune would eventually rise to similar heights of academic glory.

It hadn't, but not through any deficiency in the aesthetics of the campus.

But as much as he loved the antiquity portrayed by those buildings, it was the broad, smooth expanse of the quadrangle itself which moved Malcolm most deeply. It was as evocative, in its own way, as Trafalgar Square or St. Mark's in Venice, a great public space where generations had come and gone and history, at least of a sort, had been made. His own history not least of all, for Malcolm had been a college student here. Decades ago, his youthful self inhabited these gothic revival precincts, meandered the dreamy cloisters and alcoves, sat on the weathered stone benches, reclined on that almost artificial looking grass. Those college days had been the last time—no, really the only time—he was happy.

Witnessing the return of students to the college each fall he was drawn back to those days, to pensive, bittersweet musings on what had been and what hadn't. Each year's new crop of students, discovering the campus in their own way, reminded him inevitably of his own experiences, his own friendships, his own triumphs and disappointments. And every year there was one young man among the throng of entering students who reminded him of his own special one, that friend for whom he would have done and given everything.

This year the young man is no analogue; the resemblance not merely a product of imagination and wishful reminiscence. This year, that young man is quite literally the embodiment of that dear, lost love. Because this year, that young man is Malcolm's godson Griffin. Outwardly, Griffin is his father Garrett's *doppelganger*. Inwardly, Griffin is—well, Malcolm has no idea, actually, who Griffin is inwardly. His musician's psyche has up to now been totally indecipherable. He is not his father, that's all Malcolm is sure of.

Still, there is one thing Malcolm does know about Griffin. He knows it because there are a handful of eternal verities one understands instinctively. There hasn't been a male college freshman yet born of whom it wasn't true. If by some accident such an individual actually exists, Malcolm prays never to encounter him, just as he prays never to come face to face with the antichrist. One's entire future rests on this single truth. A freshman boy needs a special friend. No, not needs; must have. Just as that same boy must have oxygen in the air he breathes, must have water, must have nutritious food. The imperative is as elemental as that.

So it is for Griffin, because it must be.

It has taken some doing to provide the conditions necessary for that friendship to flourish, but Malcolm has been equal to the task. There was a price to be paid, and he paid it. There was nothing he could do that was left undone, and nothing he was unable to do that he wouldn't have done had it been possible.

The harvest was visible outside his window.

Not every day, necessarily, but often, he sees them out there crossing the quadrangle, Griffin and his special friend, his companion, his partner on the perilous passage through these most precious days and years. What the nature of their friendship needs to be, Malcolm can't even begin to guess. That is something different for each young pair. Perhaps their fate will be different. Perhaps their challenges will be less daunting. Perhaps they will achieve the impossible—a happy ending, however they may define it. Seeing them out there, the sun blazing off Brock's blond hair, his handsome head bent to hear the words of his shorter, smaller companion, Malcolm gave himself up each time to his perennially disappointed but daily rediscovered faith.

SAN FRANCISCO: 1975

S onny Dallas' dilemma, as he saw it, was that he had always wanted to be loved for who he was. On the face of it, this was a simple enough aspiration. But Sonny's life was crammed so full of complications that simple as it seemed, it proved as unattainable as anything could possibly be. No matter how well things started out with someone new, sooner or later it all came crashing in, the Olympic medals, the house in Hillsborough, the Rolls-Royce, Felicia and the girls, and that was that.

He'd had a few mistresses over the years, but when they cared at all they cared too much, which made them just like Felicia and he certainly didn't need two of those. And the sex was no better than it was with Felicia, which made it all rather pointless not to mention expensive. This didn't matter in practical terms but offended his sensibilities. Sonny was extravagant to a fault, but demanded value for his money.

What Sonny needed was some bizarre hybrid. A wife/mistress built and equipped like one of his favorite hustlers. This species, of course, didn't exist even in fiction. But Sonny's platonic ideal of it persisted, year in, year out. And every now and then it compelled him out of his daily routine and onto the hunt.

Usually when he was in one of these moods he booked a room at the Fairmount and ordered a hustler. The agency he employed knew and accommodated his taste. He was never disappointed. At least sexually. But the young men never adored him for himself in even the most superficial of ways, so even though he would never have complained about value for money in these transactions, how did one put a price on intangibles?

Which was why he had come to this particular bar tonight. Why he was standing by himself chain smoking his Pall Malls and watching the ice cubes melt in his scotch, hoping against hope and fighting against the discouragement that mounted with each tick of his Rolex. He should know better. He did know better. Grails were for seeking, not necessarily finding.

The bar filled up. He ordered a second scotch. The dream flickered like a guttering candle but wouldn't quite go out. Just as he was about to give up for the night there was a sudden shift in the atmosphere of the place, subtle but unmistakable like the barometric pressure plummeting before a storm or radio interference caused by sunspot activity. He turned to follow the gaze of the nondescript man a few feet away from him.

There, just inside the doorway from the shadowy foyer. Sonny's heart didn't skip a beat for just anybody. But this one was exactly Sonny's type. A breathtaking physique, an exotically handsome face, a thick mop of raven hair hanging almost to the extravagantly muscled shoulders. Sonny was the quintessential connoisseur of this type. He had spent literally decades observing and stalking them. His estimates were never wrong, and as the guy slipped his white athletic shirt over his head, Sonny totaled it up: five feet nine and a half. One hundred ninety-seven pounds. The chest, shoulder, and arm development was breathtaking, and you could have laundered dress shirts on those abdominals. If that waist measured a millimeter over twenty-nine inches, Sonny would be a monkey's uncle.

There was no time to lose. Somebody was going to make a move. Sonny would be damned if he'd let anybody else get there first. He moved across the room, shouldering aside drag queens, hustlers, other associated barroom detritus, eyes locked on his target, who, he decided, reminded him of a renaissance Italian prince ready to swashbuckle his way through a trail of mountain villages, raping, plundering, and never, ever cheating on his bench presses.

Up close, the glossy raven hair was smoother and finer textured than Sonny had noticed from across the room, almost asiatic in fact. The skin was alabaster perfection, and the oversized nipples were tauntingly, almost obscenely, plump. There was a Slavic cast to the cheekbones, but it was the eyes that put Sonny's Italian fantasy to rest. They were a spooky shade of silvery blue, glinting like chips of an iceberg. Sonny mentally rattled off the possibilities, Finnish, Ukrainian—hell, he could be half Swedish and half Manchurian.

"Evening," Sonny ventured.

"Hello."

The voice was deep and not too loud.

"What are you drinking?"

The eyes, those fabled windows of the soul, told Sonny absolutely nothing. If they were windows of any kind, the shutters were closed.

"Calistoga, thanks."

"That's all?"

"Yes, thanks."

"The name's Sonny, by the way."

"I'm Cooper."

WILLIAMSTOWN,
KENTUCKY: 1979

B rock bolted down the pizza like a man who'd just spent six months on a deserted island with nothing to eat but coconuts. He couldn't remember the last pizza he'd had. Probably the night he'd won the Kentucky bodybuilding championship, back last spring. After he finished his meal he hurried back to his hotel. He had to call Juliette and tell her about his placing in the finals. Second in his height class. In a national contest. His first ever national competition. Second in his class and third place overall. It wasn't as good a result as he'd hoped for when he left home, but the minute he arrived at the venue and saw his competition he realized he'd be lucky to qualify for the finals at all. So it wasn't a bad result by any estimation. He couldn't believe how proud he was of not having won.

And backstage afterward that photographer had approached him. Lance Garrison. *The* Lance Garrison. He'd been seeing Lance's work in the bodybuilding magazines for several years now. Cover shots, even. Lance Garrison wanted to shoot him. Seeing himself on the cover of one of those magazines would be even better than winning the contest outright. He'd have a record of how he looked at his best. It would be something he could show his sons.

It would mean a trip to San Francisco. There was an intriguing possibility.

———

Mrs. Murchison, his mother's maid, had been staying with Juliette while Brock was away. She answered the phone. He wasn't alarmed to hear her voice. Realizing how late it was, he was hoping to hear that Juliette was already in bed. But Mrs. Murchison said Juliette wasn't home. She had gone into labor a couple of hours earlier. Her mother and father had come and taken her to the hospital. Brock called there and was eventually able to talk to his mother. Everything was fine. There was no cause for concern. Juliette was doing well. The baby probably wouldn't arrive for a couple of hours yet at least. Maybe not until morning.

———

Juliette wasn't due for six weeks yet. He'd never have left her on her own if he'd known this was going to happen. He'd have scrubbed his entry for the competition. He packed quickly and took a taxi to the airport, not sure when he'd be able to get a flight. His original plan had been to fly back Monday morning, but that wasn't an option now.

———

They arrived in Cincinnati behind schedule after having to circle for over an hour because of bad weather. There were no flights on to Lexington until morning, and he could drive home sooner than that. So he headed for the Hertz counter, where a sleepy eyed young woman with bottle blond hair signed him up for a Monte Carlo.

———

When he got to the hospital it was all over. Juliette and his son were both doing well. Juliette's parents were jubilant. Brock's mother looked at him like he'd lost his mind when he said he should have been there. His father had missed the births of all but two of Brock's brothers.

———

Brock cradles the baby to his chest as he feeds him the bottle. The day Juliette and the baby came home from the hospital, he instituted his new rule. Juliette must use a breast pump so that Brock can take charge of the overnight feedings. He won't have Juliette getting up at two a.m. She needs her sleep. And he needs this time with his new son. He won't be the kind of father Big Jim was, oblivious to his offspring until the day each one was old enough to hold a football. He won't cheat his child that way. He won't cheat himself.

Later this morning they'll take this one to Grace Presbyterian to be christened. Brock would be happier not to, but it can't be helped. Recently, Dr. Ferguson's sermons are betraying signs of having been influenced by ideas distressingly similar to what Brock used to hear from the Students for Traditional Values. There hasn't been a clear declaration yet, just some vague references, as if the pastor is testing the waters. Brock has been pretending to ignore this, but he knows Juliette knows he has noticed it. When and if the time comes, he won't hesitate to turn his back on the church forever. He knows she won't argue the point. He doesn't expect her to follow him into this voluntary exile, but the child won't go to church with her. Brock won't have his son absorbing anything like that, even subliminally.

Brock has been imagining this day for years. The christening was supposed to fall on the day of his first anniversary. And he would have thrown the biggest party Grant County had ever seen. There would have been live music, the barbecue to end all barbecues, and, at the end of the evening, a fireworks show as elaborate as anything you'd see on the Fourth of July. But with his anniversary still six months away and snow on the ground from the last storm, he's had to modify his expectations. There will be a party, of course, but indoors. His parents' pool is closed until Derby Week. There will be a live band and dancing, but only what will fit into the outbuilding where his father stores his collection of antique cars. They've been moved to the Chevrolet showroom until after the event. The fireworks display is still scheduled, but on a smaller scale. Only the hardiest of souls will venture outside to watch it. Everyone else will view the spectacle as best they can through the windows of his mother's family room. It's more symbolic than anything. It's the best he can do. Maybe the next baby will be born at a more temperate time of year.

The more pressing problem is that the child still lacks a name. Brock and Juliette haven't been able to settle on anything. Part of the problem is that Brock has too many male relatives, none of whom can be singled out for the particular tribute of having the baby named for them. Part of the problem is too much input. Auntie Olympia favors names from Italian opera. Brock's mother watches too many soap operas. Juliette's mother and grandmother insist that names from the Old Testament are the most suitable. Brock's father campaigns in support of honoring various and sundry NFL luminaries. Juliette's father advocates names from classical antiquity. Papa Charlie, the Van der Jagt patriarch, wishes to honor some Confederate general or other. It's enough to drive the new parents crazy. So they've just been putting it off. Juliette's mother hasn't complained, but Brock senses her disapproval. His own mother is frantic. There is no telling what emotional damage has already been done to the child by leaving him without a name to be addressed by. He's already at risk for failing kindergarten, and that disaster will only compound itself unless something is done soon. She makes suggestions several times a day, and Brock, out of natural perversity he presumes, marks each one off the list of possibilities no matter how euphonious and appropriate it may be. Juliette and he will choose their son's name. And since their first choice is impermissible (they both understand that all too well) then people had just better leave them alone to figure it out.

But the fact remains. Their time is about to run out. When Brock carries his baby up the aisle of the church and presents him to the minister, he'll have to speak the name. He stares into the fathomless eyes gazing up at him. One thing he is certain of. With a glance, Griffin would be able to tell him what to call this child.

"Buddy," he says, speaking in the voice he uses for this creature alone, "please. Just tell me who you are."

PART FIVE: MARIETTA'S LIED

1979

We must take the current when it serves, or lose our venture

William Shakespeare—*Julius Caesar*

I

Kent stifled a moan as Cooper gradually—at a glacier's pace, really—went soft and slipped out of him. Cooper wasn't quite the biggest guy Kent had ever slept with, but he was right up there in the whoppers hall of fame. There was a reason Cooper's penis was known around the Bay Area as "The Hindenberg". Unlike a lot of guys with oversize equipment, who could barely get themselves inside you without using their hands to help out, Cooper actually managed to get fully hard. Like granite, really. Another thing Cooper had going for him that most of the other really big guys didn't was technique. Not to mention staying power. Lots of guys came almost the minute they got inside you and then deflated more or less immediately. Like popped balloons, pretty much. But Cooper was one of a handful of guys who made a more lasting impression. Orgasms were all well and good, but what Kent really lived for was these few moments with that big thing still tight in there, twitching slightly as it made its continued presence known. That truly was the best. That was heaven. Still, despite all Kent's will power and obsessive ingenuity, the moment of departure inevitably arrived. It always made him a little sad.

"Better get home," Cooper grunted, giving Kent's left nipple a final tweak and rolling out of bed.

"You never stay afterward," Kent said, hoping it didn't sound too much like a complaint. Cooper hated whiners.

"Gotta check on the dogs," Cooper said.

Kent wasn't sure the dogs existed. They might only be a convenient excuse. He was only twenty but he was pretty sure he already knew enough about convenient excuses to write a book on the topic. He'd certainly heard enough of them. Cooper wasn't the first guy to use his dogs as a reason not to spend the night. Sometimes Kent suspected the word dog was more accurately spelled "wife", though he was pretty sure Cooper didn't have one of those.

"We could get together at your place some time," he suggested, but not too strenuously. You had to walk on eggs with a guy like Cooper, who insisted on calling the shots.

"We could do that," Cooper said, pulling on his black leather jeans.

Kent was pretty sure he didn't mean it. He was going to have to try harder.

———

The dogs were fine when Cooper got home, particularly once he broke out the Milk Bone box. They greeted him with their usual fervor and then got to work on their treats. It didn't take them long. Only then did he let them out into the yard. Pre-treat, they were too excited by his return to attend to business. They'd just stand at the door until he let them back in and end up waking him in the middle of the night to go out again. Once they'd had treats to calm them down they'd do their stuff out there and he'd sleep through the night.

The light on the answering machine was blinking, and he listened to his messages while waiting for the bathtub to fill. Several wrong numbers. A couple of tricks asking plaintively why he hadn't called, leaving him trying to recall what faces went with those disembodied voices. Buzz the office manager reminding him about his Monday appointments. And the dreaded rasp of Holly Montezuma.

"Hey big boy, who was that delicious creature I saw you with at Dennis and Ronnie's housewarming?"

Holly Montezuma wasn't an invited guest at said function. In her more mundane identity, Enrique "Henry" Sandoval the cater waiter, she had seen and overheard enough to prompt this call.

"Does Chanel know about him? Or is it up to me to break the news?"

"Deranged princess," Cooper muttered.

Kent wasn't an invited guest at the Ballard-Malandrini housewarming any more than Holly. He just showed up. He was doing that more and more often these days. Cooper was ignoring it but if it went on much longer he'd have to do something.

The last message of all was from Kent himself. He had called while Cooper was on his way home.

Typical of Holly Montezuma to inquire about Kent. Years ago, Sonny Dallas had accused her of "transparent duplicity". Once the concept was explained to her, she adopted it as her signature style. Everybody knew who Kent was—that season's reigning go-go boy. He was everywhere, invited or not, apparently on the assumption that a cute enough guy was always welcome. Even Big Steve's gang, usually indifferent to the genre, took note. Nick Romanovsky, the gang's first string Lothario, designated Kent a Platonic Ideal—with just enough ambiguity in his tone to both intrigue and dismay Cooper—and Kent had taken tea with Ned Westerleigh, though not actually in Ned's apartment. Cooper was conversant with Kent's various and conflicting putative biographies well before actually meeting him. That was at a charity oil wrestling extravaganza a couple of months back. They had been paired as competitors. Alpha Drag Queen Chanel Rococo's bizarre idea of entertainment. Kent put up an impressive struggle considering their sixty pound weight differential. Cooper had to give him credit for that. Most of his previous opponents hadn't really made much effort beyond the histrionics. An out of focus photo of their match ran in the *Bay Area Reporter* a week or so later. Kent bought a print of it from the staff photographer and stuck it to his bedroom mirror. Cooper tried his best to ignore it. He wasn't there that often.

After a long soak, Cooper showered off. He never felt really clean after a bath. He only took baths when he needed to turn off his brain. He still needed to wash the grease out of his hair. Slicked back was a great look for him, particularly when he wore his black leather jeans, but he couldn't imagine going to bed like that and ruining the pillow cases. Other people's pillow cases weren't his concern.

Nor were Holly's veiled threats about blabbing to Chanel. There was no doubt Chanel already knew about Kent and Cooper's fuck buddy status. Kent was practically shouting it from the housetops, and Chanel was far from deaf.

———

"It's brilliant when you analyze it," Tristan said, watching his husband spot Nick on bench presses.

"What is?" Cooper asked.

"Don't play innocent," Big Steve growled. "You know what he's talking about. The way you've pitted those two against each other."

"I didn't."

"Like hell," Big Steve snorted.

"Really," Tristan said, "it's perfect. The drag queen versus the go-go boy. It's like a gay science fiction thriller."

"What's Nick grinning about?" Cooper asked.

"The collision of archetypes," Tristan chortled.

"You apparently aren't aware," Big Steve said, "that your little pal has been hedging his bets. Since you're taking your sweet time about making an honest twinkie out of him, he's lined Nick up as his reserve pitcher."

"You really didn't know?" Tristan asked. "You must be the only one in the city."

"Really, Niko? Congratulations."

"Not like you to have missed a thing like that," Nick grunted.

"Was I supposed to dust Kent for fingerprints?" Cooper asked. "Administer sodium pentothal and interrogate him?"

"Sounds like fun," Tristan suggested.

"You've got it all wrong," Cooper insisted. "The only reason I'm seeing him is because he told me he wasn't looking for a boyfriend."

"Because he thinks he already found one," Tristan laughed. "I can't believe you fell for that. It's the oldest one in the book."

"Our agreement is we're both seeing other people."

"And boy is Nick happy about that," Big Steve said. "Terms like those are like giving him a license to steal."

"What about it, Nick?" Cooper chuckled. "Want to do me a favor and take him off my hands permanently?"

"Hell no," Nick grunted, setting the bar into the rack. "Don't you dare cut him loose. Thinking about you all the time has him so hot and bothered he'll do anything I want. Regular little sex piglet."

———

"You missed a very nice party at Dennis and Ronnie's," Elizabeth said.

"I was planning to go, but then the Weitzmanns insisted I join them for dinner Saturday," Buzz said, blushing slightly. "I wasn't expecting that at all."

"So our boy Trevor came through," Cooper said. "Didn't I tell you he would?"

"You did, boss," Buzz smiled. "You did."

Buzz was ridiculously handsome, Cooper thought. And completely oblivious to it, which made him even sexier. Sexiest of all was a really hot man several years older than Cooper calling him "boss". Cooper sometimes fantasized about pushing Trevor in front of a bus. He'd have done it already but he suspected moving on Buzz would be the same story as with Nick. There was no getting around it, though. When people talked about husband material, they were thinking about Buzz Montgomery whether they had ever met him or not. San Francisco, or at least the gay part of it, seem to be populated entirely by archetypes these days.

"So how did it go?" Elizabeth asked.

"I'm still numb," Buzz said, "but Trevor's over the moon. That's what counts."

"Details, Buzz," Ned demanded.

"Not much to tell," Buzz shrugged. "Trevor told his parents about us and they were fine with it."

"You WASPs," Elizabeth laughed. "The world could end, and you'd say 'it wasn't really that big a deal.'"

"Oh, it's a big deal, all right," Buzz said. "I mean, put yourself in their place. As far as they knew when they got to town on Friday afternoon their little boy was a perfectly normal college freshman."

"He is perfectly normal," Cooper insisted. "Except for constantly changing his hairstyle. And color."

"But think of it from their perspective, Cooper," Elizabeth said.

"Perspective, huh? I'll give you some perspective," Cooper said. "Above all, Jewish fathers are realists. Trevor is an only son. The Weitzmanns are going to make nice. Trust me on that."

"It must have been a shock, though," Buzz said. "Trevor hadn't said a word to them about staying around for summer school instead of going back to Arizona. Much less that he'd practically moved into my place—and not as a roommate."

"I'm sure it helped that they already knew you," Elizabeth said.

"Right," Buzz winced. "It's every mother's dream for her son to marry his male high school English teacher some day. The age difference alone. . ."

"Former English teacher," Ned pointed out. "Besides, you're only what—eight or nine years older than Trevor?"

"Twelve years. And not all that former," Buzz said. "It's less than a year since he graduated. His mom took our picture together that night after the ceremony. She'll probably burn it as soon as she gets home."

"You're not feeling guilty, are you?" Cooper asked. "Because I could tell you how it is when college boys go after older men. They don't take no for an answer."

"I just hope we're not making a mistake," Buzz said.

"None of that negative thinking," Elizabeth cautioned. "We don't allow it in this office."

———

Cooper could easily have picked Chanel up at her place, but he believed that using public transportation was good for her character so he told a white lie about a late meeting with clients and insisted that they meet at the restaurant. Not one of their regular places, but it was currently in vogue so Chanel could hardly say no. The real reason Cooper suggested it was that one of Kent's go-go buddies waited tables there so word of their appearance would spread with the speed of light.

"How's the twinkie?" Chanel asked, a disapproving expression on her face as she surveyed the menu.

"What twinkie would that be?" Cooper asked. "Last time I looked San Francisco was crawling with twinkies. It's practically an infestation."

"Don't play dumb. I know you saw him Saturday."

"Ran into him at a party, is all."

"Right."

"Pull in your claws, girl," Cooper laughed. "We're just friends. I'm allowed to have friends."

"Fuck buddies is what I heard."

"Like you don't have a couple of those of your own."

"I just thought you had better taste than that," Chanel said, pretending she didn't care after all.

———

"Harry Gordini's is just around the corner," Cooper said as they left the restaurant. "We could stop in for drinks."

He had no intention of spending the rest of the evening with Chanel and knew that the best way to forestall it was to suggest something she'd object to. There was an unflattering story making the rounds about her and Harry's current bouncer, a confrontation in which the allegedly half-witted galoot had nevertheless gotten the better of her. In front of unimpeachable witnesses, better yet. Never underestimate a man with shoulders that broad, was how Cooper thought of it. He had been called a galoot himself. Plenty of times.

"On a Wednesday evening, Cooper?" Chanel rolled her eyes. "Nobody goes to Harry's on Wednesdays."

"Suit yourself."

"I wouldn't say no to a round at Rascals."

"Great idea," Cooper smiled. "I told Kent I'd try to stop by. He's dancing there tonight."

By the time she figured out that wasn't true, she'd be pissed off about something else. Check and mate.

———

They didn't go to Rascals. Of course not, once Cooper made Kent seem imminent. They discussed several other possibilities but ended up not going anywhere. He drove her home, managed not to go inside for a nightcap, and was at his favorite new place on Castro Street by nine. The guy he took home was the all-American type, with wheat colored hair, freckle dusted cheeks, and a cute gap between his front teeth. Afterward, while he napped, Cooper checked his messages.

Chanel, thanking him for dinner in a cryptic tone of voice that he knew was calculated to arouse his curiosity and so didn't. Buzz, with a question about a property in escrow. A couple of former tricks, as always. The American Cancer Society. A heavy breather. And last of all, what he'd been hoping for.

"Cooper, it's Kent. Don't forget I'm dancing at Bolt tonight."

Mission accomplished.

II

Professor Demetriou got suspicious if essays seemed too polished, so Griffin spent the last fifteen minutes of the exam period scratching out, scribbling in margins, and drawing arrows here and there until he felt he had achieved the requisite appearance of chaos and disorganization without actually affecting the clarity of his response to the question "compare the philosophical assumptions underlying abstract impressionism in painting, the International Style of architecture, and serialism in music". The answer, obviously, was that they shared in common the imperative to disassemble the hierarchies inherent in traditional forms and structures in the arts, replacing them with more democratic interrelationships among their elements. But Professor Demetriou detested answers that he deemed "too facile" or "lacking in nuance", so Griffin had gone out of his way overcomplicating matters until he was practically crosseyed. As the only undergraduate in the seminar, he believed he had lots to prove. Though at this point it was hard to see why he should bother.

—

Griffin had been dreading it, but he couldn't put it off any longer. He knocked on the door.

"*Entrez.*"

Jean-Pierre's studio always reminded Griffin of the anteroom at some cathedral. It wasn't the décor, particularly, just the atmosphere. There was nothing priestly about his piano teacher, however, who was his usual vivacious self that morning.

"*Ah, bon,*" Jean-Pierre greeted him. "It's good you dropped by. I'm leaving for Paris right after graduation tomorrow and I was afraid I might not get a chance to speak with you."

"Here I am," Griffin said.

If he had let himself, he'd have had a crush on this handsome Frenchman with his perfect grooming and astonishing charm. Not that falling for his teacher would have done him any good. Things like that never turned out well. He had heard plenty of stories. Life at the conservatory was one big soap opera.

"So, my young friend," Jean-Pierre smiled sadly, "this is it. *Je suis desole.*"

"I thought we agreed it isn't the end of the world."

"It isn't. But I spoke with Madame Grammatikova last night," Jean-Pierre said. "I'm supposed to make a last ditch effort to keep you here. I promised her."

"That's what this feels like, all right."

"Don't make that face. It isn't that I don't want to convince you to stay. It's that I respect you too much. I understand your reasons. I know your mind is made up."

"I don't want Madame and my godfather raiding their retirement savings to keep me at the conservatory."

"Admirable, my young friend, admirable. I don't doubt that I'd make the same choice under the circumstances."

"Of course I wish things were different," Griffin said, willing his voice not to crack. "I'll miss you terribly."

"But I'm not going anywhere. I'll only be in France for six weeks. You know you're welcome to come see me any time. As a friend, you understand? And whenever you're performing you have to promise to let me know."

"You know I will, Jean-Pierre."

"You'll be fine at the university. Michael Krakowiak is a wonderful teacher. I know him well. Very different from Grammatikova, of course. Also very different from me. It will be good for you to work with someone who has a completely different approach. It will be an opportunity for you to continue your development."

"We've been through all this."

"I know," Jean-Pierre said. "I'm just trying to provide you with encouragement. And some perspective."

"All right."

"I know you're disappointed about the scholarship. So am I. I want to help you understand what went wrong."

"Nothing went wrong," Griffin said. "I'm just not good enough."

"Not true. *Pas du tout*. And that's why I'm happy for this opportunity to speak with you. I won't have you leaving under such a misapprehension."

"What do you mean—misapprehension?" Griffin asked. "Either I'm good enough for the committee to want me to do graduate work here or I'm not."

"If it were only that simple. What you fail to understand is the politics of the situation."

"Politics?"

"You made a very bad mistake, dear Griffin," Jean-Pierre frowned. "A serious tactical error. You didn't apply to any of the big name schools. Didn't I tell you you must try for Julliard? Or Eastman?"

"But I don't want to move again. I've barely gotten used to it here."

"I know. But you're still not listening. I didn't say you actually had to go to any of those places, did I?"

"Didn't you?"

"No. I just told you to apply. If you had, I could have gone to the committee and said 'we can't lose him to Curtiss'. And that would have been that. The first phone call from New England Conservatory to verify your references would have scared them into a bidding war. That's how it works. But you're too independent for your own good. You didn't listen to me and you made it easy for the committee to turn down your scholarship application. They still think you'll be returning in the fall. They never believed you intended to leave when the only other place you applied to was the university. You made them think you really didn't need the money, you see. They gave it to someone they are certain really does."

"Jesus," Griffin shook his head.

"It won't matter in the long run. You'll see. The master's degree program at State is very nearly as good as ours. And I'm serious about Michael Krakowiak. I think he's just the thing for you in your current phase. But you have to understand that failing to get that scholarship doesn't have anything to do with your talent or your hard work. Please try to remember that."

Griffin shrugged.

"Now, if you'll indulge me," Jean-Pierre said, "I'd really love to hear you play the *Corelli Variations* once more."

Griffin's stomach growled as he stepped off the bus a block up the hill from Union Square. Breakfast had been earlier than usual because of his exams. He felt like he could eat a horse, but in this neighborhood everything appetizing was too expensive and everything he could afford was indigestible. Better hold out until he got home later, though that would make it difficult to concentrate on practicing.

The doors of the club stood open in honor of the unusual warmth and sunshine. In daylight the place was just somewhere for nicely dressed businessmen to grab a quick lunch, but the posters in the tiny lobby advertising that evening's entertainment alluded to its truer, more glamorous identity as perhaps the city's chicest piano bar. Griffin stepped as inconspicuously as possible through the dining room, feeling horribly shabby. Back in the office, Harry was handing out pay envelopes in person.

"A little extra in yours, Griffin," he smiled. "A graduation bonus."

"Thanks, boss."

"You have time for a quick bite?"

As uncomfortable as he was accepting favors, particularly from older men, Griffin knew he was a hopeless liar.

"Actually, I'm starving."

"Terrific. I'll have Gus send us in a couple of London broils."

"Sounds great."

"You really ought to let us fatten you up some. You here to practice? Lunch crowd will clear out soon. It's almost closing time."

———

Griffin sometimes felt like he spent his whole life on buses. From home to the conservatory. From the conservatory to the record shop. From the shop to Harry Gordini's. It was slow but it was cheap. It was reliable, and he never had to worry about parking. It wasn't comfortable. Sometimes it didn't feel particularly safe. And it was always slow. But so far he had never failed to get where he was going, and because he always set out long before any reasonable human being would have considered necessary he was almost never late.

He had learned to make use of the time in all kinds of ingenious ways. He had learned to tune out his fellow passengers. He had learned how not to appear frightened even when he was. He had developed the ability never to miss his stop, no matter how deeply engrossed he was in a textbook or musical score. Not bad for a guy who had never been on public transport before arriving in San Francisco. The school buses of his boyhood didn't count. His almost encyclopedic knowledge of routes and schedules made him feel like the ultimate urbanite, though to be honest it was the only relevant skill he felt he had mastered. Everything else about city life flummoxed him almost to the point of paralysis.

But today, with his degree finished and the beginning of graduate school several months away, the normal pressure was off and he was merely bored with the routine. He picked up a copy of the *Reporter* someone had left behind and leafed through it idly, stopping at the full page ad for a new club opening on Castro Street. The ad featured the photo of a sweat slicked go-go boy with an expression of ecstasy on his cute face. Staring at the image, Griffin couldn't help feeling that the boy was possessed of esoteric wisdom to which he wasn't privy, even if it was nothing more significant than where one could acquire underwear like that. Pondering it further, it occurred to him that perhaps there was nothing more essential in his new existence than the correct choice of g-string and that he had wasted his entire life learning about everything but that. Not that having the g-string would matter a hill of beans absent the body to go with it. Not to mention the fortitude or at least kiss my ass attitude required to appear in public with so much of your skin exposed.

Photos of this particular go-go boy were everywhere lately. The ad Griffin was staring at was merely the tip of the iceberg. His image could be seen on flyers stapled to utility poles. His all too apparent charms featured prominently in montages in shop windows Griffin walked past on Castro Street. A shrine of sorts dedicated to him graced the staff washroom at Harry Gordini's place. Clipping after clipping had been thumb tacked to the wall until there were literally hundreds of him, like some ubiquitous Hindu deity. He was, Griffin mused, a symbol of the age.

Indeed, he was almost too beautiful to be human. But the sweat seemed real enough.

—

Ever since Scott and Jared moved out the top floor apartment had been empty. And with Millicent still in the rehab facility recovering from her stroke, Griffin and the cats had the entire house to themselves. Strictly speaking, the garden was not his responsibility, but if he didn't care for it who would? Just before her stroke,

Millicent had planted her vegetables and set out her tomato plants. The thought of all that dying due to lack of attention offended Griffin's farmboy sensibilities. So most afternoons found him back there weeding, watering, and exterminating pests under the wary eyes of the cats, who wanted nothing to do with him except when he fed them and cleaned their litter box. He had brought it down from Millicent's apartment and installed in his place. The cats moved in but spent most of their indoor time hiding from him, as if they believed they had been abducted.

Word was that Millicent's progress was disappointingly slow. She might never be able to live on her own again.

Her garden flourished, however. It burgeoned. The crop promised to be bountiful, though God only knew how he would dispose of it. The whole scene lacked only a chicken coop and a pen full of pigs to take him back to his old Kentucky home.

———

Griffin was re-alphabetizing the record bin marked "composers assorted—F" when the bell on the shop door rang. The man who had entered looked a few years older than Griffin, but that was true of just about anybody who'd finished tenth grade. In this instance he chalked it up to the man's five o'clock shadow. Griffin had lived and worked in this part of San Francisco for long enough that encountering a stunning man was not especially rare. But even given that this man was extraordinary, practically a supernatural manifestation. The chiseled features, glinting eyes, slicked back black hair: he could easily be a model. Below the neck the archetype shifted: shoulders almost too broad to credit if Griffin hadn't actually been staring at them, massive arm and chest muscles stretching the thin fabric of the spotless t-shirt so taut that the man's next breath, or even impulse, might well rip the garment to shreds. He was the most totally built specimen Griffin had seen in real life since his upstairs neighbors absconded.

"Can I help you?" he asked, mildly surprised that he still had the power of speech.

"I hope so," the man's voice was deep and smooth, like someone you'd hear on the radio. "It's a gift for a friend. I need a recording of an aria. It's called 'Margarita's Lied'."

A radio host, but only if you lived in New York. The accent was unmistakable.

"Do you know what opera it's from?"

"My friend wasn't sure," the man shook his perfect head. "Something in German. She knew that much about it. I'm sorry I can't give you more to go on. I've been to several places. Nobody's been able to help."

"Margarita's Lied" didn't ring any bells. But the idea of disappointing this spectacular man: Griffin would sooner have set himself on fire and jumped off the Golden Gate Bridge.

"I'll be happy to buy a recording of the entire opera if that's the only way to get the aria."

"Just give me a second," Griffin stammered, starting to panic. Anything. Anything at all to keep the man in the shop for a moment more. He had to know this. He had to. It was exactly the kind of request Kip expected him to handle. He had never failed before. This would be the first time. Worse than that, it would be a tragedy. If he failed in front of someone like this, he might just as well give up on his life.

"If you can't help, you can't," the man said. "It's O.K. I'll get her something else. It's her fault for not having better info."

And then. Who was it? That soprano he accompanied freshman year. It was on her senior recital program. Yes, Marie Wilson. It had been her God damned encore.

"Not 'Margarita's Lied'," he blurted. "'Marietta's Lied'. From *Die Tote Stadt*. Erich Wolfgang Korngold."

"Bingo," the man smiled. "Korngold. Chanel didn't know the title of the opera but she did know the composer's name. How could I have forgotten a good Jewish name like that?"

"He's mostly famous for composing film scores," Griffin stammered. "*Captain Blood* was one. And the Errol Flynn *Robin Hood*. He left Austria for Los Angeles in the late 1930's."

"Lucky bastard."

"Operas, T," Griffin said, heading for the shelves along the back wall.

"I thought you said 'dee' something or other," the man protested. "Shouldn't you be going for Operas, D?"

"*Die* is just a definite article in German," Griffin explained, sure that he sounded insufferably pedantic but unable to stop himself. "In English we don't alphabetize everything starting with 'the' under T."

"Got it."

"As I remember there are several good recordings. The Schwarzkopf and the Leontyne Price are very highly rated."

After the man left, Griffin found a copy of the aria in an arrangement for voice and piano in the sheet music section. It was the same edition that Marie Wilson had used. The copy was in shreds. He would have to buy plastic sheet protectors to store it in. What an amazing vision that man had been. Griffin tried to imagine what kind of woman a guy like that would buy an opera recording for.

———

The shop had been empty for the last forty-five minutes, so Griffin was able to turn the sign and lock the door on the stroke of eleven. On the way out through the back he set the alarm and double checked the dead bolt. Two doors down the alley, he entered a dimly lit stockroom. Stepping between stacks of boxes, he heard customers out front. Once again, books were more popular than classical music. Big surprise. He emerged into the shop. Brightly lit, it was several times as large as the annex where he worked, ground zero of what Kip referred to as his empire. That night, Kip himself presided at the front counter, his expression that of a concierge at one of the luxury hotels downtown. With his close cropped silver hair and immaculately groomed mustache he lacked only the requisite uniform. For that matter, he could just as easily have been a guest at one of those establishments.

Griffin handed Kip the money pouch and key ring.

"Everything all right?"

Griffin had never been able to identify the accent, faint but distinctive. He sensed, however, that it didn't quite mesh with the unassailably WASPish name. Kip Truman.

"Fine," he said. "Extremely quiet the last hour. I was able to re-alphabetize a couple aisles of stock."

"You never know what to expect on a Friday night," Kip said.

"Right."

"Finished with your exams?"

"Last one this morning."

"So you'll be ready to take daytime shifts starting Monday."

"If you can use me."

"Ace quit. Yesterday."

"Oh."

Kip's friends were always called Ace or Trip or something racy and masculine that wasn't really a name, exactly. And they always quit eventually. Sometimes eventually wasn't very long. Griffin understood that their departures ranked as something more serious than staffing difficulties for the shops and had finally decided to label them minor domestic tragedies, though Kip never said anything that actually confirmed this interpretation. Kip never said anything about those guys beyond their names and shift assignments. But he was too secretive about it, Griffin thought, for them merely to be employees. In any case, while he regretted whatever distress Ace's departure might have inflicted on Kip, he welcomed its promise of additional shifts.

"What time is graduation?" Kip asked.

"Eleven."

"Celebrating afterward?"

"Nope. I'll just be an hour or so late for my shift."

"You sure?"

"I'm sure."

III

Cooper was getting dressed for work when Big Steve came into the locker room. Big Steve was the biggest bodybuilder at the gym and perhaps the whole city. At five feet ten and 220 pounds, Cooper was not small, but at six-six and a hard three twenty-five, Big Steve dwarfed him and everybody else they knew. He grabbed Cooper, lifted him, swung him wildly, and set him down again. Ordinarily, Cooper was a fervent believer in the concept of personal space, but this was different. This was Big Steve, and there were men all over San Francisco who would have killed to be manhandled by him like this, who would go to their graves regretting that they never had been.

So Cooper submitted happily to the assault. It wasn't just that they were fellow bodybuilders or even that they were gay men. They were both New Yorkers. Their accents were nearly identical, as were their attitudes. They had that undefinable something, that edge, that whatever it was that people claimed to hate but, Cooper was certain of it, secretly admired. Cooper and Big Steve embodied the stereotype. The brash, obnoxious New Yorker. To their neighbors, these oh-so-mellow citizens of the City by the Bay, the differences between them, one Jewish, one Catholic, one from a blue collar background, the other upper middle class, one from Manhattan, the other from Brooklyn, were completely obliterated by that vivid persona. For Cooper, being tossed around like a toddler by this behemoth was like a quick trip home.

"Take off the shirt," Big Steve commanded. "Let's have a look."

"How's T?" Cooper asked, peeling off his undershirt.

"T. is great this morning," Big Steve grinned. "Damned near perfect, as a matter of fact."

Big Steve's fingers examined Cooper's upper body like a blind man reading Braille.

"Nice job on the abs, my friend."

As the high priest of his own particular sect of the bodybuilding cult, Big Steve had promulgated his own Decalogue, toting the stone tablets down not from Sinai but more likely Olympus. His first commandment, predictably enough given his magnitude, was "Size Matters." The second, less obvious, was "Cuts Do Too." It was the third, "Thou Shalt Have Abs," that departed from bodybuilding orthodoxy. In America, even the most prominent bodybuilders tended to neglect their abs. They might be enormous, with shoulders, arms, pecs, thighs for days; they might present extravagant V-shapes with broad upper bodies tapering down to tiny waists; their bellies might be firm and flat, but they didn't have abs, sculpted, chiseled, defined washboards, ridge upon solidly toned ridge. Generations of European bodybuilders had abs. For them, abs were a given. But often they didn't achieve very impressive size. They were practically indistinguishable from gymnasts and wrestlers. The ideal physique was huge and cut and featured real, honest to God abs. That was Big Steve's gospel, so his approval of Cooper's belly was a supreme validation. Hearing it Cooper felt almost lightheaded.

"Tell you the truth, though," Big Steve grunted. "Our boy T. is a bit frustrated lately."

"What's the problem?"

"These," Big Steve laughed, giving Cooper a stinging slap across the pecs.

"Huh?"

"It bums him out. 'Cooper and I are the same size and body type,' he says. 'and I work out as hard as he does, so why the hell aren't mine as big as his?' Oh, he's got a bad case over your pecs."

"Wait a damned minute," Cooper protested, sliding his undershirt back over said musculature. "T. has one of the ten best bodies in the whole city."

"Undoubtedly," Big Steve agreed. "As do you."

"And there's not a thing wrong with his pectoral development."

"'Course not. But you've got to admit his aren't as filled out as yours. Hence his funk."

"That's crazy."

"I told him it's genetic, really. He may never have pec size like you do; you'll never be blond; you'll both always be four inches shorter than Jared Bartok. It's just how things are."

"T.'s got better symmetry than I do," Cooper said. "And a better tan. I can't tan like that."

"Listen, you interested in doing the Western Regionals again this year?"

"Been thinking about it," Cooper said. "Wouldn't mind adding another trophy to the collection."

"Nick and Tristan are both sitting this season out," Big Steve said. "You'd have my undivided attention."

"Second place in my class last year," Cooper said.

"And in the overall placings."

"That's the point. Tristan's up against the same thing. That class is the most competitive one in the competition. First five guys in the overall rankings last year were from our class. I'm really not interested in going again unless I'm confident of improving my placing."

"Makes sense," Big Steve nodded.

"So I'm going to sit this season out, too. Really work hard getting ready for next year, you know?"

———

"How was her highness' birthday party?" Ned asked, stirring his Earl Gray.

"Like you'd expect," Cooper said, wincing at the recollection. "A combination of a papal coronation and a Roman slave auction. Everybody was there except Jay Gatsby, the Lindbergh Baby, and the missing Romanov heirs."

"You left out the Maltese Falcon," Buzz laughed. "I'm sure Trevor caught sight of him."

"The Maltese Falcon was a he?" Elizabeth asked, looking puzzled. "I thought it was a statue."

"Trevor's too young to know the difference," Buzz said. "He's under the impression that the Maltese Falcon is a sort of Mediterranean equivalent of Zorro."

"He's not that much younger than me," Cooper said, "and I know about the Maltese Falcon."

"I wasn't at the party," Ned pointed out.

"Lucky you," Cooper said. "You've got too much class to be invited to a bacchanal like that."

"Correct answer," Ned chuckled. "Though one does long for a good bacchanal from time to time."

"I never actually got home Saturday night," Cooper said. "I ended up showing the Becker-Adamsons those properties in Pacific Heights still wearing my party frock."

"How picturesque of you," Ned said, "but you should never camp, my boy. Not with shoulders like those. Unless your understanding of the term involves pup tents and Coleman lanterns."

"Speaking of shoulders," Buzz said. "The last Trevor and I saw of you, you were doing the fireman's carry with little Kent Norberg."

"Speaking of picturesque," Elizabeth giggled, "how undressed was he?"

"Kent or Cooper?" Buzz asked.

"Either or both."

"Cooper not at all," Buzz said. "Kent almost completely."

"Had to get him out of there," Cooper said, "before the host called the cops. He'd set up shop in the upstairs powder room."

"Shop?" Elizabeth looked baffled.

"He was giving blow jobs to all comers, the way we heard it," Buzz explained.

"For money?"

"For attention, mostly," Cooper said.

"A tall order in a crowd like that," Ned mused. "Not surprising he felt driven to such an extreme."

"What he needed was a good spanking," Cooper said, "but of course he enjoys that, so it really defeats the purpose."

"In all my years in this city," Ned said, "I can't remember a season going by without some boy like that trying to attain notoriety."

"Took him home and tucked him in, of course," Cooper said.

"You're a real boy scout, boss," Buzz laughed.

"How did her highness like her prezzie?" Ned asked.

"God, Ned, I thought she'd play that fucking record until the grooves wore out."

"You owe me."

"Who I owe is that kid at the record shop. The bitch got the title of the aria wrong. It confused the hell out of everybody I asked. Until I ran into that kid. Of course I didn't help matters by forgetting the name of the composer."

"Kip didn't wait on you himself?"

"Wasn't there. Just this skinny twinkie. Hell, not even a twinkie—looked like he was about fifteen years old. Reddish hair. Not a carrot top. A lot darker than that. Real nervous type. Looked like he was about to pee himself the whole time."

"Fox red," Ned said.

"You could call it that."

"I know who you mean. Rather cute, actually."

"Think so?"

"You didn't notice?" Ned asked. "No, you wouldn't. That type isn't sufficiently Wagnerian to attract your attention. Well for the record, he's adorable. He always reminds me of Huckleberry Finn's shy baby brother."

"Not Kip's usual type," Cooper said. "That's for sure."

"Oh, he's not one of Kip's boys. He's just a simple employee."

"I didn't know there was such a thing in that place," Cooper said. "Anyway, I stumped him, too. At first. Just like everywhere else I'd been. But he thought real hard for a minute and just came out with it. He's some kind of genius, apparently."

"He plays Tuesdays and Wednesdays at Harry Gordini's," Ned said. "Elizabeth and I have heard him several times. He's quite good."

"Astonishing, actually," Elizabeth said. "Almost to the point where you suspect supernatural intervention."

"No kidding?"

"Practice, Elizabeth," Ned said. "It's the result of lots of practice, that's all."

"So how about the Becker-Adamsons?" Buzz asked. "Are they going to buy a house, or are they just trying to get you into the sack?"

"We'll be writing an offer on a property by the end of the week."

"Which means no sex until after the close of escrow," Buzz laughed.

———

"Hey, Coop."

"Stone! My God. I thought you dropped off the face of the earth."

In his hurry to get up from the desk, Cooper nearly knocked over his coffee. It had been a long time since a simple hug felt so good. Stone's hair was shorter and a shade or two darker than it had been the last time Cooper saw him. His face was leaner, more mature looking. His shoulders were broader than ever.

"Sorry I haven't been in touch," Stone said. "Never was much good at correspondence."

"When did you get back?"

"A few days ago. Needed some time to get my bearings. Didn't seem like I'd been gone for the best part of five years until I actually got back."

"Where are you staying?"

"The Ned Westerleigh Home for Wayward Youth," Stone grinned, finally looking like his old self.

"Old bastard didn't say anything."

"I asked him not to. Great place you've got here. Ned told me all about how you and he got hooked up. Agency going great guns and everything."

"Sit down, man. Sit down. Can I get you coffee? A bagel?"

"Nothing, thanks," Stone said. "Ned's housekeeper does a mean breakfast."

"That he does," Cooper nodded.

"Feel like I won't need to eat again for a week."

"Talk. I want to hear everything."

"Well, Esteban turned out to be a big old crook. Can't believe I didn't figure that out before I was nine thousand miles away from home. We had to get out of Argentina in a hurry. I've been living in Montevideo the last three years."

"And Esteban?"

"He passed away two years ago. Pancreatic cancer."

"God, I'm sorry."

"I'm not," Stone said. "Things had gotten pretty bad between us."

"How have you been getting by?"

"My savings. And there was some money in Switzerland. Esteban must have forgotten he'd given me access to the account."

"A lot of money?"

"I'm not rich. There's enough left to get me started back here. Like you to help me buy a place. Nothing fancy. Couple of bedrooms. Ned says the Castro is getting really nice."

"I can show you some properties any time you like."

"You have time this afternoon?"

IV

Griffin was just about to cook up a box of macaroni and cheese for dinner when there was a knock on the front door. It was Butch, holding a pair of pizza boxes. At his feet sat a grocery bag. A sixpack of Dos Equis for him and some Canada Dry for Griffin, if past visits were any guide.

"Butch, hi. This is a surprise."

"Hey, there, buddy. Bet you haven't had your graduation party yet."

"Actually, no."

"Well here it is," Butch said. "Get out the paper plates."

"This is so nice of you," Griffin stammered, choking up.

"That's me all right," Butch said, "your guardian angel."

"It's been a long time since we did this. How did you know I'd been thinking about that all day at the shop?"

"Guardian angels know all kinds of shit."

———

"Great movie, huh?"

"Yeah."

"Just kidding," Butch guffawed. "I know you hated it. You always hate the best ones, for some reason. But you never complain, and you always watch them with me right through to the end. You're a helluva sweet guy, Griff."

Griffin was always speechless when Butch talked like that.

"Yep," Butch said. "Really gonna miss my sweet little buddy."

"Butch," Griffin said, finding his voice. "What are you talking about? You sound like you're going somewhere."

"I am," Butch said. "Back in the Corps, to be exact."

"What?"

"For real," Butch said. "I just can't get the hang of things around here. Nothing turns out like it's supposed to. Tired of the hassle, you know?"

"Was somebody mean to you?"

"Nope."

"Seriously, Butch, because if that's all it is, you'll get over it. You always do."

"Hell, boy, it's not nearly that simple. Been thinking about goin' back in for a long time. Practically since I got out. Time to shit or get off the pot."

"Won't it be awfully tough?"

"'Course it will. It's the Marines, not the Girl Scouts."

"I mean, for a guy like you," Griffin said.

"Oh, that," Butch said. "Not so bad. I can always do it with women enough to get by. And there are plenty of guys who're available for a sausage party if you get them liquored up right. Piece of cake, really."

"I'm astonished."

"Hey, little guy," Butch said. "Don't go worrying about me, O.K? I'll be fine."

"I always worry."

"Well don't," Butch said. "And you'll be fine, too."

"Sure."

"Listen to me. I mean it."

"O.K."

"One thing, though," Butch said.

"What?"

"Just for old time's sake, you know?"

Butch was still the only guy Griffin had ever had sex with. And the way things looked, that situation might last for the rest of his life. For the few moments he was still capable of coherent thought, he catalogued the sensations so he'd have them to remember in his old age. The huge boa constrictor arms. The big, pouty lips. The pungent stuff Butch used on his hair. The sandpapery jawline, that perpetual stubble. The wooly chest. The grotesquely oversized and yet strangely fascinating nipples. And that enormous—well, at least it seemed enormous. Griffin had nothing to compare it with except his own.

———

"You're not staying the night?" Griffin asked as Butch rolled over and started pulling on his jeans.

"I'd surely love to," Butch said. "You're one hell of a great cuddle. Bad idea, though. Very, very bad. Besides, catching an early bus in the morning."

"So soon? I was going to fix you a going away dinner."

"Aw, that's sweet. Sorry to miss that. Appreciate it though, that you wanted to do it."

"Butch?"

"Listen, kiddo, gotta go, really."

"O.K."

"No, don't get up. Want to remember you just like that," Butch knelt by the bed and gave him a long, slow kiss.

"I wish you weren't going," Griffin said, finally tearing up.

"Oh, now, none of that."

"Sorry," Griffin said. "I can't help it."

"It's all right," Butch said, stroking his face. "Go ahead if you need to. You can cry for both of us."

At that, Griffin felt his heart breaking.

"Not very good at writing letters. Just makes me feel stupid, you know? Tryin' to put things on paper. Never was any good at it. Just a big old, ignorant—enough about that. Hope you won't be too disappointed not hearing from me."

V

Every time her highness Chanel Rococo asked Cooper to escort her somewhere—to a concert, a party, one of her many personal appearances—he swore it would be the last time he said yes. It wasn't that he didn't enjoy these events. He invariably had a good time. Chanel was always entertaining. She knew a lot of fun and interesting people who did lots of fun and interesting things. He knew that acting as hunk-in-waiting to one of the city's most vivid (not to say most notorious, because that's always a moving target) drag queens of their generation was a questionable pastime with regard to his professional aspirations, but he never allowed that to concern him unduly. San Francisco wasn't Philadelphia.

His resistance really stemmed from a growing certainty that Chanel considered herself entitled to his attention. Ever since he moved out of that decaying ruin she and her cohorts shared in Haight-Ashbury and rented his own place up the hill from Castro Street, she'd gotten downright proprietary. She didn't ask any more, she told. She even went so far as to select his wardrobe for each event as if he wasn't capable of dressing himself, or couldn't be trusted to. He had never taken orders from Sonny, though he often enough found himself acceding to requests he didn't particularly like. But Sonny had been his lover, not just someone he hung out with. He had finally realized that it was time to call it what it was. Chanel was acting just like a wife. But if she was, it was Cooper's fault. He let her get away with it.

Tonight she almost went too far. Once again the event was a party. He was vaguely aware that it was to have a science fiction theme. When he got to her place she had his outfit all laid out for him. She was already dressed. Her outfit was a kind of evening gown, layer upon layer of electric blue chiffon hovering round and about an inner sheath of satin that fit her as tight as a drumhead and limited the length of her stride to an extent that was unexpectedly comical, which Cooper knew hadn't been the desired effect. As long as she stood still, however, she looked for all the world like the queen of some alien planet inhabited by a race of especially glamorous Amazons.

There was nothing particularly objectionable about the costume she had chosen for him, a kind of futuristic spacesuit, he guessed, in some shiny, silvery looking fabric that fit him like it had been applied with a paint sprayer. Even the cape, which matched her gown, wasn't that terrible. But he'd never dressed up for her before and he suddenly decided that enough was enough. He insisted on going home to change into his second best tux, which made them later than was fashionable. Then her highness insisted on stopping at the Safeway on Market Street for a "suitably amazing and futuristic dessert" to take with them. After much agonizing on the part of her highness, this turned out to be one of those plastic tubs of tapioca meant to be taken on picnics, accompanied by a can of whipped cream and a jar of maraschino cherries. The protracted selection process made them still tardier. And next, when they got back to the parking lot, the Jaguar wouldn't start. For once it wasn't the battery. The engine turned over fine. It just wouldn't fire. So Cooper got out and raised the hood. He stood gazing at the gleaming but slumberous powerplant, his mechanical knowledge pretty much exhausted by that point and her highness mad enough to spit nails.

"Got car trouble?"

Cooper straightened up. It took a long three count before he recognized the kid from Kip's record shop. He was carrying a sack of groceries in each arm. His question seemed remarkably stupid, but Cooper held his tongue. The kid set his groceries down beside the driver's side door and bent over the engine compartment, an intent look on his pale face. After a long, silent moment, he straightened back up.

"It's your carburetors," he announced with what Cooper thought was a surprisingly authoritative tone. He might have been a world famous specialist announcing his discovery that the symptoms his patient had been complaining of were the result of a rare tropical disease. Except that in this case, the verdict was delivered in the kid's hopelessly cornball accent. Cooper couldn't help grinning.

"Really."

"In your toolkit you should have a mallet."

"I don't have a toolkit."

"Cooper," her majesty croaked, "go find us a taxi, please. We're disastrously late."

"All Jaguars come with a toolkit," the kid insisted.

"I don't think. . ."

"It'll be in the spare wheel well underneath the trunk floor panel."

"Be my guest," Cooper shrugged.

"Cooper, did you hear me?"

"Cool it, Chanel."

The kid opened the trunk, rummaged, and emerged with a mallet Cooper had no knowledge of until just then. Cooper found this as unexpected and as comical as a magician actually producing a bunny from a top hat.

"I knew you had one. All these E-types came from the factory with a mallet for loosening and tightening the knock off hubs."

"Cooper, this is stupid."

The kid stared thoughtfully into the engine compartment for what seemed like an eternity, while a couple of fat raindrops splatted on the windshield.

"Oh, great," her highness drawled. "Opie plays gas station, and now it decides to rain."

The kid closed his eyes, opened them again, and gave the forward carburetor the slightest of taps with the mallet.

"Give her a try," he said.

"Cooper, I swear to God."

Cooper got behind the wheel. Foot on the clutch. Gearshift in neutral. Turn key. The engine whoomped emphatically to life.

"My God," Cooper said. "You actually did it."

"Used to fix my godfather's Jaguar that way back home. Those carbs are as temperamental as opera singers."

The rain was picking up by the minute. The kid lowered the hood and tossed the rubber mallet back into the trunk. The lid slammed shut.

"Give you a lift?" Cooper offered.

"No thanks."

"You can sit on Chanel's lap."

"Like fuck he can."

"It's not far to the bus stop," the kid said.

"You'll get soaked."

"You folks are already late," the kid said, rain dripping off the tip of his nose. "Get going."

"Honestly Cooper," her highness complained as he accelerated up Market Street.

"What?"

"When you're late for an extremely important engagement, you don't waste time messing about under the hoods of cars. Sometimes I think you don't have a brain in that gorgeous head of yours."

———

"You've got to stop doing this," Cooper said.

"Doing what?" Kent asked. When he tossed his head his antennae bounced. The rest of his costume was a g-string that looked like it was made of tinfoil. And like it would come off in the gentlest breeze.

"You may be cute enough to crash any party on the planet, but you can't just act however you want once you arrive. It doesn't work like that."

"The drag queen started it," Kent shrugged. "I finished it."

The drag queen in question wasn't one of Chanel's associates, thank goodness. Still, the scene was bad enough.

"You punched her in the nose," Cooper said. "It's probably broken."

"She had it coming. You go around all the time talking about how big your cock is and you pick fights with grown men, you'd better be ready to duke it out."

"Drag queens do pretty much whatever they want," Cooper said. "Outrageous behavior is expected of them. It's what gets them invited to parties like this. People think it's entertaining. Boys like you, on the other hand, have to behave. If you don't, sooner or later people won't think you're cute any more and you won't get past the front door."

"Says you," Kent said. "I hate this party anyway. Take me home."

"I can't take you home. You know that. I'm here as Chanel's escort. I can't just leave."

"Sure you can. It's simple. We walk out. Come on, I'll show you."

"Think again," Cooper said, shaking his head.

"You're pussy whipped is what."

"I'm a gentleman."

"Right," Kent snorted. "You know, Cooper, I can't believe you actually have sex with that hag."

"Who says I have sex with her?"

"She does. She talks about it all the time. Way she makes it sound the two of you are practically engaged."

"Huh?"

"In fact you already would be if you had your way. She's putting you off. Isn't convinced you're really ready to settle down. Needs to make sure you've really changed your bad boy ways. That's her story. Surprised you didn't know about that."

"And you believed it?"

"Isn't it true?"

"Of course not," Cooper laughed. "It's what she does. Exaggerates. Makes up stories. Every drag queen ever born plays fast and loose with the truth."

"I can't believe you let her get away with it. It's like you don't care what she says about you."

"Why should I? Everybody knows nothing she says is to be taken seriously."

———

"The way you defend that little bastard makes me want to puke."

"Come on, Chanel," Cooper said. "Just get in the car, O.K?"

"I mean it," she insisted. "You've really got to give more thought to how you choose your friends."

This, whether she knew it or not, was the pot calling the kettle black as far as Cooper was concerned.

"In the car, Chanel."

"What's your hurry? Got somewhere else to be?"

He did, but he knew better than to say so. If she got wind of what he had planned for later, she'd break his windshield.

———

"Let me spot you," Cooper said.

"Hey," Stone said, setting the barbell on the rack. "Thought I might run into you here."

"Man, you've gotten huge."

"Look who's talking. We're still like identical twins below the neck."

"Crazy, huh?" Cooper laughed. "Must not be much to do in Montevideo but go to the gym."

"Yeah," Stone grinned.

"So what did you think of those properties we looked at the other afternoon?"

"They were great, Cooper," Stone said, "but none of them really talked to me, you know?"

"Got a couple of new places just listed," Cooper said, "if you'd like to see them."

"I'm free—oh, pretty much full time," Stone laughed. "We'll go out whenever you can fit me in."

"How about tomorrow afternoon?"

"I'll stop by your office."

VI

S he shouldn't have called him "Opie". That had been a low blow. You don't say a thing like that when someone you don't know is going out of his way to do you a favor. Griffin should have just let them sit in the rain waiting for a taxi. He didn't regret helping Cooper out, but that—drag queen he guessed she was, that was another matter. He had a friend at the conservatory, Mike, who considered himself an expert on drag queens because he was housemates with one. The way Mike described it drag queens were like fairy godmothers with better fashion sense. But this Chanel, she was just a harpy, that's all. He had been soaked to the skin and chilled to the bone when he got home. But you couldn't accept a ride on the lap of a drag queen who called you "Opie". Not if you had any dignity at all.

Still, it had been a small price to pay to see that amazing man again. Griffin had a name to go with the face now. Cooper. Presumably it was a last name, but the way Chanel had been saying it, it seemed like maybe a first name. Back home a lot of boys had their mother's or grandmother's maiden names for first names—Griffin himself, for instance, though in his case it was his great-grandmother's maiden name. So it wasn't impossible. There were Coopers all over Grant County. Griffin had gone to school with several. But he couldn't imagine this Cooper being related to any of them.

In the weeks since their intitial encounter in the shop, Griffin's memory of Cooper had faded so that he had almost convinced himself he had imagined it. Or at least imagined how spectacular Cooper was. Now he knew better. Cooper, whoever else he might be, was the handsomest man in the world, not just a hallucination. And definitely one of the most built. Although he was hardly taller than

Griffin, his shoulders were as broad as Griffin remembered Brock's being. He must have all his clothing custom tailored, with proportions like those.

Griffin wondered if Chanel was the "friend" Cooper had bought the present for. If that was true, it meant—what? Despite Mike's explanations, Griffin didn't get drag queens other than knowing of their existence. They didn't bother him. They simply were. You saw one on the street and you noted the phenomenon, but you didn't understand any more than you understood photosynthesis beyond what it said in your biology textbook. Since you couldn't imagine what a being like that had to do with you, you just registered it and went on about your business. It was as abstract, really, as the laws of thermodynamics. No, what confused Griffin was a guy like Cooper. In the record shop that night it hadn't occurred to him that Cooper might not be straight. There hadn't seemed to be anything gay about him. But why would a straight guy hang out with a beautiful woman who was so obviously not a woman at all? For that matter, why would a gay man want to hang out with a guy who looked and acted like a woman? Wouldn't it make more sense for a gay man to hang out with another gay man like himself? The more Griffin pondered the question, the less sense it made.

Seeing Chanel and Cooper together on their way to some fabulous gathering in their fancy clothes and driving off into the rain in that midnight blue Jaguar roadster had been just like a scene from a movie, except because Chanel was what she was, it wasn't. That was their business, not Griffin's. He understood that. She shouldn't have called him "Opie", though. She really shouldn't have. He was just being helpful. He had helped them out, dammit. He could just as easily have walked right past and paid them no mind. Except it had been Cooper, so that really hadn't been a possibility.

He stepped off the bus toting his music satchel. He walked the remaining half block up Powell, turned the corner, fished the key out of his pocket, turned it in the lock, stepped into the dark silence which reeked of liquor and tobacco smoke. He turned on a few lights. He slipped the cover off the Steinway, folded it, laid it over the back of a chair. He sat down at the keyboard and began his warmup, improvising a little on "Marietta's Lied." When Cooper showed up that night asking for it, Griffin had known next to nothing about the aria or the opera it came from. His researches turned up a fact which intrigued him whenever he thought of it. The date of the opera's premiere performance was the same as his birthday.

———

Griffin was playing the last few bars of the Chopin G minor Ballade when he sensed he wasn't alone in the room. He felt the tiny jolt of adrenaline that an audience, no matter how small, invariably occasioned and finished the piece with more panache than he ordinarily displayed in practice.

"Bravo," a voice called out, and he heard two sets of hands clapping.

The man standing next to Harry was tall and silver haired. He had the face of an aging Boy Scout and the posture of a military officer.

"Griffin, hi," Harry said. "Have you met Ned Westerleigh?"

"Um, no," Griffin stammered, rising from the piano bench.

Mr. Westerleigh offered a large, perfectly manicured hand.

"I know who you are," he smiled. "The amazing Griffin MacDonald. I've heard you play. Repeatedly."

"Nice to meet you."

"No, my boy, the pleasure is all mine. And now that we've actually met we must get to know each other. You'll come to tea. Shall we say Wednesday? Four o'clock?"

"Thank you."

"Harry will give you my address. Now, don't disappoint me."

"I'll make sure he gets there," Harry laughed. Then, once Mr. Westerleigh was out the front door, he said, "you will go, Griffin."

"I will?"

"Only an idiot turns down an invitation from Ned Westerleigh. There are people who'd kill for one."

"Oh."

"Honestly, there's nothing to be afraid of. He's a perfect gentleman. You don't have to worry about being groped or chased around the sofa."

"I wasn't. . ."

"Oh yes you were. You young guys think anybody over forty is a dirty old man."

"We do?"

"Don't play dumb," Harry laughed. "I've been over forty long enough to know how it works. Ned was no end of impressed with your playing. I swear to God, I've heard some good ones in my time, but kiddo, you take the cake."

"Thanks, Harry."

"And you couldn't get a scholarship to stay on at the conservatory. Un-fucking believeable."

"It's not the end of the world."

"Listen, Johnny Domino needs a few days off. Says he's going on a rest cure. Which means he's off to Palm Springs to check out this season's rent boys. How'd you like to play a couple of weekend gigs?"

Johnny Domino, though on his driver's license it said Seymour Lowenstein, was the club's headliner. He had been for decades, since long before Harry bought the place. He wasn't a particularly wonderful pianist but he was an amazing entertainer. His knowledge of standards and show tunes was encyclopedic. No one could remember him ever being stumped by a request. Not to mention, his patter was so old school as to be practically as familiar to audiences as the Lord's Prayer.

"You're joking," Griffin said.

"Nope. Whaddya say?"

"I'm not sure I'm up to it."

"'Course ya are, kiddo. It's not like you have to be him. Nobody'll be expecting that. You'll play a few tunes, take audience requests. Just like your weeknight sets. It's a piece of cake."

"The requests scare me. I don't know enough songs."

"You do fine," Harry said. "I never hear any complaints."

"Sure, on Tuesdays and Wednesdays. I know what kind of crowds are here on weekends."

"So you don't know something somebody requests," Harry said. "So what? It's not the end of the world, believe me. You play something else, is all. Kiddo, you're cute enough to get away with just about anything."

"If you say so."

"I say so." Harry pulled a wad of bills out of his pocket and peeled off two fifties. "Here. Buy yourself something snazzy to wear."

VII

"You two," Cooper laughed, spotting Tristan on his bench presses while Big Steve looked on. "I mean, is that your answer to everything? We should all settle down with steady boyfriends?"

"Technically," Tristan panted, letting the bar down onto the rack, "Big Steve thinks you should all have husbands."

"Right," Cooper snickered, "like you can just snap your fingers and there he is, Mr. Wonderful."

"Finding Mr. Wonderful isn't the problem," Big Steve said.

"Sure it's not."

"Seriously. Terrific guys are all over the place. In your case, the problem is you're not looking."

"Easy, Big Steve," Tristan warned.

"O.K." Big Steve said, "you're looking, but for the wrong thing. And in all the wrong places. That Kent twinkie that you're constantly out and about with. The one who causes all those scenes. He thinks he's got you wrapped around his finger, you know. And then there's that drag queen. Don't even get me started on that one. Your taste is atrocious."

"I said, easy," Tristan glowered.

"No, T.," Cooper said. "He's right. I admit it. I've got to be more careful about stuff like that."

"But in more general terms," Big Steve said, "all you young guys are looking for the wrong thing."

"How so?"

"You're looking for the finished product when what you really need to find is the raw material."

"You sound like my Nanny Freitag."

Big Steve shrugged.

"But really, is that the secret? 'Cause I have to say T. looks pretty much like a finished product to me."

"He does now," Big Steve grunted, "but he didn't that afternoon he walked into camp."

"January, 1969," Tristan nodded. "East Butthole, Viet Nam."

"What he looked like that day was a kid who didn't know who he was or what he wanted," Big Steve said. "Which made sense, because otherwise he wouldn't have been there in the first place."

Cooper nodded.

"But I could tell. Believe me. One look at him was all it took. He had what it takes. The raw material."

"How did you know?" Cooper asked.

"I think it's usually in the eyes."

———

Cooper hadn't thought of himself as the marrying kind since breaking up with Sonny. That had been a dead end he didn't want to drive down again. But he was smart enough to see the advantages. In all other aspects of gay life, he had been a faithful disciple of Stefano Fabiani since T. first approached him in the gym his sophomore year at State. But in this one thing he was a skeptic. Big Steve believed pairing off was the answer to all the ills suffered by the gay population, and more than that was the ultimate fulfillment of homoerotic desire. It was surreal, listening to a guy that big and hot talk heavy theory. It would have been way too much to swallow if it hadn't been for the compelling example Big Steve and his partner presented. Occasionally Cooper found himself drifting off into some reverie in which he and his boyfriend emulated them. Occasionally, that is, because Cooper was generally too busy for reveries, not to mention too practical. And besides, he had no idea who to cast in the role of boyfriend.

His practicality insisted that what Big Steve advocated was all but impossible for mere mortals to achieve regardless of Big Steve's assertion about the availability of great guys. The supply of men like Big Steve and Tristan was severely limited. Just because you wanted someone like that didn't mean you could find him. And you couldn't build a partnership like they had with just anybody, though Cooper had to admit that he still had fantasies about their buddy Nick Romanovsky from time to time. Sonny had, several times actually, accused Cooper of cheating on him with Nick. And it had probably been in an effort to corroborate his denials that he had steered clear of Nick so resolutely since the breakup. Not that Nick was really such a good candidate, actually, despite his chiseled face, smoldering eyes, and Mr. Universe build. Inside all that impressiveness beat the heart of a true opera queen, addicted to romance written in flaming letters blazing against a night sky, while Cooper wasn't at all sure that true love existed. Consensual arrangements mutually beneficial and satisfying to both parties was more how he thought it should work, so Nick was perhaps not the ideal match. In addition to that basic incompatibility of temperaments, there was the awkward reality that Nick had been carrying the biggest and brightest of torches for T., yes, Big Steve's T., for God only knew how long—since the dawn of time, for all Cooper could tell. T., for his part, was so gaga over Big Steve as to be practically a somnambulist and thus remained oblivious to the drama that was so apparent to everyone else. And Cooper didn't need all that emotional stuff. He just wanted someone to hang out with, fuck regularly, and be seen with in public as a couple, complications and emotional entanglements kept to a minimum, if you please. But it seemed pretty much impossible to find the right kind of guy for that, presentable, pleasant, trustworthy, and emotionally undemanding.

So after much consideration he had decided that though he accepted Big Steve's premise in principle he wasn't sold on its general applicability, and he had no strong inclinations in that direction himself. But despite his ambivalence and the difficulty of finding a suitable mate, he was committed to thinking practically and the idea was increasingly attractive on professional grounds. Each month the number of male couples coming to the agency to shop for homes increased. Cooper sensed that those men would approve of him more heartily if they saw a photo of a boyfriend displayed prominently on his desk. They all expressed interest in the Labradors they saw photos of there instead, but clearly in their minds the dogs were an imperfect substitute. There was no question he was losing out on some deals because of it.

And how much more effective might he be at his job if his domestic arrangements were ordered differently and he wasn't out so many nights finding sex? There was a reason beyond social pressure, he had come to believe, that highly successful businessmen were never single. So though he hated to admit that the straights might be right about anything, it certainly made him think.

———

"Can you believe it, Elizabeth?" Ned exclaimed. "The boy studied with Grammatikova. *The* Grammatikova. It's extraordinary."

"Who's that?" Cooper asked, looking up from his *Wall Street Journal.*

"Who's that? Who's that? Listen to him Elizabeth. Youth these days. Hopeless, I tell you."

"Ned," Elizabeth interrupted him, "I'm sorry to have to tell you, but I don't know who Grammatikova is, either."

"Of course you do," Ned insisted. "You've heard me tell the story. My mother's dear friend from St. Petersburg. Their families fled the revolution together. Well, not literally together, mind you. But you know. . ."

"Oh, certainly," Elizabeth said. "The name just slipped my mind."

"Like sisters they were. I have a photograph of them taken in London in 1918. I was only an infant at the time. Grammatikova very nearly became my aunt by marriage."

"I didn't know you were half Russian, Ned," Cooper said.

"Only one fourth. My maternal grandfather married a Russian woman. He was with the British mission in St. Petersburg. As military attaché. It seems my Uncle Sebastian was quite taken with Grammatikova. That was certainly a lucky escape for her. What a bounder he turned out to be. She was the toast of London for a season, but that father of hers dragged them off to America. He thought they'd get rich over here. She could have been the virtuoso of her generation with the right representation. Instead she ended up teaching in that little backwater college. And this young man was her student there. It's really the most amazing coincidence."

"What young man?" Cooper asked.

"That boy Griffin who plays weeknights at Harry's place," Elizabeth said. "The one who helped you find that record album for Ms. Rococo."

"He came to tea yesterday," Ned said.

"Ned Westerleigh adopts another stray." Elizabeth rolled her eyes.

"You really must go hear him play, Cooper. Your education isn't complete without hearing a student of Grammatikova perform."

———

"It's fantastic," Stone said. "It really is. I love that fireplace. The kitchen is perfect. But I just don't know."

"If you don't buy it," Cooper said, "I've got half a mind to pick it up myself. It's a ridiculous value."

"I'm sorry," Stone said. "I feel like I'm wasting your time. I wasn't expecting it to be this hard."

"I get it," Cooper said, "you've only been back in town a few weeks. Everything's up in the air. Maybe you're just not ready to buy a home."

"Yeah," Stone said. "Maybe that's it."

"Or maybe there's something you're not telling me."

"Man," Stone said, "Ned warned me you'd sniff it out."

"It's O.K." Cooper said. "I don't want to know if you're not ready to tell me."

"It's just, well, I'm shopping for two."

"I see."

"I thought it would be easy to pick something out for us. But I look at these places and I have no idea what he would think of them."

"Well, hell, man, you should have brought him with us to view properties."

"He's still in Montevideo," Stone said. "We're waiting for his work permit to come through. Ned's looking into it."

"Guess you've got a thing for South American men."

"He's not South American. He's Czech. He and his parents left Prague in '68 just before the Russians went in."

"Thought most of those folks came here," Cooper said, "or went to Germany."

"Jiri's dad was under the impression that he had relatives in Uruguay who would help them get settled. Once Jiri's family got there, his dad couldn't find them. Jiri's parents are both doctors. They managed just fine."

"Is Jiri a doctor, too?"

"His brothers both are. He's a research biochemist."

"Shouldn't have any problem getting work up here."

"He's been offered a position at Berkeley. It's just this paperwork thing."

"I'm sure Ned will sort it out."

"Of course," Stone said. "Listen, I think I know what the problem is."

"Tell me."

"We need a place with really good natural light in one of the bedrooms. Jiri paints water colors in his spare time. He's a wizard."

"I know just the property," Cooper said. "It's a fixer-upper, but the views are amazing, and you won't believe the light."

VIII

In a vintage clothing store a few doors down from the record shop, Griffin bought a dove grey suit that looked like something from the 1940's, thinking it might go well with his coloring. He ventured as far as North Beach looking for a barber shop that didn't seem too intimidating. Before he knew it, it was Friday. Then Friday evening. He showered, shaved, slicked his new cut into place with the same brand of pomade he remembered from a different lifetime. He had bought it special for the occasion. Gazing at himself in the mirror for a last time before leaving home, he knew he had missed the target. He couldn't see vintage glamor staring back at him, just a shy, awkward kid playing dressup.

On the bus his appearance made him feel conspicuous, but his fellow passengers didn't seem to notice him at all. The bus ground along Market Street toward the towers of downtown. With the shadows of the summer nightfall deepening, the city lights seemed more evocative than he could remember ever seeing them.

———

Griffin didn't recognize Cooper at first. The black hair wasn't slicked into place, but flopped over the forehead in the style, Griffin imagined, of the European nobility. He only realized who Cooper was when he caught sight of that seven foot tall drag queen on his arm. They were accompanied by two others. The three drag queens wore evening gowns and rhinestones, Cooper a tuxedo. They looked like they'd just come from the opera. Griffin seemed to recall that it was *Turandot* this weekend. Out of the corner of his eye, he saw Bruce the host showing them to a reserved table.

Back to business. His first two sets of the evening had gone far better than he expected. The tip jar was overflowing. Now he just had to make it through the next thirty minutes and go home happy.

———

The sing along of "Moon River" ended to gratifying applause, and Griffin breathed yet another sigh of relief. Five minutes and counting. But suddenly it looked like he had counted his chickens too soon. Here she came. Was her name Charmant? No, that wasn't right. What was it? Yes. Chanel.

"'Marietta's Lied', from *Die Tote Stadt,*" she hissed at him. "I believe you know it. In F, if you please."

It wasn't until she situated herself at the bow of the piano and assumed the posture of a recitalist that Griffin realized she intended to perform. There was an uneasy hush in the room. Shouldn't someone get up and stop this? He could sense her growing impatience. He didn't know what else to do. He improvised a little introduction and paused for her to pick up the melody. It was a simple enough tune. He wouldn't have thought it was histrionic enough for the likes of her. The first few bars were practically a recitative, and she managed to sing this with a quiet conviction that was almost compelling enough to disguise her warbling falsetto as mere stylistics. Perhaps he had underestimated her.

Now came the first real interval, not that wide a jump, really, just that trusty old perfect fourth. "Here Comes the Bride" was the mnemonic traditionally taught for it in introductory music theory classes. It shouldn't have been a problem for her. But in F major, as she had demanded, it lay in the worst possible band of her vocal range. Obviously she intended to soar, but so had Icarus. Instead, she produced a hideous sort of croak that even the force of her personality couldn't sell as intentional. She stopped dead. Griffin paused. He waited. The silence was as horrible, somehow, as her last, indescribable note.

She whirled to face him.

"You stupid little cretin," she shrieked. "I said, in F major."

Next thing he knew her drink was all over him, and Bruce the host was dabbing at him with a towel, and Harry was yelling, "Get her out of here, Cooper. Get here out of here right now."

Griffin took the towel from Bruce and dried his face and hands.

"You O.K?" Harry asked.

"Sure, boss, I'm fine."

"You might as well take off. Your set's nearly done anyway."

"No," Griffin said, running the towel over a couple of damp keys. "One more number."

He sat back down, adjusting the piano bench for something to do while he thought. He stared down at his hands, resting them lightly on the keys. Johnny Domino would have known exactly what to play that would serve as an appropriate riposte to a drag queen rampant. But Griffin couldn't think of a thing but his classical repertoire.

Then, almost before he knew it, his left hand was zipping through those blazing figures in the bass and on cue his right hand pounded out those high, dramatic chords. Chopin. The "Revolutionary" Etude. Perfect. And as he played, he felt, or at least thought he felt, the crowd rooting for him.

———

Griffin answered the dressing room door expecting to see Harry.

"Hi."

"Hello."

"I just wanted to see if you're O.K."

"I'm fine. Thank you."

"Can I come in?"

Griffin stood away from the door.

"We've met before," Cooper said, staring at him.

Griffin nodded. He could buy three weeks' groceries for what Cooper's cologne probably cost.

"Well, not actually met," Cooper corrected himself. "I'm Cooper."

"Griffin."

"Please accept my apologies," Cooper said, shaking his hand.

"You didn't do anything."

"Oh, but I did. Chanel had been drinking. I should have cut her off earlier in the evening. Come to think of it, I should have taken her straight home from the opera. I want you to understand that I ordinarily exercise better judgment."

"Drinking's no excuse."

"You're right. But she sure uses it as one. I should have stopped her. I could have. I can usually make her behave. After a fashion. I just never thought she'd do something like that."

"Really," Griffin insisted. "You're not responsible."

"You're too nice. You sure handled it well."

"Right."

"You heard them out there. You brought down the house with that encore you played. That's what I call revenge. For a drag queen, the one who gets the standing ovation wins."

"Doesn't matter," Griffin said. "She wasn't there. She didn't see it."

"Don't worry. Her spies are everywhere."

"Oh?"

"That was a joke, O.K? But believe me, she'll hear about it. She'll know you got the better of her."

"That's not. . ."

"I know," Cooper said. "It was self defense. Everybody here tonight gets that. She started it, you finished it."

"Thanks, I guess."

"I'd really like to do something to make this up to you."

"No," Griffin shook his head. "There's no need."

"You sure?"

"Yes."

———

When Griffin got to the club the next evening, there was a vase full of long stemmed roses waiting on the piano.

"They came this afternoon," host Bruce said, breathless, handing him the card. "Guess you've got an admirer."

Griffin opened the card.

"Not an admirer," he said. "It's just a peace offering."

"Chanel Rococo sent you roses?"

"No. That Cooper guy who was with her."

"Cooper Luxemberg! Cooper Luxemberg sent you roses?"

"He felt bad about what happened."

"Cooper Luxemberg," Bruce goggled. He turned to address the waiters and bartenders. "Hey, everybody. Griffin's roses are from Cooper Luxemberg."

———

The place was packed, even more so than usual for a Saturday night. Bruce told him that for much of the evening there was a line out front to get in, something that almost never happened. Harry told him he's a sensation. Griffin thought it was like motorists slowing down to gawk as they passed the scene of an accident. As he played, he felt the crowd's curiosity coming at him in waves. This was probably how a circus freak felt.

Madame Grammatikova had taught him how not to wilt under pressure. Her other relevant lesson was that talent spoke for itself. Truly gifted people never had to show off. So he played it cool and classy, as if he might actually be either of those things. During his third and final set he got into some kind of groove, almost convincing himself that he was all alone with the piano. He couldn't have said what he was actually playing, just that he was playing it with style.

He finished the set and got up from the keyboard a little dazed. Pandemonium broke loose in the packed room, clapping, whistling, cheers. A few people were actually standing on chairs. There were scattered cries of "Bravo" and "Encore". Harry rushed over.

"Play something else!"

"I can't. I'm exhausted."

"Anything, Griffin. Just one more number."

Griffin sat back down, and the room went spookily quiet. What the hell? Then like a bolt of lightning it came to him. Sure, why not? It was a simple melody, actually very pretty. And last night nobody had gotten to hear anything but the first few bars. He started to play. Out of the corner of his eye he saw a few nods of recognition, a couple of knowing grins. By the time he played the last phrase, with that unusual, almost spooky sounding series of cadences, he realized that he had just performed his signature tune for the first time.

———

He left the club by the alley exit, desperate for solitude. But damn that Harry. Cooper was waiting back there.

"Thanks for the roses," Griffin said, cradling the bouquet in his arm. "You really shouldn't have."

"I typically do exactly what I shouldn't," Cooper said. "I'm kind of famous for it."

"Uh huh."

"Can I give you a lift?"

"Thanks, but it's not far to the bus stop."

"That's three times now."

"What's that?"

"Three times you've turned me down."

"Oh."

"Three times is all you get. Most people don't even get away with doing it twice."

"Cooper, honestly, the roses are more than enough."

"Dinner Monday," Cooper said. "I know you have the night off, 'cause I checked with both of your employers. So you'd better not stand me up."

"All right."

They walked side by side to the street corner.

"Here's my car," Cooper said.

"Running fine, is it?" Griffin chuckled. "Starts up on the first turn of the key?"

"Very funny. You coming?"

"Not this time."

"Monday then. I'll call you."

"What if I don't give you my number?"

"Harry already did. Kip as well. I don't leave a thing like that to chance."

IX

Cooper wasn't used to seeing Kent fully clothed and in daylight. He almost didn't recognize him standing across the street from the gallery.

"Finally coming to your senses," Kent laughed.

"What are you talking about?" Cooper asked, receiving Kent's hug as casually as possible. He knew rumors were already circulating about the rift with Chanel and didn't want to throw fuel on the fire by looking too chummy with someone else, especially Kent, who must have heard the rumors or he wouldn't be there. Gallery openings weren't his thing, as a rule. It was too hard to be center of attention, something that Kent wasn't good at unless he could take his shirt off at least.

"That drag queen of yours just left."

"She's not my drag queen," Cooper said.

"Tell her that. She looked naked without you on her arm. I bet it's no accident she was by herself."

"I have no idea what you're talking about," Cooper laughed.

"Everybody's talking about that scene at Harry Gordini's the other night. Figured you might not want to be seen in public with her after that blowup."

"I thought you were dancing at Rascals this afternoon," Cooper said.

"Did I say that?" Kent grinned. "Must have been confused."

Confused like a CIA operative behind the Iron Curtain, Cooper thought. How transparent. He should have known that Kent would try and use Friday evening's fiasco to his advantage.

"Let's go inside," he suggested, not wanting to get sidetracked. Kent was a great one for that.

———

"Didn't know I'd posed for him, did you?" Kent gloated.

"If you're not careful, one of your tricks is going to sue for false advertising," Cooper laughed.

"What are you talking about?"

"You're not as big as he made you in the picture."

"I certainly am."

"Not even when your trick is blind drunk are you that big."

"Think not? How about we go back to my place and I let you measure it?"

———

"Jesus, Cooper," Kent complained, "you're leaving?"

"Gotta get home."

"I don't fucking believe it. I make you come three times and you won't spend the night."

"I like sleeping in my own bed."

"Then let's go to your house."

"Sleep tight," Cooper grinned.

———

From the bathtub Cooper heard Chanel's whiskey baritone coming through the answering machine.

"Cooper, God dammit, pick up. I know you're there. I know to the minute when you got home and where you were before that. You can't shut me out like this. I won't stand for it."

———

"Rumor has it that Chanel Rococo has gone into hiding," Ned said, filling the tea-kettle in the kitchenette of the Luxemberg-Montefiore Realty. "Some scene at a gallery opening yesterday. Corinne de Menthe and her gang, apparently."

"Drag wars," Buzz observed.

"I wouldn't know," Cooper said, intent on mixing his second protein shake of the day. "I haven't spoken to her since Friday night."

"You're joking," Elizabeth said, spreading cream cheese on a bagel.

"Cross my heart," Cooper said. "I'm no longer taking her calls."

"Cutting her off, are you?" Buzz asked. "I'll alert the press."

"As a matter of fact, yes. Yes, I am."

"Just like last time," Ned chuckled, "and the time before."

"You'll see," Cooper insisted. "Those were just warnings. This time I really mean it."

"There'll be hell to pay," Buzz laughed.

"If it sticks," Ned said.

"Miss Chanel can be awfully insistent," Elizabeth pointed out. "I'm not sure I'd put money on you, Cooper."

"Does anyone here know anybody more stubborn than I am?"

"Point taken, my boy."

"Oh, my God! Is that the time?" Elizabeth blurted. "I'm due to show the Hudginses the Porter property in twenty minutes. Damn, I hate Mondays."

"Elizabeth," Buzz called after her. "You left your briefcase."

———

"Congratulations, Stone," Cooper said. "You are officially in escrow."

"That's great," Stone said.

"Ned told me about Jiri's work permit. When's he arriving?"

"Some time next week," Stone said, blushing slightly. "Got to work out the travel arrangements."

"Let me know if there's anything I can do to help."

"Man, you're the best. I feel like the luckiest guy in the world right now."

"You deserve it," Cooper said. "Listen, I know about Jiri's job, but what are you planning to do? Not stay home and knit, if I know you."

"Ned says I should study for a real estate license."

"Does he?"

Stone nodded.

"Well, you've got a job with us the minute you pass the exam."

X

I t was like being in a movie. The gleaming sportscar. Its seductive growl as they drove through twilit streets. Cooper's ravishing surfaces and breathtaking suavity. The luxurious hush of the restaurant. The deference of the staff, all of whom treated Cooper like a young prince. The sparkle of the flatware and dishes, the succulence of the meal, all of it, every detail, every sensation, seemed perfectly choreographed. It was a world where nothing had been left to chance. Everything had been planned to surprise and delight. It was, Griffin believed, the opposite of reality. It was some film director's vision of dinner. Eventually the cameras would stop running, the director would shout "Cut!" and real life would reassert itself.

Except there was no sign of that happening. And since with every passing moment it seemed less and less likely that it would, Griffin had to redefine everything for himself. His overly philosophical brain barely managed that task, transforming the moment into a vignette from a universe he had never visited except in his imagination. But even his imagination wasn't helping. All he could think was that he didn't belong there, in that place or with that man. Worse than that, he had no idea what to say. He had never felt dowdier. He had never felt more awkward. He had never been more tongue-tied.

Every time he encountered Cooper, Griffin sensed his sanity deserting him. He felt and thought all kinds of things that he didn't want and couldn't allow himself to feel or think. Simply put, Cooper was not humanly possible. Hallucinations could look like that. Fantasies certainly could look like that. Your fondest dream might well look like that. But not a real, living, breathing, flesh and blood guy who bought you roses and asked you to dinner. Even if it was only because he was suffering from guilt once removed.

Of course Griffin knew all too well that such creatures did exist. He had been in love with one once. Hell, he still was in love, might as well admit it, no point in denying it. No point in anything to do with Brock, who, face it, was just as mythic in his own way as Cooper. But that was different. Because when you lay in side by side cribs in the church nursery you had no awareness of demigods. And as the child next to you grew into one, the process was so gradual and you came to apprehend it so slowly that no matter how supernatural your buddy became he paradoxically remained as familiar as your own skin.

And in the case of Brock it had been different for an additional reason. Due to Brock's many other qualities, qualities peripheral to his extravagant physicality, Griffin had been able to remain until the last, or at least pretend to remain, completely unaware of where his silent idolatry was tending. But this. There were no mitigating circumstances of history and friendship influencing matters now. He was simply and totally overwhelmed. If Cooper were to tell him to jump off a bridge, he might well do it. It had been that way with Brock, but in Brock's case Griffin had always known that whatever he jumped from, Brock would be waiting below to catch him. Brock might have inspired at least the prospect of total capitulation, but their history together had taught Griffin infinite trust. That provided the crucial element of balance necessary for maintaining his sanity. With Cooper there was no history, so there could be no trust. Nevertheless, the impulse to jump was as overpowering as anything Griffin had ever experienced. And what he was feeling wasn't some nebulous phenomenon composed of a lifetime's shared experience and common perceptions and simple boyhood innocence. No, now it was all too clearly defined and all too surely adult and terrifyingly alien.

Given all that, Griffin understood what was at stake for him. Despite the irresistible aesthetic and physical experience Cooper represented, Griffin would have been way happier if he could just turn back the clock to Friday night and never get off the bus and walk into Harry Gordini's club. He would still know of Cooper's existence of course. And he would still feel what he felt every time he encountered Cooper somewhere. But it would be from a distance. And in time he might well be able to discipline himself into a degree of detachment which would allow him to preserve a little dignity and autonomy while his infatuation burned itself out.

His only hope lay in his certainty that as much as he had invested in the proceedings, Cooper had nothing at all. It was just dinner. It couldn't possibly be anything else. Because there was no way a guy like Cooper could possibly want anything more than that from a guy like Griffin. The notion was as impossible in its own way as Griffin's love for Brock had been. He was just caught up in this bizarre drama set in motion by a drag queen's pique. Cooper and he would play out the script, and then Cooper would move on to the next act his life was writing for him. And Griffin would start digging himself out of this pit. Barehanded, because where did you acquire an implement for such a task?

———

It should have ended with the crème brulee. Griffin ate it; Cooper watched. Or with the ride home in Cooper's Jaguar, the sound of its purring engine echoing off the darkened buildings. Or with a firm, manly handshake at his own front door. In contemplating the evening, Griffin's imagination hadn't been able to go any farther than that. Until they arrived at Cooper's tiny house up the hill from Castro Street, Griffin hadn't realized that Cooper thought of this as an actual date rather than a mercy dinner. But here he was, in a place Brock never would have taken him, a place Butch, for all his "aw shucks" charm couldn't have, a place he had never expected to be with a man this incandescent. Cooper apparently had extremely questionable tastes in bedmates, otherwise this wouldn't be happening. And all Griffin could think about, because mostly right then he couldn't think at all, was that nothing like this would ever happen to him again as long as he lived. Other things might happen. But never with a man like this.

Those few times with Butch had been playful and tender and as passionate as Butch could make them without terrifying Griffin into more or less permanent celibacy. That had been Butch's gift to him, he suddenly comprehended, awakening him to certain physical realities without pushing him beyond his all too pedestrian limits. No such calculus was in force in this bed. This was no holds barred. This was like the difference between a Jeep and a Ferrari, between a harmonica and a Stradivarius. The comparisons stormed his consciousness like barbarians sacking a castle. Cooper was—no other word for it—transcendent.

As long as he lived, Griffin decided during the last instant he remained capable of coherent thought, these would be the moments against which all others were measured.

———

The dogs observed Griffin with drowsy interest as he pulled on his clothing. He had been afraid they might stir and wake Cooper, but they seemed to be in on the conspiracy. Indeed, he had an uncanny feeling that they were mind readers. He was frantic to avoid the morning after face to face in which Cooper's disappointment would inevitably be apparent.

If time could be made to stand still, with Cooper sleeping peacefully and Griffin staring reverently at him—well, no use contemplating that. But the idea of touching only once all that opulent masculinity was almost enough to keep him there despite the risk. Time should have stopped, really, last night. Griffin was famished for more. Even just one more touch. The face was too sensitive. The slumbering *ubermensch* might wake. He pressed his lips against the smooth skinned, fantastically muscled shoulder, just for an instant. Once, he told himself, hoping it was true but profoundly doubting it, was better than never.

The dogs escorted him to the door, silent as forest predators. He scratched their muzzles and slipped outside. Striding down the narrow driveway past the dew-fogged Jaguar, he felt like a pebble disappearing beneath the surface of a glassy pond.

XI

"The dogs are ruining my sex life," Cooper complained.

"What?" Tristan looked blank.

"That's one I haven't heard before," Big Steve chuckled.

"It's been going on for a while now. Every time I take a guy home, they go psycho."

"Every time?" Big Steve raised an eyebrow. "I thought you never took guys to your place."

"Right," Cooper said. "Usually we go to the trick's place."

"So what are we talking?" Big Steve said.

"Four times," Cooper said, "in eight weeks."

"Enough to constitute a pattern," Big Steve nodded.

"What do you mean, psycho?" Tristan asked. "Like barking and carrying on?"

"Peeing in the bed psycho. Shredding the guy's clothing while we're asleep psycho. Snapping at him psycho. Blocking the door so we can't even get inside the house psycho. I'm telling you it's bad."

"It doesn't sound like them at all," Big Steve said.

"It sounds like some weird jealousy thing," Tristan suggested.

"Or maybe one of your dates did something he shouldn't have to one of them. Dogs always remember a thing like that."

"I don't think that's it," Cooper said. "That wouldn't make them go after everyone I bring home, would it?"

"It might," Tristan said.

"But probably not," Big Steve said.

"The thing is, other people come over all the time," Cooper said. "It only happens with tricks."

"Definitely weird,"Tristan said.

"Well, all I know is I can no longer get laid in my own house. I can have all the sex I want as long as I do it anywhere else. Day in, day out, it's no big deal. But I can't live that way indefinitely."

"What have you tried so far?" Big Steve asked.

"Bribing them with treats. Locking them outside. The usual stuff. Nothing's working. It would drive me nuts if I let it."

"Dogs sure are funny,"Tristan said.

"They're also smart," Big Steve said. "Your three especially."

"You couldn't prove it lately."

"No, really," Tristan insisted. "Your Isis is probably the smartest dog on the planet. And Calpurnia's whole litter got her brains. Your other two, our Carlotta, Matt and Ashby's dogs."

"That's right," Big Steve said. "And I bet Eeyore and Bear are taking their cue from Isis, aren't they?"

"Like always."

"She's trying to tell you something," Big Steve said. "Obviously. And you're not getting the message."

"Right," Cooper laughed. "And I know what it is. 'Daddy we want you to be celibate'."

"How long did you say this has been going on?" Big Steve asked.

"Almost two months."

"Can you remember who the last guy was that they weren't like this with?"

"Nope," Cooper said, way too fast in spite of himself.

"You shouldn't lie to your friends,"Tristan said. "Next thing you know you'll start lying to yourself."

"O.K.," Cooper said. "Yeah, I remember who it was."

"You don't have to tell us,"Tristan assured him. "Yet."

"But if you really want to get to the bottom of this," Big Steve said, "track down that guy. Take him home with you again and see what the dogs do."

Big Steve's advice didn't surprise Cooper, though he wasn't that crazy about having his own suspicions confirmed. Supremely skeptical about things like karma and fate, he nevertheless had a profound reverence for the wisdom of the canine species. There had always been a Schnauzer or two around the Luxemberg apartment during his boyhood, and those dogs had been at least as smart as Cooper's brothers. There were individual animals, of course, who exhibited amazing stupidity, but in general Cooper believed that dogs were a good deal smarter than most people. And given that, he had to take his dogs' aversion to the men he brought home seriously. It wasn't random. It wasn't capricious. He was being instructed. It wasn't the first time they had appointed themselves his tutors.

But while he was always prepared to accept their guidance, at least within limits, he wouldn't have them running his life. It wasn't because they were dogs. He wouldn't take that from anyone. Not even someone as distinguished as Big Steve could get away with it. And he wasn't sure he was ready to take such a serious step as was implied by the current meddling. He was happy enough with his life. Why should he rush into settling down with anyone? There was no reason not to take his time. Once he tested his suspicions he'd be in the position of having his hand forced.

By three Labradors.

How was he ever going to explain that one? It wasn't the kind of story that would portray either Cooper or his chosen in a particularly flattering light: "My dogs told me to propose to him." He could just imagine the reactions. The weird laws associated with that Murphy character made it the kind of story that would inevitably come out. And at the most embarrassing possible moment, because that part was the most inevitable of all. So he had every possible incentive to keep on playing dumb with the dogs and ignore Big Steve's advice and his own nagging annoyance at being absolutely unable to control his destiny.

Assuming Big Steve was right and the Labradors were indeed attempting to direct him, Cooper had business to take care of. He always thought he had plenty of time to figure things out. He had planned and prioritized. Body? Check. Brain? He'd have his degree finished in a couple more semesters going part time. Career? Coming along nicely, thanks very much. Relationship? Eventually, perhaps, but no hurry. Seriously, he was only twenty-three. What gay twenty-three year old worried about settling down with someone? That kind of thing was for breeders. Hell, even his straight cousins, with their mother and grandmother breathing down their necks, had taken their own sweet time. The idea was absurd.

Cooper knew his dogs. And he knew Big Steve was right about his dogs. That could only mean that time was not on his side. But before he committed himself to the course of action they were laying out for him every time the drama repeated itself, there were things he had to know. Things you couldn't go to a library and look up in a book. Things you couldn't go to school for. Still, everything could be learned if you knew where to do your research.

———

Nick Romanovsky's apartment was in a tall old building on Nob Hill. Cooper had been there a few times, but never by himself. He'd never trusted either of them. Checking his hair in the rear view mirror one last time, he winced at the thought of how awkward he must have sounded on the telephone. He wondered what, if anything, Big Steve or T. might have said to Nick about his problem with the dogs. Clutching his thirty dollar bottle of French wine, the only peace offering he'd been able to think of, he headed for the front door.

Nick was apparently just back from jogging. He wore his sweat with real panache. If he was at all curious about Cooper's visit, he didn't let on. That was an attorney for you. You couldn't ever tell what they were thinking. It was a skill Cooper wouldn't mind developing.

"Mind if I hop in the shower for a minute?" Nick asked.

"I'll open this," Cooper suggested. "Give the wine a chance to breathe."

"Great."

The apartment was sparsely furnished. Nick hadn't gone down the all too predictable road of aping the period detail of the building with his décor. He'd chosen mid-century pieces mostly, with some art deco. All of it carefully selected, Cooper noted. Nothing kitschy. Just clean, simple, masculine. Exactly the way Nick wanted to be thought of. When Cooper got around to really decorating he had to remember this, design as a kind of self presentation. He had barely located the corkscrew and wine glasses by the time Nick reappeared, damp haired, wearing sweatpants and a t-shirt. There wasn't a hint of innuendo about him. So far, so good. Cooper didn't want this getting tacky.

"Great views on this block," he said.

"So they tell me."

"Sorry," Cooper laughed. "Occupational hazard. A house you're visiting is never just a house. We always think in terms of listing descriptions and potential commissions. Not to mention prospective buyers. I could sell this place by the end of next week. Two or three times, actually."

"Right," Nick grinned. "Guys like me are always calculating how people would look in the witness box."

"Ouch," Cooper laughed.

"Nice stuff," Nick said, studying the label on the wine bottle.

"The guy at the shop promised me."

"And it's not even sundown."

"We can save it, if you want," Cooper said.

"Are you planning to be here that long?"

"What?"

"Sorry," Nick said. "Didn't mean to be rude, Cooper, but surely you've got plans later. It is Saturday afternoon. And as far as I know, Kent Norberg hasn't left town or gotten himself married off to a sugar daddy. Not that that would stop him."

"I wanted us to spend some time together," Cooper said, knowing as the words came out of his mouth how ridiculous he sounded.

"Sorry," Nick laughed, "but you'll have to do better than that."

"No, I'm the one who should be sorry," Cooper said. "I'm too used to bullshitting people. I forget I'm not supposed to try it with my friends."

"Are we friends?"

Of course Nick wouldn't make this easy. Why would he? Why wouldn't he be on his guard?

"Well, I mean, T. and Big Steve and you and I. . ."

"Sure," Nick smiled, a little sadly. "The four musketeers. Or six or eight, depending on who else you're counting. Still, if you say we're friends, we're friends."

"All right," Cooper said. "We go to the same gym and the same bars and we know the same people. Other than that, I don't know you from Adam's housecat. We've never bothered trying to be more than we are."

"And you thought this would be a chance for us to get to know each other better."

"Not even that," Cooper shrugged. "I need a favor, that's all. Is that honest enough for you?"

"It's a nice start, thank you," Nick said. "What kind of favor are we talking about? Should I get my checkbook?"

"It's personal," Cooper squirmed. He deserved this. He knew that. But it didn't make it feel any better.

"No checkbook. O.K."

"You're going to make me say it, aren't you?"

"Am I?" Nick grinned. "Say what?"

"Jeez, you must be a real demon in the courtroom."

"That's the idea," Nick said. "All right, relax. I've tortured you enough. I'll play nice now."

"God," Cooper exhaled, "remind me never to piss you off."

"Don't worry. You're too hot ever to do that."

"Right."

"O.K. I get it. There's something you've never tried. And everybody's heard that there's nothing Old Nick doesn't know about what goes on between guys."

"Something like that."

"I should quit practicing law and open an office for this," Nick said. "Now what could it be?" He made a face like he was thinking really hard. "What could there possibly be that Cooper Luxemberg has never, ever done in the sack?"

"I thought you were going to be nice."

"You don't have anything to worry about," Nick said, suddenly sounding sincere. "Seriously, bud, when it comes to certain matters, I'm as solid as they come. Ask Big Steve."

"That's why I'm here."

"And I'm guessing that the issue is you've never taken it up the ass. Am I right?"

"Bingo," Cooper said, not accustomed to blushing.

"Really."

"Honest to God."

"Oh, I don't doubt it," Nick said. "Not a surprise, really. One does hear things about one's friends."

"God, you make that word sound so dirty. Can we go back to being enemies already?"

"Actually, I was just starting to like the friends thing," Nick said. "I thought it had a nice ring to it. Maybe we should call ourselves imperfect strangers. How does that sound?"

Cooper grinned.

"Now, Big Steve does wax eloquent about you from time to time."

"Does he?" Cooper asked.

"And I have the impression from listening to him that you're not much interested in theory."

"Huh?"

"More a hands-on kind of guy to hear him tell it," Nick said.

"I guess."

"Well, you've come to the right place."

"Have I?"

"Oh, you have, all right," Nick said, "but there are two conditions."

"What?"

"One, nobody knows about this. I don't want to drop into some club next week and hear people quoting you on the subject of my technique. My anything at all, for that matter."

"Fair enough," Cooper said, "but T. and Big Steve will probably figure it out."

"You can rest assured. But they don't count."

"Got it. What about condition number two?"

"I don't believe in quickies," Nick said. "If you're serious about this, I'm going to give you the works."

———

When Cooper got to the restaurant Stone and Jiri were there waiting.

"Gentlemen," he greeted them. "Good news. The sale recorded this morning, and I'm here to give you your keys."

"Fantastic," Stone said.

"We're so happy," Jiri smiled.

Cooper had met him for the first time a few days earlier. Floppy light brown hair, gray eyes behind wire rimmed glasses, olive complexion, medium height, slender build. He was good looking, but nothing spectacular. If he'd ever been in a gym it would have been to collect laboratory samples for some biological experiment. Cooper saw guys like this everywhere. He hardly gave them a second look. They worked in offices or banks. Some of them taught school. Their boyfriends looked just like them. T. called them the "gaygeoisie". Ned said they were the future. Big Steve didn't call them anything, but when he saw a pair of them walking down the street hand in hand he invariably smiled with approval.

"We are so thankful to you," Jiri said. "Stone tells me what a good friend you are to him. We want to buy you lunch."

"Not on your life, buddy," Cooper said. "Lunch is on me. I just came into some money."

———

A few days later Cooper and Nick met for coffee in one of those little places in North Beach. With their Italian suits, silk ties, and perfectly groomed hair, Cooper thought they looked like actors portraying high powered young stockbrokers. Ironic in the extreme, given the topic of conversation. As usual when unsure of himself, Cooper was a little boisterous. The amused glint in Nick's eye told him his gaucherie wasn't effective camouflage in this case.

"So," Nick said when Cooper finally paused to catch his breath, "when will you be stopping by for a rematch?"

Remembering the rasping kiss of Nick's expertly wielded straight razor, the exotic musk of the body oil, the nipple play which seemed to go on for hours, and eventually the sensation that was even more uncomfortable than he'd imagined but most of all his own astonishing, totally unexpected response to it, Cooper felt himself start to blush.

"Probably never," he said. "Sorry, I know how that sounds."

"Exactly what I expected," Nick said. "You weren't there to figure out if you were a bottom. You already knew you weren't. You were there to find out what all those guys are experiencing when they're with you."

"Something like that."

"It's essential knowledge for men like us."

"Right," Cooper said, "but now it's even harder to believe guys actually like that. Afraid it might have put me off the whole sex thing."

"You'll get over that," Nick said. "Thing is, we're all wired differently. Some guys can't imagine liking to do what you do."

"Unbelievable."

"Not really. Just a question of perspective. You know, Coop, a very wise man once told me that no man with a virgin asshole is truly gay."

"The only wise man I know is Big Steve," Cooper said, "but I somehow can't see it."

"Nevertheless," Nick shrugged. "You have to remember, he was in the service at an age when most of us still didn't have our driver's licenses. He wasn't always the man we know."

"Well, well."

"I'd venture to guess," Nick continued, "that your reactions surprised you a little."

"Honestly, yes."

"Don't sweat it. I told you I was going to pull out all the stops. The tricks I was playing—a dead man would have gotten off. A dead straight man."

"Right."

"But now that you've experienced the hands-on, you find yourself curious about the theory after all."

"What are you, some kind of mind reader?" Cooper asked.

"Just a guy like you. Been through it myself."

"So what? I go to Big Steve now and have him explain it to me?"

"I'm a man of many talents," Nick said.

"I'll say."

"I mean, I can do theory too."

"Sorry."

"You're an asshole," Nick grinned, "but you're a really hot asshole."

"Gee, thanks," Cooper said, wincing at the pun.

"Gays almost all start out as bottoms, I think. It's because we instinctively seek out tops to initiate us."

"Wasn't that way for me," Cooper said.

"Me either," Nick said, "but I wouldn't say we're typical."

"No. I see your point, though. It's probably that way for lots of guys."

"But when you're talking about experienced, settled guys, an awful lot seem to be switch hitters. They like the variety, both sexually and emotionally. And by being adaptable in that way, they end up having more sex. Not everybody's like you, Cooper. All you have to do is walk out your front door. Hell, you probably don't even have to do that. You probably just have to open your front door."

"Look who's talking."

"Fair enough," Nick admitted, "but the point is, most guys find it substantially more difficult than that. Switch hitters have an edge. They can adapt to whatever opportunity presents itself."

"Point taken."

"Then there are the bottoms. Some guys are natural bottoms. Some guys are bottoms because they're natural masochists. Some guys are bottoms because they only go with straight guys. And some switch hitters become bottoms more or less permanently because they pair off with tops."

"Sounds like T."

"It does," Nick nodded, "but it's not. T. is a very special case."

"No kidding."

"Finally there are your tops," Nick said. "Most guys who claim to be exclusive tops are either physically afraid of being fucked or afraid of what they think it would say about them if they let themselves be fucked. Those are the loud, obnoxious, aggressive tops."

"They're everywhere," Cooper laughed. "They're like a plague of locusts."

"Exactly. But they're not real tops. They're just posers."

"Got it."

"Your true tops are a very small group. It's not really about what they do in bed. It's about their essential selves. They top because it's who they are. They can even take it up the ass every now and then and it doesn't make them any less top. But it's not who they are. Finally, rarest of all, there's the true top who chooses to live as a bottom to please the man he loves. Some people say that kind of top doesn't exist because a true top would never do that. But you and I know at least one."

"T." Cooper nodded.

"It's too bad," Nick said.

"About T.?"

"About you and me," Nick said.

"What about us?"

"T. tried to get me interested in you a while back."

"Really."

"He and Big Steve have this idea they need to get me married off. In the case of you and me, Big Steve convinced T. he was just hung up on the visuals."

"Oh."

"We'd never have worked out as a couple," Nick said. "Too much alike."

———

"How are the dogs?" Tristan asked, pulling on a sweatshirt.

"Still driving you crazy?" Big Steve asked.

"'Fraid so."

"Thought you were going to do something about that," Big Steve glowered.

"I did," Cooper said. "I figured out who the guy is."

"So?"

"That's as far as I've gotten."

"And?" Tristan asked.

"And that's all."

"You're going to leave it like that?" Big Steve growled. "You're useless is what you are."

"I guess I am," Cooper agreed.

"Cooper's not useless," Tristan said. "He's got his reasons. The dogs will get over it sooner or later."

"I know who the guy is," Cooper said. "But he's not—well—he's not the kind of guy I really want to go any farther with."

"What's it got to do with what you want?" Big Steve demanded.

"Huh?"

"We don't choose," Big Steve shouted. "The universe chooses for us. Listen to your dogs, dammit. You'll fuck everything up if you don't."

XII

They looked, Griffin thought, like Macbeth's three witches masquerading as Presbyterian ladies of a certain age. They had come into the shop together, incongruous as polar bears in that part of town at that time of night. He scrupulously refused to eavesdrop as they tittered, giggled, and exclaimed over the opera albums. They seemed more the type for Lawrence Welk and his Champagne Music Makers, but opera fanatics came, Griffin knew from long experience on duty here, in all sizes and shapes. His first clue that not all was as it seemed came when one of them turned to another one and said, "No, dear, not the go-go boy. The pianist. Don't tell me you've forgotten that gorgeous red hair?"

He was thrown into confusion and spent several minutes trying to convince himself that he hadn't heard her correctly. Finally one of them approached the counter, and as she drew nearer her all too prominent adam's apple gave the game away. But the solution to that mystery only revealed a deeper one. These frumpy little aunties had about as much in common with Chanel Rococo and her troupe as a leopard did with an orangutan.

"My dear," she said. "I can't contain myself a moment longer. I simply have to ask you. Do I have the honor of addressing the divine young artiste who's been performing so exquisitely at Harry Gordini's establishment of late?"

Obviously, she already knew the answer to that question.

"Um, yes, ma'am."

He'd been halfway expecting some sort of reprisal but hadn't imagined that the attack might take this form.

"Then please allow me to introduce myself. My name is Corinne de Menthe. And these are my associates, Miss Helena Handbasket and Miss Ebola Borscht."

Her companions giggled and saluted him with unison Queen Elizabeth style waves.

"It's a pleasure to meet you, ladies," Griffin smiled, thinking it was about time for his life to flash before his eyes.

"No, no, dearie," Miss Borscht croaked, "the pleasure is all ours."

"Indeed," Miss Handbasket averred.

"You see, we were present at Harry Gordini's revered nightclub," Miss de Menthe explained, "on a certain evening not very long ago."

"Oh?"

"We were incognito on that occasion," she continued conspiratorially, "which is undoubtedly why you don't recall seeing us there."

"Um yes," Griffin said, "or, I mean, no."

"You know, darling," Miss Handbasket said in a hick accent almost as thick as his own, "you're even more charming in person."

"He *was* in person that night, you idiot," Miss Borscht hissed.

"I'm quite certain he knows what I mean," Miss Handbasket said.

"He may, dear, but you certainly don't," Miss Borscht cackled.

"What a night that was," Miss de Menthe enthused. "One doesn't generally expect the climax of the drama to occur *after* the final curtain. Opera is not supposed to work that way, everyone knows."

"If it did," Miss Borscht offered, "most ticket holders would probably demand refunds."

"Undoubtedly," Miss Handbasket nodded.

"We'd been waiting *years*. Hadn't we girls? Absolute, desolate, endless *years* for such an event," Miss de Menthe moaned. "We were like the Three Kings of Orient Tar, bearing gifts and scanning the eastern skies for a star that never seemed to appear."

"That's not how it goes," Miss Handbasket objected.

"We weren't bearing gifts, either," Miss Borscht pointed out.

"But we were very nearly moved to bare our fangs," Miss de Menthe declared. "Weren't we, girls?"

"Among other bodily parts, yes," Miss Borscht confirmed.

"And then, imagine how entranced we were when you put that upstart princess in her place with that divine encore of yours. Chopin, of all things. Chopin wielded like a battleaxe—what genius. And before we had the chance to spring to your defense."

"That *nouveau riche* trollop," Miss Handbasket snarled.

"That flea bitten, syphilitic hag," Miss Borscht cried.

"When you came in just now," Griffin said, choosing his words with even greater care than usual, "I wondered if perhaps the three of you were associates of hers."

"Oh, dear," Miss de Menthe said, turning even pinker.

Her companions hooted extravagantly at the ridiculousness of the thought.

"Sweetie, it wouldn't be suitable at all," Miss Handbasket moaned. "In fact it would never occur to us to have anything to do with that Joanie Come Lately. Not women of our position. Why, Miss de Menthe is a member of the D.A.R. You've heard of that organization, certainly. Everyone knows of it."

"I'm not sure," Griffin said.

"*Descendents* of the American Revolution of course," Miss de Menthe purred.

"And I myself," Miss Handbasket continued, "am the great-grandchild of a famous naval captain, you see. A very courageous officer who went down on his ship."

"*With*, my dear," Miss Borscht corrected her. "*With* his ship."

"He went down *on* his ship," Miss Handbasket insisted, "subsequently being highly decorated and living to a ripe old age. Though I'll admit that in his later years he suffered terribly from that chronically dislocated jaw. Meanwhile, at the end of hostilities, the vessel was converted into a floating bordello, as was only fitting given its illustrious history."

"I believe the word you meant to employ in that description was *notorious*," Miss Borscht said.

"Quit your bickering, you two," Miss de Menthe snapped. "So you see, Griffin darling, an alliance of any kind whatsoever with that she-jackal. . ."

"That hyena," Miss Borscht interposed.

"That croco-gator," Miss de Menthe affirmed.

"Why it's unthinkable," Miss Handbasket insisted. "Simply unthinkable."

"So my dear little one, have no fear," Miss de Menthe said. "She Whose Name Must Never Pass the Lips of the Righteous won't dare make a move against you. We've put out the word that you're under our protection, you see. And in the unlikely event that any silly little slip of a scullery maid should take it into her head to ignore such a warning. . ."

"Coming from such estimable figures as ourselves," Miss Handbasket suggested.

"Things will go very badly for her indeed," Miss de Menthe continued. "So never forget: should you ever need our aid, we'll be at your side to defend you."

Miss de Menthe had grown rather breathless toward the end of this oration.

"In the blink of an eye." Miss Borscht nodded so hard as she said this, Griffin thought she might dislodge her wig.

"In less than that," Miss Handbasket confirmed. "In a trice."

"But. . ."

"Don't worry about how to find us," Miss Borscht assured him. "Our spies are everywhere."

XIII

"Take young Griffin MacDonald, for instance," Ned said, brandishing his tea mug like a television weatherman using a pointer to indicate an approaching cold front on his giant map. "The difference between Griffin and Kent Norberg for instance isn't as obvious as one might think. Put the two of them in matching g-strings—or matching dinner jackets for that matter—stand them side by side, and ask the great gay public to tell you which one is the go-go boy and which one is the classical pianist: no one would be able to tell for certain. The meaningful distinctions are internal."

"A tad obsessed with Kent these days, aren't you, Ned?" Cooper chuckled.

"Not at all. I'm citing those youngsters merely as examples to illustrate my point."

"Quite frankly," Cooper said, "I can't imagine anyone getting Griffin into a g-string. Even at gunpoint. That's assuming he even knows what one is."

"Interesting question," Buzz said.

"But just say you did," Ned insisted. "You'd be amazed at the transformation. I'd wager my next two commission checks on it."

"I'd be amazed at something," Cooper agreed, "but this point of yours? I know I came in in the middle, but I'm not following you at all."

"The bifurcation of our community into Apollonian and Dionysian elements," Ned declared. "Not to say camps."

"It's gay graduate school," Buzz grinned. "Professor Westerleigh's advanced seminar on the formulation of conceptual frameworks in non-traditional socio-sexual contexts."

"Apollonian and Dionysian elements, huh?" Cooper mused. He knew he was supposed to know the terms. He'd better listen carefully and figure it out from the context. Ned's explanations were invariably clear enough as long as you paid careful attention. "Don't stop now. I'm fascinated."

"The categories are typified," Ned continued, "by two factions we're all familiar with. Jules de Croteau and his Flying Circus up in Pacific Heights and Big Steve Fabiani and his band of Spartan Warriors."

"In other words," Buzz said, "everyone's either a hero or a hedonist."

"And never the twain shall meet? Sorry, Ned, I'm not buying it."

"Don't put words in my mouth, Cooper."

"There's hardly room in there, Ned," Buzz laughed.

"I never meant to suggest that the bifurcation is absolute. Social groups don't work that way. Of course there's some blurring of boundaries."

"I'll say," Cooper laughed. "Our Buzz here blurs those old boundaries every time he beds his boyfriend."

"Look who's talking," Buzz countered, coloring slightly.

"A nice point," Ned nodded. "Inevitably, the interactions between the two camps will often be sexual in nature. Given the context, that's probably the case more often than not. The point is, in the example you cite. . ."

"Buzz isn't an example," Cooper protested. "He's our loyal friend and trusted associate."

"Yes, yes, of course," Ned admitted.

"Thank God," Buzz said. "I was beginning to feel like a laboratory experiment."

"You're not, Buzzy," Cooper said, "but Trevor almost certainly is."

"Gentlemen, gentlemen," Ned persisted, "the point is that there's no question, is there, which one of the groups represents the Apollonian ideal?"

"That was the point?" Cooper asked.

"Is there?"

"Well," Cooper mused, "Trevor is many things, but no one would describe him as a Spartan warrior. Unless he has talents I'm not aware of."

"He does," Buzz said, "but not that kind. Ned's right."

"Uh huh," Cooper grinned, "and that would make you the Spartan warrior of the house, right?"

"I don't think the distinction is that clear, really," Buzz said. "I mean, look at Nick Romanovsky. He's as Dionysian as they come, if only half of what you hear about him is to be believed."

"Yet he's the King of Sparta's right hand man," Cooper nodded. "A prince of the realm, one might say."

"You might indeed say that," Ned nodded, "but I'd put it another way. I'd describe our Nick as the consummate Apollonian, albeit driven by his romantic frustrations to act out in a spectacularly Dionysian fashion."

"Romantic frustrations?" Buzz asked, looking baffled. "Romantic frustrations? Is this the same Nick Romanovsky we're talking about?"

"It is, indeed."

"Thank you, Dr. Freud," Cooper said.

"I met him, you know," Ned nodded. "I spent several weeks with him in Vienna. The tail end of his career, you understand. He was already gravely ill."

"You studied with Freud?" Buzz was flabbergasted.

Cooper knew better than to be surprised.

"Studied is too strong a word," Ned said. "Followed him around with my ears wide open would describe the situation more accurately. But I certainly learned a good many things."

"So that takes care of Nick," Cooper said. "An Apollonian in Dionysian drag. I can almost buy it."

"For now," Ned said. "All he lacks is one triggering event to precipitate his return to his authentic state."

"Triggering event?"

"You'll know it when the time comes," Ned nodded.

"All right," Buzz said. "I'll give you Nick. But what about Cooper? How does he fit into your conceptual framework?"

"I wouldn't presume to analyze Cooper," Ned smiled. "Not even behind his back. Cooper defies augury."

"Not to mention compelling people to quote from Shakespeare," Cooper laughed. "Though I'm not sure how anyone could see a similarity between Hamlet and me."

"Augury's not the same as analysis," Buzz objected.

"Isn't it?" Ned asked. "Big Steve would say that if you really know a man, you're likely to know what he's going to do next."

⌒

Cooper watched Nick doing lat pulldowns.

"Bad night?"

"Had to bail out your buddy Kent," Nick grunted. "Drunk and disorderly."

"He's your buddy, too."

"Rethinking that," Nick said. "Not sure it's good for my career, you know?"

"Exactly," Cooper chuckled.

"Honest to God," Nick said, "it almost got really ugly. Little idiot tried to French kiss the arresting officer."

"Nobody's cute enough to pull that off."

"He hasn't figured that out yet."

⌒

"Don't let Big Steve railroad you," Tristan said.

"Not planning to," Cooper said, performing curls.

"He matchmakes for everyone, you know."

"Right."

"Usually it doesn't work out," Tristan said. "Ever wonder why Nick doesn't have a husband?"

"Not any more."

"Oh?"

"Never mind."

"Oh," Tristan said. "Well, Nick is just the most apparent of Big Steve's failures."

"Being part of a couple isn't for everybody," Cooper said, finishing the set and panting heavily.

"Exactly."

"Hate to have Big Steve down on me, though."

"I wouldn't worry about that," Tristan said. "He's a big fan of yours."

"But I'm not following his advice. I know how he can get."

"Neither is Nick. And they're as tight as ever. So don't sweat it."

"I hope you're right. 'Cause I'm not sure I'm up for what he's suggesting."

⌒

When Cooper got out of the shower, Stone was just changing into his workout clothes.

"You and Jiri getting settled all right?"

"Great, thanks."

"Glad to hear it."

"You're Jiri's hero," Stone smiled.

"He's a very sweet guy."

"Listen."

"What?"

"About Jiri. I know he's no beauty."

"What do you mean? He's very good looking. Ned thinks he's adorable."

"Don't patronize me, Cooper. You're my oldest friend. You're probably the best friend I've ever had. You know what I mean."

"O.K."

"Jiri's no sex god, either. What he is is kind and sweet and gentle. Boring stuff, right? I know exactly what I sound like."

"What you sound like," Cooper said, "is a man in love. That's nothing to apologize for. I get it, swear to God."

"All right."

"There's only one thing that would disqualify him in my book," Cooper said.

"What's that?"

"Does he make you happy, Stone?"

"Wrong question, man."

"Oh?"

"Here's what I've learned from him. Making him happy is what makes me happy."

———

"This came for you, boss," Buzz said, laying the envelope on his desktop. "Hand delivered."

Cooper recognized the handwriting immediately.

"Oh, God," he muttered.

"She wanted to give it to you herself, but I told her you weren't in. She knew I was lying. She looked like she was spoiling for a fight. But I guess with Ned in the office she was afraid to try anything."

"Thanks, Buzz."

He attacked the envelope with a letter opener that had a replica of the Jaguar 'leaping cat' hood ornament as a handle.

"*Dear Cooper, since you're refusing to return my phone calls—assuming that Cunt (oops!!! I mean, Kent) isn't erasing all the messages, which I wouldn't put past her—I'm forced to resort to other methods.*"

He stopped reading, slid the letter back into the envelope, and tossed the envelope into the trash. She didn't get it. The escort of any spiteful, misbehaving woman—whatever her gender—was as lacking in class as she was. It had nothing to do with Kent.

XIV

The university wasn't a bit like the conservatory, Griffin thought as he rapped on Professor Krakowiak's door. For all you could tell about what went on behind the doors in this corridor, he might be in a Chemistry building. Or the school of Business and Public Administration, whatever that was.

"Come in."

Griffin stepped inside. Professor Krakowiak, a tall blond man who looked like the retired captain of an Olympic rowing squad, was looking intently at a young guy almost exactly Griffin's size and shape, though the similarities ended there.

"I'm sorry," Griffin stammered. "I didn't realize."

"It's all right," Professor Krakowiak said. "Kent was just leaving."

"No, I wasn't"

Kent was so good looking it hurt Griffin just to glance at him. It didn't seem possible for anybody to be that cute.

"Actually, you were."

"Really?" Kent seemed unable to believe that he had suddenly become superfluous.

"I'm quite certain of it," Professor Krakowiak said. He made a very convincing authority figure. Not at all like Jean-Pierre. Still, Kent didn't move.

"I said go, Kent."

A pout like that ought to be federally regulated, Griffin thought, as Kent stalked out of the studio. The hip action he put into his exit, as well.

"I'm Michael Krakowiak," the professor said, flashing a piratical grin, "and you must be my new student, Griffin MacNeill."

"MacDonald."

"Sorry. Why don't you have a seat? No, not there. At the piano. You're not here for conversation."

"Sorry."

"I was just listening to your recital tape last night. Professor Schein sent it over. Incidentally, that's the last time you'll ever hear me use his academic title. You really can't refer to somebody that way after holding his hair out of the toilet while he puked. He used to wear it way past his shoulders. Gorgeous. Flags were flying at half staff all over Paris the day he had it cut off. I have to say, I really liked what you did with *Gaspard de la Nuit*."

"Thank you," Griffin said, squirming into position on the piano bench.

"I did think, though, that 'Scarbo' almost got the better of you."

"I was in over my head," Griffin admitted. It had been a miracle he got through the piece at all.

"That's when pianists are at their most exciting," Krakowiak said. "When they're on the ragged edge. When they play it safe, they're boring. Nothing worse than a boring pianist. Except someone who's boring in bed. That's the one unforgivable sin. I always find that Jean-Pierre's former students have formidable technique. However, I generally have to work with them on their expression. Such a timid little tribe you all are. So inhibited. Well, never mind that. We'll pull the repressed passions out of you. Don't bother trying to convince me you don't have any, because I know better. Ever played any Liszt? *Liebestraum* doesn't count."

"Except for the *Allegro agitato molto* I played as an encore at my junior recital, no."

"Get a score of the complete *Transcendental Etudes*," Krakowiak said. "Have a look at 'Mazeppa' and '*Harmonies du soir*.' Oh, and get a copy of the *Dante Sonata* as well. That'll keep you off the streets. Now let's have you warm up. How about 'Marietta's Lied'? I promise not to sing along."

XV

Ned Westerleigh gave two kinds of parties. The first type rivaled anything the Emperor Nero might have staged and could, indeed, have taught Jay Gatsby a thing or two about entertaining. For these events Ned rented a hotel ballroom, hired a platoon of private security, and stood back to watch the fun. Or at least the ensuing chaos. There were no invitations and no guest list, just word of mouth. The results were spectacular in a decadent kind of way that Ned both deplored and considered imperative in more or less equal parts. Just as you couldn't make an omelet without breaking a few eggs, you couldn't maintain a certain position in a certain segment of society without compromising your standards a little. Or at least appearing to, which was really as far as he ever went. He was only up to this kind of entertaining once every two or three years, which was usually about the length of time required for the furor generated by the previous event to dissipate.

The second kind of party took place in Ned's flat and was altogether more intimate, not to mention as ruthlessly genteel as any function at Buckingham Palace. There were printed invitations—highly coveted, to be sure. And even a dress code of sorts. There was a highly restrictive guest list, and Ned meant it. No one had ever successfully crashed one of these parties. The concierge at Ned's building simply didn't admit anyone who wasn't on the list and even refused a few individuals who were when they showed up shirtless or already drunk, for instance, or whose dates he judged to be unsuitable. The concierge was one of Ned's protégés. He didn't really consider himself to be employed by the building, thinking of himself instead as Ned's personal retainer. Which was actually pretty accurate. As far as he was concerned, Ned's preferences were as deserving of reverence, and enforcement, as the Ten Commandments. There had been lamentable scenes but none of them had

taken place at the party itself. The histrionics were restricted to the lobby downstairs, or, more typically, the sidewalk out front. If Chanel Rococo hadn't thrown
that drink—or that fit—at Harry Gordini's, she might well have become one of
the few drag queens ever to experience the event. Ned didn't disapprove of drag
queens on principle, only in practice. Few were demure enough in their deport-
ment to pass what he referred to as the "antacid test". Nine weeks on, Chanel was
still leaving messages on Cooper's answering machine. So far he'd only answered
the first one.

Though as one of the city's most eligible young men he could have had his
pick of companions for the evening, many of them actually suitable for such an
event, Cooper elected to attend stag. This fact was noted by the concierge when he
checked in.

"No guest tonight, Mr. Luxemberg?"

"No, Derek."

"A gay bachelor indeed," Derek grinned, meaning it in every possible sense of
the term. "Go on up."

———

It was that rarest of parties, Cooper thought. One he could actually enjoy. Almost
everyone he considered a close friend was present but nobody he truly disliked.
Scott and Jared were there staring into each other's eyes and oblivious to everyone
else. Buzz and Trevor were present as well. Buzz was an observer, Cooper noted,
while Trevor was a schmoozer. Typical Jewish American Prince, even if his mother
was Chinese. Even Matt and Ashby had managed to clear their terrifyingly con-
gested calendars. In matching dinner jackets they looked like two grooms on the
top of a wedding cake, if you could imagine such a thing.

A harpist alternated with a string trio. This was fronted by Elizabeth's newest
beau, a gorgeous Italian, and it, in turn, alternated with a young Asian woman at
Ned's grand piano. The catering was sublime. The bartenders were divinely attractive, well mannered, and expert. Contrary to appearances, they hadn't been hired
solely for their looks. Contrary to what gossip would assert come Monday morning, they were fully clothed.

———

From Ned's extensive roof garden you could see the lights of Alcatraz. Cooper found the view bracing. When the party got to the point where he really needed to clear his head, nothing was better. He wasn't alone with his thoughts, however.

"Is that the celebrated Cooper Luxemberg I spy?" a figure greeted him from the other side of an arbor patterned after one Ned had seen in at a villa on the Amalfi coast.

"Dr. Altman, I presume," Cooper said. "How on earth did you manage to get a night off? And this one, of all nights?"

"I asked for it," Jamie laughed.

"It's that simple?"

"That simple," Jamie nodded. "Most of that stuff about doctors' schedules is a myth. Hell and damnation, man, do you never stop getting better looking? It's almost enough to make me reconsider my rule against dating fellow Jews."

"Don't sweat it," Cooper laughed. "I have the same rule myself."

———

"I thought Stone and Jiri were coming," Cooper said.

"I was hoping they would," Ned nodded. "That Jiri. Absolutely divine little creature. Nice to have someone to speak Russian with, even though he claims to hate it."

"He's growing on me," Cooper admitted.

"He's still a little nervous around crowds," Ned said. "I'm giving a dinner party for them in a few weeks. You're on the guest list."

———

"I can't believe Nick brought a date," Cooper said. "He never takes a date anywhere. Except to bed. Who is he, anyway?"

"Dario teaches literature at Berkeley," Tristan explained. "His parents ran afoul of the Perons once upon a time and had to leave Argentina. He grew up in Geneva. His parents still live there."

"Funny," Cooper mused, "from his accent, I would have guessed someplace more Olde Englishe."

"He attended Winchester and Oxford."

"Ned must be peeing himself," Cooper said. "I mean, Ned must approve."

"As does my husband," Tristan nodded.

"I do," Big Steve agreed.

"Gorgeous, isn't he?" Tristan observed.

"I heard an ancient queen at the buffet insist that he was some Mexican movie star," Cooper said. "I didn't recognize the name."

"Jorge Rivero," Big Steve nodded. "Could be his identical twin. But he's not actually Nick's date."

"No?"

"What Big Steve means," Tristan said, "is that we believe he's Mr. Till Death Do Them Part."

"I didn't know Nick was the marrying kind," Cooper said.

"Everyone is the marrying kind," Big Steve said. "Even you. Though I notice you're still single."

———

And now Nick, as well.

Cooper scanned the room. T. and Big Steve. That went without saying. They were an institution. Scott and Jared, just back from Europe. Ashby and Matt in those identical dinner jackets. Even Buzz and Trevor, silly as Trevor was. Buzz was solid enough for both of them. All the men Cooper admired and respected, with their mates. The men he preferred to spend his time with. The men who taught him things, made him laugh, showed him what to value.

Not to mention Stone and Jiri, blissful in the snug little nest he'd found for them.

And now Nick, too. Because Big Steve was undoubtedly correct. This was no date. This was Nick committing himself publicly.

"I think," Cooper said on his way out the door, "I understand what you mean by a 'triggering event.'"

"Indeed," Ned nodded. "People insist that experience is the best teacher. But I find that close observation has a great deal to recommend it as well."

———

When Cooper pulled into the driveway, something that shouldn't be there was sitting on the front steps. Instantly alert, he took his time getting out of the car.

"I thought you'd never get home," Kent said getting to his feet.

"What are you doing here?"

"It's been a couple of weeks since I heard from you. I thought I'd drop by. Can we go inside? It's freezing."

"Wait here a minute. I'll bring you a sweatshirt."

"Huh?"

"I didn't invite you over."

"You're kidding."

"I'll be right back."

Cooper stepped inside, half expecting Kent to try and follow him. He must have been sufficiently intimidated, or at least sufficiently surprised, not to. Cooper flicked on some lights and gave the dogs their treats. Kent would wait. The dogs shouldn't have to. He went into the bedroom and retrieved a sweatshirt some trick or other had left back in the days before the dogs staged their crazy insurrection and he was still able to bring tricks home. The dogs were chomping as he stepped back outside.

"I don't fucking believe this," Kent fumed. "It's two a.m. and you're not going to let me come in. Not to mention, you didn't invite me to Ned Westerleigh's party even though you could have. I know you didn't take anyone else. Yancy called from Ned's pantry and told me you were there alone. I was all prepared to forgive you for that if you were nice. You really are a cold-hearted bastard."

"Here," Cooper said, handing him the sweatshirt. "Looks like it should fit you."

"Do you have any idea how many guys would kill to have me show up at their front doors?"

"Uh, yeah," Cooper said, "I've got a pretty good idea."

XVI

When Griffin got to Harry Gordini's, Bruce the host was training a new guy. He was gorgeous. His name was Kent. He seemed familiar. Griffin couldn't be sure if this was because they had actually run into each other before or if Kent was just so good looking that he unconsciously wanted to believe they had met. In any case, Kent was likely to be great for Harry's business.

Finally it came to him. The guy from Professor Krakowiak's office. Was he a musician, too?

He wouldn't be around long, in any case. Before you knew it some doctor or attorney or banker would swoop down and carry him off to a condo on Nob Hill. That's how it always was with boys like that. They seemed to live charmed lives. That's what being beautiful got you. Whether or not they actually lived happily ever after was another question entirely. But they at least got that boost up the ladder.

Harry had hired yet another bouncer. Butch's first two replacements hadn't worked out. The new guy was called Kick. His real name, an Eastern European one, was apparently unpronounceable. Harry had hired him with his usual eye for masculine pulchritude. He had no discernable personality but he was certainly intimidating enough to quell any misbehavior. Griffin caught him looking at Kent from time to time. His expression was that of a warrior just returned from battle who has spied a t-bone steak sizzling on the grill and is determined not to let it overcook.

Halfway through the set, Cooper walked in. Griffin pretended not to notice. He had just about managed to convince himself the whole thing was a dream.

———

Kick sat down at Cooper's table for a couple of moments. They obviously knew each other, presumably from the gym. After Kick went back to his duties, Kent stopped there just long enough to give Cooper a big hug and then rushed off on some errand or other. Boys that cute hugged whoever they felt like hugging whenever they felt like hugging them. For that matter, Kent, too, was exactly the kind of guy Cooper would be friends with. Birds of a feather.

A drink arrived for Cooper, and he acknowledged it by throwing a snappy salute at a trio of middle aged men seated at a corner table. Griffin knew them as Wednesday night regulars, lavish contributors to his tip jar. They generally requested arias rather than show tunes. When they greeted him, which was rarely, they were unfailingly solicitous but without any of the innuendo which invariably flummoxed him. Every time he encountered them he sensed that there was something strangely familiar about them, but he'd never been able to figure out why this was. It was interesting that they knew Cooper. But only mildly. Apparently everyone knew Cooper.

Harry stopped at Cooper's table. They shared a joke, and Harry gave him a slap on the shoulder.

All this Griffin saw without looking. He couldn't look directly. He'd turn to stone if he did. Out of the corner of his eye was bad enough.

———

San Francisco was a city of dreams. Every spire, dome, and tower in the skyline attested to the fact. Dreams permeated the streets like fog. Dreams whistled at the corners of buildings and rattled their windowpanes. Dreams sang in the clanging of the cable cars. Dreams were the hunger Griffin saw in the eyes of his fellow students, of strangers encountered on the streets, of his co-workers here at Harry's. Dreams glimmered in his own eyes looking back at him from the bathroom mirror. Everyone, it seemed, had some dream or other when they first came to the city. Some dreams came true as fortunes were made, careers were built, love affairs were consummated. Some dreams, though unfulfilled, persisted over years and decades, perhaps lifetimes. Some dreams, all too apparently, died like the last gleams from guttering candles, like the faint glow of the setting of the sun, like the fading pigments of fallen leaves decomposing in the city's gutters. That elderly gentleman staring hungrily at Kent the host-trainee—he must have had dreams once but now his expression told only of exhausted desperation. What dreams had tantalized him over a lifetime only to bring him here on a rainy weeknight?

Griffin's dreams were like a distant horizon. They receded as fast as he chased them. More and more they tended to be obscured by meteorological conditions or other interposing phenomena. More and more he saw himself as a hamster in a wheel, running and running and getting nowhere, lacking even the most rudimentary understanding of why he still ran. He no longer regretted Julliard or any of the other fabled schools Madame had held up as his goals. The competition at the conservatory was as much as he could handle. The challenges of the school, both musical and intellectual, nearly overwhelmed him. He had never known what hard work was, what fear was, what loneliness was, until following his dream to San Francisco. That was what came from living in a bubble. When it burst, the world grew unimaginably larger and more challenging. You learned daily from experiences which left the taste of ashes in your mouth that you were less equipped to survive in it than you had supposed. You learned that the limits were more concrete than you had imagined. That they were more or less the only reality that mattered. That was something no one had bothered to tell him, but looking back he thought he recalled seeing the knowledge in his grandparents' eyes.

Once you sold yourself to dreams, there seemed to be no escape. There was no going back, certainly, to a tidy little ivy covered school that was itself no more than some other fool's dream, fulfilled in a barely recognizable form. There was no going back to friends who had been as oblivious as you were yourself during those lazy days when it seemed like you had all the time in the world to get where you imagined you were going. There was no going back even farther, to the slumbering farm, the somnolent heifers rousing themselves to be milked on freezing mornings before dawn, the drowsing pigs lounging in their muddy shade on steaming afternoons, the irascible hens pecking frantically at your hands—the hands your whole future depended on—to prevent you from stealing the eggs from their nests. No going back to corn that needed to be shucked, potatoes that must be dug from the ground on just the right date and under just the right phase of the moon, peas that required shelling, rows and rows of vegetable garden to be weeded, hoed, watered, and protected against the depredations of countless pests. No going back to cleaning gutters and raking leaves and mowing grass and chopping firewood and all the thousand other mundane tasks that had filled Griffin's boyhood and adolescence, the tasks that had nurtured and apparently fulfilled generations of his people but left him only exhausted and dreaming that somewhere else there was another life that would awaken him. His days and nights in this city of dreams had taught him one lesson at least. There was no going back to any Eden whatsoever. If you could even find your way. Time, indeed, was the greatest distance of all.

There was only forward, one step and then another, staring blindly as if there might be something to catch sight of ahead in the dimness and fog. As if you knew what you hoped to find around that corner, on the other side of that closed door, at the break of that next day—the rising of yet another sun.

Meanwhile, there was here and there was now. There was the firm flat bench underneath him, the cool smoothness of the keys against his fingertips, the fluid motions of his wrists and forearms. There was sound. There was rhythm. There was concentration. There was the ecstasy without consequence or guilt that resulted from a perfectly articulated phrase, a tone so exquisitely generated by the pressure of his foot on the pedal and the ideal force applied by his fingers and then transferred through the invisible components of the action onto the strings as to defy any analysis, a mystical transformation of black markings on a sheet of paper into something which lived and breathed and inhabited both time and space. There was the certain understanding that in that moment there was no music without him and there was no him without the music. That there was no clearly defined point at which the piano started and he began. That the instrument was, perhaps more than anything or anyone else could ever be, his truest friend and lover, because no matter whatever or whoever happened to him, no one nor any thing could ever be so honest and faithful.

There was, above all, the glorious oblivion that was the music's ultimate gift back to him. All the fear, all the frustration, all the hopelessness lay outside the sound of that music, outside the charmed circle centered on the piano itself, which was his altar of both worship and sacrifice. He played on, fending everything off, all sorrow, all hope, all anticipation of future, and all disappointment in the past, until finally it was time to go.

This particular evening this presented a bit of a problem. By now "Marietta's Lied" was widely known as his signature tune. People would notice if he played anything else as his signoff. Someone in the crowd might even call out for it before he could leave. He took a deep breath. There was no alternative. He had to brazen it out. He hated the thought that Cooper might perceive it as a signal. He didn't want to seem to be trying to remind Cooper of that particular night or of any subsequent night when they had encountered each other. But really, there was no avoiding the act itself or any possible consequence. He could only trust in Cooper's own fabulousness to obscure the tune's significance. Cooper probably didn't remember it anyway. If he'd ever registered it in the first place.

XVII

Cooper knocked on the dressing room door. After a moment it swung open. "Hi, Griffin."

"Oh," Griffin said, obviously surprised to see him. "Hi."

"Can I come in?"

"I guess."

"So how have you been?"

"All right," Griffin said. He didn't look like he believed it.

"Harry says you've really been packing them in."

Griffin shrugged and stared at his feet.

"Seriously, you're turning into a local celebrity."

"Harry exaggerates."

"It's not just Harry. You've really got people talking."

Griffin shrugged again. This tack was getting Cooper nowhere. Griffin had never been any good at small talk. Might as well get to the point.

"I think you and I should go get coffee somewhere."

"I don't know," Griffin said. "I've got to be up early."

"You've forgotten rule number one already?"

Griffin looked sheepish.

"That's right," Cooper laughed. "Nobody says 'no' to Cooper. I promise I won't keep you up too late."

———

Cooper pulled into the narrow driveway.

"I thought we were going somewhere for coffee," Griffin muttered.

"This is somewhere," Cooper said. "You can't tell me it's not. You're not that much of an existentialist. And I make damned good coffee."

"All right. I guess."

Griffin's reluctance was palpable as they climbed the front steps. Cooper turned the key in the deadbolt and braced himself for the onslaught. He opened the door and stepped inside quickly, ready to fend off the dogs in the unlikely event that he was mistaken. He wasn't. He hadn't expected to be. That would have been too simple. Or too complicated, depending on how seriously you decided to take Big Steve's advice. Isis grinned at him, her tail swinging lazily. Bear and Eeyore flanked her, their expressions goofily ecstatic.

"Dogs," Cooper said, "look who's here. You remember Griffin."

He motioned Griffin inside. Isis yelped, but it was far from the blood thirsty challenge she had been issuing to all comers. It was, in point of fact, the sound she always made when Tristan brought Carlotta and Neptune around for a family reunion. Cooper watched as Griffin crouched and allowed his face to be licked. The dogs overwhelmed him in their euphoria. Cooper grabbed Griffin by the arm and hauled him to his feet.

"They're such great dogs," Griffin said.

It was the first time Cooper had ever seen an honest to God smile on that face. He leaned in for a quick kiss on the mouth, and the smile vanished.

"What's wrong?"

Out of the corner of his eye, Cooper saw the dogs echo his question with their tails.

"I don't think I can do this," Griffin stammered. "I'm sorry."

Griffin was trembling. Cooper had never been responsible for anyone but himself before. He'd gone to whatever lengths necessary to avoid such a situation, in fact. Involvements that entailed that requirement were for other people. But the Labradors' mandate was unmistakable. He assumed that like every other task he had taken on this new one could be learned and eventually mastered.

"Hey now," he said, placing a hand on Griffin's shoulder to steady him. "It's going to be different this time. I promise it's going to be O.K."

www.ingramcontent.com/pod-product-compliance
Lightning Source LLC
Chambersburg PA
CBHW051432260626
47162CB00001B/63